Hell Left Behind

by Eric Wright

A Novel

Supernatural Thriller, Horror

Published 2024

Foreword for Hell Left Behind

In the realm of literature, few genres can challenge the depths of our fears and aspirations as compellingly as horror and suspense. Hell Left Behind provides a harrowing journey through a post-apocalyptic world where the boundaries between the living and the dead blur, exploring the themes of survival, betrayal, and the relentless pursuit of truth.

As you step into the pages of this story, you'll find yourself immersed in a world where shadows linger and terror thrives. At the heart of the tale is Deacon Sawyer, a determined leader fighting not only against the external horrors that plague his camp but also the demons of trust and fractured relationships that threaten to tear his community apart. The struggles faced by Deacon and the group resonate deeply within us, as they grapple with their humanity amid nightmarish encounters and the ever-present threat of darkness.

Author Eric Wright takes readers on an emotional rollercoaster, weaving a rich tapestry of vivid characters and gripping narratives that immerse you in their plight. From the haunting presence of Wrathful Spirits to the pulse-pounding intensity of confrontations with supernatural forces, each chapter propels you deeper into the heart of a struggle that transcends mere survival—it is a fight for identity, hope, and the very essence of what it means to be human.

As you turn each page, expect to confront not only the fears of the characters but also the shadows within yourself. The intricacies of trust, sacrifice, and perseverance are masterfully interlaced throughout the narrative, challenging you to consider how far you would go to protect the ones you love.

In Hell Left Behind, the stakes have never been higher, and the consequences of choice weigh heavily on every character's shoulders. Whether you are a fan of horror, psychological thrillers, or simply enjoy stories that keep you on the edge of your seat, this book promises to captivate your imagination and grip your heart.

Prepare yourself for a journey through hell and back, where every revelation leads to another shadow, and the struggle for hope is fraught with peril. We invite you to join Deacon Sawyer and his companions on this harrowing adventure—because in the depths of darkness, hope fights back.

Welcome to Hell Left Behind.

— Eric Wright
Writer, Director, Producer
October 31, 2024

Prologue

In the hushed remnants of twilight, when shadows grow long and the air thickens with secrets, a familiar darkness emerges from the depths. It is here that hope dances on the edge of despair, where the lost souls of the past linger, crying out for retribution, and the living are haunted by choices made in fear. This is the world left behind—where echoes of nightmares still resonate and the boundaries between life and death blur in the relentless grip of sorrow.

Deacon Sawyer had once been a protector, a guiding light for those who sought shelter from the maelstrom of chaos that roamed the earth. He had fought valiantly against flesh-hungry Hounds and the terrifying spirits that preyed on the living, rallying survivors in their darkest hours. But the world had changed; survival was no longer guaranteed, and betrayal lurked in corners once thought secure.

On an unremarkable night, tragedy struck unexpectedly. In the midst of defending his camp against overwhelming odds, one of his closest friends vanished without a trace, swallowed by the shadows that crept ever closer. Frank's disappearance sent ripples of doubt and suspicion through the once-unified camp, eroding the very fabric of trust they had built. It was not enough to battle the physical monsters; they now had to confront the spectral horrors lurking within themselves.

As the darkness thickened and spirits rose to seek vengeance for their unresolved grievances, Deacon found himself standing on a precipice—accused and alone, fighting not just for his survival, but for the souls of those he had promised to protect. With every haunting wail that rose from the lost, he realized that much more was at stake than mere survival; they were engaged in a battle for their very humanity.

Tonight, as the stars began to fade and the shadows danced ominously around the campfire, a storm approached on the horizon—a tempest of wrathful spirits demanding their due and secrets waiting to be exposed. And as the weight of the past bore down upon him like a heavy shroud, Deacon understood that the greatest battles weren't always fought in the open—they often unfolded in the heart, the mind, where the true monsters dwelled.

In this world left behind, time is fluid, and the line between right and wrong blurs under the pressure of regret. The spirits of the past beckon, and Deacon must wrestle with the ghosts of his choices if he hopes to lead his friends from the edge of oblivion. The journey ahead is fraught with peril, where every decision echoes with consequences and every whisper of the wind carries the weight of souls longing for release.

What remains lies scattered among the shadows—a hell left behind, a reckoning on the horizon, and a fight against the darkness that threatens to consume them all. Deacon's story is about to unfold, and like the phantoms roaming the woods, he must confront the shadows lurking in the corners of his own soul. For in this world, where hope battles despair, only one truth remains: The past never truly leaves us; it follows us, waiting for the right moment to strike.

CHAPTER 1: THE DEVIL'S PLAYGROUND

The desolate landscape stretched under a blood-orange sky, remnants of civilization shattered and scattered like forgotten memories. Rusted cars lined the cracked asphalt of what had once been a bustling highway, and the silence was deafening—punctuated only by the distant echoes of gunfire and the eerie whisper of the wind.

Deacon Sawyer, clad in tactical gear, emerged from the shadows of a dilapidated building. His determined gaze surveyed the abandoned stretch of highway ahead. An uneasy tension hung in the air, thickening as the sun dipped lower, casting long shadows that danced across the pavement.

"Stay sharp," he mumbled to himself, the words a whispered reminder of the fragility of their situation.

Behind him, the group moved cautiously, each member aware of the lurking dangers just beyond sight. Reverend Thomas, holding a makeshift flashlight, stepped forward, his eyes wide with concern.

"Deacon, this place… it feels wrong. What if they're out there watching us?" the reverend urged, his voice trembling slightly as he scanned the area.

"They are," Deacon replied, steadying his resolve. "But we can't linger. We need to find shelter before nightfall."

Frank Carter, fidgeting with a rusted blade, chimed in, trying to lighten the mood despite the tension. "Let's just hope we don't run into any Sin Eaters tonight. I'd prefer to keep my sins to myself, thanks."

A loud crash suddenly erupted from a nearby wrecked vehicle, causing everyone to tense up, muscles coiling in instinctive readiness.

"I'll take whatever comes at us. Let's show them what we're made of!" Jake "The Hulk" Henderson, towering and muscular, readied his fists, his voice a low growl.

"Not yet. First, we scout," Deacon ordered, raising his hand. "Colonel Stone, what's your take?"

Colonel Max Stone stepped forward from the shadows, his expression calm and focused. "This area's too open. We need to move quickly, keep to the buildings. The Whispering Shadows love places like this—the less cover, the better for them."

Deacon nodded in agreement but felt a flicker of doubt cross his mind, an unsettling thought buried beneath layers of training and experience.

"Remember, brother, it's in our weakness that His strength shines through," Reverend Thomas reminded him, placing a supportive hand on Deacon's shoulder.

"Right… let's move," Deacon replied, shaking off the heaviness that threatened to close in.

The group began to make their way forward, cautiously navigating the fallout of a world gone mad.

A DISTANT FIGURE IN THE FOG

A faint shadow flickered at the edge of their vision and then disappeared, sending chills down everyone's spines.

"Did you see that?" Jake asked, his eyes narrowing.

"Yeah. Something's out there," Frank replied, unease creeping into his voice.

As they approached a cluster of cars stacked haphazardly, a guttural growl reverberated through the air. Deacon motioned for everyone to stop, signaling them to take cover.

The view shifted to reveal the source of the noise—a grotesque Sin Eater, a demon with a gaping maw and twisted features, lurking beside a mangled vehicle. It sniffed the air, its gruesome tongue flicking out like a serpent.

"Weapons out. On my count," Deacon commanded, his heart racing as adrenaline surged.

The group took a defensive stance, fear and determination mixing in their gazes as the demon inched closer, its eyes glinting with hunger.

"For courage and faith," Reverend Thomas murmured, taking a deep breath.

"One... two... three!" Deacon shouted.

They simultaneously unleashed their firepower at the demon. Gunshots echoed ominously, cutting through the stillness.

The Sin Eater let out a horrific scream as the bullets found their mark. It lunged forward, but Deacon was quicker, a well-aimed shot from his sidearm taking it down. With a spray of darkened blood, the creature fell to the ground, lifeless.

The group stood together, breathing heavily, their adrenaline racing in the aftermath of the confrontation.

"Nice shot, Deacon. But we can't keep doing this," Frank said, trying to catch his breath.

"I could've taken it. Just saying!" Jake jested, flexing his muscles with an easy grin.

Deacon furrowed his brow, looking around at his team, the weight of leadership pressing heavily on him.

"Let's move—not just to survive, but to find a way to fight back," he stated, resolve hardening in his voice.

Reverend Thomas raised a fist, determination gleaming in his eyes. "And we will. Together."

As they pressed forward into the deepening twilight, the camera pulled back to reveal the highway fading into darkness, the ever-present threat of demons lurking just out of sight, ready to strike at the first sign of weakness.

CHAPTER 2: REFUGE AMONG RUINS

ABANDONED WAREHOUSE - NIGHT

The group approached a crumbling warehouse nestled at the edge of the highway, its windows shattered and doors hanging ajar like the lifeless husks of a forgotten past. Old signage dangled precariously, swaying in the evening breeze, a reminder of what used to be. The heavy air was thick with an impending sense of dread.

Deacon scanned the building cautiously, signaling for everyone to halt. The once-bustling hub of activity now stood silent and foreboding.

"Keep an eye out. No more surprises," he instructed, his voice steady despite the anxiety creeping into his stomach.

The group nodded, their expressions tense as they surveyed the darkened structure.

ABANDONED WAREHOUSE - NIGHT

Deacon entered first, stepping through the splintered doorway. His flashlight beam cut through the gloom, illuminating the remnants of a long-past era. Dust hung in the air, and the scent of decay mingled with the dampness. Old furniture lay in disarray, a wheelchair tipped over and old magazines scattered across the floor.

Frank followed, glancing around warily. "This place is a dump.

You sure it's safe?" he asked, skepticism coloring his tone.

Colonel Max Stone entered next, his keen eyes already scanning the surroundings. "It's better than being out there in the open. We can fortify this place. Better to have walls than none at all," he noted, a light smile touching his lips as he spoke.

Jake, ever the bold one, moved deeper into the warehouse, his muscles tense, readiness emanating from him. "I'll check the perimeter!" he declared, eager for action.

"Jake, wait! Stay in earshot," Deacon called after him, his voice firm.

"Got it, sir," Jake replied, grumbling but compliant.

As Jake patrolled, the remaining group gathered near the entry, Reverend Thomas casting a reassuring presence, lighting a small lantern that flickered in the thick silence. Its glow cast dancing shadows on the walls, momentarily dispelling the darkness.

"This place could become our sanctuary... if we allow it," Reverend Thomas whispered, his voice a soothing balm to the tension in the air.

Frank crossed his arms, eyeing the dilapidation around them. "Sanctuary or a coffin? We need to be practical," he countered, his skepticism still evident.

Deacon nodded, appreciating Frank's concern. "We'll set up a watch. We need to gather supplies, find food. No more running. We stand our ground here," he declared, trying to instill confidence in the group.

Just then, the sound of a SHATTERING GLASS nearby made all heads turn. The group tensed, hearts racing, ready for potential danger.

Determination hardened his features as he raised his weapon, instinct taking over. "Stay low," he instructed.

"Looks like a couple of crates fell over… or something even worse," Jake mused, his voice low.

The group exchanged wary glances; tension thick as they drew closer together.

Colonel Stone kept his gaze focused. "We need to be ready for whatever comes through that door," he warned.

Suddenly, a small ANIMAL scurried past—a scruffy dog. The group collectively inhaled sharply, tension momentarily breaking as the dog stopped and looked up at them with cautious curiosity.

"It's just a dog," Frank exhaled, relief washing over him.

Rounding on them, Reverend Thomas knelt beside the dog, extending a cautious hand. "Hey there, fella. You lost too?" he asked gently.

The dog, a mix of breeds, approached cautiously, sniffing at Thomas's hand, almost sensing the shared fear beneath the bravado.

"We can't forget it could be a trap—nothing is ever just a dog," Deacon said seriously, keeping his weapon trained in the direction of the noise.

Just then, a loud THUD echoed from outside, shifting the atmosphere back to alertness.

"I think we're not alone," Jake whispered, bracing himself.

Deacon motioned for everyone to space out, readied for whatever might come through the doorway.

Everyone squared their shoulders, weapons raised, eyes darting in anticipation.

"Stay together. No one moves alone," Deacon ordered, his voice a steady anchor amid the impending chaos.

Frank's voice broke through the tense silence. "What do we do about the dog?"

Reverend Thomas, still kneeling, looked at Deacon. "If it's meant to be our companion, we shouldn't abandon it," he suggested.

Deacon weighed the thought. "If it can help, we keep it. If it's a threat—"

Before he could finish, another crash sounded, louder this time. The dog reacted, barking and growling, its instincts kicking into overdrive.

"At least it's alert," Jake remarked with a smirk, ready for combat, but the unease lingered.

Suddenly, the warehouse doors burst open, and a horde of FLESH RIPPERS charged in, their twisted bodies a grotesque sight, growling hungrily. The air thickened with the stench of decay and malice, a palpable fear thrumming through the group.

"Get ready! Hold your ground!" Deacon shouted at the top of his lungs.

The chaotic ROAR of FLESH RIPPERS filled the air as they descended upon the group. Wood splintered under the weight of the oncoming horde, yet Deacon stood firm, determined to protect his team.

"Everyone, cover your flanks!" he commanded.

Colonel Stone swiftly provided tactical commands, while Jake remained steadfast, his fists clenched, ready to pounce.

Frank and Reverend Thomas took defensive positions,

weapons aimed and throats dry with adrenaline.

"What do we do if they get past us?" Frank shouted over the chaos.

"We hold! We've got to protect each other!" Deacon urged, his eyes scanning for weaknesses.

As the first Flesh Ripper lunged for Deacon, he expertly sidestepped, firing a precise shot that took it down. The group erupted into action, a chorus of gunfire and primal snarls.

The dog barked ferociously, rallying beside Deacon, sensing the danger that loomed.

"Now—let's move!" Deacon yelled, a fire igniting in him as they fought back against the encroaching threat.

CHAPTER 3: SHADOWS OF UNCERTAINTY

ABANDONED WAREHOUSE - NIGHT

In the wake of battle, the atmosphere inside the abandoned warehouse was thick with dust and adrenaline. The light from the lantern flickered against the walls, casting elongated shadows of the weary survivors. Deacon, Frank, Jake, and Colonel Stone stood in a defensive formation, weapons still drawn, watching as the last of the Flesh Rippers fell lifelessly to the ground.

Deacon wiped sweat from his brow, feeling the weight of leadership pressing down on him. "Is everyone alright?" he asked, scanning the faces of his team, relieved to see them all standing, albeit shaken.

"We made it," Frank said, his voice steadier now. "But we can't keep facing wave after wave like this."

"It won't get easier," Colonel Stone observed, glancing out the broken windows into the darkened wilderness beyond. "We need to fortify this place before they come again."

ABANDONED WAREHOUSE - MEDICAL AREA - LATER

The group gathered in a makeshift medical area crammed with supplies scattered about. Emily, who had managed to save one of the injured survivors during the fight, now worked furiously, wrapping bandages around their wounds with steady hands.

"Just hold on, you've got this," Emily murmured, her voice calming amidst the chaos. The survivor grunted in pain but nodded appreciatively.

Deacon watched her for a moment, admiration flooding through him. "Nice work, Doc," he said, stepping closer. "You're even better than I remembered."

Emily looked up, meeting his gaze. "There's a lot more at stake now than ever before. We need to keep everyone alive."

"I know, and I appreciate what you're doing," Deacon replied, his voice low enough that it was just for her ears. "You've proven your worth many times over already."

Just then, the door creaked ominously, echoed by a sudden chill that swept through the room. Everyone turned their heads, readying their weapons.

"Who's there?" Frank demanded, tightening his grip on his blade.

The tension was palpable when they heard the soft patter of feet followed by a low whimper. The scruffy dog, still trembling from the battle, cautiously entered the room and approached Emily, its tail tucked and ears back.

"Hey there, boy," she said softly, kneeling down to pet him. "You did good out there."

The dog responded by leaning into her touch, a flicker of courage returning to its eyes.

ABANDONED WAREHOUSE - MAIN ROOM - LATER

As the adrenaline began to fade, the group regrouped in the main warehouse area. Colonel Stone and Jake took positions near the entrance, still on alert for any incoming threats, while Deacon gathered everyone around to discuss their next steps.

"All of us are alive. That's a win in my book," Deacon started, his gaze sweeping over the team. "But we need to plan better. Moving forward, we must fortify our defenses and scout for supplies. The longer we stay in one place, the more likely those demons will return."

Emily raised her hand. "And I think we should also consider looking for more survivors. There may be others out there just as lost and scared as we are."

Frank nodded in agreement. "If we can expand our numbers, we increase our chances of survival. But we need to proceed with caution. We've seen how quickly chaos can descend upon us."

Deacon rubbed his chin thoughtfully, contemplating the risks. "So, we split into groups for scouting. One team can search for supplies, and the other can check the surrounding area for any survivors. Agreed?"

As the group nodded, the atmosphere shifted slightly—a sense of collaboration igniting among them.

"Don't forget to keep an eye out for other groups," Colonel Stone cautioned. "Not everyone will be friendly. We should have some protection measures in place."

Just then, the warmth of the lantern light flickered more erratically as the wind howled outside, carrying with it the uncertainty that lingered in the air.

"Whatever we do, we have to stick together," Deacon said, reinforcing their bond. "No one moves alone."

DEACON'S CAMP - ALONGSIDE THE HIGHWAY - NIGHT

As they gathered their supplies for the night—you could hear the crackling fire illuminating their weary faces, defiance still flickering behind their eyes.

Nadine, who had previously been quiet, stepped forward. "I want to help. I can join whoever goes out, and I can help with gathering supplies," she offered earnestly, desperation lighting up her gaze.

Frank hesitated for a moment, remembering his earlier concerns about her and her past. "Are you sure? It's dangerous out there."

"I know. But I'm not afraid anymore. I won't let fear paralyze me," Nadine replied, determination etched on her face.

A shared glance between Deacon and Emily spoke volumes about the internal battle they were facing.

"Very well," Deacon finally said, admiration breaking through his skepticism. "You can come with us, but you need to follow my lead and stay close."

ABANDONED WAREHOUSE - MAIN ROOM - NIGHT

As the group began discussing the night's objectives, a bundle of excitement mixed with anxiety filled the air. Unbeknownst to them, darkness loomed not just outside their camp but also within—threatening to unravel the fragile bonds of trust and strength they had begun to forge.

"Let's get to work," Deacon said, resetting the focus on the task at hand. The night wore on, filled with preparations and plans, but an uneasy fog settled in the back of their minds—an awareness that the nightmare was far from over.

CHAPTER 4: THE UNEXPECTED VISITOR

ABANDONED WAREHOUSE - LATER THAT NIGHT

As darkness enveloped the abandoned warehouse, the only source of light came from the flickering lanterns that cast eerie shadows on the cracked walls. The air was thick with anticipation—everyone was on high alert, exchanging stories and strategies for the coming days while their adrenaline from the earlier battle faded.

Deacon stood near a makeshift map laid out on a table, consulting with Colonel Stone and Emily. Their voices were low, yet the urgency was palpable. Meanwhile, Frank and Jake gathered supplies, preparing for the journey ahead.

"Alright, we need to cover as much ground as possible," Deacon instructed, his finger tracing potential routes on the map. "If we split into two groups, we can search for food and medicine while keeping an eye out for other survivors."

Emily glanced up from the inventory list she was compiling. "And we should check the perimeter. Any signs of recent activity could indicate trouble. We can't be caught off guard like before."

Just then, a soft WHIMPER cut through the stillness of the warehouse. The scruffy dog, now visibly more comfortable, wandered closer to Deacon, nudging him for attention.

"Seems like he's taken a liking to you," Frank said with a grin, noticing the bond forming between Deacon and the dog.

Deacon chuckled softly as he scratched behind the dog's ears. "Well, at least someone trusts me," he replied, casting a quick look at his group before turning serious again.

Suddenly, the sound of footsteps echoed outside the warehouse, causing the group to tense up. Weapons instinctively raised; their eyes darted toward the entrance.

"Everyone, stay quiet," Colonel Stone ordered, his expression hardened to determination.

ABANDONED WAREHOUSE - NIGHT

Outside, a figure approached through the fog, shrouded in darkness. The crunch of leaves beneath their feet provided a rhythmic sound that amplified the group's anxiety.

"Hold your positions," Deacon whispered, readying himself for whatever came next.

The group prepared for the worst, but as the figure stepped into the dim light of the warehouse doorway, relief flooded through them, though uncertainty still lingered.

"Who goes there?" Frank called out, stepping forward hesitantly, the weapon still tightly gripped in his hand.

The figure stepped closer, revealing a YOUNG WOMAN (late teens, wide-eyed but determined), her clothes ragged and dirty. She held her hands up, showing she meant no harm.

"I swear, I'm just trying to survive! I'm not with any group," the young woman called out, her voice trembling slightly.

ABANDONED WAREHOUSE - NIGHT

Deacon caught her gaze, assessing her carefully. "How did you find us?" he asked, his tone steady but cautious.

"I heard noises and saw the light," she replied, her eyes darting to the weapons they carried. "I thought you might be friendly."

"Could you be any more reckless?" Colonel Stone interjected, his voice laced with suspicion. "You could have brought friends… or worse."

"Wait," Emily interjected, stepping in front of Deacon. "If she's here alone, she needs help like the rest of us. We can't just turn her away."

"Name?" Deacon asked bluntly.

"Carla," she replied, her voice wavering. "I… I used to be part of a group, but they… they turned on me."

"What do you mean 'turned on you'?" Frank asked, unfurling surges of concern.

Carla hesitated, gathering her thoughts. "They started being reckless. Some wanted to raid nearby shelters, and when I spoke up against it, they threatened me. I had no choice but to run."

Deacon exchanged glances with Colonel Stone, his expression thoughtful. "If you're telling the truth, we can offer you a chance to stay with us, but trust is earned here. We can't afford mistakes."

"I understand. I'm just looking to survive," Carla said earnestly, her eyes pleading for validation.

"Let's say we decide to let you stay," Frank said, still skeptical. "What skills do you bring to the table?"

"I can cook, I know basic first aid, and I can handle myself in a fight if I need to," Carla said, a flicker of confidence returning to her eyes. "I just want to help."

Deacon rubbed his chin thoughtfully, weighing the risks. "Emily, what do you think?" he asked, needing her insight.

"I think everyone deserves a chance," Emily said softly. "We can't lose our humanity in this fight against the darkness."

With a firm exhale, Deacon nodded. "Alright, Carla. You can stay, but you'll be under close observation. Follow our rules, and you'll be safe here. Break our trust, and there will be serious consequences."

"Thank you," Carla replied, visibly relieved as she stepped fully into the shelter of the warehouse.

ABANDONED WAREHOUSE - MAIN ROOM - NIGHT

As the group began to gather again, the atmosphere shifted slightly. The tension still loomed, but now there was a hint of shared determination among the members.

"Let's regroup and finalize our plans," Deacon suggested, casting a glance around the room. He felt a sense of responsibility amplifying with each new face.

The conversation resumed, and as they spoke about strategies for scouting supplies and improving defenses, the flickering lanterns illuminated a new alliance forming, one marked by flickers of hope in a world steeped in despair.

CHAPTER 5: ALLIANCE IN THE SHADOWS

DEACON'S CAMP - NIGHT

The campfire flickered warmly against the chill of the night air, casting dancing shadows on the faces of the weary survivors. The atmosphere buzzed with a renewed sense of purpose following the arrival of Carla. Deacon, Frank, Colonel Stone, Emily, and Reverend Thomas gathered in a tight circle to finalize their plans for the next day.

"Now that we have Carla on board, let's outline our immediate needs," Deacon began, his voice steady and commanding as he laid out the custom-made map on the ground. "We need food, medical supplies, and we need eyes on the perimeter."

"Agreed," Colonel Stone replied. "I suggest we split into two teams. One to check the nearby stores and one to scout the area for any unexpected visitors."

Frank interjected, "Maybe we can alternate and have Carla join one of the teams to keep an eye on her skills. If she's as good as she says, it'll boost our chances."

"I can handle myself," Carla offered with a determined glint in her eye, eager to prove her worth. "I promise I won't let anyone down."

"Alright," said Deacon, nodding in approval. "But remember, this isn't just about fending off demons; it's about staying vigilant against all threats, including human ones. Trust is hard to earn out here."

Reverend Thomas stepped in, his voice calming. "Let's not forget the importance of morality in our decisions. Each encounter shapes who we are beneath the surface—let's be the light in this darkness."

ABANDONED WAREHOUSE - MEDICAL AREA - NIGHT

Meanwhile, as plans formulated, Emily worked alongside the survivors in the medical area. She placed the supplies she had gathered on the table, ready to assess what they had left and what they still needed.

Nadine stayed close; her curiosity piqued by Emily's methodical approach. "How did you learn all of this?" she asked, observing Emily's gentle and focused demeanor as she sorted through bandages and medical gear.

"I was a nurse before all this happened," Emily replied, not skipping a beat. "In times like these, we must leverage our skills to help each other survive. Medicine doesn't stop just because the world has changed."

"You're right," Nadine acknowledged. "I just want to contribute, to feel useful again."

"Keep that spirit," Emily said warmly. "We will need every bit of strength we can muster."

DEACON'S CAMP - LATER THAT NIGHT

As the group wrapped up their discussions, a low rumble of laughter echoed out from the food area where Jake and another survivor were attempting to prepare a meal.

"Let's see if we can make something edible out of this," Jake called out, holding up a dented can of beans triumphantly, his earlier bravado returning.

Deacon smiled for the first time that evening. "Every little victory counts."

The conversations and laughter continued until the fire began to flicker lower, and the shadows deepened. As weariness settled in, Deacon gathered the group for final thoughts.

"Tomorrow, we have a lot to do. Stay alert, stick to the plan, and we'll pull through," he urged, a hint of pride in his voice for the makeshift family they were forming around him.

"Together," Reverend Thomas added, raising his fist. "We face whatever comes, side by side."

CHAPTER 6: UNFORESEEN CHALLENGES

WOODS - EARLY MORNING

The dawn painted the sky with hues of pink and gold as the group prepared to split into their scouting teams. The air was crisp, filled with the scent of damp earth and the promise of a new day. Deacon, Frank, Colonel Stone, Carla, and Jake gathered their gear, mentally preparing for the day's challenges.

"Alright, we'll keep the routes simple," Deacon instructed, checking the map one last time. "Frank and Carla, you'll head north toward the old grocery store. Stone and I will take the south route to check the pharmacy. Keep your radio on—communication is key."

"Got it," Frank replied, adjusting his gear and glancing at Carla. "You ready to earn your keep?"

Carla smirked. "Let's just get this done. I won't let you down."

Jake, already bouncing on his feet, added, "And I'll make sure Deacon doesn't get himself into too much trouble."

"Yeah, right," Deacon retorted with a chuckle. "You just try not to break anything."

ABANDONED WAREHOUSE - MEDICAL AREA - EARLY

MORNING

As the teams made their way outside, Emily busied herself in the medical corner, checking supplies with Nadine beside her.

"I thought we could use what we have left to prepare for any injuries," Emily suggested, sorting through gauzes and antiseptics.

Nadine nodded, a touch of enthusiasm dancing in her eyes. "I'll help. Maybe I could also scout around the perimeter at some point?"

"That's a good idea, but stay close to the warehouse for now," Emily replied, knowing that Nadine needed the practice but also required supervision.

ABANDONED GROCERY STORE - LATER THAT DAY

Frank and Carla arrived at the GPS-marked location of the grocery store, the building looming ahead like a giant skeleton. The silence around them was thick, broken only by the crunching of debris beneath their feet.

"Let's move quickly," Frank urged, glancing nervously over his shoulder. "This place gives me the creeps."

As they stepped inside, the air was stale, and every step echoed eerily. The shelves were partially stocked with long-expired goods, covered in dust and grime.

Carla scanned the area, her eyes sharp. "We need to find canned goods and anything still packaged. We can't waste time here."

Suddenly, a loud CRASH reverberated from the back of the store, followed by a series of guttural growls.

"Did you hear that?" Frank whispered, panic creeping into his voice.

"Yeah, but what was it?" Carla replied, her grip tightening on her makeshift weapon.

"Let's check it out, but stay low," Frank said, urging her to follow him as he moved toward the sound, heart pounding in his chest.

With every step they took closer to the noise, the shadows seemed to grow taller, the danger palpable.

WAREHOUSE - OUTSIDE - EARLY MORNING

Meanwhile, Deacon and Colonel Stone moved down the southern path towards the pharmacy. The trees loomed overhead, blocking much of the morning light.

"The last team that came through here reported seeing signs of survivors," Colonel Stone said, his voice grave. "But we can't be too hopeful."

Deacon nodded, scanning the tree line. "We've seen how quickly things can turn. We need to gather supplies and get back to camp safely. No heroics today."

SUDDENLY, A LOUD CRACKING NOISE

The sudden sound echoed through the woods, causing Deacon to halt mid-step. He instinctively raised his weapon, heart racing. Colonel Stone mirrored his actions, eyes narrowing as they searched the shadows.

"Stay alert," Deacon whispered, his voice low but urgent. "We don't know what's lurking out here."

ABANDONED GROCERY STORE - MOMENTS LATER

Inside the grocery store, Frank's grip tightened around his makeshift weapon as he and Carla crept cautiously toward the source of the sound. Shadows stretched ominously across the floor as they moved deeper into the darkened aisles.

"Whatever it is, we need to be quick," Carla muttered, her eyes darting around the dusty shelves.

Another growl reverberated through the stillness, followed by a guttural roar. Frank's heart pounded in his ears as bile rose in his throat.

"On three," Frank said, staring into the darkness. "One... two... three!"

They pushed around the corner, weapons drawn, to reveal a CHAOTIC SCENE. A pair of NIGHTMARE HOUNDS, sleek, shadowy canines with glowing eyes and snarling jaws, were hungrily tearing at a mangled cart filled with long-rotted food.

"Back! Back!" Frank shouted, panic surging as he instinctively backed away.

The Nightmare Hounds jerked their heads toward the sound, their eyes flashing with predatory instincts. One of them lunged, teeth bared, as Frank barely managed to dodge its attack.

"Run!" Carla yelled, adrenaline surging as she rushed toward the exit.

Frank followed, pushing through the door just as the Hounds lunged again, scraping the ground with their claws. They burst outside into the open air, scrambling for safety as the creatures skidded to a halt at the threshold, sniffing at the remnants of their prey.

ABANDONED GROCERY STORE - CONTINUOUS

As Frank and Carla stumbled outside, gasping for breath, they skidded to a halt. Frank's heart raced, but he quickly raised his weapon, scanning their surroundings.

"They're not following," Carla panted, her face pale but determined.

"Good. Let's make sure it stays that way," Frank replied,

steeling himself. "We need to get back to Deacon and the others."

WOODS - LATER

Meanwhile, Deacon and Colonel Stone continued along the path, keeping their senses heightened. The tension in the air thickened, every rustle of leaves and snap of branches causing them to tense.

"Something is definitely up," Colonel Stone muttered, stopping to scan the trees. "I can feel it."

"Let's keep moving. We're almost there," Deacon urged, shifting the weight of his weapon as they pressed on.

Suddenly, a SHADOW darted between the trees. Deacon and Stone froze, scanning the area.

"Did you see that?" Deacon asked, his voice tense.

"Yeah," Colonel Stone replied, noting the direction it had gone. "Let's investigate. It could be another survivor, or—"

Before he finished, the same low growl echoed from a thicket nearby, freezing the duo in place.

DEACON'S CAMP - EARLY MORNING

Back at the camp, Emily and Nadine worked together to organize and store supplies they had amassed. The air was heavy with an uneasy awareness of the ongoing tension.

"I'm glad we're preparing for the worst," Nadine said, her hands busy sorting medical supplies. "But I can't help but feel we're sitting ducks out here."

Emily looked up from her work, concern etched on her face. "We have to trust Deacon and the others will return soon. They have to."

Just then, the sound of the campfire crackling was interrupted by the soft whimper of the dog, which had settled near them.

"Maybe he senses something we don't," Nadine said, scratching behind the dog's ears. "Animals can be more in tune with their instincts."

Suddenly, the atmosphere shifted as they heard a LOUD BANG emanating from the woods, causing both women to jump.

"What was that?" Emily said, her heart racing.

"Whatever it is, we should prepare ourselves," Nadine replied, adrenaline surging through her veins.

WOODS - MOMENTS LATER

Deacon signaled Colonel Stone to stay quiet as they moved toward the source of the noise. They crept forward cautiously, weapons raised, hearts pounding in their chests.

"On my signal, we approach," Deacon whispered, determination in his eyes.

Just then, Frank and Carla emerged from the thicket, their faces pale and breathless.

"Deacon!" Frank shouted, relief flooding his voice as he spotted his leader. "We ran into trouble... Nightmare Hounds! We barely got away!"

"What? Are you okay?" Deacon rushed forward; concern etched in his voice.

"We're fine, but we need to get back to camp. We have to warn everyone," Frank replied, glancing back nervously as if feeling the threat still nipping at their heels.

The group quickly regrouped, sharing critical information in frantic whispers. The tension was palpable, but they rallied together, determined not to let fear control them.

"Let's move now!" Deacon commanded, the fire of leadership

igniting in him. "Stick close together."

Deacon led the way, his senses heightened, adrenaline coursing through him as they prepared to face whatever lurked in the shadows. Outside, the sun dipped lower, casting long shadows that seemed to reach out like hands, pulling them back into darkness.

CHAPTER 7: THE DARKNESS WITHIN

DEACON'S CAMP - NIGHT

The camp seemed peaceful beneath the cover of stars, but an undercurrent of tension rippled through the group. Deacon's team moved quickly, their weapons poised as they approached the edge of the camp, casting wary glances into the looming darkness of the woods beyond.

"Keep your eyes peeled," Deacon urged, his voice steady despite the gravity of the situation. "We don't know what's out there, but if it's anything like the Nightmare Hounds, we'll need to be ready."

Nadine, holding tightly to the scruffy dog she had taken a shine to, glanced at Emily. "Do you think we can trust the others we met? They seemed… desperate."

Emily nodded thoughtfully; her brow furrowed. "Desperation can lead to rash decisions. We need to be vigilant, but we also can't lose sight of what we stand for. Compassion can't become a casualty of this nightmare."

As they continued to survey the perimeter, a sudden rustle came from the trees. Instantly, the group froze, weapons raised, hearts pounding in unison.

WOODS - NIGHT - SIMULTANEOUSLY

Deacon and Colonel Stone, positioned at the front of their

group, shared a tense glance. The question hung in the air: friend or foe?

"Someone's coming," Deacon whispered, straining to hear through the night's stillness.

"Hostiles?" Colonel Stone asked, his grip tightening on his weapon.

"Could be," Deacon replied, taking a cautious step forward. "Let's wait and see."

Suddenly, a FIGURE burst from the shadows, collapsing to the ground before them—a scruffy, out-of-breath MAN in ragged clothing clutched his side, looking up at them with wide, terrified eyes.

"Please! I mean no harm!" he gasped, desperation in his voice. "I've been running for days!"

"Identify yourself!" Colonel Stone barked, his voice sharp and commanding.

"Jacob! Jacob Finch!" the man wheezed, pressing his palm against the dirt to steady himself. "I saw your camp and thought maybe… maybe you'd take me in?"

Deacon exchanged glances with his team, weighing their options. Trust was a fragile thing in their world, and every moment spent in hesitation could mean danger.

"Why should we trust you?" Deacon demanded, his eyes piercing. "What are you running from?"

Jacob glanced over his shoulder, fear evident on his face. "You wouldn't believe me if I told you. The group I was with… they weren't right. They wanted to raid your camp, take everything. It's only a matter of time before they come for you too!"

The team shifted nervously, the weight of Jacob's words hanging heavy in the air.

"Can you show us who these raiders are?" Frank asked cautiously, stepping forward but keeping a safe distance.

"They're ruthless and hungry," Jacob urged, his voice trembling. "A band of survivors turned raiders. The last I saw, their camp was destroyed, but they were fierce. I barely escaped."

Deacon's resolve hardened as he considered the implications. If they were indeed being targeted, they needed to fortify their camp—and fast.

"What do you bring to the table?" Deacon questioned, a determination in his tone. "If we let you in, what can you do to help?"

"I've scavenged before; I know where to find supplies. I can help defend your camp, and I can be your lookout!" Jacob insisted, desperation turning to urgency. "Please, you have to believe me."

Deacon hesitated but sensed a flicker of truth in Jacob's fervor. The uncertainty of the world weighed heavily upon them.

"Fine," Deacon said, pulling the group closer. "But know this: one misstep, and you're out. We don't have room for lies."

Jacob nodded vigorously, relief flooding his features. "Thank you! I swear I'll prove myself!"

WAREHOUSE - NIGHT

As they brought Jacob back to the camp, the atmosphere remained tense. They entered the dimly lit warehouse, their hearts racing, ready for anything. Emily took Jacob aside, checking for wounds or signs of distress, her innate compassion guiding her.

"I can't believe they were going to raid us," Emily said, her voice low enough for only Jacob to hear. "We're all just trying to survive out here."

"I know how it feels to be vulnerable," Jacob said, meeting her gaze. "But it only takes one act of kindness to change everything."

Reverend Thomas stepped in, overhearing the conversation. "It's true. We can't let fear turn us against each other. This life will try to harden us, but we must hold on to our humanity."

As Deacon gathered the team, sharing recent intel, the weight of their new reality settled in—a constant state of vigilance against lurking dangers.

"Tonight, everyone must remain alert," Deacon announced, his tone somber. "We may have a new ally, but we are all still at risk. If Jacob's words are true, our defenses need fortification."

"Count me in," Jacob said, determination in his eyes as he stepped forward. "I'm here to help."

The group nodded, and a renewed sense of purpose ignited in the room. They knew that they would have to work as one to survive the threats ahead—both those that came from outside and those that simmered just beneath the surface.

Suddenly, the hairs on the back of Deacon's neck stood on edge. "Did you hear that?" he said, pausing.

A distant howl echoed through the night, chilling and primal. The tension in the room thickened, and the group felt the shared understanding of what lay ahead.

"Stay ready, everyone," Deacon commanded, eyes sharp, aware that the Devil's playground had yet to reveal its full horrors.

CHAPTER 8: SHADOWS GATHER

DEACON'S CAMP - NIGHT

As the howl faded into silence, the flickering firelight illuminated the faces of Deacon and the others, whose expressions mirrored the tension in the air. They gathered closer together, weapons at the ready, eyes scanning the perimeter where darkness gnawed at the edges of the camp.

"Everyone, stay alert. That wasn't just any noise," Deacon warned, his voice low and steady. "We've got to be prepared for anything."

Frank, still visibly anxious, clutched his weapon tightly. "What do you think it was? Another horde of Flesh Rippers?"

"Could be," replied Colonel Stone, his eyes narrowing as he surveyed the shadows. "But it could also be something worse. We need to spread out and keep watch. Jake and I will take the north side; you, Frank, and Emily handle the east, and Nadine can scout along the south perimeter with Jacob."

"Got it," Frank replied, glancing at Nadine. "Stay close to him, alright?"

Nadine nodded; her expression now serious as she prepared herself for the task ahead. "I won't stray far," she promised.

As the teams moved into position, the fire crackled, casting dancing shadows and providing the only warmth against the cold night air. The dog stayed by Emily's side, its ears pricked and alert, sensing the tension that hung in the atmosphere.

ABANDONED WAREHOUSE - HOLDING AREA - NIGHT

In the dim light of the warehouse, Emily and Jacob found a moment of respite as the others set their watch.

"Tell me about your group," Emily said, both curious and cautious. "How did you end up alone?"

Jacob shifted uncomfortably, glancing toward the flickering shadows. "We were a small group at first, just trying to survive. But as time went on, people changed. Trust eroded, and eventually we had to fight for resources."

"Were you all close at one point?" Emily asked softly, her eyes searching his.

"Yeah, like a family. But desperation makes people do terrible things. Once a couple of folks decided to raid other camps, those of us who wanted to stay ethical were quickly outnumbered." He paused, the weight of his words heavy. "That's when I knew I couldn't stay."

"Survival shouldn't mean losing who we are," Emily replied, her voice firm yet kind. "We must hold onto our humanity as best as we can."

Jacob nodded, his expression transforming from despair to determination. "I hope I can find that again here. This place... it feels like people actually care."

Just then, the distant howl returned, echoing louder this time, sending a shiver down Emily's spine. She gripped the dog's collar tightly, steadying herself.

"Let's get back to the others," Emily said urgently, and together they moved back toward the main area of the warehouse.

DEACON'S CAMP - NIGHT

At the perimeter, Deacon and Colonel Stone were on high alert, their senses heightened. Shadows flickered at the edges of the camp, and every rustle of leaves felt amplified in the silence around them.

"Stay close, but maintain distance," Colonel Stone advised, keeping his tone low and measured. "If something comes at us, we need to have space to maneuver."

Deacon nodded, scanning the trees and the line of darkness that loomed ahead. The night seemed alive, filled with hints of movement, and his instincts prickled with unease.

"We'll hold this line. But if they come, we need to be decisive. No heroics," Deacon said, eyes narrowing. "Let's fall back to the warehouse if we feel overwhelmed."

"I agree," Colonel Stone replied, positioning himself for a better vantage point. "We need to know when to retreat."

Just then, a rustling sound erupted from the bushes beyond the camp's edge. Deacon immediately raised his weapon, urging Stone to do the same.

"Did you hear that?" Deacon asked, his voice a whisper.

"Something's moving," Stone said, a steely resolve set in his gaze.

Suddenly, they caught a glimpse of movement—a lone figure stumbling from the trees, cloaked in shadows.

"Identify yourself!" Deacon shouted, stepping forward cautiously, prepared for a fight.

The figure halted; hands raised in surrender. "Please, I mean no harm!" A WOMAN's voice emerged, trembling but clear.

Deacon exchanged a glance with Colonel Stone, both on high alert.

"Come forward slowly!" Colonel Stone commanded, weapon still raised.

DEACON'S CAMP - NIGHT - MOMENTS LATER

As the figure drew closer, the woman emerged from the shadows—a disheveled but determined woman in her late twenties, her clothes torn and dirty, her eyes wide with despair.

"I've been searching for a safe place," she pleaded, urgency lacing her words. "I swear I won't be any trouble. Please, just let me stay the night."

Deacon assessed her carefully, feeling the weight of her desperation. "What's your name?" he asked, his voice steady.

"Lila," she replied, voice trembling with emotion. "I lost everyone I care about. I just need a place to hide from the demons."

Colonel Stone exchanged uncertain glances with Deacon. "How do we know she isn't leading something toward us?" he asked, skepticism coloring his voice.

"We don't," Deacon admitted. "But we can't ignore her plea. If she's telling the truth, we might be able to help her."

"Maybe she can be of some use to us," Frank chimed in from behind, where he had just rejoined Deacon and Stone. "She could know something valuable."

Deacon's gaze turned back to Lila, who watched them with a mix of hope and fear. "Alright, Lila," he said slowly. "You can stay, but you'll be under strict observation. We can't risk putting the group in danger."

"Thank you! I promise I'm no threat," Lila said, relief flooding her face.

As Lila stepped cautiously into the warm glow of the campfire, the shadows around them deepened, and the weight of uncertainty remained heavy in the air.

WAREHOUSE - NIGHT

As the group settled back into the relative safety of the warehouse, the atmosphere shifted yet again. They were stronger together, but the lurking dangers beyond their temporary refuge were far from eliminated.

"Let's finalize our plan," Deacon said as they gathered in a circle. "We need to prepare for what's coming, and we may want to consider scouting for extra supplies tomorrow. With Lila here, we might have more resources than before."

Each member nodded, and a feeling of unity began to blossom among them, despite their individual fears and doubts.

"Together, we can face whatever darkness lies ahead," Reverend Thomas declared, raising his hand in encouragement. Lila watched, feeling herself being absorbed into the newfound strength of the group.

As they shared strategies and bonded over their shared struggles, a sense of hope flickered against

the darkness that surrounded them. Though the path ahead remained fraught with peril, for the first time in a long while, they felt the faint embers of resilience igniting within.

CHAPTER 9: RISING DAWN

DEACON'S CAMP - EARLY MORNING

The first light of dawn streamed through the trees, casting a golden hue across the camp. Deacon stood outside the warehouse, his back to the rising sun as he took a moment to breathe in the crisp morning air. Though the night had been long and fraught with challenges, he could feel a sense of renewed determination among the group.

As he adjusted his gear, he heard the familiar sound of footsteps behind him. It was Jake, stretching and yawning, trying to shake off the remnants of sleep.

"Morning, Deacon," Jake greeted, a hint of eagerness in his voice. "Are we really going to scout today? Shouldn't we rest a bit more after everything?"

Deacon chuckled lightly, shaking his head. "Rest is a luxury we can't afford, my friend. If we want to survive, we need to be proactive. Plus, we have Lila now—she might provide some valuable information about our surroundings."

Jake nodded, already dismissed from his sleepiness. "All right, let's do this then. I've got your back."

ABANDONED WAREHOUSE - MORNING

Inside, the mood among the group was bustling with energy as they assembled supplies for the day. Emily was reviewing their medical stock while Reverend Thomas helped her organize.

"Looks like we might be running low on antiseptics, and we should check our bandages as well," Emily assessed, her brow furrowed in concentration.

"Not to mention food. We could use a full haul today," Reverend Thomas replied, glancing at the packets of food and empty cans scattered across the countertop.

Just then, Lila entered the room, a hopeful expression on her face. "Can I help? I know some places nearby where we might find supplies, and I'm good at scouting."

"Of course, Lila," Emily replied, smiling at her eagerness. "We could use your local knowledge."

"Let's get everyone together," Frank said, stepping in from outside with Deacon right behind him. "We can finalize our teams."

DEACON'S CAMP - LATER THAT MORNING

The team gathered together in a circle around the campfire, the sun rising higher in the sky. Deacon stood at the center, unfurling a map on the ground.

"Alright, here's how it's going to work," he began, pointing to various locations marked on the map. "Frank, Lila, and Reverend Thomas will head into town to check for any remaining shops or supplies. Keep a steady pace; be on the lookout for anything suspicious. Keep your radio on."

"And what about us?" Jake interjected, crossing his arms.

"Jake and Colonel Stone will scout the perimeter and assess any potential threats. Stay focused and cover ground systematically. Anything, and I mean anything, that catches your eye, report back." Deacon reinforced, his voice steady.

Nadine shifted nervously, glancing at Emily. "What about me?

What should I do?"

Emily looked at Nadine encouragingly. "You can come with us. Your fresh perspective could help us spot anything we might miss."

Nadine nodded, though a flicker of anxiety lingered in her eyes. "Okay, I'm in."

EXT. WOODS - DAY

As the teams split up, Deacon took a moment to watch them go, adrenaline ready to fuel their expedition. They ventured into the surrounding woods, the sunlight draping the path ahead like a golden promise, yet uncertainty lingered in the air.

"Stay close, grouped," Deacon barked as he carefully led Colonel Stone and Jake toward the tree line, their senses honed and alert.

"We need to work quickly," Colonel Stone said, scanning the area with sharp eyes. "No telling who—or what—could be lurking in these woods."

As they progressed, each step brought them deeper into the surreal landscape that had become their life—a continuous cycle of decay and survival.

ABANDONED STORE - SAME TIME

Meanwhile, in the town, Frank, Lila, and Reverend Thomas moved cautiously through the debris, the remnants of society crumbling around them. The shops, once vibrant with life, now stood hollow, their windows shattered, giving them a glimpse into the echoes of the past.

"I see some cans over there," Lila pointed out, her voice a mix of excitement and apprehension. "Let's check if they're still good."

They slowly approached an old grocery store, its aisles still stocked with long-forgotten treasures.

"Be careful, everyone," Frank whispered as they moved cautiously through the store. "We don't know who else might be here."

Suddenly, another loud noise echoed from deeper within—a scraping sound, low and threatening.

"What was that?" Reverend Thomas whispered, eyes darting around.

"Let's investigate, but stay close," Frank urged, leading the way as the three of them readied their weapons.

EXT. WOODS - DAY

Outside, Deacon, Jake, and Colonel Stone reached the edge of a clearing. Deacon paused, squinting into the distance, alert for any signs of trouble.

"Look," Jake pointed, motioning towards a cluster of trees where something shifted. "Do you see it?"

"Yes," Deacon replied. "Stay low and quiet. We'll flank it from both sides."

As they steeled themselves, a distorted SHADOW moved again, catching Deacon's trained eye.

"What are we dealing with?" Colonel Stone asked, holding his weapon tightly.

"Find out," Deacon commanded, taking a deep breath as he prepared to confront the unknown.

ABANDONED STORE - SAME TIME

Back in the grocery store, Frank and the others crept toward the source of the noise, glancing over their shoulders. As they rounded a corner, they found themselves face-to-face with a trio of GUILT APPARITIONS, shadowy figures writhing in malicious glee, their cries echoing through the aisles.

"No!" Reverend Thomas gasped, gripping his flashlight tightly. "These are manifestations of regret... the weight of our past misdeeds."

Frank's pulse quickened as the apparitions began to fade in and out before them, whispering dark memories that clawed at their thoughts. "We can't let them get into our heads!" he yelled, shaking off the mounting panic.

"Yeah, but how do we fight them?" Lila asked, trembling slightly.

"Stay focused," Reverend Thomas said, raising his voice above the haunting whispers. "They can only take power from what we give them. Remember who you are, and they will have no hold!"

Determined not to let the spirits overpower their resolve, Frank gritted his teeth, tightening his grip on his weapon. "Let's move!" he shouted, rallying Lila and Thomas toward the exit.

WOODS - MOMENTS LATER

Meanwhile, in the woods, the shadow moved again, drawing closer. Deacon's instincts blared warning bells in his mind. He motioned for Jake and Colonel Stone to prepare for whatever emerged from the cover of the trees.

"On my signal, we break left and right," Deacon said, his voice a tight whisper. "We don't want whatever it is to flank us."

The tense silence stretched taut, interrupted only by the rustle of leaves. Then, without warning, a FIGURE burst from the underbrush—a **YOUNG MAN**, gaunt and wild-eyed, stumbling as if chased.

"Help! Please!" he yelled, falling to his knees, hands raised in surrender. "I didn't mean to trespass! I was just—"

"Stay back!" Jake growled, raising his weapon defensively.

Deacon, however, felt a flicker of empathy. "Wait—let him speak. We don't know what he's running from."

The young man gasped for breath, words tumbling out in a rush. "There's a group... a hostile group! They're coming this way! I barely slipped away."

Colonel Stone narrowed his eyes, his posture easing slightly as he lowered his weapon. "What group? Is this a joke?"

"No! They're dangerous!" the young man pleaded. "They've been raiding the area—taking everything from any survivors they find. I heard them talking about hitting your camp next!"

Deacon glanced at Jake, who wore a skeptical expression. "How do we know he's not leading them to us?" Jake asked, brow furrowing.

"Because if he was, he wouldn't have warned us," Deacon replied, stepping cautiously closer to the young man. "What's your name?"

"Evan," he replied, eyes wide and earnest. "I'm just trying to survive. Please, you have to believe me!"

"Trust is something we can't afford to waste," Colonel Stone stated, crossing his arms. "Not until we know for sure you're not a threat."

Deacon took a deep breath, feeling the weight of the decision pressing down on him. "You're not armed, right? If we let you stay, you've got to prove you're on our side."

Evan nodded vigorously. "I'll do whatever it takes. I just need a chance."

"Let him stay with us," Deacon said, looking between his team.

"If he's telling the truth, we may have an ally in the fight against raiders."

Stones' face softened just a bit. "Fine. But keep an eye on him. We'll give him a chance, but it's a short one."

As they allowed Evan to join their ranks, the atmosphere around them shifted—a new dynamic forming among the group.

ABANDONED WAREHOUSE - LATER THAT NIGHT

Back at the warehouse, Emily, Nadine, and Reverend Thomas worked to treat the wounded survivor from earlier. The sound of laughter echoed from the scavenged medical supplies, blending warmth with the chilling uncertainty of their existence.

"I think I found some painkillers!" Nadine called out, pulling a bottle from a patch of sunlight filtering through the dusty windows.

Emily smiled and took it, grateful for the help. "Good work! We can use these for our patients."

Just then, the lights flickered, causing everyone to pause and glance around nervously. "Power fluctuations?" Nadine asked, concern creeping in.

"Could be," Reverend Thomas replied, glancing at the shadows. "Let's keep an eye out."

WOODS - MOMENTS LATER

Meanwhile, outside the warehouse, Deacon, Colonel Stone, Jake, and Evan began to make their way to the perimeter. The camaraderie from earlier was transformed into a palpable tension as shadows danced along the path.

"This is where you saw them last?" Colonel Stone asked Evan, his voice a low growl, echoing through the undergrowth.

"Just beyond those trees," Evan said, pointing nervously. "They were organizing into groups. I overheard them—definitely planning an attack on your camp."

"Then we need to move quickly," Deacon said, determination surging through him. "Jake, take point. Evan, stay close to me."

As they moved closer to the trees, eyes peeled for any sign of movement, the hairs on the back of Deacon's neck stood on end.

"Everyone stay low," he commanded, the urgency of their situation clear.

Suddenly, the bushes rustled again, and the group froze, weapons raised, alert for danger.

FLASHLIGHTS DANCE ALONG THE TREES

Then, from the shadows, another figure emerged, calling out breathlessly. "Wait! Please don't shoot!"

Deacon and his team exchanged alarmed glances, instincts screaming that they were walking into a trap.

"Identify yourself!" Stone shouted; his weapon trained on the unknown figure.

"Chill out! I'm one of you!" a WOMAN gasped, stepping into the light, hands raised. She was disheveled but held an unmistakable air of defiance.

"Who are you?" Deacon barked, maintaining a firm stance.

"Rachel," she replied quickly, her eyes scanning the gathered group, assessing them. "I've been on the run from a hostile group just like you. I overheard them discussing plans to raid your camp. You need to be careful!"

Deacon raised an eyebrow, uncertainty eating away at his resolve. Another person claiming to be a survivor, another potential threat.

"We don't take in strangers without a fight," he warned, still readying his weapon.

"Please, I just want to survive!" Rachel pleaded; desperation evident in her voice. "I know where their camp is. I could help you."

"Help us?" Jake scoffed, unwilling to lower his guard. "How do we know you're not leading them right to us?"

"Because I'm risking my life just talking to you right now!" Rachel shot back, emotion weaving through her words. "I want the same thing you do—life, safety, and family."

Deacon paused, looking at his team, sensing the unease in the air. "Let's give her a moment," he decided, glancing at Colonel Stone, who nodded.

As they hesitated, the woods around them became silent, and a low whisper of the wind filled the air with a haunting reminder of the dangers that lay just beyond their sight.

"Alright, Rachel," Deacon said after a moment, lowering his weapon cautiously. "You can join us. But know this—one slip, and I won't hesitate to take you down."

Rachel nodded, a flicker of gratitude crossing her features, and as Deacon invited another potential ally into their fold, he felt the weight of the night settle heavily around them—a reminder that in this world, trust was a fragile commodity.

CHAPTER 10: SUSPICION AND STRATEGY

ABANDONED WAREHOUSE - NIGHT

As the evening deepened, the atmosphere inside the warehouse became increasingly charged. The flickering lanterns cast shaky light across the gathered survivors, their faces reflecting a mix of determination and worry. Lila, still processing the unexpected appearance of the new woman, Rachel, watched closely as Deacon conversed with her.

"Tell us what you know about this raider group," Deacon urged, crossing his arms. The scrutiny in his piercing gaze felt heavy.

Rachel took a deep breath, her expression firming. "They're ruthless. They started as a group of survivors like us, but desperation twisted them into bandits. They raid camps, take resources, and don't hesitate to eliminate anyone who stands in their way."

"Have you seen them?" Frank's voice trembled slightly, a mix of fear and curiosity. "How many are we talking about?"

"Maybe ten or twelve," Rachel replied, her eyes darting. "That's if they haven't taken on more members since I left. They're dangerous because they know how to manipulate others. They play on fear and build a sense of loyalty among their grunts to keep them in line."

"Sounds like we could be in for a tough fight," Colonel Stone said, his brow furrowing. "We'll need to fortify our defenses even more."

"Or we could strike first," Jake interjected, his enthusiasm bubbling under the surface. "If we can take the fight to them, we can gauge their numbers and maybe disband them before they even reach us."

Deacon shook his head. "No, we don't have enough intel to risk an offensive. We need to gather more information first. I don't want to lose anyone unnecessarily."

"But what if they launch an attack here?" Rachel insisted, a tremor of urgency in her voice. "We need to be prepared. I can lead you to their last known location."

Deacon studied her for a moment, weighing the possibility. "If you can guide us and prove your trust, it might give us the upper hand," he said finally. "But we need to work as a unit. That means all of us—not just you leading a group into the dark."

"You'll have to trust me," Rachel replied earnestly. "This is my chance to atone for surviving when others didn't."

The group absorbed her words, a heavy silence hanging in the air. Reverend Thomas broke the tension, placing a hand on Rachel's shoulder. "Forgiveness is possible through unity. We'll reach out to the light together."

WOODS - NIGHT - MOMENTS LATER

As night melded into deeper shadows outside the abandoned warehouse, Deacon gathered the group to prepare for their scouting mission. Flashlights and weapons were checked, leaving a palpable energy in the air as they set off toward the woods.

"Stick together!" Deacon reminded them as they stepped beyond the threshold.

The trio of Frank, Carla, and Rachel formed one scouting party, while Deacon and Colonel Stone led Jake into the depths of the unknown.

EXT. WOODS - CONTINUOUS

The forest enveloped them, darkness creeping in thick as the trees stretched overhead. Sounds began to whisper from within the shadows, but the group pressed on, hearts pounding with each rustle in the underbrush.

"Keep your guard up," Colonel Stone directed, his military instincts sharp. "Remember what's at stake."

They cautiously advanced, eyes scanning the surroundings for any sign of movement. As they moved deeper, the tension escalated, each snapping twig heightening their senses.

Suddenly, Deacon halted, raising a hand. "Do you hear that?"

A low murmur reverberated through the trees, chilling as it blended with the night air. The sounds filtered in—an almost melodic tone mixed with guttural growls.

"Sounds like a campfire," Jake whispered, eyes darting around nervously. "But not ours."

"Could be their camp," Deacon murmured, his gut twisting. "We need to reconnoiter before making any moves."

They crept closer, instincts guiding them as they positioned themselves behind a large tree, peering through the foliage toward the small cluster of light ahead.

RAIDER CAMP - NIGHT

A makeshift encampment lay spread out before them, with several tents pitched haphazardly among the trees. A flickering fire illuminated rough faces—raiders gathered around, their laughter mingling with crude songs, hardly masking their predatory aura.

"Look!" Colonel Stone hissed quietly, pointing out two massive men standing guard at the entrance. "They're definitely here."

"Let's count heads," Deacon said, settling into observation. "If we know their numbers, we can act."

As they watched, they counted the raiders and took mental notes on their weapons and wary movements, carefully plotting their next steps.

ABANDONED WAREHOUSE - NIGHT - SIMULTANEOUSLY

Meanwhile, back in the warehouse, Emily and Nadine had fallen into a rhythm gathering supplies and checking the medical stock they had.

"What do you think is going on with Deacon and the others?" Nadine asked, a hint of concern lacing her voice.

Emily paused, weighing her thoughts. "It's hard to say. Revealing their position could lead to trouble… but they also need to gather intel we lack."

Suddenly, the lantern flickered ominously, and the temperature around them seemed to drop.

"Do you feel that?" Nadine asked, her voice lower than a whisper, eyes wide with unease.

"Yeah, something isn't right," Emily said, glancing toward the entrance. "We should tighten security. If the raiders come, I want to be ready."

Emily grabbed a few extra medical supplies and weapons, preparing for the worst, believing that their safety depended not only on strength but `also on vigilance.

RAIDER CAMP - NIGHT

As Deacon continued to observe the raider camp, a dreaded realization washed over him. "They're getting restless," he murmured, noticing the tension between the raiders and their haphazard organization.

"Let's backtrack before they spot us," Colonel Stone said, sensing the urgency.

"Wait!" Jake said, pointing toward a smaller figure sneaking around the perimeter of the camp. "Look over there!"

It was a young girl, no more than ten, her clothes tattered and filthy as she stealthily navigated between the tents, a frightened look on her face.

"Why is she out here?" Deacon whispered, horror creeping in. "She shouldn't be here."

"Maybe she's being used as a spy or a messenger," Colonel Stone suggested, grim determination in his voice. "We can't leave her here."

Deacon felt a mix of resolve and dread swirl in his stomach. "We need to help her," he decided. "But we must be careful. It could turn the raiders against us."

"What if we take her with us into the woods? We can get her to safety," Jake offered, nodding firmly.

"Fine," Deacon confirmed. "Jake, stay behind. I'll stay with Stone to approach the camp quietly. We'll grab her and bring her to safety. Everyone else, stay hidden. We move fast."

With a silent nod, Jake crouched down to remain concealed as Deacon and Colonel Stone carefully maneuvered through the underbrush toward the camp.

RAIDER CAMP - CONTINUOUS

Deacon's heart raced as he and Stone edged closer to the flickering firelight. The sounds of raucous laughter and shouts from the raiders enveloped them, contrasting sharply with the child's vulnerable presence.

"There's the girl," Stone whispered, his eyes locking onto the small figure moving cautiously near a tent. "We need to get her before they notice."

As they crept closer, Deacon noticed that the girl was watching the raiders with fear in her eyes, clearly desperate to escape but unsure how to do so.

"Just a few more steps," Deacon murmured, keeping his grip firm on his weapon.

Suddenly, a loud shout rang out from the camp. A rugged raider cursed as he knocked over a crate. "Watch where you're stepping, idiot!" he yelled, laughter erupting around the fire.

The girl flinched, her eyes widening further as she darted towards the shadows, tension rising as she risked drawing attention.

"Now's our chance," Deacon said, moving quickly toward her as Stone covered him. They emerged from the brush into the dim light of the fire.

"Over here!" Deacon called softly but urgently, motioning to the girl.

She paused, looking torn between trust and her instincts.

"Come on, we're here to help," Deacon urged, his voice calm and inviting. "They're not safe; you need to get away from them."

The girl hesitated, glancing back at the raiders, who had begun to quiet down, sensing that something was amiss.

"Now!" Stone urged, taking a cautious step forward.

With a deep breath, the girl bolted toward Deacon. He met her halfway, crouching to her level as he grasped her shoulder gently. "You're safe with us. Stay close."

As they turned to retreat, a shrill voice cut through the air. "Hey! Where do you think you're going?"

RAIDER CAMP - NIGHT

A raider had spotted them, raising his weapon and shouting to the others. "Intruders!"

Pandemonium erupted around the camp as Deacon's heart pounded. "Run!" he shouted, urging the girl forward as chaos swelled behind them.

Deacon grabbed the girl's hand, pulling her along as they sprinted through the trees, the sounds of the raiders barking orders and footfalls pounding behind them.

Stone followed closely behind, keeping Deacon and the girl shielded as bullets whizzed past, the air thick with the rush of adrenaline and fear.

"We have to get to the camp! We can't let them surround us!" Deacon yelled, leading them toward the familiar landscape he hoped would offer some safety.

DEACON'S CAMP - MOMENTS LATER

Panting and terrified, the trio burst out of the woods, rushing toward the camp. Emily, Nadine, and the others looked up in alarm as the frantic sounds of pursuit drew closer.

"Deacon!" Emily shouted, alarmed, seeing the fear in their eyes. She rushed towards them, embracing the girl momentarily. "You found her!"

"Get inside!" Deacon barked, pushing them all forward. "We've got company!"

As they entered the camp, the sounds of the raiders grew closer, shouting orders as they pursued their prey. Colonel Stone remained standing guard, weapon ready, eyes sharp as Deacon hurriedly closed the entrance.

ABANDONED WAREHOUSE - MAIN ROOM - NIGHT

Once inside the warehouse, everyone took cover, weapons drawn and voices lowered. The atmosphere buzzed with heightened tension as they prepared for the impending confrontation.

"We won't let them take us without a fight," Deacon declared, eyes scanning his team as they sought refuge.

"What's the situation with your scouting mission?" Emily asked quickly. "Did you learn anything that can help us?"

"Raider camp is close; they're organized and ready for a fight," Deacon replied breathlessly, his adrenaline still surging. "We have to prepare."

Jake exchanged glances with the group, his demeanor serious. "So, what's the plan?"

"We need to fortify our position and set up traps around the perimeter," Colonel Stone suggested. "If they breach our defenses, we need to minimize our losses."

"We can use everything we have," Deacon said, rallying their spirits. "I want everyone to check their weapons, and let's set for a defensive formation."

A sudden CLATTER came from outside, followed by a loud voice shouting, "I know you're in there! Come out with your hands up!"

Deacon tightened his grip on his weapon, eyes narrowing at the entrance. "They're trying to intimidate us," he muttered.

"We need to set an example."

"Maybe we should negotiate," Emily suggested cautiously. "They might be willing to talk before charging in."

Deacon hesitated, weighing their options. "We don't know their intentions. What if they're just looking for an excuse to attack?"

"Then let's make them rethink their strategy," Stone said with resolve. "Lead with strength. Show them we're not afraid."

"Agreed," Deacon replied, feeling the weight of leadership settle firmly on his shoulders. "Prepare for the worst, but be ready to defend what's ours."

As the clamoring voices grew louder, the group readied themselves, adrenaline coursing through their veins in anticipation of what was to come.

CHAPTER 11: THE CLASH OF SURVIVAL

DEACON'S CAMP - NIGHT

The atmosphere was thick with tension as the raider voices grew closer, their taunts echoing through the darkness. Deacon and his team stood in the dim light of the warehouse, weapons raised and hearts racing—prepared for whatever was about to unfold.

"Remember, we're defending our lives, not just our supplies," Deacon said, glancing around at the determined faces of his team. "Stick together; we can't let them divide us."

"Let's show these raiders what we're made of," Jake added, an eager fire shining in his eyes. The others nodded, their resolve hardening.

A loud BANG resonated as one of the raiders kicked the door, testing their defenses. The team braced themselves, weapons pointed at the entrance, ready for an all-out assault.

OUTSIDE THE WAREHOUSE - MOMENTS LATER

"Open up, or we'll come in after you!" a male raider shouted, his voice heavy with threat. "You have ten seconds before we make this a bloody affair!"

Deacon glanced at the others; their anxiety palpable. "We stick to the plan. No one shoots until I give the order," he instructed, scanning the area for potential vulnerabilities.

Suddenly, a loud CRASH erupted as the raiders made their move. The wooden doors splintered as they were breached, sending splinters flying through the air. Shadows poured into the dim space, revealing the ragged figures of live raiders, their eyes glinting with malice.

"Get ready!" Deacon shouted as the first raider, a hulking man with a scarred face, rushed through the entrance, followed by two more.

ABANDONED WAREHOUSE - NIGHT

With the gunfire ringing through the air, Deacon quickly assessed the situation. "Fire at will!" he commanded, signaling the team to unleash their weapons.

Shots rang out, echoing off the walls as Deacon took aim, focusing on the nearest raider. The chaos erupted, bullets flying and cries of shock and pain reverberating as the team engaged the armed intruders.

Colonel Stone moved like a trained soldier, his experience evident as he fired accurately, taking down one of the raiders in his sights. Frank joined in, his heartbeat racing as he fought alongside Deacon and the others—a sense of unity forming amidst the frenzy.

In the corner, Emily and Nadine worked quickly, fortifying the makeshift barricades against the incoming threats. They needed to ensure the area remained defended against whatever raiders fell back or attempted to flank their position.

"Keep your head up, Nadine!" Emily shouted, her brow glistening with sweat. "We need to hold the lines!"

"Yes, I'm on it!" Nadine replied, determination lighting her eyes even as she arranged crates and debris to reinforce their position.

CAMP - NIGHT

Outside, chaos enveloped the area as the raiders fought to press through the breach. The first raider charged deeper inside, brandishing a baseball bat, swinging wildly at the group as he crashed into one of the crates, splintering it beneath his weight.

"Push them back!" Deacon roared over the din of battle, his own heart pounding as he moved toward the front lines. He spotted Rachel, behind a crate, taking aim with her weapon, her face set with fierce determination.

"Stay focused!" he instructed, feeling the weight of their mission on his shoulders. This was not only about survival, but about protecting every soul in their ragtag camp.

Just then, another wave of raiders surged through the door, and the fight intensified. The warehouse was filled with flashes of gunfire, guttural roars from the demons, and collective roars of defiance from Deacon's team.

In the turmoil, Deacon spotted one of the raiders, a wiry man with a wild mane and wild eyes, trying to sneak around the side toward where Emily and Nadine were working.

"Watch out!" Deacon yelled, sprinting toward them.

He reached just in time to push Emily aside as the raider lunged toward her, knife glinting in the dim light. The force sent Deacon crashing against a column, but he quickly regained his footing, his body instinctively moving to protect his team.

"Get back!" he shouted, disarming the raider with a well-placed kick before drawing his own weapon, feeling the adrenaline surge. The struggle was fierce, but Deacon was determined to protect them all.

ABANDONED WAREHOUSE - NIGHT CONTINUED

Jake and Colonel Stone held their ground, pushing back against the raiders with a coordinated effort.

"Let's flank them!" Colonel Stone shouted, his commanding voice cutting through the chaos, directing Jake to their left. Together, they maneuvered, taking down another raider with a swift series of shots.

Just as it seemed they were regaining control, a loud scream sounded—the last raider's desperate cry echoing as a flash of movement drew everyone's attention.

A massive FLESH RIPPER charged into the fray, its twisted body a horrifying sight, its growls mixing with the sounds of battle.

DEACON'S CAMP - NIGHT

Everyone froze at the sight of the monstrous abomination smashing through the remnants of the camp, pushing raiders left and right as it sought to join the fight. The air filled with desperation; chaos intensified.

"Not today!" Deacon yelled, shaking off the shock and regaining focus. "Everyone, back to your positions! We can't let it break through!"

Emily's heart raced as she turned to Nadine. "We need to prepare to deal with that thing!" she shouted, urgency overwhelming her calm.

"I'll grab more supplies!" Nadine replied, the dog barking at the chaos, sensing the danger.

Deacon moved to the front lines, reloading his weapon confidently. "With every shot, we fight against despair!" he roared, rallying the team.

"Together! Hold your ground!" Colonel Stone bellowed,

moving to flank the monster as it crashed into the camp, teeth bared and growling, eyes locked on its prey.

Their firepower erupted again, echoing with a fierce resolve, determined not just to survive but to reclaim their right to fight. The atmosphere crackled with tension as both sides advanced, knowing that victory meant the difference between life and death.

CHAPTER 12: INTO THE FRAY

ABANDONED WAREHOUSE - NIGHT

The chaos inside the warehouse escalated as the arrival of the Flesh Ripper sent shockwaves through the group. The creature lunged forward, its jaws snapping wide as it aimed for Deacon.

"Fall back! Fall back!" Deacon shouted, taking aim at the soul-sucking beast.

The air filled with the sounds of clattering boots, gunfire, and frantic cries as the group pushed back against the raiders and the Flesh Ripper alike. Adrenaline coursed through Deacon's veins, fueling an unyielding determination to protect his makeshift family.

Colonel Stone worked in tandem with Jake, their movements fluid as they fired shots aimed at the mighty creature. The Flesh Ripper roared, the sound reverberating off the walls as it spun towards them, an embodiment of primal terror.

"Deacon! Keep it distracted!" Colonel Stone shouted as he repositioned himself, lining up for another shot.

"On it!" Deacon said, steeling his nerves. He focused his attention on the Flesh Ripper, watching its movements, calculating its next strike.

"I'll flank left; you go right!" Jake proposed, preparing to sprint past Deacon, his muscles coiling like a spring.

"Right!" Deacon confirmed. He steadied his breath, waiting for the opportune moment. Just then, the Flesh Ripper lunged toward him, drool pooling on the floor as it snapped desperately.

Deacon sidestepped, barely avoiding the creature's jaws, and fired off two quick shots aimed at its head. The bullets hit their mark, causing the Flesh Ripper to stagger, momentarily thrown off balance.

DEACON'S CAMP - NIGHT - CONTINUOUS

While the fight raged within, Nadine rushed around, gathering supplies that could aid the group against the sinister threat. In her mind, she replayed the lessons learned from Emily—the medical supplies would be crucial in the unfolding battle.

Suddenly, she heard the cries of struggle from the other side of the warehouse. Her instincts kicked in. "I have to help!" she muttered, but just as she made to join the others, the scruffy dog barked excitedly, almost as if urging her to stay put.

"Nobody's going to leave you behind," she reassured the dog. "But I can't just stand here."

With a determined nod, she moved toward the commotion, grabbing a heavy metal pipe as a makeshift weapon to defend herself, adrenaline making her heart race.

ABANDONED WAREHOUSE - NIGHT - CONTINUOUS

Back inside, the fight reached a fever pitch. Frank and Emily worked side by side, firing their weapons and helping to hold the line against the raiders, whose numbers swelled with the chaos.

"Keep moving! Don't let them corner us!" Frank yelled; his voice barely audible over the chaos.

"Almost out of ammo!" Emily shouted back, reloading her weapon in a swift, practiced motion. She glanced around for anything left that could help. "We need something stronger!"

Just as she uttered those words, a wounded raider stumbled into view, clutching his side and grimacing in pain. Without thinking, Emily took aim.

"Get down!" she warned, her instincts guiding her as she aimed at the raider, keeping her focus sharp.

The raider, desperate and dangerously flailing, lashed out in a last-ditch effort but instead fell to the ground, momentarily forgotten amid the ruckus.

The Flesh Ripper roared once more, its attention turning away from Deacon, who seized the moment to sprint toward Emily.

"Get the supplies!" he yelled, signaling her to take cover.

WOODS - NIGHT

Outside, Colonel Stone continued to lead the charge against the Flesh Ripper, and Jake was right there beside him. They coordinated their movements and aimed meticulously.

"Now!" Colonel Stone commanded, and they both fired together, hitting the beast square in the chest. It let out a horrific shriek, staggering back, but not falling just yet.

"Let's keep it distracted—back to the corridor!" Jake suggested, pointing at the opening that led toward the rows of hospital equipment that could potentially be turned against the creature.

Stone nodded, moving toward the hallway, maintaining fire as the Flesh Ripper drew closer, its eyes fixated on their movements. "Draw it in! It won't follow if it thinks there's an escape route."

As they retreated, the rest of their group pulled together, forming a tighter barricade as they regrouped near the entrance like a dam against the flood of chaos.

ABANDONED WAREHOUSE - NIGHT

Inside the warehouse, tension hung in the air as Deacon called for a move. "Everyone, near the medical area! We'll make our stand there!"

The dog began barking uncontrollably, sensing the building strife and the potential danger at hand. Nadine, weapon in hand, ran to catch up with the others who had begun to move.

"Stay close!" Deacon shouted over the ongoing fray as they staggered toward the back where Emily had set up supplies.

As they reached the makeshift medical area, Deacon evaluated their surroundings, and his mind whirled with possibilities. If they could fortify this area and create a defensive position, they might just stand a chance.

"Grab anything that might help us!" he commanded, as the group hurried to gather supplies—bottles of antiseptic, bandages, and anything heavy enough to use as an improvised barrier.

DEACON'S CAMP - NIGHT - SIMULTANEOUSLY

Outside, chaos erupted as the stolen volley of gunfire continued, the incessant growls and roars sharp against the sudden silence of the woods.

"Get that door barricaded!" Colonel Stone barked as he reloaded, keeping focus on the Flesh Ripper that bulldozed toward them, relentless in its pursuit.

Jake positioned himself behind a cluster of crates, eyeing the beast's movements. "We need to distract it. Maybe one of us can lead it away while the others flank!"

"Are you crazy?" Colonel Stone replied, turning serious. "You can't put yourself at risk like that!"

"I won't let it get to the others!" Jake replied, his resolve unwavering. "Give me a chance!"

A series of SHOUTS and GUNSHOTS erupted back inside the warehouse, mingling with the sounds of battle.

"I hope your instincts are right!" Colonel Stone said begrudgingly, turning his attention back to the Flesh Ripper as it approached, only a few paces away.

"I'll cover you!" Jake surged forward, knowing that the time to act was now. As the creature lunged, Jake shouted, drawing its attention toward him.

"Hey, over here!" he yelled desperately, motioning for it to chase him.

The Flesh Ripper turned, snapping its jaws as it bore down on Jake, its gnashing teeth glinting in the scattered light. Stone realized that Jake's gamble could pay off—or cost them dearly.

ABANDONED WAREHOUSE - NIGHT - CONTINUOUS

Inside the warehouse, the atmosphere was thick with tension and fear as the others prepared for the impending clash. Deacon, Emily, and the remaining survivors moved urgently, packing the area with supplies that could be used as defensive measures against the chaos outside.

"Everyone, grab anything that can be used to barricade the entrance!" Deacon commanded, scanning the room for makeshift weapons. "We need to buy ourselves time."

"Got it!" Nadine replied, her voice steady as she moved to a stack of crates, dragging them closer to the entrance. The scruffy dog followed her, barking encouragingly, instinctively sensing the urgency.

"Come on! We don't have all night!" Frank shouted, pushing chairs and tables against the door while keeping his eyes fixed on the shadows beyond.

Emily, focused on treating the wounded survivor, glanced up briefly to survey the tension among the group. "Once we're barricaded, we can plan our next move. We can't afford to lose anyone else," she reminded, trying to encourage the others.

"We'll hold this line," Deacon said resolutely, pulling a few more supplies closer to create a formidable wall of defenses.

DEACON'S CAMP - NIGHT - SIMULTANEOUSLY

Outside, the battle escalated as Jake lured the Flesh Ripper away from the entrance of the warehouse. The creature lunged forward, its massive jaws snapping dangerously close as Jake dodged to the side, adrenaline surging through him.

"Come on, you ugly beast!" Jake shouted, leading it further into the woods as he glanced back to see Colonel Stone readying a shot.

"Keep moving!" Colonel Stone yelled, taking aim. "I'll draw it back toward the camp!"

Jake sprinted forward, heart racing as he glanced over his shoulder. The Flesh Ripper was fast, but he was faster. He zigzagged through the trees, using every ounce of his strength to stay ahead.

"Just a little bit closer!" he urged himself, picturing the warehouse behind him as a sanctuary, the only safe space they had left.

As the creature raged closer, Colonel Stone took full advantage of the distraction. He adjusted his aim and fired, striking the Flesh Ripper in the flank. The shot echoed like thunder, sending shockwaves through the air.

ABANDONED WAREHOUSE - NIGHT

Back in the warehouse, the noise outside caught their attention. Deacon's heart raced as he caught a glimpse of the chaos through the makeshift barricade.

"We need to regroup!" Deacon shouted, adrenaline spurring him to move. "If they breach, we can't let them find weak points!"

"More raiders could come too!" Nadine shouted from her position. "We need to be prepared for both!"

Just then, the loud banging returned from the door, causing the group to jump. Things could quickly become hazardous if they didn't stay sharp and alert.

"Stay together!" Frank yelled, standing guard with Emily beside him, weapons steady. "We protect this space!"

CAMP - NIGHT - CONTINUOUS

As Jake broke free from the woods and rejoined the group, he was winded but alive, his heart pounding as he took position next to Colonel Stone.

"Is everyone alright?" Jake breathed, trying to catch his breath, scanning the group for signs of trouble.

"We're holding it together," Deacon replied. "But we can't let them wear us down. Colonel—you and Jake spearhead the next approach. We'll act as reinforcements. If we can draw them away from the entrance, we'll keep our people safe."

"Understood," Colonel Stone said, his voice filled with quiet conviction. "Let's knock them back and reclaim this space."

Just then, the trio of raiders appeared on the edge of the wood line, having heard the noise of their struggle. "We know you're in there!" a raider shouted, arrogance lacing his words.

Deacon stepped forward, using this as an opportunity. "Gather around, everyone! We're facing this head-on!"

ABANDONED WAREHOUSE - MAIN ROOM - NIGHT

Frank and Emily took strategic positions near the main entrance, their determination palpable as the air thickened with desperation.

"What do you think their strategy will be?" Emily asked, her eyes keen as she scanned the entrance.

"They'll try to overwhelm us with numbers," Frank replied, sweat trickling down his brow. "But if we stay coordinated, we've got a fighting chance."

"Here they come!" Nadine warned, her voice cutting through the tension.

CAMP - NIGHT - CONTINUOUS

The raiders surged forward, brandishing weapons and racing towards the warehouse, their laughter intermingling with a sense of impending doom. Deacon steadied himself, ready to defend what was theirs.

"On my command…" Deacon murmured, readying his weapon as the raiders drew closer.

"Fire!" he bellowed, and the group opened fire, the unified sound of gunfire echoing against the night.

The raiders staggered under their assault, multiple shots ringing, illuminating the grim reality of battle as they fought against the tide of chaos.

"Remember to watch your angles!" Colonel Stone yelled, advancing alongside Jake, forming a defensive wall against the onslaught.

ABANDONED WAREHOUSE - NIGHT

Back inside, the tension was thick as the team monitored their defenses, readying to move into the fray if needed.

"Aim true! We've got to protect our ground!" Deacon shouted, heart thundering in sync with the explosive chaos just beyond their walls.

As the raiders crashed against their defenses, it was clear that they wouldn't go down without a fight.

And so, the battle raged on, the fate of their makeshift family teetering on a blade, as they fought not only against external demons but against the internal fears that threatened to tear them apart.

CHAPTER 13: BONDS TESTED

ABANDONED WAREHOUSE - MAIN ROOM - NIGHT

Chaos reigned inside the warehouse as Deacon and his team faced off against the wave of raiders. Gunfire echoed through the air, ringing out in blasts that drew closer to the confines of their refuge. Deacon's focus sharpened, every instinct honing in on protecting those he'd sworn to lead.

"Watch your flanks! Keep your heads cool!" he yelled, directing Frank and Emily as they took aim at an advancing group of raiders, some brandishing makeshift weapons while others fired indiscriminately.

The sound of bullets ricocheted against the walls, punctuated by harsh grunts and the shouts of pain. Sweat dripped down Deacon's brow as he surveyed the scene, adrenaline fueling his every move.

CAMP - NIGHT - CONTINUOUS

Outside, Colonel Stone and Jake stood together, bracing their shoulders against the onslaught. The raider's push was relentless, their numbers overwhelming, but each of them held a fierce will to protect their new family.

"Stick to your positions!" Colonel Stone barked, aiming down the sights as one of the raiders approached the front of the warehouse.

"I've got right! You take left!" Jake replied, pumping his weapon in preparation.

As the raiders pushed against the barricade, Jake's muscles tensed, ready for the fight ahead. "I'll shove my boot right up the first bastard that comes through!" he declared, a wild grin spreading over his face despite the chaos.

ABANDONED WAREHOUSE - NIGHT

Inside, the situation grew increasingly dire as Deacon's team fought tooth and nail to maintain their hold on the warehouse. One of the raiders pushed through the weak point in their defenses, and Emily shot him point-blank, sending him sprawling backward.

The adrenaline-fueled momentum surged through the group, but beneath the pressure, the strain of trust began to show.

"We need to pull back!" Frank shouted, reloading quickly. "It's too much!"

"No! We can't let them think they can break us!" Deacon shot back, determination lighting his eyes. "We'll hold our ground—no matter the cost!"

Suddenly, a cacophony of screams erupted as one of the Flesh Rippers charged into an undefended corner of the warehouse. Chaos erupted anew, shattering their fragile defense.

"Deacon!" Emily yelled, sensing the creature closing in on the others. "We need to deal with that first!"

WOODS NEAR THE PERIMETER - NIGHT

Outside, the sounds of battle roared, the pressure of survival pushing each group into the limbs of the forest. Lila, Frank and Reverend Thomas had taken a position to scout the outer edges of their camp, ready to alert the others if necessary.

"Do you think they're okay?" Lila murmured, doubt creeping into her voice as she stared into the distance where gunfire erupted sporadically.

"They're capable," Frank said, though uncertainty flickered in his eyes. "They've faced worse. We have to trust them."

Reverend Thomas placed a calming hand on Lila's shoulder. "Their fates are intertwined with ours. We must remain hopeful."

Suddenly, the sound of heavy footsteps approached from the darkness, urgent and erratic. The trio turned their heads sharply as the shadows shifted, revealing another figure stumbling towards them from the tree line.

"Stop! Who goes there?" Frank barked, raising his weapon defensively.

ABANDONED WAREHOUSE - NIGHT - SIMULTANEOUSLY

Back inside the warehouse, the battle raged on as Deacon and Colonel Stone stood shoulder to shoulder against the Flesh Ripper.

"Keep it distracted!" Colonel Stone commanded as he fired at the creature, glancing at Deacon for support.

"On it!" Deacon replied, redirecting his focus. He sidestepped the demon's lunging attack, drawing closer as it snapped at him with jagged teeth.

In a swift move, Deacon lodged a knife in its side, causing it to howl in agony and turn its attention toward him. The room filled with chaos as the team rallied to work in concert, determined not to let the creature get the upper hand.

"Let's push it back!" Jake yelled, moving in close to land a few hits on the weakened beast.

One of the raiders, overtaken with fear, tried to flee but was tackled by another who had gotten cornered.

"Don't let them run!" Colonel Stone shouted amid the fray. "Everyone we allow to escape can return with reinforcements!"

"More resources!" Frank yelled, firing another shot and glancing at Emily, who was scrambling to check on the wounded survivor. "Make it quick!"

WOODS NEAR THE PERIMETER - NIGHT

Outside, the figure in the shadows stepped fully into view—gasping for breath, it was Jacob, looking disheveled and frantic.

"I need help!" he gasped, clearly chased. "There's a group coming this way!"

The trio shared alarmed glances.

"We need to get back to camp now!" Lila shouted, urgency coursing through her veins.

"Move!" Frank ordered, leading the way back toward the camp, their hearts racing as they calculated the worst that could come—the possibility of betrayal and the reality of threats magnified by the shadows.

ABANDONED WAREHOUSE - NIGHT

Inside the warehouse, the Flesh Ripper was relentless, its howls mingling with the crack of gunfire as Deacon issued commands, guiding his team through the onslaught.

"Stay united! Don't break ranks!" Deacon called, his voice cutting through the chaos.

As they pressed forward, Deacon felt the dynamic shift; the raiders caught between the monster and the survivors.

Confused and desperate, some simply turned to flee. The chaos became an opportunity.

Just then, a loud crash echoed from the entrance as the raiders frantically tried to break free from the advance of the Flesh Ripper.

"Get those barricades reinforced!" Deacon shouted, realizing they were close to losing their foothold.

With renewed resolve, the group fought back, turning the tide of the conflict.

DEACON'S CAMP - MOMENTS LATER

Frank, Lila, and Reverend Thomas burst into the camp just as the chaos rose within the warehouse and saw bodies of the raiders and the Flesh Ripper lying scattered. The air was thick with gunpowder and blood, but the field was theirs.

"They made it!" Reverend Thomas exclaimed, relief flooding through him as they rushed toward the entrance.

Suddenly, they realized that they weren't done yet; there remained shadows shifting within the trees.

"Deacon! They're still here!" Frank shouted; eyes filled with an urgency that mirrored the chaotic energy surrounding them.

ABANDONED WAREHOUSE - NIGHT - CONTINUOUS

Just then, Deacon's voice boomed over the noise. "We need to regroup! Everyone back!"

As the shadows shifted ominously, the realization hit them—the fight was not over. Deacon turned to the remaining team members inside, his expression sharpened with urgency.

"Colonel Stone! Bring any supplies you can find. We need to obstruct their advance!" he commanded, adrenaline racing through him.

Jake nodded, taking position beside Deacon as he scanned the entrance for any signs of the raiders and the Flesh Ripper. "Let's make sure we seal this place up tight," he said, determination in his voice.

Frank, Lila, and Reverend Thomas rushed to gather whatever debris they could find, trying to create a barricade to prevent any raider from slipping through their defenses.

"Over here!" Lila called, pulling at a heavy metal shelf that had fallen earlier. "We can use this to block the entrance."

As they began stacking supplies, the sound of a distant roar echoed through the night air—a reminder that they were still in the danger zone.

WOODS - NIGHT - MOMENTS LATER

Outside the warehouse, shadows lurked at the edge of the trees, and the sound of footsteps grew louder.

"They're coming!" Jake warned, tense and alert, heart racing as he turned to face the woods just beyond their shelter.

Colonel Stone returned with additional materials, the look on his face grim and serious. "We need to keep our wits about us. If we don't hold this line, we might lose everything."

"Right!" Deacon said, feeling the weight of leadership pressing against him. "Colonel Stone, take a side with Jake. Frank, Lila, stay near me and keep the others focused."

"Let's keep communication clear," Frank added, adrenaline surging through him as he caught his breath. "If one of us gets in trouble, call for backup. No one goes in alone."

As they readied themselves at the entrance, Colonel Stone scanned the woods for movement, weapon drawn and eyes hard.

"I don't like this," he muttered. "Not one bit."

Just then, the first raider emerged from the shadows—a lean, wild-looking man, a smirk plastered across his face. "You think you can hold us off? This place will be ours before you even know it!" he taunted, clutching a crowbar in one hand, waves of other raiders forming behind him.

"Looks like we've got guests," Deacon said, his grip tightening around his weapon.

The group braced themselves as the raiders advanced, fueled by a maddening sense of confidence, believing themselves superior to the weary survivors.

ABANDONED WAREHOUSE - NIGHT - CONTINUOUS

"Together!" Deacon roared, shouting words of encouragement as they faced the oncoming tide.

The first wave of raiders rushed toward them, their faces filled with rage, claws of desperation grasping for the supplies and safety they had fought so hard to secure. As the first raider crashed against their barricades, gunfire erupted, filling the air with the sharp cracks of firearms mixed with cries of fury.

The warehouse echoed with the sounds of battle—the chaos palpable, old walls reverberating as survival became a visceral fight. Deacon pushed back against the nearest raider, adrenaline guiding his movements as he fought with everything he had.

Jake stood shoulder to shoulder with Colonel Stone, working in perfect harmony as they cut down raider after raider.

"Keep firing! Don't give them an inch!" Stone barked, feeling the energy of resolve swell around them.

Lila aimed thoughtfully, releasing a shot that hit a raider square in the shoulder, sending him reeling back. "I can't believe how many there are!" she exclaimed, adrenaline-fueled empowerment shining in her gaze.

"Focus, and keep moving!" Frank yelled, wrestling with a raider who had crashed through their defenses. Using quick reflexes, he wrestled his weapon free and pulled the trigger, sending the intruder scrambling backward.

WOODS - NIGHT - SIMULTANEOUSLY

Outside, the pressure mounted as the raiders pushed deeper into the camp. The cacophony of chaos exploded as they stumbled forward with reckless abandon. Suddenly, a loud roar erupted from the back—one Flesh Ripper had broken free of its confines, drawn by the sound of battle.

"Watch out!" Jake shouted as the monstrous creature barreled into view, teeth bared and eyes glowing with fury.

"Step back!" Colonel Stone ordered, pivoting his stance ready for the beast. "Fall back to the inner defenses!"

Deacon could see it emerging in the darkness, a nightmare made real. "Get to safety!" he yelled, moving to steer the others away from the incoming onslaught.

The Flesh Ripper crashed against the barricade, its roar shaking the very foundation of their camp. Bodies fell, and the struggle intensified.

ABANDONED WAREHOUSE - NIGHT - CONTINUOUS

Inside the warehouse, the group fought tirelessly, focus driven by the frantic need for survival.

"Everyone, push!" Deacon cried out, continuing to direct their efforts toward repelling both raider and beast alike. "We can't let them break through! Hold the line!"

Tension coursed through every fiber of Deacon's being as he fought to keep his crew alive while reflecting on the weight of leadership he carried. Decisions loomed large in his mind; trust began to flicker like the firelight around them—fragile yet vital.

As the remnants of the group pressed against the oncoming tide, the hope to reclaim their world began to ignite once more.

CHAPTER 14: MOMENTS OF RECKONING

DEACON'S CAMP - NIGHT

The fight reached a fever pitch as the Flesh Ripper barreled into the warehouse, crashing into makeshift barricades with formidable force. The growl of rage echoed through the air, a reminder that survival was the name of the game.

Deacon squared his shoulders, adrenaline sharpening his focus. "Everybody, to the back!" he shouted, rallying his team as they prepared for the onslaught. "We need to cut it off from our supplies!"

Frank rushed toward Nadine, who was still frozen with fear. "Come on! Get moving!" he urged, grabbing her arm and pulling her along.

"We can deal with the raiders later, but we have to handle that thing first!" Deacon urged, motioning towards the monstrous demon as it bared its teeth, eyes glinting hungrily in the firelight.

ABANDONED WAREHOUSE - MAIN ROOM - NIGHT

As the team regrouped in the main room, the pressure mounted to an all-time high. Colonel Stone assessed their makeshift defenses, frustration bubbling at the surface as he prepared for the worst.

"Focus your fire on the legs!" he commanded. "Try to take it down! It's a tough one, but together we can manage it."

Jake, fueled by adrenaline, moved to form a defensive line with Colonel Stone and Deacon. "I'll distract it!" he shouted, charging toward the beast with sheer defiance in his eyes.

"No!" Deacon barked, but Jake was already sprinting forward, weapon raised, preparing to divert the creature's attention.

As Jake emerged from the shadows, he unleashed a barrage of gunfire at the Flesh Ripper, the bullets hitting their mark. "Over here, ugly!" he yelled, drawing the creature's furious gaze.

DEACON'S CAMP - NIGHT - CONTINUOUS

The raiders, sensing an opportunity amidst the chaos, surged forward through the back, but Emily and Reverend Thomas took tactical positions near the entrance, firing off shots to hold them back.

"Don't let them in!" Emily shouted, moving to cover as she flicked her gaze towards the fire illuminating the perimeter.

Nadine picked up anything she could find—a stick, a rock—preparing herself to protect the camp. "I'm not afraid!" she reminded herself, adrenaline overcoming her initial fear.

Carla stood beside her; determination written across her features. "We can do this. We stand together!"

A loud crash resonated from the door as a raider broke through, and Nadine swung the stick, her heart racing. Connection! It landed hard against the intruder's arm, and they stumbled back, stricken.

"Nice hit!" Carla yelled, feeling the shift in momentum.

ABANDONED WAREHOUSE - NIGHT - CONTINUOUS

Back inside, Deacon focused on luring the Flesh Ripper away from the barricade and toward the center of the room. "Stay sharp!" he called out.

The beast roared again, furious as it lunged towards Jake, its claws extended, hunger radiating from every fiber of its being.

As Deacon prepared to act, he noticed a nearby group of fallen supplies. "Using fire!" he muttered, realizing he could turn the tide. In a moment of calculated daring, he grabbed a nearby bottle filled with flammable liquid. He quickly prepared it, knowing they needed a strategic advantage.

"Stone, cover me!" he shouted as he sprinted toward the creature's flanks.

Colonel Stone took aim, firing at the beast's legs to keep it occupied while Deacon positioned the makeshift Molotov cocktail, ready to ignite the chaos.

"Do it!" Jake urged as he continued to draw the beast's attention away.

With a deft flick, Deacon ignited the liquid, a flash of fire bursting forth, and hurled the explosive toward the Flesh Ripper.

The impact was immediate. The flames erupted against the creature, causing it to howl in fury.

"Back! Everyone back!" Deacon shouted, motioning to the others as he took cover.

The explosion of fire singed the air, and the creature thrashed wildly, its howl reverberating through the night as it tried to escape the blaze, which spread rapidly along its grotesque form.

DEACON'S CAMP - NIGHT - SIMULTANEOUSLY

Outside, the raiders began to realize their predicament, the chaos around them intensifying. One of the raider leaders, a burly man with a scar across his cheek, took notice of their struggling beast.

"Focus on the survivors!" he shouted, waving his men forward. "They're too distracted!"

"Move! We can't let them draw our attention!" responded another raider, pushing forward into the fray.

The raiders surged toward the entrance of the warehouse, seeking to capitalize on the pandemonium. But Emily and Reverend Thomas stood firm as the front line.

"Now, hold your fire until they're close!" Reverend Thomas yelled, his voice steady against the clamor.

As the raiders approached, it was clear their numbers had swelled in the chaos—their confidence driving them higher as they aimed to overwhelm.

"We can't let them in! If we do, there's no telling what they'll take," Emily urged, feeling the pressure intensify.

Just as the raiders sprang into the opening, she and Thomas fired a coordinated volley that caught them off guard, sending raiders scrambling back.

"We're still strong! We push back!" Emily shouted, adrenaline fueling her resolve.

ABANDONED WAREHOUSE - NIGHT - MOMENTS LATER

Inside, the Flesh Ripper thrashed on the ground, still burning, its anguished cries filling the air.

"Keep firing, but aim for the head!" Deacon yelled, urging everyone to maintain their focus.

As the team worked together to take down the beast, the energy in the room shifted toward them, a fierce camaraderie pushing forward in their battle against overwhelming odds.

The dark reality of their lives pressed against their shoulders; the Flesh Ripper's guttural growls interspersed with bursts of gunfire created a wild symphony of survival.

But just as it seemed they would finally take down the monstrous creature, the walls of the warehouse shook as more raiders surged through the entrance, flooding the room with chaos.

"Get ready! They're here!" Colonel Stone yelled, adrenaline making his pulse quicken as he prepared for the onslaught.

The moment crystallized into a whirlwind of movement—fear turning to determination as Deacon and his team held the line against the gathering storm of foes.

CHAPTER 15: THE BREAKING POINT

ABANDONED WAREHOUSE - NIGHT

The atmosphere inside the warehouse exploded into chaos as both the Flesh Ripper and the raiders converged on Deacon and his team. The sound of gunfire mixed with the creature's tortured roars, creating a cacophony that threatened to overwhelm them. Deacon, his chest heaving, focused on the immediate threat.

"Everyone, regroup!" Deacon commanded, stepping closer to Colonel Stone, who was already firing into the advancing raiders. "We may need to fall back into the inner sanctum!"

"Fall back? Are you crazy?" Jake shot back, disarming a raider who had slipped through their defenses before elbowing him away. "We can hold this line!"

The raiders poured into the main room, their faces twisted into vicious grins, emboldened by the chaos around them. Just as Deacon assessed the situation, a large burst of energy knocked him off balance—a heavy thud announcing the arrival of further chaos as the Flesh Ripper flailed in desperation.

Jake and Stone pushed closer to Deacon's side, forming an impenetrable wall. "Stay tight! Stay sharp!" Stone yelled as he fired at the raiders.

"Watch the rear!" Frank yelled in response, but before he could shout further, another raider caught him by surprise and tackled him to the ground.

"Frank!" Deacon shouted, turning just in time to see his friend struggling against the weight of the raider, who was desperately trying to overpower him. In a split-second decision, Deacon dashed forward, aiming his weapon at the raider.

"Get off him!" he shouted as he fired a shot that found its mark, sending the raider sprawling away from Frank just as he regained his footing.

"Thanks!" Frank gasped, breathing heavily, looking up at Deacon with a mix of gratitude and urgency.

As the chaos continued, Reverend Thomas moved in closer, aiming his weapon at the merging tides of enemies. "We need to funnel them and keep them from overwhelming us!" he shouted, voice strong even amid the tumult.

Carla, resolute and filled with a sense of purpose, took advantage of the moment. "Jake, can you hold the left flank? I'll assist with the barricades!"

"On it!" Jake replied, pushing back against the crowd with a swing of his weapon.

DEACON'S CAMP - NIGHT - SIMULTANEOUSLY

Outside, the sounds of battle echoed into the encroaching night as Lila and the others scanned the perimeter, weapons poised and ready.

"Shouldn't we help them?" Lila asked anxiously, her grip tightening as she scanned the dark edges of the woods, aware that unknown threats still lingered in the air.

"We can't risk exposing ourselves," Nadine reminded her, glancing nervously at the shadows. "We have to stay vigilant.

If more raiders come, we need to prepare."

"Listen," Lila said earnestly, "if we can get a sense of how many are out there, we can warn Deacon and the others, see if we can draw them away."

A loud explosion of gunfire erupted from the warehouse, causing them to jump instinctively. "We don't have much time!" Nadine replied, trying to keep their spirits high. "Let's see what we can do!"

ABANDONED WAREHOUSE - NIGHT - CONTINUOUS

Back inside the warehouse, the battle raged on, a vicious swirl of chaos as the team fought back against the raiders. They stood united, struggling against the rising tide of enemies in the dim light.

Deacon shouted commands, trying to keep everyone coordinated and focused while also dealing with the noise erupting from the Flesh Ripper, which was even now focusing its unfathomable rage on the raiders.

"We can do this! Hold your ground!" Deacon rallied, firing into the throng.

Just then, one of the raiders lunged toward him with a jagged knife, but Deacon twisted aside, leading the man directly into the path of the Flesh Ripper. The creature took advantage of the confusion and lunged, sinking its teeth into the raider's shoulder with a sickening crunch.

Deacon seized the opportunity, pushing back against another raider who was trying to flank them. "We're almost there!" he urged, his eyes hardening with resolve.

"Look out!" Jake warned, receiving no answer as another group of raiders pushed through from behind, causing the team to be compressed further against the wall.

Just then, a loud roar deafened them, and the adrenaline surged again as Deacon felt the atmosphere shift. The Flesh Ripper, its mouth-stained crimson, turned its attention back toward the survivors, eyes glued to Deacon's group.

"No! We need to resist!" Colonel Stone shouted, forcing the raider back. "We can't let fear conquer us!"

WOODS NEAR THE WAREHOUSE - NIGHT

"Hold the perimeter!" Lila cried out as she and Nadine took cover behind a large tree, watching as the chaos unfolded. The shadows outside felt alive as the sounds of battle intertwined with distant growls.

"There's something moving over there!" Nadine's eyes widened, pointing toward the thicket. "Stay low!"

"Do you think it's more raiders?" Lila asked, her heart pounding aggressively.

"Possibly," Nadine replied. "We need to be ready for anything. If they're coming for reinforcements, we need to warn Deacon!"
ABANDONED WAREHOUSE - NIGHT - CONTINUOUS

Inside, the fury of battle intensified as the raiders pushed the limits of Deacon's team. The Flesh Ripper roared again, a visceral reminder of their struggle.

Deacon executed a calculated dodge as he braced himself against the heavy table, heart hammering as he aimed at the beast and fired, his aim true.

"Get back!" Frank shouted as he used the distraction to pull Colonel Stone into a flank. "We can't let them overwhelm us!"

As rounds of fire continued to echo through the warehouse, each moment became fraught with urgency and desperation. But amidst the rising tide of chaos, energy surged, binding the survivors as they fought not only for their lives but for each other.

Suddenly, a blinding light flooded the interior as Lila called out from outside. "Deacon! We're out here!"

"What are you doing?" Deacon shouted, startled but realizing the moment. "You need to stay hidden!"

But Lila and Nadine leaped from cover, determined to join the fight.

"This is not the time! Get back!" Deacon yelled, but the girls pressed forward, defiance in their eyes.

And in the thick of the fight, amid the roars of the Flesh Ripper and the chaos of battle, a new determination began to bloom—one that would challenge their strength, alliance, and resilience against the encroaching darkness forever.

CHAPTER 16: STRENGTH IN NUMBERS

DEACON'S CAMP - NIGHT

The sudden illumination from the lanterns outside caused a ripple of astonishment and confusion among both raiders and survivors. Lila and Nadine stood firm; their eyes filled with resolve as they faced the thronging chaos before them.

"Stand back! We're with Deacon!" Lila shouted, gripping a crude weapon she had fashioned from a piece of scrap metal. Her voice carried a weight of defiance that seemed to momentarily freeze the combatants.

Inside the warehouse, Deacon caught sight of Lila's bold stance, adrenaline surging through him. "What are you two doing?" he yelled amidst the tumult, his voice filled with concern and frustration.

"We're not leaving! We're here to fight with you!" Nadine called back; her hands clenched tightly around the weapon.

"Watch your backs!" Deacon shouted, redirecting his aim at an oncoming raider who lunged toward Lila. With a sharp report, his shot rang out, hitting the raider squarely, sending him tumbling backward into the shadows.

ABANDONED WAREHOUSE - NIGHT

The atmosphere sharpened, tension coiling around them, as the raiders regrouped after Deacon's interruption and began to close in, fueled by desperation. The Flesh Ripper was still thrashing against their barricades, its furious roar echoing through the confusion.

"Fall back!" Colonel Stone barked, moving quickly to establish a defensive formation near the entrance, his instincts as a former military officer kicking in. "Everyone, pull toward the center!"

As the team regrouped, Emily and Reverend Thomas returned to the fray, providing a steady beating rhythm for their collective efforts.

"Reinforcements!" Emily called out, her voice steady as she caught sight of Lila and Nadine joining their ranks. "Let's push them back!"

The air thickened with the sounds of disarray as the raiders pressed against their defenses, the throaty growls of the Flesh Ripper mingling with the frantic exchanges of the two opposing groups.

"Everyone, hold the line!" Deacon shouted; his resolve unyielding as he rallied his team once more. "We're not losing this!"

A sudden surge of energy rippled through the survivors, rooted in their unity.

WOODS NEAR THE ENTRANCE - NIGHT

From the edges of the woods, an alarming sound broke through the din of battle—a deep growl radiating through the trees. The shadows shifted ominously, spinning the air with a sense of impending dread that permeated the night.

"Something else is coming!" Lila warned, scanning the dark

edges of the camp.

"Stay vigilant!" Frank replied, feeling the mounting pressure in the air. "We can't afford to be blindsided!"

Suddenly, a familiar form appeared—Jacob, breathless and wild-eyed, emerged from the thicket, panic etched across his face. "They're coming! A whole horde of them!" he yelled, his voice frantic.

"What do you mean a horde?" Colonel Stone pressed, concern knitting his brow. "How many?"

"More than a dozen!" Jacob shouted. "They were gathering just outside our perimeter and preparing to strike! You need to fortify your defenses!"

ABANDONED WAREHOUSE - NIGHT

"Everyone, we're not just fighting raiders anymore," Deacon warned, his voice steady as steel, trying to instill courage into every member of the team. "We need to save our energy and stand our ground for whatever comes next. We can't let them break our spirit!"

As he finished his sentence, the Flesh Ripper let out an ear-splitting roar, sound echoing across their camp as it struggled against its restraints, fueled by rage and vengeance.

"Distract it!" Jake shouted, rushing toward a nearby crate filled with supplies, grabbing an old flare gun. "I'll draw its attention!"

"No! You can't single-handedly take that on!" Deacon objected, panic flickering in his voice.

"Just cover me!" Jake replied with conviction, moving toward the creature.

DEACON'S CAMP - NIGHT

Jake carefully positioned himself just beyond the monster's reach and fired the flare gun into the air. The loud WHOOSH of the flare ignited, sending brilliant red flames spiraling skyward, illuminating the surroundings with a crimson glow.

The Flesh Ripper jolted, its focus shifting toward the bright light, howling in confusion and anger as it chased after Jake, who ducked behind some crates.

"This way, you ugly beast!" Jake taunted, adrenaline surging, but his heart raced against him as he backpedaled.

Colonel Stone took advantage of the distraction to take aim. "Now's our chance!" he commanded, firing at the demon's exposed flank.

ABANDONED WAREHOUSE - NIGHT

Inside, the raiders continued their assault, but the tide was turning. Frank and Emily worked seamlessly together, using their shots with precision and purpose, pushing back against any intruders that dared to challenge their hold.

"Keep it steady!" Frank shouted, dodging a swinging fist from a nearby raider, recovering quickly to deliver a solid blow to the intruder's gut before he fell back against another raider.

Nadine and Reverend Thomas joined forces, using their weapons to cover one another, their camaraderie solidifying in the heat of the battle, shifting the dynamic further toward survival.

"Remember, it's not just about the fight!" Reverend Thomas shouted, keeping spirits high. "We're fighting for our lives and our future!"

DEACON'S CAMP - NIGHT

Out in the woods beyond the camp, Jake continued to taunt the Flesh Ripper, leading it further away from the others. "Come on! Come get me!" he yelled, adrenaline surging with each bound back and forth as the creature lunged after him.

A BARRAGE of shots rang out from Colonel Stone and Frank as they kept the raiders at bay, holding the line that defined their sanctuary.

"Don't let them fall back," Colonel Stone commanded. "We push forward!"

As the group continued to hold their ground, shadows began to close in on them. Small figures emerged, grotesque and twisted, leading them to the realization that the raiders' plan had spiraled into chaos, a melding of both predator and prey.

ABANDONED WAREHOUSE - NIGHT

The noise from the outside blended into a tumultuous din as Deacon began to understand their situation. "Everyone, we need to shift tactics!" he proclaimed, urgency flooding his voice. "Focus fire on the raiders, then flank the Flesh Ripper!"

"We'll use our surroundings," Emily said, her voice clear as she moved to her position, readying her weapon for the next shot.

As the sounds of the struggle roared on, Deacon felt a surge of fierce pride for his makeshift family, a group that had banded together against unimaginable odds.

With renewed purpose, they pressed forward, driving the melee into a frenetic clash as the forces of darkness converged upon them.

DEACON'S CAMP - NIGHT

The atmosphere was charged with a collective desperation as the survivors fought. Deacon's heart raced, not only from the adrenaline coursing through his veins but also from the heavy weight of responsibility he felt for every single soul in this camp.

"Now! Push!" he called, rallying the fighters. Frank, Jake, and Colonel Stone pushed through, firing at the remaining raiders, their resolve steeled against what lay ahead.

The Flesh Ripper, restless and wounded, continued its furious pursuit of Jake, who had led it away from the main fight. Suddenly, it whirled, snapping its massive jaws in frustration, lunging close enough to brush against Jake.

"Too close!" Jake gasped, narrowly dodging to the side, the creature's foul breath ghosting past him as he zigzagged through the wreckage of their camp.

"Jake, get clear!" Deacon shouted from within the cover of the barricades, anxiety vibrating in his voice. "Fall back to the others if it gets too close!"

Just then, another wave of raiders barreled into the clearing, undeterred by the Flame and the chaos, emboldened by their numbers. They shouted, marching into the fray as they saw their comrades faltering.

"Reinforcements!" Colonel Stone shouted, urging Deacon forward. "We need to push them back while we still can!"

ABANDONED WAREHOUSE - NIGHT

Inside the warehouse, the atmosphere thickened with determination. Emily and Reverend Thomas fought hard to keep the raiders at bay. They formed a guard line, weapon ready, shouting to keep morale high.

"Aim for the center! Keep them from breaking through!" Emily yelled, steadying her breath as she fired methodically.

"Hold fast!" Reverend Thomas urged. "We will prevail if we stay true!"

The team worked in tandem, responding to the chaos around them as the Flesh Ripper roared once more, the sound reverberating through the thin walls of their shelter.

"Now!" Deacon shouted. "To the second exit! We flank them!"

With a coordinated effort, the group moved swiftly, forming a determined line at the back of the camp, preparing to cut off the raiders as they surged forward without restraint.

DEACON'S CAMP - NIGHT

Outside, Jake was desperate to evade the Flesh Ripper, shifting away from its monstrous jaws. As he sprinted toward the relative safety of the warehouse's shadow, he caught sight of Colonel Stone aiming, ready to line up another shot.

"Jake!" Colonel Stone shouted. "Get down!"

Jake dove to the side just as Stone fired, the shot ringing true. The bullet struck the Flesh Ripper in the side, causing it to howl angrily, stumbling back.

"Nice shot!" Jake exclaimed, scrambling up to his feet. "But we need to keep moving!"

Colonel Stone quickly shifted aim toward the incoming raiders, firing again, trying to pin them down. "Cover me. We need to finish this!"

Suddenly, a figure stepped forth from behind the flames—Rachel, face grim as she wielded a baseball bat, determined to stand her ground.

"Get behind me!" she cried as she charged at the raider nearest to her. She swung the bat hard, connecting with a sickening thud that sent the raider sprawling.

"Rachel, what are you doing?" Deacon shouted, surprised and impressed.

"You need all the help you can get!" she replied, eyes fierce with determination.

ABANDONED WAREHOUSE - NIGHT

Meanwhile, within the walls of the warehouse, the remaining survivors regrouped and prepared for another wave. Each breath felt heavy as they braced for the impact.

Frank looked to Deacon. "Should we flank them now?"

"Not yet," Deacon replied. "We need to draw them closer to the center—then we can strike hard."

Just then, the rattle of gunfire erupted as the remaining raiders advanced, their numbers pushing forward. "Now!" Deacon shouted, signaling the group to prepare.

A chorus of determination filled the air as the survivors unleashed a barrage of fire on the raiders, each shot ringing true and plunging into the shadows of uncertainty.

The tide swelled, and the raiders faltered, their bravado starting to slip as the team executed their plan flawlessly, each survivor working in unison.

DEACON'S CAMP - NIGHT

Outside, the Flesh Ripper continued its rampage, narrowly missing Jake as it swung again. "Deacon! Up there!" Jake pointed to the rotting beams overhead—to the crate of supplies hanging dangerously.

"Let's bring it down!" Deacon called, motioning for Colonel Stone. "We can trap it!"

"Yes!" Stone shouted, adrenaline surging. They quickly adjusted their strategy, leading their shots towards the weak point above as the team inside redirected their focus.

"Now!" Deacon yelled, feeling the weight of momentum shift in their favor. They took aim, and with a synchronized volley, their combined fire hit the crate, sending it crashing down onto the Flesh Ripper.

The beast howled in pain as debris fell away, stunning it into temporary paralysis.

"Push! Now!" Deacon shouted, urging his team to move quickly as they pressed into the fray with relentless determination.

ABANDONED WAREHOUSE - NIGHT

As they fought back the raiders, Deacon felt the tide of the battle shifting heavily toward their favor with every scream and gunshot.

"Stay strong!" he yelled as the Flesh Ripper writhed on the ground. "Keep fighting! We can win this!"

Just as hope began to fill their hearts, another ripple of shadows erupted at the entrance of the warehouse. Deacon and Colonel Stone exchanged worried glances as the door creaked ominously open once more.

"Everyone, shift positions!" Deacon commanded, anxiety pooling in the pit of his stomach as darkness spilled forth.

But as they prepared for whatever new threat emerged, they were greeted by familiar faces—Nadine and Emily, faces streaked with dirt but undeterred.

"We're here to help!" Nadine shouted, holding a weapon high.

With the combined strength of their newfound allies, Deacon felt the surge of leadership overcoming the uncertainty he had felt mere moments ago.

"Together!" he roared as the tide turned once more.

The battle had yet to be won, but they would fight as one.

CHAPTER 17: THE LIGHT IN THE DARKNESS

ABANDONED WAREHOUSE

As Nadine and Emily rushed into the fray, a shared fury pulsed through everyone. Deacon felt a renewed sense of purpose swell within him, invigorated by the defiance and bravery of his team. The Flesh Ripper's furious roars hung in the air, but now they had a better view of the chaos unraveling within the warehouse.

"Reinforcements!" Nadine exclaimed, gripping her makeshift weapon. "We heard the sounds from the perimeter and rushed back to help!"

"Keep it steady!" Deacon called as he took his position beside them, preparing for the next wave of raiders. "We have to finish what we started!"

Emily quickly assessed the scene and glanced at the wounded survivor. "I'll help him—we can't lose anyone now!" With focused determination, she rushed to the side of the injured, working to apply bandages and stabilize him amidst the chaos.

As the battle continued, the combination of firepower and sheer willpower strengthened their defenses. Frank and Colonel Stone formed a unified front, directing their shots precisely at the raiders, while Lila used the distraction to prepare her weapons.

DEACON'S CAMP - NIGHT

Outside, the raiders caught sight of their dwindling numbers as their morale wavered. The Flesh Ripper howled in pain, caught between the chaos of the struggle.

"They're losing it!" one raider shouted, glancing back at his comrades. "We have to retreat!"

"No! We're going to take what's ours!" their leader shouted defiantly, trying to galvanize the remaining fighters. But his confidence was crumbling as panic set in.

As tensions escalated outside, Deacon felt the pressure rise. "Gather yourselves! We need to push back!" he shouted, aiming steadily at the sound of approaching footfalls.

ABANDONED WAREHOUSE - NIGHT

With renewed resolve, Nadine shouted, "We're not letting them take this from us! We'll fight for our home!"

The survivors rallied, drawing strength from the chaos that was both terrifying and exhilarating. Emily, now free from the responsibility of the wounded survivor, joined in support near the barricades, providing backup cover.

"Keep your fire steady!" Frank commanded, excitement surging through him as they began to press forward against the raiders.

Suddenly, the Flesh Ripper turned its attention toward Deacon again, the beast snarling as it readied to charge.

"Watch out!" Lila shouted, raising her weapon, panic washing over her momentarily. "It's coming for you!"

"Move!" Deacon yelled, creating space as he dodged the beast's angry lunge.

WAREHOUSE - NIGHT

Just as the Flesh Ripper lunged toward Deacon, Colonel Stone fired with precision, hitting the creature right in the flank. It howled again but remained focused, and in that moment, Deacon seized his opportunity.

"Now!" he urged, launching a heavy iron rod they had fashioned as a makeshift weapon, connecting firmly with the demon's skull.

The impact stunned the creature momentarily, causing it to stagger back, giving everyone else the opportunity to engage with the raiders.

"Shoot! Keep firing!" Jake roared, rushing back into the fray and firing at the raiders while simultaneously dodging the erratic movements of the Flesh Ripper.

Nadine, feeling the adrenaline rush through her veins without hesitation, swung at a raider who rushed forward but was promptly met with a punch that sent him sprawling.

"Take that!" she yelled, exhilaration sparking inside her as she gained confidence.

Inside the warehouse, the team reformed their line, resolute, weapons raised, ready for whatever the raiders would throw at them—both figuratively and literally.

ABANDONED WAREHOUSE - NIGHT

As they fought back against the raiders, Deacon glimpsed someone moving through the shadows near the entrance of the warehouse. "Who's there?" he shouted, swiftly aiming his weapon.

"Wait! It's me!" Jacob was shouting, emerging from the edge of darkness. "I found more survivors!"

Deacon's heart raced with anticipation. "Bring them in! We need all the help we can get."

"Quick!" Jacob shouted, leading another weary-looking group of survivors into the fray. It was a small team, but they were armed and resolute.

"Now we really have a fight on our hands," Colonel Stone grunted, seeing the potential for reinforcements.

"Let's give them a welcome!" Deacon said, steeling himself as he envisioned pushing the raiders back once and for all.

DEACON'S CAMP - NIGHT

The merging teams inside the warehouse formed an unbreakable bond, and as the swirling chaos intensified, they felt an unspoken pact solidifying between them, defining their resolve.

"Together!" Deacon shouted, rallying everyone around him. "Now is our moment to take back what's ours!"

The group charged forward, a unified force against the chaos. They pushed against the raiders, rallying with both determination and the fiery spirit of survival.

As they fought, Lila caught sight of the Flesh Ripper faltering nearby. Fueled by adrenaline, she took careful aim and fired, hitting the monster squarely.

"Take that!" she yelled, pride surging through her as the shot connected, her confidence finally surging.

ABANDONED WAREHOUSE - NIGHT

Inside, Deacon felt the tide shift as his team fought back with fervor; they were emboldened by the new arrivals and the fresh spirit of camaraderie.

With a final bid for victory, the combined force of Deacon's team surged forward, taking down raider after raider with precise shots and unwavering unity, each moment forging their connection in the fires of battle.

"Push!" Deacon yelled, adrenaline rushing, and they rallied together, determined to reclaim their home.

As the raiders began to falter and panic spread among them, the Flesh Ripper dealt a final blow, howling in pain.

But just then, the doors shuddered again as the final wave surged forward, nearly overwhelming the camp.

"Get ready!" Deacon shouted, but a chill ran down his spine—there was no backing down now.

They had fought bravely, but the struggle wasn't over.

CHAPTER 18: THE HEART OF THE STORM

ABANDONED WAREHOUSE - NIGHT

The cacophony inside the warehouse reached a fever pitch as Deacon and his team pushed against the surging wave of raiders. The air was thick with the smell of gunpowder, sweat, and fear—a volatile mixture that heightened every instinct in their bodies.

"Hold the line! We can't let them break through!" Deacon shouted, his voice hoarse but commanding, urging everyone to focus on the threat before them.

Reverend Thomas stood beside Frank, both of them firing in tandem at the incoming raiders. Thomas's face was resolute, strengthened by unwavering faith that coursed through him. "Remember our strength comes in our unity!" he called, trying to boost the morale of the group as their shots rang out.

"Push back!" Frank urged, sweating profusely as he reloaded, eyes darting around to ensure their perimeter remained secure. The energy of desperation electrified the air, each heartbeat a reminder of their precarious situation.

Just then, the Flesh Ripper thrashed against the barricades, its growl merging with the sounds of the melee. Deacon caught sight of a raider slipping through a gap—a desperate attempt to break into the heart of their defenses.

"Cut him off!" Deacon yelled, rushing forward as he pushed against the surge.

DEACON'S CAMP - NIGHT - OUTSIDE THE WAREHOUSE

Outside, the tension swelled as Lila, Nadine, and other newfound survivors positioned themselves behind makeshift barricades, preparing to protect their home.

"You ready?" Nadine whispered to Lila, determination blazing in her eyes.

"More than ever," Lila replied, gripping a weapon firmly. "We fight for everyone."

Suddenly, the ground shook beneath them as the Flesh Ripper lunged toward the entrance, compounded by the raucous battle of raiders. Lila tightened her grip, her heart racing.

"We'll hold this line!" Lila shouted, as the sound of combat crackled in the night, raiders trying to push through the defenses.

The moment was pregnant with urgency.

ABANDONED WAREHOUSE - NIGHT

Inside, chaos enveloped the group. Deacon and Stone were relentless, firing at every raider that threatened to breach their defenses.

Colonel Stone caught sight of a raider trying to circle around. "Over here!" he shouted, taking aim and firing as the man fell.

"Direct hit!" Jake grinned, exhilaration coursing through him as he dove into the fray beside Deacon, adrenaline fueling his movements.

"We're almost there!" Deacon yelled as they fought, listening to the fire echoing in the warehouse. "Let's push them toward the exit."

With renewed vigor, the group pressed forward, their resolve shining brighter than the fear that threatened to consume them. As the Flesh Ripper continued to roar in pain and confusion, they carved a path against the tide.

OUTSIDE THE WAREHOUSE - NIGHT

Outside, the tension rose higher as the raiders began to strategize. "Let's flank them from the side! They won't see it coming!" one of the raiders yelled, attempting to form a plan.

Just then, the sound of laughter erupted from the back, reminding Lila and Nadine of the chaos still brewing beyond their control.

"We can't let them reach the others!" Nadine urged, determination coloring her tone.

"Let's charge them!" Lila exclaimed, adrenaline pumping. "If we let them know we're opposing them, they'll second-guess their numbers."

Nadine nodded, feeling the thrill of her own bravery. "You're right! We have to do everything we can!"

ABANDONED WAREHOUSE - NIGHT

Inside the warehouse, Deacon felt the tide shifting. "We've got to pull everything we've got together!" he yelled as he positioned himself beside Emily.

As they fought back against the raiders, Deacon saw the raider leader drawing closer, rallying his group. "You think you can hold us off?" the leader taunted, emboldened by the sheer numbers backing him.

Deacon squared his shoulders, adrenaline coursing through him. "Not if we have anything to say about it."

"Flesh Ripper, move!" Colonel Stone yelled, taking aim at the beast as it snapped, roaring amid the chaos.

"We can't let it breach the defenses!" Deacon shouted, directing the group's fire toward it as adrenaline surged through him.

The Flesh Ripper roared once more, the resonating sound cutting through the clamor as its monstrous form obliterated portions of the barricade.

CAMP - NIGHT

Outside, Lila and Nadine charged into the clearing confronting the surge of raiders, determination setting their spirits ablaze. "For Deacon! For the camp!" Nadine shouted, fueled by the moment.

Without hesitation, Lila swung her weapon with all her might, catching one of the raiders off-guard. "Let's show them!" she yelled, adrenaline rushing as she fought fiercely.

The raiders staggered back, caught off-guard by the calculated defense of the survivors—their confidence in overwhelming numbers began to waver.

ABANDONED WAREHOUSE - NIGHT

Inside, the scene intensified, sweat mixing with the dirt as the Flesh Ripper continued its onslaught. With every blast of gunfire, the survivors pressed on, fighting side by side with resolve burning in their hearts.

"Push! Don't let them take ground!" Deacon bellowed, moving with purpose amid the chaos, eyes fierce and unyielding.

Finally, he turned to Colonel Stone, who was firing methodically. "We need to regroup! Prepare to counter-attack!"

"On your lead!" Stone replied, locking eyes with him.

In that moment, they took a step back, allowing the raiders to push forward—luring them deeper into their trap.

"Now! Cut them off!" Deacon commanded. The team surged back into the fray, catching the raiders off-guard as they turned to fight against the approaching tide of anxiety.

CAMP - NIGHT

Outside, Lila and Nadine returned to support, feeling newfound strength propelling their actions. They joined the others, the energy among the survivors creating an almost palpable atmosphere of bravery.

"Together! We hold this line!" Nadine shouted, her voice rising over the clamor, feeling the depth of celebrated unity among them.

With each battle cry, hope surged and fear began to fade. They were strong together, united by purpose and unbreakable bonds.

ABANDONED WAREHOUSE – NIGHT

Deacon felt the tide shift not just outside but also within. As the raiders faltered, caught by surprise, they began to retreat under the unified pressure of Deacon's group, pushing them back toward the entrance like a tide washing out an opposing force.

"We've got them on the run!" Deacon shouted, heart racing with exhilaration. "Let's finish this!"

The remaining raiders looked for an escape route, their bravado fading as they realized the tables had turned. The Flesh Ripper, still raging, began to thrash wildly, disoriented and enraged from the collective assault of Deacon's team.

"Keep firing at that thing!" Colonel Stone commanded, refocusing the group's efforts on stabilizing their position. "We need to take it down before it breaks our barricades completely!"

"On it!" Frank shouted, steadying his aim as another wave of raiders stumbled back, trying to calculate their next move. "If we can bring down that monster, we can dismantle the rest of them!"

DEACON'S CAMP - NIGHT

The remnants of the raider force realized they were trapped between the relentless Flesh Ripper and the determined survivors. Their leader stomped his foot in frustration, cursing under his breath, "We'll regroup! Fall back!"

Just as they turned to retreat, Lila and Nadine charged forward, weapons raised. "Not so fast!" Lila shouted, emboldened by the surge of adrenaline.

With the combined might of Deacon's team, they pushed forward, aiming to capture any raider who sought to escape—their desire to protect what was theirs burning fiercely.

"Cut them off at the trees!" Nadine yelled; her voice fierce as she directed the charge. The survivors surged, creating a wall of determination against the remaining raiders.

ABANDONED WAREHOUSE - NIGHT

Inside, a final hail of gunfire erupted as Deacon's team retaliated against the thundering Flesh Ripper. It lunged wildly, attempting to swipe at those who moved toward it, its instincts frantic and desperate.

"Get clear! Move!" Deacon commanded as the creature roared again, and the group split, allowing space for the instinctive shift in their game plan.

As Deacon took aim, he steeled himself for what was next. "Now! Find a way to pin it down!" he shouted, feeling the urgency compelled by their proximity to victory.

In a bold maneuver, Jake rushed toward a stack of fallen supplies, working to create an improvised barricade that could trap or slow the creature—not allowing it to escape back into the shadows.

"I've got this!" he shouted, and just as the Flesh Ripper charged again, his timing was impeccable. The supplies tumbled into the path of the beast, causing it to lose its footing and stumble briefly, which gave the group a clean shot.

"Now's our chance!" Colonel Stone yelled, aiming sharply ahead.

"Keep it distracted!" Deacon shouted as he moved to flank it once more.

DEACON'S CAMP - NIGHT

Outside, Lila, Nadine, and Reverend Thomas kept the raiders engaged. "Stay on your toes!" Lila yelled as they maneuvered through the crowd, providing cover fire for each other. They would not allow the enemy to break through their lines.

Suddenly, a raider tried to break away, and Nadine pivoted, catching him by surprise. "Not today!" she shouted, striking him across the legs and sending him sprawling.

With each raider they took down, the fight ignited their spirits further. They were not merely defending; they were reclaiming their lives.

ABANDONED WAREHOUSE - NIGHT

As the battle raged on, the Flesh Ripper, temporarily stunned, roared in fury, thrashing around wildly, swinging its massive claws at anything near enough to grasp.

"Hold your positions!" Deacon bellowed to his teammates; eyes fixed on the beast's movements. "We end this now!"

Leaning into the charge, Deacon prepared for another round of coordinated shots. He glanced at Jacob and the new survivors who had joined them, nodding in solidarity. "On three!"

Everyone steadied their weapons, ready to fire. "One... two... three!"

The combined effort of gunfire erupted again, striking at the Flesh Ripper with renewed determination, bullets pounding into the creature as it howled in pain.

The sounds of chaos melded into an overwhelming roar as Deacon lunged toward the creature, weapon poised. With one final push, he aimed and fired into the beast's skull, sending it crashing to the ground in a powerful thud.

DEACON'S CAMP - NIGHT

Outside, the remaining raiders hesitated as the massive roar of the Flesh Ripper fell silent. One of the raider leaders, realizing they were surrounded and outmatched, waved a white flag above his head, signaling surrender.

"Alright! We give up!" he called, voice echoing into the night air. "No more fighting! We just want to go!"

"Take them down!" shouted Lila, eyes flashing with determination, preparing for another round.

"Wait!" Deacon shouted, holding up a hand to his team. The chaos paused as everyone looked to him, their breaths heavy. "We can't keep fighting aimlessly!"

"What are you suggesting?" Colonel Stone asked, adjusting his weapon, still ready for anything.

"Let's talk. We can't lose ourselves to anger. They might be reasonable," Deacon proposed, feeling the weight of his leadership pressing heavily upon him.

"Are you kidding?" Jake exclaimed. "They've already attacked us!"

"The world is different now. We have to find a way to coexist in this wasteland," Deacon replied, staying resolute.

Just then, the sound of raiders trampling around echoed alongside the growing silence, as the remnants of chaos began to settle.

"Put your weapons down!" Lila called, steeling herself against the uncertainty.

"What choice do we have?" one of the raiders grumbled, fuming but begrudgingly lowering his weapon.

With the culmination of battle drawing to a close, Deacon felt the tremors of hope breaching the enveloping darkness. Maybe there was a way to forge a path from here, to build what had been lost out of the ashes of the fight.

"Now let's negotiate for peace," he said, heart heavy but filled with the flicker of possibilities.

CHAPTER 19: NEGOTIATIONS IN THE DARK

ABANDONED WAREHOUSE - NIGHT

The atmosphere inside the warehouse had drastically changed. The roar of the Flesh Ripper had ceased, replaced by the heavy silence of a battlefield at dusk. Deacon stood resolute at the forefront, rallying his remaining survivors as the raiders lowered their weapons, a cautious truce settling over both groups.

"Let's not make this worse than it needs to be," Deacon said, his voice steady but firm. "We're all in this fight for survival. If we can find a way to coexist, we might just save each other from this nightmare."

The raider leader, a gritty-looking man with a patchy beard and bloodied clothes, stepped forward warily, his hands raised, mirroring Deacon's tentative peace offer. "We don't want any more trouble," he said, his voice edged with skepticism. "But you threw a barrier in our way. We just wanted what we thought was ours."

"And what's yours in a world where everything is broken?" Deacon replied, his gaze unwavering. "We all want to survive. We have supplies that could benefit both our groups if we share resources rather than fight over them."

The tension in the air was thick, the remnants of fear and animosity swirling between the two factions. Colonel Stone moved slightly closer to Deacon, keeping his weapon readied but lowered.

"Let's hear him out," Stone urged quietly, sensing the moment might be their best chance. "We can't keep fighting forever, and fuel isn't infinite."

Behind Deacon, Reverend Thomas stepped forward, conviction lighting his eyes. "We cannot allow fear to dictate our actions. Instead, let compassion lead us," he said, his voice calming and poised. "We can choose to end this cycle of violence."

Lila and Nadine stood resolute beside them, steadfast in unity, feeling emboldened by those around them.

"Are you all serious?" the raider leader scoffed; skepticism etched across his craggy features. "You expect us to just take your word for it? We came here for resources, not sermons!"

"If you want resources without violence, this is your chance!" Nadine countered, her voice steady. "We're willing to work together."

DEACON'S CAMP - NIGHT

Outside, the remnants of the camp stood eerily still. The flickering lanterns swayed in the breeze, casting shadows that danced across the weary faces of the survivors and raiders alike.

"Time to make a choice," Deacon said, clenching his jaw. "Together, we can survive. Apart, we both may not see tomorrow."

The raider leader shifted, glancing at his ragtag group, who looked weary but conflicted. Several had lowered their weapons; some exchanged uncertain glances, weighing their options.

"If we agree... what's to stop you from just turning this around and killing us later?" the leader asked, sincerity laced with fear.

"Nothing," Deacon admitted honestly. "But understand this: I won't put my people at risk by breaking trust. We all have something to lose. If we can build a semblance of cooperation, perhaps we can forge a better life together."

At the flicker of his words, a tall, wiry raider stepped forward, arms crossing in contemplation. "And what do you offer us?" he questioned, suspicion still lingering in his voice.

"Protection," Deacon replied resolutely. "We can share what we have so long as we share responsibility. Cooperation will fortify not only our strengths but our weaknesses too."

ABANDONED WAREHOUSE - NIGHT

Inside, Emily shifted restlessly, watching the negotiation unfold. She shot Deacon a look of concern, uncertainty shadowing her face. "Are you sure about this?" she whispered.

"We have to be." Deacon nodded. "It's the only way to break this cycle. We need every hand we can get."

As they held onto the tenuous threads of negotiation, the tension hung in the air like a fragile strand, ready to snap at any moment.

OUTSIDE THE CAMPSITE - NIGHT

The raider leader stepped closer, eyeing Deacon with a mixture of curiosity and distrust. "And what's your plan for the Flesh Ripper? It's one of your problems now, too," he said, nodding to the fallen beast nearby, its grotesque form crumpled against the remnants of the barricade.

"Together, we'll deal with it," Deacon said. "We can all learn from the mistakes of our past. We can start over. But it means putting the past behind us."

A murmur rippled through the raider ranks; skepticism mingled with consideration. The atmosphere felt pregnant with hope and hesitation, unsure whether to lean toward trust or fall back into chaos.

ABANDONED WAREHOUSE - NIGHT

"Let's not forget how we got here," one of the raiders called from the back, bitterness evident in his tone. "You think you can negotiate after all the bloodshed?"

"Blood has already been shed, true—but it doesn't mean more needs to follow," Reverend Thomas interjected thoughtfully. "Instead of letting anger dictate our paths, let us choose wisdom. We can work together to vanquish this threat."

"Listen, we're all at the brink of survival!" Nadine added, her voice rising, echoing through the tumult of emotions. "If we don't work together, there won't be anything left for any of us!"

Staring down their differences, the raiders hesitated, caught between the looming threat of conflict and the promise of cooperation.

OUTSIDE THE CAMPSITE - NIGHT

Finally, the raider leader stepped back, evaluating the situation as his men and Deacon's team quietly surveyed one another—uncertainty lingering yet beginning to ease.

"Alright," the leader relented, arms dropping slightly. "We'll give this a shot. But know that if any of you betray us, we won't hesitate to take what we want."

"Fair enough," Deacon replied, relief flooding through him as he extended a hand toward the leader. "We'll start fresh. Together."

The leader clasped Deacon's forearm, a gesture signifying the uneasy truce as both sides acknowledged the fragile bonds of camaraderie.

ABANDONED WAREHOUSE - NIGHT

As the atmosphere began to thaw, Emily stepped closer, gesturing to the injured. "What about those we lost along the way? We need to find a way to honor their memory," she urged, hoping for a lesson that could transcend defeat.

The raider leader nodded solemnly, his hardened expression softening slightly. "You're right. Loses have been felt on both sides. If we work together, we can ensure that both our groups will endure."

A flicker of hope brushed across the crowd as they engaged in quiet discussions on how to rebuild and unite the fractured remnants of their existence. The shadows of the past had yet to fade, but now there was a chance—the possibility of survival and a brighter future forged together.

DEACON'S CAMP - NIGHT

As the tension diminished, Deacon surveyed the group, both raiders and survivors standing side by side, a fragile alliance beginning to take form. "Alright, everyone!" he called out, raising his voice to draw attention. "We need to assess our situation and determine our next steps. We've got to stay vigilant—there could still be threats lurking out there."

Nadine stepped forward; her expression fierce yet hopeful. "We should gather supplies from what's left," she suggested. "If we can secure what we need, we can start working together more efficiently."

"Agreed," the raider leader said, his presence commanding attention. "I can lead a team to scavenge what we can find. If there are more of us, we can cover more ground."

"Let's clarify our roles," Deacon replied, nodding at the leader. "We'll mix our groups. We can't just look at this as 'us' and 'them' anymore. Everyone has something to contribute, insights we can all share."

The weary but determined group began to break into smaller factions, setting aside grievances as they forged a united front. Lila and Nadine joined forces with a couple of raiders who offered their knowledge of the surrounding terrain, ready to scout efficiently.

ABANDONED WAREHOUSE

Inside the warehouse, Reverend Thomas worked alongside Emily, tending to the wounded survivor who had been caught in the fray. The sight of their injured compatriot brought back a wave of sorrow, but that sorrow was mingled with a flicker of hope.

"We can't forget what happened," Thomas said softly, securing a bandage around the survivor's wound. "We honor them by pushing through and ensuring their sacrifices mean something."

Emily nodded, her voice trembling slightly as she spoke. "This is a chance to create a legacy—a new beginning."

Outside, the digging of new roles began, the sound of work mixing with cautious conversations as measures of trust began to emerge.

DEACON'S CAMP - NEAR THE WOODS - NIGHT

As the groups formed, the raider leader found himself standing beside Colonel Stone. The two exchanged glances filled with unreadable tension.

"Let's get down to business," Colonel Stone said. "We need to discuss our defenses. If those raiders come back, we need to be ready."

"Agreed," the raider leader replied. "And we'll need to scout food sources too. There's a nearby settlement that might still have supplies—we can check it together."

Colonel Stone nodded, his demeanor shifting slightly as he began to view the raider in a new light. "I appreciate the cooperation. By working together, we might hold both our organizations together."

Together, they formulated a plan—a combination of survival strategies that addressed their precarious reality.

ABANDONED WAREHOUSE - NIGHT

Back inside the warehouse, Deacon gathered his team, the air thick with determination. "Listen," he began, "tonight, we've taken a step toward unity. But we must remain sharp. There could be raiders still lurking. We'll need to set watch rotations and patrols."

Everyone nodded in agreement, recognizing the delicate balance they were treading.

As they set their plans into motion, the atmosphere erupted into a collaborative spirit, laughter and banter echoing through the surroundings as they whispered hopes and ideas for the future. Bonds were beginning to be crafted from the despair of their shared struggles.

OUTSIDE, NEAR THE CAMP - NIGHT

In the woods, Lila and Nadine scouted together, keeping low and listening carefully for signs of life. The tension hung in the air, but it felt different now—there was potential in the future, a chance to change.

"Look there!" Lila pointed to a set of footprints in the mud. "We're getting close to that settlement."

"We should mark this and return," Nadine suggested, feeling her confidence grow. "If we can find food and supplies, it will strengthen our alliances."

With that, they made swift work of tracking the footprints, marking essential places of interest.

ABANDONED WAREHOUSE - NIGHT

Back at the warehouse, conversations flowed. Deacon stood at the center, observing everyone as they prepared their food and tended to the remaining wounds.

Every action felt necessary, a step closer to reclaiming what had been lost.

"We need to create a system—let's have everyone contribute to a communal effort," Deacon announced. "We feed each other, gather our supplies, and look out for one another. This is the foundation of our alliance."

Emily nodded in agreement. "We need to prioritize safety and communication. If we can remain connected, we can endure."

As the group continued to bond—the lines between raiders and survivors beginning to blur—Deacon felt the flicker of new beginnings.

They were not just defending against darkness; they were forging a new path through it—one that demanded strength, but also compassion. With each moment they stood united, they built something more significant than merely surviving—the chance for a brighter future, defying the shadows lurking beyond.

CHAPTER 20: DAWN OF A NEW ALLIANCE

DEACON'S CAMP - NIGHT TO MORNING

As the night wore on, the sounds of battle faded, replaced by the steady rhythms of exhaustion settling in. The survivors and raiders worked side by side, their collective efforts intertwining like threads in a tapestry—each individual contributing to the fragile hold they now had over their shared existence.

The dawn broke slowly, casting a soft light over the camp, revealing the scars of the night—broken barricades, scattered supplies, and the remnants of a struggle that had tested them both physically and emotionally.

ABANDONED WAREHOUSE - MORNING

Inside the warehouse, Deacon gathered everyone for a morning briefing. The survivors and the raiders now shared the space, the air filled with anticipation and uncertainty about what the day would bring.

"Alright, everyone," Deacon began, looking around at the hopeful faces illuminated in the morning light. "We made it through a tough night. But now, we need to address what lies ahead."

Rachel, standing beside him, chimed in. "We need to divide our resources carefully. With everyone contributing, we can establish a solid foundation."

"Exactly," Deacon replied, appreciative of her support. "We must set patrols to scan the immediate area to ensure no threats are lurking nearby. We also need to secure food and medical supplies."

Reverend Thomas raised his hand, a calm demeanor strong as usual. "Let's also not forget to tend to the wounds. We have to ensure that everyone is at their best to continue this fight together."

Colonel Stone stepped forward; his military training evident as he laid out the strategies for the day. "I suggest we set three groups: scouting, gathering supplies, and a guard to stay on watch. We can take some of the raiders with us—if they're willing to contribute. Trust will be built through cooperation."

Lila spoke up, her voice full of determination. "I'll join the scouting party. We need to check out the footprints from last night and see if we can find the settlement you mentioned."

"Count me in too," Nadine added, excitement coursing through her. "I want to help gather edible supplies."

WOODS NEAR THE CAMP - MORNING

As the groups formed and prepared for the tasks ahead, Deacon felt a careful optimism blooming among them. They set off into the woods with a map in hand, guided by the freshly unearthed footprints and the glimmers of hope strung throughout their newfound alliance.

Lila and Nadine led the scouting group through the tree line, eyes peeled for any signs of danger, while Jacob and Rachel joined them to add their insights.

"This way!" Lila whispered, pointing to a path slightly hidden beneath the foliage. "If we stick low, we should be able to avoid any potential watch."

They moved like shadows, fluid and silent, yet driven with purpose. Every sound—a rustle, a snapping twig—had them on high alert, reminding them of the night's terror.

ABANDONED WAREHOUSE - MORNING

Meanwhile, back at the warehouse, Colonel Stone coordinated the supply gathering, delegating responsibilities with precision. "Alright, we'll split into teams. We need to hit the stores that are closest but move quickly and cautiously. Grab anything you can find."

Frank joined a small group tasked with checking an old hardware store nearby. "Let's go before we lose the advantage of surprise," he said, glancing at the others.

"Keep weapons ready just in case," Colonel Stone reminded everyone as they split into groups, forging out toward potentially fruitful areas.

WOODS NEAR THE MYSTERIOUS SETTLEMENT - MORNING

Lila, Nadine, Jacob, and Rachel advanced cautiously, following the contours of the trail. "It should be just beyond this next thicket," Jacob said, pointing ahead.

As they continued forward, a dim outline of buildings came into view, shrouded in morning light. "Is that it?" Lila whispered, astonishment mixing with caution.

"Yes, that's the settlement. And it looks abandoned," Jacob observed, tension evident in his voice.

Nadine felt a sense of dread creep in as they approached the outskirts. "Should we check it out? What if it's a trap?"

"Let's be cautious," Rachel advised, shifting her grip on her weapon. "We can split and scout the area to determine if it's safe before moving in."

ABANDONED SETTLEMENT - NIGHT

As they approached the settlement, they spotted remnants of structures—walls crumbling with time, debris scattered across the ground indicating previous fights and challenges that had plagued the place.

Lila led the way, carefully peering around corners and into shadows. "We should check the buildings one by one. If we find anything useful, we can bring it back," she suggested.

Each member moved stealthily, tension hanging in the air like a warning as they entered one of the buildings. Dust particles danced in shards of sunlight that penetrated the cracked windows.

"Search for anything that looks edible or usable," Nadine instructed, carefully checking shelves and cabinets.

As they scavenged, Rachel's sharp eyes noticed a forgotten cache of supplies near the back of the room—a collection of canned foods, blankets, and a few medical kits, left untouched in the shadows.

"Look at this!" Rachel exclaimed, her voice low and excited. "We hit the jackpot!"

"Get it all!" Lila urged, moving swiftly to help gather the supplies. "This will help everyone back at camp."

As they filled their packs, a sudden sound sent a chill down their spines—heavy footsteps outside the building.

"Quick! Hide!" Jacob whispered urgently, pushing them toward a set of leftover furniture.

ABANDONED SETTLEMENT - NIGHT

Outside, a group of ragged looking survivors approached, their movements cautious, weary. The figure leading them, a tall woman with a wild mane of hair and eyes sharp as knives, cleared her throat and shouted, "Anyone here? Show yourself!"

Lila and the others exchanged terrified glances, knowing that their safety depended on remaining silent.

"What do we do?" Nadine hissed, panic creeping into her voice.

"We wait and see," Rachel replied, fear tightening her grip on her weapon.

Their breath held, the moment stretched as the tension of the situation escalated, their hearts pounding in rhythm with the impending storm outside.

CHAPTER 21: ENCOUNTERS AND DECISIONS

ABANDONED SETTLEMENT - NIGHT

The atmosphere was thick with apprehension as Lila and her group crouched behind the makeshift barricade of furniture, their breaths shallow and hearts racing. The murmur of the approaching survivors filled the air, a blend of uncertainty and desperation palpable in their voices.

"Anyone here? We don't mean any harm!" the leading woman called out again, her tone gruff yet tinged with weariness.

"We need to stay quiet," Jacob whispered urgently, his wide eyes scanning for exits. "They might not be friendly."

"Or they could be just like us," Rachel countered, trying to temper the fear rippling through the group. "We can't assume everyone is out for blood."

Lila nodded, her heart beating in her throat as she weighed their options. "If we stay hidden, we could listen and find out more about them. If they are peaceful, we can negotiate."

Just then, the group outside shifted, moving closer to the entrance of the building. Lila's pulse quickened as she fought against the impulse to flee or fight.

ABANDONED SETTLEMENT - NIGHT

"We're starving! We barely made it here!" the woman barked, her voice carrying urgency as she spoke to her group. "We need supplies, and we're not looking for a fight, but we'll defend ourselves."

"We should at least check it out," one of the other survivors said, glancing toward the door. "They sound desperate."

The tall woman, exasperation flashing in her eyes, replied, "We don't have time for a standoff. If they're dangerous, we need to find out now."

ABANDONED HOUSE - NIGHT

Inside, Lila's heart pounded as she leaned closer to the wall, trying to catch snippets of their conversation. "They sound unsteady," she murmured, her voice barely a whisper.

Suddenly, the sound of breaking glass resonated from outside. "Shit! Move!" the woman shouted; panic sparked as the group realized they weren't alone.

Lila quickly crouched low, adrenaline coursing through her veins as she exchanged worried glances with her companions. "We should prepare for them to come in!"

"Ready your weapons," Rachel whispered, gripping her makeshift fighting tool as her pulse quickened.

WOODS NEAR THE CAMPSITE - NIGHT

In another part of the woods, back at Deacon's camp, tension lingered as morning approached, slowly giving way to light. The raiders positioned themselves, considering their next move as they whispered among each other, eager yet cautious.

"Is this how you want to end?" the raider leader scoffed, scanning the weary faces of his followers. "Letting them dictate the terms of our survival?"

"They took down our comrades last night! We need to strike!" another raider shouted, anger boiling beneath the surface.

"No, we need to play it smart," the leader countered grimly. "If we rush in blindly, we'll lose everything. We can negotiate terms—ensure our survival by regrouping."

Across the camp, the members of Deacon's team remained steadfast, preparing themselves for whatever alliance may come their way, hoping for a chance at stability.

ABANDONED HOUSE - NIGHT

Back in the abandoned house, Lila listened intently to the commotion outside. The air was thick with uncertainty as the residents began arguing in hushed tones.

"We should raid them! They look like they have food!" one voice shouted.

"I think they're scared," another said. "We can't just go in swinging."

Just then, the door creaked open slightly, and Lila's heart halted.

"Make sure they don't enter!" she hissed, adrenaline coursing through her as she prepared to defend against whatever chaos lay before them.

Suddenly, a man's voice echoed through the doorway, weary but commanding. "We don't want to fight! We just want to survive!"

Lila exchanged glances with Jacob, who looked equally uncertain. There was desperation in their voices—but were they survivor allies or raiders seeking more victims?

"We'll keep our distance for now," Jacob suggested, feeling the moment weigh heavy with implications. "If they do want to negotiate, we can at least give them a chance."

As the tension hung in the air, Lila nodded, still readying her weapon.

"We will not be pawns in this game," she said quietly, steeling herself for whatever was to come.

WOODS NEAR THE CAMPSITE - NIGHT

As Lila and her companions braced for confrontation, back at Deacon's camp, the rising sun began to illuminate the landscape, transforming the battle-scarred scene into a hauntingly beautiful morning.

Colonel Stone stood guard, surveying the surroundings, his instincts heightened as the remnants of the previous night's chaos faded into memory.

"Let's move our watch closer to the perimeter," Stone said to Jake, who nodded, ready to carry out the order. "We need to ensure we're alerted if those raiders attempt anything."

Just then, a dull thud echoed from the tree line, capturing their attention. "What was that?" Jake asked, instinctively turning toward the sound.

"Keep your eyes sharp," Colonel Stone commanded, readying himself. "We remain vigilant!"

As the morning broke, the effects of last night's struggle reshaped the landscape of the camp, awaiting the promises of a new day—perhaps one that could unite their fractured world.

ABANDONED HOUSE - NIGHT

Inside the abandoned house, the group felt the tension mount. Lila and the others braced themselves as the door creaked open fully.

"We're not here for a fight!" the leader of the newcomers

shouted; his expression resolute yet defeated. "We just need help!"

Lila's heart raced as logic clashed with instinct. "Why should we trust you?" she replied, her voice steady despite the turmoil within.

"Because we all want to survive," the man said, backing up in a show of support while his comrades remained ready. "If we work together, there might still be hope. We know the area, and we can assist each other."

Lila lowered her weapon slightly, considering the implications. "If you've been sidelined, how do we know you'll remain loyal?" she pressed, skepticism entwined with caution.

"Let's face it," the leader continued, a note of desperation creeping into his voice. "Our enemies are the same. We have to move forward or risk annihilation."

In that moment, as he extended his hand toward Lila, the tension shifted—the uncertainty heavy in the air, their decisions on the brink.

"That's a risk we're willing to take," she said finally, feeling the weight of the choice they were about to make.

As she exchanged glances with Jacob and Rachel, a surprising understanding blossomed among them; the darkness of the night blended with the tentative hope of dawn—an opportunity to forge a new path through the remnants of their shattered world.

ABANDONED HOUSE - NIGHT

Outside, the raiders watched with wary anticipation, the atmosphere hanging heavy with suspense. The sun began to rise, illuminating the area in warm tones that belied the chaos of the previous night.

Deacon, standing at the edge of the warehouse, could see the newcomers hesitating at the doorway, wondering if they'd really crossed the threshold from enemies to allies. He could feel the weight of their collective decision pressing against him as he weighed their intentions.

"Trust is a fragile thing," he said finally, stepping forward to make his voice heard. "If we are to work together, we must set ground rules."

The raider leader nodded, conviction softening the ember of hostility that marked his features. "Agreed. We need clarity to avoid any missteps."

Deacon continued, "First, we ensure that no further violence occurs between our groups, by any means. We cannot afford unnecessary bloodshed."

The atmosphere shifted again, the tension dissipating slightly as those in the warehouse acknowledged the wisdom of his words.

"Second, we establish a shared supply route. We all share and divide resources, evenly, based on each group's need," Deacon added, sounding more confident with each proclamation.

The raider leader glanced back to his companions, who exchanged nods, arriving at a silent consensus. "We can work with that," he replied, newfound hope glimmering in his voice. "As long as we get what we need to survive."

"Lastly," Deacon raised a finger, "we communicate openly about any potential threats—before they arise. No secrets."

"Fine by me," the leader said, trembling with the realization of how this could reshape their fates. "We've had enough of hiding our plans."

ABANDONED HOUSE - NIGHT

Inside, Lila, Jacob, Rachel, and Nadine held their breath as they witnessed the negotiations unfold. Each word seemed to anchor the fragility of their new alliance.

"If we can work together," Lila said quietly, her voice soft but firm, "maybe we can face the larger threats ahead. We all know the dangers out there. We can make this work."

Rachel nodded in agreement. "It's time to put our differences aside. We need strength in unity if we're going to survive."

DEACON'S CAMP - NIGHT

As daylight broke fully over the landscape, Deacon took another step closer to the door, assuring the group could indeed find common ground.

"Let's set a watch rotation for both sides," he said, gesturing toward both the existing survivors and the newcomers. "Each side respects the others' territory as we plan to move forward."

"Agreed. We'll patrol at intervals and communicate through signals. A whistle system might work. Just loud enough for everyone to hear," the raider leader suggested, an air of cooperation finally forming.

"What if we share the supplies we scavenged?" Nadine interjected, a spark of inspiration lighting her eyes. "Perhaps we can divide them evenly until each group can find their own?"

As they exchanged ideas, foundations of trust began to take root. The introduction of shared supply caches might lead to the beginnings of an unbreakable alliance.

ABANDONED WAREHOUSE - NIGHT

Inside, the air settled into an uneasy yet hopeful calm as the last remnants of the battle lingered in their minds. Deacon stood resolutely among them.

"Let's take stock of what we have left," he instructed, rallying the group. "We need to ensure that we're ready for whatever comes next."

As they began to group supplies and share resources, the mutual respect built through necessity began to fortify their new community. Trust hung in the air like a fragile string—delicate yet full of promise. They could still find a way through the darkness.

Suddenly, a sharp noise echoed from outside—the soft crunch of leaves beneath footsteps, the unmistakable sound of movement approaching again.

Deacon's instincts kicked in immediately, and he motioned for silence, everyone freezing in their places. "Get ready," he whispered. "We may not have all the answers yet."

DEACON'S CAMP - MORNING

Outside the warehouse, figures began to emerge from the trees—other survivors, clearly weary and desperate but determined. Deacon squinted against the light to assess new arrivals, his heart racing.

"Who goes there?" he called, readying himself for any response.

"We come in peace!" a voice shouted back, and Deacon relaxed slightly, lowering his weapon.

More survivors stepped into the clearing, appearing worn but alive, their eyes wide with both trepidation and hope as they took stock of the camp.

Relief flooded through Deacon as he recognized the faces of those, he had feared lost. "You're safe now! We've formed an alliance!" he proclaimed, feeling the weight lift as the collective breath of hope heaved in the air.

"You found others!" a familiar voice called out, and Emily stepped back to meet him, eyes glistening with tears mingling with joy. "We can make this work, Deacon."

As the sun's rays poured into the clearing, it seemed possible—a chance to forge bonds anew, amidst trials unseen and the promise of stronger alliances blossoming in the face of despair.

CHAPTER 22: A NEW DAWN

DEACON'S CAMP - MORNING

The air shimmered with promise as the sun rose over Deacon's camp, illuminating the weary faces of both the old and new survivors. The horizon glowed with a golden hue, casting long shadows that blended seamlessly with the remnants of the night's chaos.

Deacon stood at the forefront, taking a moment to let the gravity of their situation settle in. Around him, the newly arrived survivors exchanged cautious glances with the existing group. There was a palpable sense of tension, but it was laced with hope—a shared understanding that they had all survived the darkness of the previous night.

"Welcome," Deacon said, raising his hand in greeting to the newcomers. "If you're here, it means you've survived a battle of your own."

The group of new survivors nodded, clearly fatigued but alive, their expressions a mixture of relief and uncertainty.

"Let's gather everyone together," Deacon continued, motioning them to the central area of the camp. "We need to plan our next steps and restock our resources."

ABANDONED WAREHOUSE - MORNING

Inside the warehouse, the remnants of prior struggles echoed

—a testament to their fight for survival, now forming the backdrop of possibility. Deacon guided the new survivors to the makeshift seating made from crates and barrels.

"We're glad to have you here," Deacon said, aiming to soothe any lingering fears. "But we must be prepared for what's to come. We need to operate under a single set of rules so that we don't spiral back into chaos."

One woman from the new group, weary and haggard but fierce in spirit, raised her hand. "I'm Kira. We've been wandering for days, trying to escape the raiders that took everything from us. Our survival depended on getting here."

"Understandable," Reverend Thomas interjected, warmth radiating from his demeanor. "You're among friends now. We want to help however we can."

As they settled in, the group began sharing their stories—each survivor recounting the harrowing paths they had taken, their losses and their narrow escapes from peril.

Through these narratives, bonds of camaraderie began to weave through the assembly, creating an undercurrent of solidarity in their shared struggle.

DEACON'S CAMP - NEAR THE PERIMETER - MORNING

Outside, the logistics of daily life began to unfold. Lila, alongside Nadine and Jacob, organized a supply run that would help prepare for the day ahead.

"Let's check the perimeter and see if we can find more food or resources," Lila suggested, her mind racing as she assessed the contents of their dwindling supplies.

"What if the raiders come back?" Jacob asked, trepidation coloring his tone.

"We'll be ready." Nadine gripped her makeshift weapon firmly.

"We can't let them intimidate us again. Our lives depend on forging strong defenses."

As Lila looked around, she felt that spark of determination swell. "We'll map out the closest areas first. If we act swiftly, we should have enough time to secure what we need before anyone else arrives."

ABANDONED WAREHOUSE - MORNING

Back inside, Deacon led the assembly of survivors in strategizing their plans. "As you all know, we need to restock our defenses and supplies," he began, eyeing the newcomers. "But we must also work on building trust. We cannot survive this alone; we need all hands-on deck."

Kira spoke up, her voice steady, "We can offer our help as well. We know of a nearby abandoned convenience store that might still have supplies. It won't be without risk, but we can scout it together."

Deacon nodded appreciatively. "Great idea. If we can send a group there to gather food while keeping our eyes peeled for any incoming threats, we can get a foothold."

The group spent several minutes discussing logistics and safety measures, everyone contributing and sharing insights from their own experiences. The discussions flowed with hope and the realization that they were shaping their futures together.

DEACON'S CAMP - LATER IN THE MORNING

The sky brightened as the sun climbed higher. Lila, Nadine, Jacob, and a few of the new survivors prepared for their excursion. Deacon gave final instructions. "Stay alert, communicate any changes, and don't hesitate to fall back if things escalate."

With that, the group took off, tension laced with excitement and anticipation. They pressed deeper into the wilderness, the foliage vibrant and alive, promising opportunities while embedding shadows of potential danger.

NEARBY CONVENIENCE STORE - LATER THAT MORNING

Upon arriving at the convenience store, Lila motioned for the others to halt, crouching behind a nearby bush, peering at the dilapidated building that loomed ahead.

"Let's take stock first. If it's safe, we'll move in," she whispered, eyes narrowing as she scanned the surroundings for any signs of life.

They crept forward cautiously, adrenaline sharpening their senses. As they moved closer to the building, a sudden noise sent them spiraling into silence—a loud crash from inside the store.

"Did you hear that?" Jacob murmured, tension coiling in his stomach.

"Stay alert!" Nadine whispered back, gripping her weapon tightly as they moved to the side of the building.

ABANDONED CONVENIENCE STORE - MORNING

Inside the store, remnants of a once-bustling atmosphere came alive with memories. Shelves lay fallen, debris scattered across the floor, and abandoned items littered every corner.

Just then, Lila peeked through a broken window, the fragmented glass offering an unfiltered view of what lay beyond.

"There's something moving in there!" she whispered urgently.

"And it could be dangerous," Nadine replied, determination evident in her voice. "We need to get a visual."

Lila took a deep breath, steeling herself. "Let's move quietly. We can't afford to be reckless now."

NEARBY CONVENIENCE STORE - CONTINUOUS

Back at the camp, Deacon and the others prepared for the eventual return of the scouting party. The air was filled with a mix of anticipation and tension as they awaited reports on their findings.

"We'll stay vigilant," Colonel Stone said, scanning the woods for movement. "We need to be ready for anything since we're in unknown territory."

Deacon nodded, confidence radiating from him as he observed everyone preparing to take up watch. "We'll do everything to ensure the safety of our people."

And so, the dawn of a new day filled with uncertainty, yet rooted in the fragile blooms of hope, began to unfold, revealing the strength of a newly forged alliance against the shadows that lingered just beyond the horizon.

CHAPTER 23: SHADOWS DEEPEN

NEARBY CONVENIENCE STORE - DAY

The atmosphere outside the convenience store was tense as Lila, Nadine, Jacob, and their companions cautiously approached the entrance. The sunlight filtered through the cracked windows, casting jagged shadows across the ground. Lila's heart raced, a potent combination of fear and resolve propelling her forward.

"Let's take a look inside," Lila whispered, motioning for the others to stay close. She positioned herself near the door, her weapon ready. "Remember, we're here for supplies, not a fight."

Nadine nodded, gripping her makeshift weapon tightly. "Right. In and out. We'll be quick."

As they shuffled cautiously through the door, the creaking hinges echoed ominously, underscoring the weight of their presence in this abandoned space. The air inside was stale, with the remnants of fear and neglect lingering in the corners.

NEARBY CONVENIENCE STORE - DAY - MOMENTS LATER

Inside, the store mirrored the destruction of many others, shelves overturned and goods scattered across the floor. Faded promotional posters clung stubbornly to the walls, remnants of a better time.

Lila held her breath, scanning the room. "We need to check

the freezer section and the back storeroom," she suggested, pointing toward an aisle that appeared relatively untouched.

Jacob, staying close beside her, whispered, "I'll check the front—keep an eye out for any movement. Just signal if you see something."

Nadine nodded; her voice determined. "We'll cover you—let's move carefully."

As they advanced deeper into the store, the shadows danced in the dim light, sparking feelings of unease. Each creak of the floorboards heightened their senses.

DEACON'S CAMP - DAY - CONTINUOUS

Back at the camp, Deacon paced anxiously with Colonel Stone, watching the woods around them for signs of their scouting party. The collective tension from the night before still lingered in the air, weighty and electric.

"Do you think they'll be alright?" Deacon asked, concern edging his tone. "They've been gone too long."

"They're prepared," Colonel Stone replied, his demeanor calm but vigilant. "Lila knows how to handle herself. Plus, Nadine and Jacob are resourceful."

"I know," Deacon exhaled deeply, trying to quell the rising anxiety. "It's just... after everything that's happened, I can't help but worry. We're still very much in dangerous territory."

As the sun rose higher, illuminating the remnants of their camp, the air felt heavy. Thoughts of the night's chaos loomed large, and uncertainty hung in the atmosphere—a reminder of the precarious balance they had forged.

NEARBY CONVENIENCE STORE - DAY - CONTINUOUS

Inside the convenience store, Lila and Nadine moved carefully down the aisles, eyes sharp for anything useful.

"Look!" Nadine shouted, spotting a shelf half-buried under debris filled with canned goods. "Let's grab these!"

Lila joined her, both women working quickly to salvage what they could. "We might find some food for the group. If we can get back quickly enough, it could make a difference."

As they approached the shelf, a sudden noise startled them—a loud CRASH echoed from the back of the store, causing them both to freeze.

"What was that?" Lila whispered, instincts flaring as she clutched her weapon tightly.

"Let's check it out. But be quiet," Nadine replied, her heart racing as they moved cautiously toward the sound.

They crept through the aisles, the flickering overhead lights casting eerie shadows along the way. The air felt charged, and Lila's gut churned with anxiety.

"We need to stay low," Lila urged, inching forward, prepared for the unknown.

WOODS NEAR THE CAMP - LATER IN THE MORNING

Meanwhile, back at the camp, the team on watch remained alert. Deacon observed the tree line closely, a strange unease washing over him as he tried to shake off his worry.

"Are we expecting any more visitors today?" Frank asked, keeping an eye on the surroundings.

"We need to be prepared for anything. That's the name of the game now." Deacon responded, eyes scanning the tree line.

Just then, a rustle caught their attention, making everyone turn sharply as a FIGURE emerged from the trees. Relief flooded through Deacon as he recognized Lila and Nadine approaching, their arms loaded with supplies.

"We found some food!" Lila exclaimed, excitement lighting up her eyes as she pushed through the entrance. "And there's plenty more where that came from!"

"Thank goodness! We need every bit of it," Deacon said, his relief palpable. "What about Jacob?"

"They'll be right behind us," Nadine said, glancing back toward the woods. "We'll make sure we're ready for anything out there."

NEARBY CONVENIENCE STORE - DAY - MOMENTS LATER

Back inside the store, Jacob and Rachel hurriedly finished checking a nearby restroom area, ensuring everything was quiet. They shared a quick glance, nodding at one another, feeling the urgency but not yet ready to voice the fear building within.

"Let's grab the last of these supplies and make our way back," Jacob suggested, his instincts guiding him.

DEACON'S CAMP - DAY - CONTINUOUS

As Lila and Nadine shared the good news about the supplies, Deacon felt a sense of hope beginning to blossom.

"Perfect," he declared. "We'll create a secure passage for everyone. Jacob can scout the area while we stock the supplies. Everyone else will keep watch."

But just as he finished his thought, the sound of bush rustling erupted outside, drawing their eyes back toward the trees.

"What now?" Frank asked, nerves bubbling to the surface.

"Stay sharp!" Deacon commanded, clutching his weapon tightly. "We aren't safe yet."

Suddenly, Jacob emerged from the tree line, looking frazzled. "We have a problem!" he shouted, urgency lacing his tone. "A group is coming this way—right on our tail!"

As his words hung in the air, Deacon felt the ground beneath him shift into darkness. The fragile alliances they had begun to build were at risk once again.

"All right—no one panics," Deacon said quickly, adrenaline pounding in his chest. "Everyone, take cover! Get ready for whatever is coming our way!"

As the shadows lengthened with the approach of the new group, the sense of imminent danger surged. Would this group be friend or foe? It would come down to the choices they made in the moment—and the strength they found in each other.

CHAPTER 24: INTO THE UNKNOWN

DEACON'S CAMP - DAY

Tension hung in the air as Deacon and his team prepared for the impending arrival of the unknown group. Deacon's heart raced, every instinct within him clamoring for vigilance. A heavy silence settled among the survivors, their expressions mirroring both anxiety and determination.

"Everyone, fall back to the perimeter!" Deacon commanded, raising his voice to cut through the tension. "We need to create a defensive line."

Colonel Stone took point, pulling his weapon close as he positioned himself near the entrance. "Let's be ready for anything. Stay sharp and watch each other's backs," he instructed, his demeanor unwavering and resolute.

As they formed a barrier, the sounds of the approaching group drew nearer—heavy footsteps crunching against the twigs and leaves. The rustling intensified, and Deacon could feel the weight of those moments pressing down on them.

"What if they're here to attack?" Frank whispered, anxiety threading through his tone.

"We'll handle it—whatever it is," Deacon replied firmly, his gaze fixed on the tree line. "We're stronger together."

WOODS NEAR THE CAMP - CONTINUOUS

The shadows shifted dramatically as a group emerged from the depths of the forest, cautiously approaching the assembling survivors. Each member bore weary expressions, faces etched with the hardships of survival but with a glimmer of hope.

"Stop right there!" Colonel Stone shouted, leveling his weapon at the newcomers, ready to defend his team.

"Wait! We're not here to fight!" a voice came forth—a younger man with sunken cheeks and wild hair. "Please, we're looking for help!"

The group paused, tension hanging in suspension as they assessed the newcomers. Deacon squinted, trying to gauge the sincerity in their demeanor.

"Help?" Nadine echoed, glancing over at Lila and Jacob, whose expressions mirrored her skepticism. "Why should we trust you?"

"Because we've seen terrible things," the young man implored, stepping forward, hands raised in a gesture of peace. "We've lost everything—our camp was overrun. We barely escaped."

"What's your name?" Deacon demanded, trying to maintain authority amid the uncertainty.

"I'm Ethan," the young man replied, glancing back at his companions—two weary women and another young man, all clearly exhausted. "We traveled far from our last camp, and we've been hunted. We need shelter. We can help your group, I promise."

"Help how?" Frank questioned, still holding his weapon, uncertain but curious. "What do you have to offer?"

Ethan looked desperate, drawing in a shaky breath. "We know the area. We can scout for resources, and I'm good at traps. If you take us in, we can contribute!"

"Hmm…," Deacon said, contemplating the risks. It was a leap of faith, one he wasn't fully prepared to make, but the truth was that they needed every hand available to secure their survival.

"Look, you have two choices," Colonel Stone said with a steely gaze. "You can return to the woods with your tale or join us, but if you join us, you follow our rules."

Ethan nodded quickly; desperation etched into his features. "We understand. Just let us in. You'll see we can be useful."

"Let them in," Lila suggested, glancing at Deacon. "We can't keep fighting alone. They could help bolster our defenses."

"Agreed," Deacon replied, lowering his weapon just slightly. "But know this: any sign of betrayal and we won't hesitate to act."

DEACON'S CAMP - DAY - MOMENTS LATER

As the newcomers stepped cautiously into the camp, a silent yet palpable tension lingered in the air. The raider threat still loomed yet felt subdued, their previous aggression blending into an uneasy truce.

"Find a spot to settle," Deacon instructed, eyeing Ethan and the others. "And make sure you contribute. We need everyone's help to survive."

Nadine moved closer to Lila as they watched the new arrivals. "Do you think this is a wise move?" she asked carefully.

"I think we're all desperate enough to need it," Lila replied, exchanging a worried glance. "We can't afford to lose anyone else. We have to give them a chance."

ABANDONED WAREHOUSE - LATER

After settling the newcomers in, Deacon gathered everyone

near the heart of the camp to discuss the strategy going forward. The mood was mixed—curiosity intertwined with caution as they prepared for the next steps.

"Alright, everyone," Deacon began, addressing both old and new faces. "We need to evaluate our current resources, fortify our defenses, and ensure that everyone is trained in survival tactics. We've all suffered in this struggle, and now it's time we use that suffering to forge a better path ahead."

"Let's form teams for scouting and fixing up our perimeter," Colonel Stone advised, arranging the survivors into groups.

As conversations sparked, ideas flowed, and spirits began to lift. They spoke of food runs, setting traps, and reinforcing the perimeter against any potential enemies lurking nearby.

WOODS NEAR DEACON'S CAMP - DAY - MOMENTS LATER

Outside, Lila led a small group of scouts to search for nearby food sources—Ethan, Jacob, and another new survivor named Mara. As they moved through the forest, they honed in on their surroundings, carefully mapping out the paths.

"Look for any signs of wildlife," Lila instructed, eyes keenly searching the area. "If we can find berries or game, it will help us greatly."

"I know a few spots nearby," Ethan chimed in, his confidence growing. "We can scout and check if there's any fresh game. My group used to rely on these woods for supplies."

As they moved deeper into the foliage, cautious yet positive, Lila felt the stirrings of a fragile camaraderie blossom. They shared stories, laughed quietly about their pasts, and slowly began to intertwine their narratives of survival.

ABANDONED WAREHOUSE - DAY - CONTINUOUS

Back at the warehouse, Deacon, Reverend Thomas, and the rest of the survivors worked to reorganize their supplies.

"Communication is key," Reverend Thomas reminded everyone. "We must ensure that we're all aware of our roles. If we stick together, we can survive anything."

"Let's set up signals for patrols, so we always know who's where," Deacon suggested, formulating strategies as he spoke. "And let's keep the faith—we're building something stronger here. Together."

As the sun climbed higher overhead, each survivor—a patchwork of stories and scars—felt a flicker of hope ignite a little brighter, each step paving the way toward a trust that had been forged through fire.

DEACON'S CAMP - MIDDAY

In the woods, Lila and her group scanned for anything out of the ordinary, the sense of unity warming them against the shadows that lurked.

Suddenly, Jacob raised an alarm. "Look! Tracks! Over here!" He pointed to a series of prints leading deeper into the woods, clearly indicating the presence of wildlife.

"That could be our chance for fresh food!" Lila exclaimed, her heart racing with excitement. "Let's follow them carefully."

The group moved cautiously; eyes alert for any signs of danger. As they ventured further along the prints, anticipation tinged the air with promises of fruitfulness.

EXT. WOODS - NEAR A CLEARING - DAY

The path twisted, leading them to a small clearing where they spotted a series of deer grazing peacefully. Their graceful forms moved gently, tranquil against the backdrop of the forest.

"Do you see them?" Mara whispered; her eyes wide with awe.

"This could be exactly what we need."

"Let's try to get closer," Lila suggested, her breath catching at the sight. "We can't scare them away."

Jacob nodded, moving slowly as they approached. The group spread out, attempting to surround the deer without causing alarm. Lila's heart pounded as they stalked closer, every moment filled with tense anticipation.

Just as they neared an optimal range, a sudden CRACK broke through the air—a branch snapping underfoot. The deer bolted, and Lila gasped, her instincts kicking in. "No! We can't lose them!"

"Follow them!" Ethan urged, launching himself into the chase as the deer sprinted into the woods.

WOODS - LATER MOMENTS

The group dashed after the deer, moving fluidly through the trees. They were determined to capitalizing on the opportunity.

"Stay together!" Lila shouted as she pushed through branches, adrenaline fueling her every step. "We can't get separated!"

Finally, the deer halted, confusion lingering as they searched for a path to safety. Jacob, heart racing, positioned himself, aiming carefully and pulling back his makeshift bow.

"Easy now," he whispered to himself, focusing intensely on the movement.

In that split second, he released the bowstring, his arrow flying toward the target.

CLEARING IN THE WOODS - MOMENTS LATER

The arrow struck true, hitting one of the deer in the flank. It stumbled, raising a panic in the herd, but now they had a chance.

"Go! Let's retrieve it!" Lila shouted, rushing toward the fallen deer with the others close behind.

As they approached the deer, they could sense its panic and fear; Jacob quickly worked to calm it down while tightening the situation.

"Hold it steady!" Lila instructed, her voice steady despite the adrenaline racing through her veins.

ABANDONED WAREHOUSE – DAY

Meanwhile, back at the camp, Deacon had gathered the remaining survivors to assess their situation and discuss the new arrivals' contributions.

"Things are changing," he said, trying to bolster the morale of those gathered. "If we can keep pushing through, I truly believe we can establish a lasting peace, not just for us but for anyone who comes our way."

"Are we certain the raiders will stick to their agreement?" Rachel asked, concern heavy in her voice. "We've seen how quickly things can turn in this world."

"We'll need to keep our guard up, but we also need to give them a chance," Deacon replied, feeling the gravity of his leadership as he addressed their fears.

Just then, the sound of rustling caught their attention as Lila and the others returned to the camp, visibly exhilarated and loaded down with fresh game.

"We got one!" Lila exclaimed, her eyes sparkling with accomplishment.

Cheers erupted among the group, their spirits lifting at the sight of fresh food. Jared, one of the newest arrivals, hurried forward, eager to help. "What can I do?" he asked, excitement bubbling in his chest at the potential for contribution.

"Let's prepare it," Emily replied, already moving toward where supplies had been laid out. "We should eat together and fortify our energies."

DEACON'S CAMP - LATER THAT DAY

As the sun dipped lower in the sky, the survivors gathered around, the air filling with laughter and chatter as they prepared the meal. The scent of roasting meat mingled with the fresh aromas of herbs and spices scavenged from the woods, drawing smiles from everyone present.

"Incredible teamwork, everyone," Deacon remarked, heart swelling with pride. "We've made great strides in building something truly special here."

As they settled into their makeshift dining area, the weight of last night's turmoil began to lift. The camaraderie formed through shared struggle and triumph forged a unity among them.

ABANDONED WAREHOUSE - NIGHT - MOMENTS LATER

That evening, when the meal had concluded, the group sat around a gathering fire, the warmth creating a shield against the chill of the approaching night. Stories were shared—flickers of both joy and sorrow lighting up their expressions as they recounted their journeys.

Frank shared his tale of resilience, sparking laughter and camaraderie. "And that's how I faced down a raider with nothing but a broken shovel!" he joked, catching the wave of amusement sweeping through the group.

"Your life sounds like a wild adventure," Kira chimed in, her eyes sparkling. "Maybe I'll need to find some unconventional weapons too."

As they laughed together, the memories of last night's terror began to fade into the backdrop of hopeful possibility. Their walls, both physical and emotional, were strengthening with the bonds formed through shared struggle.

DEACON'S CAMP - NIGHT - CONTINUOUS

Underneath the stars, Deacon took a moment to appreciate the tranquility that settled over them. The horror of their battle lay behind, and as the moon rose high in the sky, it felt like a promise of new beginnings.

"Tomorrow, we continue our scouting," Deacon stated, feeling the fire of determination reignite in his heart. "We're stronger together, and we need to ensure the safety of our newest allies."

Everyone nodded in agreement, a collective glow of hope illuminating their weary spirits.

"Together, we can reclaim our lives," Colonel Stone affirmed, solidarity burning bright within his chest. "No more hiding. We'll face whatever comes next as one."

And so, surrounded by flickering flames and the laughter of newfound friends, the group settled in for a night of rest, knowing that a new dawn would bring new challenges but also the strength to face them head-on.

CHAPTER 25: ECHOES OF THE PAST

DEACON'S CAMP - DAWN

The sun rose over Deacon's camp with vibrant hues of orange and pink, spilling warmth across the landscape and chasing away the last remnants of night. The atmosphere was filled with anticipation; a new day held the promise of possibility and the weight of what lay hidden beyond the trees.

Deacon stirred awake, his mind still reeling from the events of the previous day. He stretched and glanced around, seeing the figures of his companions one by one, still sleeping, exhausted from their recent battles. Outside, the cacophony of birds chirping provided a gentle reminder of life continuing, even in these unforeseen circumstances.

As he stood, he caught sight of Colonel Stone sharpening his knife, a focused expression on his face. Deacon moved closer, intrigued by the methodical way Stone prepared for the day ahead.

"Morning," Deacon said, breaking the silence.

"Morning," Stone replied, not looking up. "Figured I'd get a head start. We need to prepare for whatever comes next."

Deacon nodded, knowing that the raiders would test their alliance. "What do you think their next move will be?"

"Hard to say. They might try to take advantage of our trust

—or they could try to avoid any confrontation," Stone said thoughtfully, setting his knife aside. "We need to be on our guard."

ABANDONED WAREHOUSE - MOMENTS LATER

Inside the warehouse, the survivors were stirring awake, the aroma of freshly brewed coffee and food cooking wafting through the air. Emily was busy preparing a communal breakfast, her nurturing spirit guiding her hands deftly as she worked.

"Good morning, everyone! We have quite a spread today!" Emily called out, her warmth bringing smiles to the gathered group.

As faces brightened, Lila and Nadine joined the crowd, their expressions still reflecting the thrill of yesterday's triumph. "Did you manage to catch some more food?" Nadine asked, her curiosity piqued.

"Just enough for everyone," Emily replied, handing out portions with care, feeling the gratitude swell around her.

With breakfast in hand, they took their places around the central area, sharing stories and laughter, fully embracing the moment.

WOODS NEAR THE CAMP - LATER THAT MORNING

After breakfast, Deacon gathered everyone, feeling the shift of unity coursing through them. "Listen up, team. We need to start making plans. Ethan, you mentioned that there's a settlement nearby?"

Ethan nodded, stepping forward. "Yes, about half a day's journey from here, but it's risky. If we head there, we'll have to be cautious. The area has had its share of raider activity."

"I say we gather a scouting party to check it out," Colonel Stone suggested. "If we can assess the situation firsthand, we may discover more resources or allies."

"Agreed," Deacon affirmed. "Let's split into two groups. A smaller team to scout the settlement, while the larger group reinforces our defenses here."

"What about the patrols?" Kira asked. "Should we send people out to monitor the perimeters today?"

"Yes," Deacon responded decisively. "We'll need to keep an eye on the woods, especially if there are any signs of the raiders returning. A proactive strategy keeps us safer in the long run."

As the strategy solidified, Lila felt an apprehension creep in. "What if they're waiting for us to leave before attacking?" she asked, concerned that the raiders could exploit their newfound trust.

Deacon caught her gaze. "We'll need to communicate at all times. If anyone senses anything, we regroup and reassess our options. We're learning to adapt as we go."

DEACON'S CAMP - LATER THAT MORNING

As the groups prepared to venture out, excitement and nerves mingled in the air. Deacon surveyed his team, feeling the weight of leadership but also the burgeoning strength of their alliance.

"Stay in pairs, stay vigilant, and trust each other," he instructed, watching as the smaller group—Ethan, Jacob, Lila, and Nadine—gathered their supplies, ready to scout the nearby settlement.

"Let's do this!" Lila said, adrenaline pumping as they set out. She felt a surge of optimism as they moved toward the unknown, aware every step would be crucial.

NEARBY SETTLEMENT - DAY

The journey felt long but fruitful; the trees began to thin out as the group approached the edge of the settlement. They slowed, instinctively checking their surroundings before stepping into the clearing.

"What do you see?" Nadine whispered, her heart racing as she scanned the area for movement.

Ethan squinted, taking in the dilapidated buildings that stood like sentinels of time. "Looks abandoned, but we need to be careful. There could be traps or hidden dangers."

As they moved cautiously through the settlement, they took note of signs that life had once thrived there—a rusted bicycle, a faded welcome sign, remnants of gardens left untended.

Lila focused her senses, feeling a strange mix of tension and nostalgia as they navigated the landscape. "We can't let our guard down," she cautioned, leading them further into the vicinity.

Suddenly, a rustle came from behind an old car, and they all froze.

"Did you hear that?" Jacob whispered; eyes wide as he scanned the edges of the clearing.

"Stay low!" Nadine hissed, gripping her weapon tightly.

NEARBY SETTLEMENT - DAY - MOMENTS LATER

Before they could react, a young girl emerged from behind the car, wide-eyed and trembling. "Please don't hurt me!" she cried, her voice trembling with fear.

"Whoa! We're not here to hurt you!" Lila exclaimed, raising her hands slowly. "We just want to help."

"What's your name?" Nadine asked softly, her heart aching at the sight of the scared child.

"Sophie," the girl replied, eyes darting between them, confusion etched on her features.

"Are you alone?" Jacob asked gently, kneeling to meet her gaze.

"Y-yes. My family... they were here, but...," she stammered, the sadness pressing heavy on her heart. "I've been hiding."

"Come with us," Lila said, extending her hand gently. "We can keep you safe. We're not like those who hurt you."

As Sophie hesitated for a moment, uncertainty flickering in her eyes, Lila felt an overwhelming wave of empathy. She understood the fragility of trust, a delicate thread in the chaos that surrounded them.

DEACON'S CAMP - NIGHT - CONTINUOUS

Back at the camp, Deacon and the others continued preparing for the day ahead. The atmosphere was charged with a mix of hope and reliance, an unspoken pact forged through their shared struggles.

As Deacon engaged with the remaining survivors, a sudden sense of possibility washed over him. "We've proven we can survive together—but we need to stay adaptable, vigilant. We can't let our guard down even for a moment."

Just then, Colonel Stone approached Deacon, a concerned expression etched into his face. "What's our strategy if the raiders decide to press their attack while we're thin on numbers? I still feel uneasy with the potential for treachery at any moment."

Deacon nodded, understanding the gravity of his friend's concerns. "For now, we've got two groups out. We'll set up a rotating watch around the camp. Anyone who hears anything unusual signals with a whistle." He paused, considering the next steps cautiously. "And if we need to retreat, we regroup at the warehouse."

"Sounds solid," Stone replied, reassured by Deacon's strategy. "We've got to stay organized, ready for anything that comes our way. Trust, but stay sharp."

NEARBY SETTLEMENT - DAY - CONTINUOUS

Back at the settlement, Lila knelt beside Sophie, her heart aching for the young girl's plight. "You don't have to be afraid anymore. We're going to get you back to our camp where you'll be safe," she reiterated, taking Sophie's hand gently.

Sophie hesitated, glancing back into the shadows of the settlement. "But what if they find us?" she whispered, fear tightening her voice.

"We won't let that happen. We'll keep you close," Nadine assured her, looking determined as they began planning their next steps.

As the group began moving carefully away from the settlement, Lila felt an overwhelming surge of responsibility. They couldn't abandon Sophie to whatever dangers still lurked within the remnants of this once-thriving place.

"Let's head back to camp," Jacob suggested gently, scanning the area once more for danger. "We need to regroup and make sure she's safe."

Just as they prepared to exit the clearing, a low rumble of footsteps caught their attention—a small group of ragged, disheveled figures emerged from behind a nearby building. Relief mixed with trepidation settled heavily over Lila's chest as she realized they were not alone.

"Who are you?" one of the new figures asked warily, holding a makeshift weapon. The young man's face was gaunt, hollowed by hardship, but his eyes revealed a fierce determination.

"We're not here to fight! We're just trying to survive!" Lila shouted, raising her own weapon slightly to show they meant no harm.

"Just like you," the newcomer replied, glancing at Sophie, who instinctively moved closer to Lila. "What are you doing out here?"

"We found her," Nadine interjected quickly, motioning toward Sophie. "We're bringing her back to safety."

The young man glanced at the small girl and then back to Lila. "There are others out here, and they've been hunting. You shouldn't be alone in this."

"That's why we're heading back," Jacob replied, his gaze shifting as more figures began to emerge from the shadows.

Slowly, more survivors stepped into the light, their faces a mix of confusion and hope as they realized they weren't entirely alone. Lila could feel an undertone of tension rising—could they be trusted?

"They can help," Sophie whispered, her small voice breaking through the uncertainty. "They've been running just like me."

Lila exchanged glances with Jacob and Nadine, who seemed equally torn between the risks and the possibilities. "We can't turn them away," she said finally, the softness in her voice betraying the weight of responsibility she felt.

"We could form a larger group," Jacob suggested, his face serious as he weighed the implications. "But we have to remain cautious. Do you trust them?"

With a determined nod, Lila stepped forward. "I say we bring them back. Safety in numbers, right?"

DEACON'S CAMP - LATER THAT DAY

Back at Deacon's camp, plans were unfolding and spirits began to lift with the morning light. Deacon awaited the return of the scouting party, feeling the blanket of anticipation settle over the camp like a weight.

"We need to ensure that everyone understands their roles when they return," Deacon said, glancing at Colonel Stone. "These new arrivals may bring more than just supplies—they have their own stories, their own traumas."

"Agreed," Stone replied, brow furrowed in thought. "But if their stories don't align with ours, we could endanger the camp."

Just as he spoke, the sound of footsteps approached—the returning group came into view, led by Lila, Nadine, Jacob, and a handful of new faces trailing behind.

"Welcome back!" Deacon called out, relief washing over him. "Did you find what we were looking for?"

"Yes! But we also found more survivors. They need our help," Lila said breathlessly, scanning the faces of the camp. The people behind her were worn but held the spark of hope within their eyes.

Deacon stepped forward, addressing both groups. "If you are here to stay, you must know that we are all committed to unity. We have survived through the darkest times, and together, we can build something more."

DEACON'S CAMP - DAY - MOMENTS LATER

As Lila and the new survivors shared their stories with the camp, the spirit of community began to take root—each tale woven into the tapestry of resilience and survival they had collectively created.

As the day progressed, everyone set to work without hesitation—scavenging supplies, mapping out safe zones, and reinforcing defenses. They tackled the remnants of the camp with newfound determination, each small act contributing to the greater good.

Deacon felt the fire of hope blossoming within his chest. They had taken another step toward not just surviving but truly living—building a new life within the shadows of chaos.

The road ahead remained uncertain, but for the first time in a long while, the survivors felt they had a chance. Together, they stood ready to face whatever lay in wait, fortified by their bonds and buoyed by the promise of a new dawn.

CHAPTER 26: THE HAUNTING SHADOWS

DEACON'S CAMP - DAY

The sun climbed higher in the sky, casting bright rays over Deacon's camp, illuminating the faces of the survivors as they continued to bolster their defenses. The energy felt alive and vibrant after the introduction of additional survivors, and for the first time, hope flickered brighter.

While work continued, Deacon gathered the newcomers around a central fire, his voice steady. "Thank you for being brave enough to join us. Let's not only survive but thrive together. We'll have a meeting to discuss our next moves and how we can integrate everyone into our daily operations."

As Lila and Nadine assisted hunters preparing food, a lighthearted banter filled the air, creating an energy of camaraderie that began to heal the collective wounds from the night's chaos.

However, as evening approached, a subtle change edged into the atmosphere. A soft breeze picked up, and an unsettling feeling crept between the shadows.

WOODS NEAR THE CAMP - NIGHTFALL

As dusk set in, those working outside noticed the encroaching darkness felt heavier. The trees swayed ominously, and an eerie silence spread like a fog, smothering the sound of the night creatures.

"Does anyone else feel that?" Jacob asked, his eyes darting nervously into the woods. "It's like the air is charged."

"Yeah, it feels... wrong," Frank replied, his instincts flaring. "What do you think it is?"

Just then, the first howl pierced through the silence—harsh and chilling, echoing from deep within the woods. Lila felt a shiver run down her spine. "What was that?"

"Nightmare Hounds," Ethan said, his expression shifting to serious as everyone turned to him. "They're demonic creatures, feeding off fear and hauntings. They can manifest your deepest anxieties."

Lila frowned, her mind racing. "So... they're real? I thought they were just stories."

"Unfortunately, no," Jacob interjected, his voice low. "I've heard those who've encountered them say they're shadows that pit your worst fears against you."

As the chilling howl echoed again from the woods, panic flickered across the faces of the survivors who listened. The new arrivals exchanged uneasy glances; the aura of confidence having slipped just slightly.

ABANDONED WAREHOUSE - NIGHT - LATER

Inside the warehouse, Deacon gathered everyone together around the fire that flickered against the encroaching shades of night. The expression of concern hung palpably in the air.

"Everyone, we need to face this threat head-on," Deacon said, his voice steady despite the quiet anxiety that loomed within. "If the Nightmare Hounds are indeed here, we need to remain vigilant. We can't let fear dictate our actions."

"Easier said than done," Kira murmured, a hint of apprehension in her tone. "They prey on fear. How do we keep them from getting to us?"

Reverend Thomas leaned forward, interjecting wisdom in the midst of tension. "Fear only has power when we allow it to grow. We face each and every haunting thought; confront the darkness within each of us."

"How do you expect us to do that when we're facing literal demons?" one of the raiders grunted, skepticism lined in his voice.

"If we're to succeed together, we must address our fears as individuals," Colonel Stone added, voice calm but firm. "Reflect on what haunts you and speak it. The more we shine a light on our fears, the less power they have."

Emily nodded, inspiring confidence among her companions. "We have to lean on each other for support. Let's work together to create a safe space to share what haunts us."

The survivors exchanged tentative glances, knowing the depths of vulnerability that could lie ahead.

DEACON'S CAMP - NIGHT - CONTINUOUS

Outside, shadows deepened and strange sounds echoed through the trees. The haunting howl of the Nightmare Hounds grew louder, set against the backdrop of silence. The world pulsed with a haunting energy, as primal instincts flared to life.

As the darkness deepened around the camp, whispers began to swirl among the survivors—a mix of concerns and anticipatory dread.

"What if they're coming for our worst fears?" Lila posed, her voice trembling slightly. "What could they manifest?"

"Just fear itself could be enough," Jacob replied, glancing toward the shadows. "We need to hold onto each other through this."

With resolve building, the survivors settled down around the fire, preparing to share their stories—each voice a thread woven into the growing fabric of unity.

ABANDONED WAREHOUSE - NIGHT - MOMENTS LATER

As stories poured forth, survivors spoke their truths, some sharing their grief, regrets, and trauma, until finally it came time for Jacob to confess something deeply personal.

"I fear failure," he began, voice raw but resolute. "The idea of not being strong enough to protect those I care for—that they might get hurt because of me—that haunts me."

Oddly, relief washed over him as he spoke. The group embraced his acknowledgment, and one by one they began to share their fears, slowly dismantling the heavy shackles that had bound them for too long.

"Mine is being alone," Lila said, the truth striking deep in her heart. "After losing everyone, I thought there was nothing left. I never want to feel that way again."

As the fire flickered brighter, each voice rang true in the quiet of the night. They shed light on their darkness, and as they did, the energy around them began to change.

DEACON'S CAMP - NIGHT - MOMENTS LATER

Suddenly, another howl pierced through the air—a warning cry that sent a wave of panic through the camp.

"Here they come!" someone shouted, and the group scrambled to their feet, adrenaline surging.

"Get ready!" Deacon yelled, instinctively taking charge. "We're facing whatever's out there together!"

The survivors positioned themselves, weapons drawn and eyes alert. The looming fear grew palpable, an electric tension coursing through their veins.

Suddenly, from the shadows of the trees, the **NIGHTMARE HOUNDS** emerged—sinister canine-like demons with eyes glowing in the darkness, their forms cloaked in shadows, each leg moving with a grace that belied their predatory nature.

"Stay close! Don't give in!" Deacon shouted, rallying his team as the creatures circled the perimeter.

As the haunting figures manifested, each survivor felt the ripple of their own fears break free, awakening deep-rooted anxieties but also resilience. They held together, and in that instant, they were no longer alone.

ABANDONED WAREHOUSE - NIGHT

"Face them!" Reverend Thomas rallied, inspiring his companions. "We're stronger than our fears!"

With hearts set aflame by newfound purpose, the group stood shoulder to shoulder, ready to invite the shadows into the light and confront the demons both inside and out.

CHAPTER 27: THE WEIGHT OF LOSS

DEACON'S CAMP - NIGHT

The atmosphere crackled with tension as the Nightmare Hounds surrounded Deacon's camp, their eerie silhouettes flickering in and out of the shadows. The air was thick with anticipation and fear, each survivor gripping their weapons tightly, adrenaline coursing through their veins.

"I can't believe this is happening," Lila whispered, the fear evident in her eyes as she peeked into the darkness, feeling the primal energy of the creatures press against her.

"Stay focused," Deacon replied, his tone resolute. "Together, we can confront them. They feed on fear, so let's use that against them."

As the Hounds crept closer, their glowing eyes locked onto the survivors' group, the tension tightened. The air grew heavy, and Deacon could feel the weight of dread pooling in his stomach—a potent reminder of what they were about to face.

"Now!" he shouted, rallying the group. As the Hounds lunged forward, a flurry of gunfire erupted, illuminating the night with flashes of light and sound.

ABANDONED WAREHOUSE - NIGHT - MOMENTS LATER

Inside the warehouse, chaos reigned as the survivors fought to push back the dark manifestations of their worst fears. The gunfire and howls filled their ears, blending into a nightmarish symphony of struggle.

"Keep moving!" Deacon urged, maneuvering to position himself near the front lines. "Don't let them break through!"

As he shot at a Hound that lunged for him, he felt the tremors of battle around him—each shot fired not just for survival, but for the flicker of hope they all desperately clung to.

"Watch your flanks!" Colonel Stone warned, aiming at a Hound that had broken through their lines, sending it sprawling.

"Push them back! We can win this!" Frank shouted, heart racing with the adrenaline of the fight. Despite the chaos, a fierce determination blossomed among the survivors as they realized they could stand together against their shared nightmares.

DEACON'S CAMP - NIGHT - MOMENTS LATER

Outside, the noise of battle began to shift. The Hounds had retreated momentarily, howling in frustration as the survivors regained their ground. Lila and Nadine took the chance to scout the perimeter while Colonel Stone and Jacob checked their weapons.

"Do you think it's over?" Nadine asked, anxiety flooding her voice.

"Let's not get too comfortable," Lila replied softly, feeling a strange emptiness settle around them as the adrenaline started to fade. "We need our eyes and ears open."

Just then, an unsettling howl pierced the air, echoing from deeper within the forest—a reminder of the darkness lurking just outside their fragile refuge.

"Those things won't give up," Jacob confirmed, watching the tree line intently. "We need to secure the camp and check for threats."

WOODS NEAR THE CAMP - NIGHT - CONTINUOUS

Determined to scout for any potential dangers, Deacon decided to venture into the woods. "I'll check the perimeter," he stated, gripping his weapon tightly. "Stay alert, and if you see anything, signal."

As he moved through the dense foliage, the dim light from the camp flickered behind him, becoming a comforting memory that he hoped to return to. Yet, the shadows were long, and every rustle made his heart quicken.

He pushed deeper into the woods, scanning the area painstakingly. A chill crawled up his spine as he wandered alone—the eeriness of the darkness watching him felt palpably menacing.

Suddenly, he stumbled upon something resting amid the brush—a gruesome sight that made his heart drop. Bodies lay sprawled across the ground, coated in dirt and blood, remnants of a violently ended group of survivors.

"Oh no..." Deacon breathed, rushing forward, his heart racing with horror. His feelings of hope began to shatter as he recognized the signs. Here were those who had also sought safety, only to find slaughter.

Deacon knelt down beside a familiar face, a survivor he had once encountered in the past during his early travels—a flicker of warmth and humanity in a world gone cold now twisted into a chilling memory.

"It can't be..." he stammered, fist tightening around his weapon as he surveyed the scene. The brutality etched into their faces struck like a knife through him—a reminder of the darkness that still lurked unchallenged.

Suddenly, a noise broke through the silence—footsteps crunching through the leaves. Deacon froze, instinctively lifting his weapon as the shadows shifted once again.

WOODS NEAR THE CAMP - NIGHT - CONTINUOUS

From the darkness emerged another group—ragged survivors, their eyes wide with fear, who looked just as lost as they had been.

"Who are you? Show yourselves!" Deacon demanded, aiming steady, heart thundering with unguarded tension.

The newcomers raised their hands, their expressions showing both fear and hope. "We're not here to fight!" one of them cried out, stepping forward cautiously. "We just want to find safety."

Deacon lowered his weapon slightly, feeling a mixture of caution and frustration. "How many of you are there?" he asked, scanning the group.

"There are five of us. We lost our camp—just needed a place to rest!" another survivor said, voice trembling. "Please, we need your help. We ran into the Hounds last night…"

As he spoke, memories of fear and loss flashed through Deacon's mind, the recollections swirling around his heart—a reminder that they were not alone in their struggle.

"Alright," Deacon relented, seeing the truth in their eyes, knowing well the hardships they shared. "But any sign of betrayal, and I won't hesitate to protect my people."

The newcomers exchanged grateful glances, relief filling the space between them as they quickly followed Deacon back toward the camp, where the flickering lights still shone like a beacon of safety.

DEACON'S CAMP - NIGHT - MOMENTS LATER

As they reentered the camp, the new survivors apprehensively eyed the remnants of battle—the lingering wounds of the previous night's chaos.

"Welcome," Deacon said, crossing his arms. The survivors stepped forward, cautiously optimistic. "We're gathering resources, but we need to ensure that we work as one. In this world, cooperation is our strongest weapon."

As Deacon welcomed them into their circle, whispers of their previous encounters with the Nightmare Hounds circulated among the group, igniting a fresh wave of fear but also determination.

"This is just the beginning," Deacon noted, surveying the rugged faces around him, against the backdrop of the fading night. "If we can survive the darkness together, we can weather any storm that comes our way."

With that, the camp began to huddle together—their shadows merging into one, stronger for the trials they had faced and building resilience for the challenges that certainly loomed on the horizon.

CHAPTER 28: TIDES OF EMOTION

DEACON'S CAMP - NIGHT

As the stars sparkled overhead, the camp buzzed with the newfound energy from welcoming additional survivors. Laughter and chatter ran through the air, mingling with the faint crackle of the campfire. For the first time in days, despite the darkness that loomed outside their fragile refuge, a sense of unity began to blossom.

Deacon stood near the fire, observing the mingling of faces—new and old—bonding over shared tales of survival. His heart swelled with a mix of pride and hope as he caught sight of Emily moving through the crowd, her spirit infectious.

"Hey, you," he called out, stepping toward her as she approached, a warm smile lighting up her face. "Looks like we're off to a good start."

Emily smiled, her eyes sparkling with admiration. "We really are. I didn't expect this much support," she replied, glancing at the gathered group. "Everyone seems ready and willing to build a new future."

"Together," Deacon affirmed, feeling the weight of responsibility settle comfortably on his shoulders. "That's what matters most."

As they stood together, the warmth of their connection

began to envelop them, and Deacon's breath caught slightly in his throat. There was an undeniable chemistry that pulsed between them, a flicker of something deeper than friendship.

"Emily," he began, his voice lower now. "I—"

But before he could finish, Emily stepped closer, her gaze lifting to meet his. Unspoken thoughts hung heavy in the air, and in that moment, the world faded away. With a shared understanding, Deacon leaned in, and their lips met in a soft kiss—tender, yet filled with longing.

DEACON'S CAMP - NEARBY FIRE - NIGHT - MOMENTS LATER

Around the campfire, Frank fiddled with his weapon, tension pooling in his gut as he watched Deacon and Emily share that moment. A tide of emotions coursed through him—disappointment, jealousy, confusion.

"Is this really happening?" he muttered under his breath, glaring down at the ground.

Colonel Stone, standing nearby, caught Frank's eye, eyebrow raised. "What's bothering you?" he asked casually, studying Frank's demeanor with keen interest.

"Did you see that?" Frank replied sharply, his voice thick with frustration. "Deacon is losing focus. He's more concerned with romance than leadership. We have serious threats at our doorstep."

Stone shrugged, appearing contemplative. "Yeah, things can get messy. There's a lot of responsibility on his shoulders. But that kiss… it could signal trouble for us all."

Frank nodded, feeling the air grow heavy with shared thoughts. "We can't afford weakness, especially now. If he can't maintain his focus, maybe it's time for someone more committed to step in and take charge."

A flicker of interest lit up Stone's features. "What are you suggesting, Frank?"

Frank straightened, his resolve forming. "I've seen how things can spiral when emotion clouds judgment. If Deacon's too distracted by—whatever that was... Maybe it's time we start thinking about future leadership."

Colonel Stone considered this; his expression thoughtful. The idea had merit—after all, leadership required a steadfast focus that could prove crucial in times of peril.

"Let's keep this under wraps for now," Stone replied, his eyes sharp. "We'll observe Deacon and see how he manages. If he slips, we need to be ready—as a camp and as leaders."

DEACON'S CAMP - NIGHT - MOMENTS LATER

Meanwhile, Deacon pulled back from the kiss, breathing heavily as he looked into Emily's eyes, warmth blooming within that moment.

"That was unexpected," he said softly, a hint of vulnerability breaking through his usually steadfast demeanor.

Emily smiled; her cheeks slightly flushed. "It felt right, didn't it?"

Deacon nodded, feeling a mixture of joy and apprehension. "Yeah. But this—everything—we're in a complicated situation."

"I know," Emily replied, her voice steady. "But we have to define our relationships, even in the chaos. It's not weakness; it's human."

Just then, Frank's tense voice cut through. "We need to keep our focus on survival, Deacon." He approached, glancing between the two. "That kiss might just be a distraction we can't afford."

Deacon felt the mood shift instantly, tension creeping back into the air. "Frank, we're all just trying to manage the chaos around us. Not everything is a threat."

"Is it distraction or is frankness saying what needs to be said?" Frank challenged, looking directly at Deacon now, his eyes filled with unresolved feelings.

Colonel Stone stepped forward, sensing the underlying friction. "Let's remember what's at stake here. We can't let emotions lead us astray," he said, his voice commanding an air of authority.

Deacon felt the weight of uncertainty pressing down. "We're all on the same side, including the newcomers," he asserted, glancing toward a few of the raiders who stood nearby, listening in. "We need each other more than ever."

"Doesn't make it any easier," Frank muttered, crossing his arms. "We can't ignore the implications of what's evolving right now."

"Look, we'll sort this out," Deacon said, trying to regain control of the situation. "But we can't let anything—especially personal feelings—hinder our focus."

As the camp fell silent, the weight of their words crystallized the mood. Deacon felt the tightening grip of leadership pull at him even further, the complexities of human emotion and the call for survival colliding in a fragmented dance of difficulty.

DEACON'S CAMP - NIGHT - LATER

As darkness enveloped the camp once more, the tension returned as the teams prepared for what lay ahead.

"Everyone needs to stay vigilant. In the coming weeks, we'll be tested more than we imagine," Deacon said, addressing both old faces and newcomers alike around the fire. "Together, we need to take on whatever challenges arise—whether it's the Hounds or each other."

In this moment of reflection, they found common ground in shared purpose, a binding thread to hold onto in a world ravaged by darkness.

As the fire flickered against the night, the mountains of uncertainty loomed large—but Deacon chose to believe in his team. Together, they would face the shadows that haunted them and reclaim the light that flickered just beyond the horizon.

CHAPTER 29: NIGHTFALL'S GRIP

DEACON'S CAMP - NIGHT

The night descended rapidly upon Deacon's camp, thick with silence and anticipation. The warm glow of the campfire illuminated the faces of the survivors as they settled in for another tense evening of watch. Despite the earlier surge of hope, the shadows clung tightly, and the tension from earlier lingered in the air.

Deacon stood at the edge of the perimeter, scanning the tree line, heart pounding as memories of the recent attacks replayed through his mind like a haunting melody. He felt the weight of leadership pressing down, the constant reminder that he must keep everyone safe.

"Are we truly prepared for what's out there?" he muttered to himself, fingers twitching around the handle of his weapon.

Colonel Stone approached; a serious look etched on his face. "We've reinforced the perimeter, but we cannot ignore the threats. Those Nightmare Hounds are still a concern. They've been getting bolder."

"Yeah, the last thing we need is for them to find a way in," Deacon replied, glancing around at the camp, full of uncertainty. "We need to keep our spirits high, but it's hard to fathom what's lurking just outside."

Suddenly, a chilling howl echoed from the woods—the unmistakable sound of Nightmare Hounds resonating through the darkness.

"Shit," Deacon breathed, instinctively gripping his weapon tighter. "Stay alert, everyone!"

WOODS NEAR THE CAMP - NIGHT - CONTINUOUS

From the shadows of the woods emerged dark shapes with piercing eyes that glimmered like embers—Nightmare Hounds, their movements sinuous and deliberate. They prowled closer to the camp, drawn by the emotions that swirled within the gathered survivors.

"Everyone, take your positions!" Colonel Stone commanded, his eyes scanning for the creatures.

As the survivors moved to prepare for battle, the air thickened with suspense. Lila, standing with Nadine, felt an icy chill crawl up her spine. "They're feeding off our fear," she muttered, gripping her weapon as the howls pierced the night air.

"We won't let them win," Nadine replied fiercely. "Fight back our fears and show them we're not afraid!"

ABANDONED WAREHOUSE - NIGHT

Inside the warehouse, Emily readied her medical supplies, feeling a heavy sense of dread settle low in her stomach. She glanced outside, listening to the sounds of chaos beginning to unfold.

"Are you okay?" Rachel asked, concern evident as Emily prepared to face the demons they had hoped to keep at bay.

"Just trying to keep everyone safe," Emily admitted, her voice low but steady. "This place feels like it's under siege—there's just a sense of foreboding I can't shake."

"Whatever happens, we face them as one," Rachel replied quietly, urgency threading through her words as they prepared to defend the camp.

DEACON'S CAMP - NIGHT

As the Hounds approached, shadows danced in the dim firelight. Deacon gathered the remaining defenders, their breaths held tight as they anticipated the dark figures that edged closer.

"Remember, we stay vigilant," Deacon instructed the group, voices steady amidst the looming dread. "They thrive on our fear, but they can be defeated—together!"

The Hounds lunged into the clearing, ethereal forms materializing from the shadows, their eyes glowing ominously. They circled the camp in a menacing dance, provoking anxiety.

"Fire at will!" Colonel Stone commanded, and the survivors unleashed a furious barrage of gunfire, the night erupting with noise and chaos.

WOODS NEAR THE CAMP - MOMENTS LATER

From the tree line, the light from the survivors' desperate defense flickered, illuminating the horrifying scenes.

"Push them back!" Frank shouted, adrenaline surging as he aimed at the nearest Hound. Another volley erupted, aiming solidly at the center of the dark figures.

The Hounds shrieked and recoiled, but their hunger remained relentless. Deacon watched as their shapes morphed, becoming more menacing with each moment, fears manifesting a reality that pulled at the edges of their sanity.

"They're feeding on our anxiety!" Jacob yelled, trying to keep his composure amidst the chaos.

"Don't give in! Remember who you are!" Deacon shouted, rallying the troops. "Fear is their strength, and we'll not give them that power!"

DEACON'S CAMP - FIGHTING BACK - NIGHT

The battle raged on, each shot fired mixing with cries of both terror and determination as the survivors fought back against the hounds. The understanding of their own fears became a collective fuel for their fight, and the teamwork began to flow stronger than ever.

Lila stepped out from the cover of the barricade, drawing her weapon and focusing on one of the Hounds. "You're not winning today!" she shouted defiantly, pulling the trigger and landing a solid hit.

As the creature reeled back, it howled loudly, pain etched into its monstrous features.

"Keep pressing!" Deacon urged, feeling the tide of battle shift with every Hound they took down.

"Get the flank!" Colonel Stone called, directing his team toward the shifting shadows.

ABANDONED WAREHOUSE - NIGHT - CONTINUOUS

Inside, Emily felt a strong sense of determination building as she patched up a few wounded survivors, her movements efficient and honed. "We're going to make it through this," she affirmed, keeping their spirits high.

As screams of pain ripped through the air, she tightened her jaw, knowing they needed to come together as one.

Despite the chaos outside, each encounter fueled a sense of determination within them. Emily took a breath, stepping out toward the entrance of the warehouse, gathering her courage as she moved to assist the defenders.

DEACON'S CAMP - NIGHT

"Keep moving!" Deacon shouted again as shadows swirled and the Hounds lunged toward them, but their spirits never wavered as they drove the nightmares back into the dark with fierce unity.

"Don't let them take over!" Frank shouted while keeping his weapon steady, his heart pounding with every pulse.

As gunfire erupted again, Deacon felt a wave of resilience surge within him. They could do this; they had fought so hard to maintain unity in the face of despair.

And then, with a unified roar, they pushed forward, reclaiming their camp, their fears transformed into raw determination. As the last Hound crumpled to the ground, a powerful silence descended, leaving only the sound of heavy breaths.

DEACON'S CAMP - AFTERMATH - NIGHT

Silence blanketed the camp, and the survivors slowly turned to evaluate the aftermath. The night, once filled with chaos, stood still, aflame with the reality of their triumph over deeper fears.

"We did it!" Jacob exclaimed, adrenaline rushing through him, looking around at the group, excitement filling the air unexpectedly.

But as exhaustion filled their bones, Deacon took a moment to assess the situation. He saw the weary faces of his friends and the new survivors who had fought bravely alongside them. Each person carried the weight of their struggles, but there was also relief. They had faced the darkest of their nightmares and emerged victorious—together.

"Let's check for any wounded," Deacon said, his voice steady as he took charge. "We need to ensure everyone is okay and regroup for the night."

ABANDONED WAREHOUSE - NIGHT - MOMENTS LATER

Inside the warehouse, Emily worked tirelessly, tending to the injured survivors as they filtered in. She moved from person to person, applying bandages and providing comfort.

"Just breathe," Emily instructed gently to a survivor nursing a shallow cut. "You'll be okay. We're all in this together."

As she turned to grab more supplies, she briefly caught Deacon's eye. He offered her a confident nod—one imbued with gratitude and respect. In that fleeting moment, their connection deepened, forged by the fire of their shared experiences.

"Emily, it's amazing how you hold everyone together," a quiet voice came from behind her. It was Rachel, a newfound survivor who had stepped closer, taking a moment to catch her breath amid the chaos.

"Thank you," Emily replied, touched by the acknowledgement. "But we're stronger as a whole. I couldn't do it without everyone's support."

Just then, Lila rushed inside, expression tense but eyes alight with excitement. "We found supplies! We hit the jackpot!" she exclaimed, momentarily breaking the somber mood.

"Supplies?" Deacon echoed; his attention piqued as he drew closer. He felt a rush of hope at the thought of replenishing what they had lost. "How much?"

"Enough canned goods and some medical supplies to help us through the next few days!" Lila reported eagerly.

"That's incredible!" Emily exclaimed, a wave of relief washing over her. "We can use that to stabilize our resources."

Deacon's expression shifted as he thought about the

implications. "We need to organize these supplies efficiently," he said, determination lacing his voice. "No one goes without."

DEACON'S CAMP - NIGHT - CONTINUOUS

Outside, the once-frantic sounds of battle had faded into the calming hush of the night. As groups began to settle back into their routines, a sense of purpose took hold, and the shadows of past fears grew dim.

Yet something still lingered—a sense that the battle wasn't truly over. A chill passed through the air as Deacon stood outside, looking toward the woods, his instincts still alert.

"Keep your watch, everyone," Deacon said, raising his voice to rally the others around the fire. "Even in moments of victory, we must remain vigilant. They could return."

Colonel Stone stepped up, his gaze scanning the tree lines. "We'll need to fortify our defenses. First light, we set patrols and check the surrounding areas thoroughly. No more surprises."

As the group muttered their agreements, a sense of determination hung heavy in the air—the survivors were ready to reinforce their defenses, ready to defend their new home together.

ABANDONED WAREHOUSE - NIGHT - LATER

Inside the warehouse, Emily finished her last round of tending to the wounded, exhaustion weighing heavily on her features. She looked up to see Deacon stepping inside, his expression softening as he took in the scene.

"You've done a great job tonight," he said quietly, admiration evident in his voice.

"Thanks, but I just did what I had to do. It's nothing we can't handle," she replied, but there was warmth in her eyes—a flicker of something deeper that had been simmering beneath the surface.

Deacon took a step closer, the atmosphere around them charged with both tension and possibility. "We wouldn't have made it through without you. You know that, right?"

Emily nodded, her heart racing. "I just want to make sure we all stay safe. Everyone is counting on us."

In that moment, their eyes locked, the connection deepening. Deacon leaned in, and they shared a tender kiss—this time filled with unspoken promises and hope for their future.

But just as the warmth enveloped them, a distant howl echoed from the woods—deep and haunting. The moment shattered, replaced by the cold reminder of the threats still lingering in the shadows.

DEACON'S CAMP - NIGHT – CONTINUOUS
The haunting cry sent a shiver through the camp, and Deacon pulled back, his heart racing. The vulnerability of their truce weighed heavily on him.

"Everyone, back to your posts!" Deacon shouted, stepping back to address the gathering survivors. "We're not done here! I want all eyes on the woods!"

A wave of anxiety swept through the group as they prepared to defend their meager holdings once more. Shadows shifted ominously at the tree line, and the sound of soft padding echoed through the underbrush.

"Could it be more Nightmare Hounds?" Frank asked, tension in his voice.

"Could be. We need to reinforce our defenses—and quick!" Deacon instructed, feeling the renewed sense of vigilance wash over the camp as they prepared for the unknown.

DEACON'S CAMP - NIGHT - MOMENTS LATER

As the group took their positions, Deacon rallied his allies against the shadows. The flames of the campfire flickered wildly, illuminating the determination in their eyes.

"Together, we face whatever comes next!" he called out as the echoes of howls surrounded them, blending with the sounds of rustling leaves.

The moment felt electric, a reminder that in this world, every day was a battle—a struggle fought not just against external demons but against their darkest fears and uncertainties.

And as they fortified their defenses and prepared for the incoming tide of darkness, their souls intertwined in a growing web of resilience, each heartbeat echoing the same mantra: They would not be defeated.

CHAPTER 30: THE BREACH

DEACON'S CAMP - NIGHT

The camp was alive with tension, each survivor standing tense at their posts, weapons ready, eyes glued to the shadows lurking near the tree line. The howls of the Nightmare Hounds echoed through the night air, a chilling reminder of the threats they faced.

Deacon moved quickly, checking in on each group as they fortified their positions. "Stay alert!" he urged, his voice firm as he felt the weight of responsibility pressing down on him.

Colonel Stone was stationed near the perimeter, scanning the edges of the woods for any signs of movement. "We've got this," he reassured Deacon as they stood together. "If we stick to the plan, we can hold them off. We just need to be strategic."

"We've faced their kind before," Frank chimed in, a grim determination etched across his features. "We can do it again."

As the darkness thickened, the tension surged, everyone feeling the unease that the encroaching shadows represented.

ABANDONED WAREHOUSE - NIGHT

Inside the warehouse, Emily and the others worked to gather any remaining supplies and reinforce supplies where they could. The atmosphere was charged with energy, each heartbeat echoing the urgency to prepare for the unknown.

"Do you think they're coming for us?" Rachel asked, her voice shaky but filled with resolve.

"They feed on fear," Emily replied, her brow furrowing. "If we let them get into our heads, they've already won."

"We just need to keep each other focused," Nadine said, determination evident in her tone. "Defend ourselves and push forward."

DEACON'S CAMP - NIGHT - MOMENTS LATER

As the night deepened, the sounds from the woods became increasingly erratic—the crunch of twigs mingled with the whispers of shadows, a fearsome melody that filled the air with dread.

Suddenly, a loud CRASH erupted from the far side of the camp—a branch snapping abruptly.

"Get ready!" Deacon shouted, adrenaline surging as he turned toward the sound, his finger tensed against the trigger of his weapon.

From the darkness, figures began to emerge—shapes darting toward them with malicious intent. The dim light illuminated the outlines of the Nightmare Hounds, eyes gleaming like hot coals in the dark.

"Here they come!" Colonel Stone shouted, raising his weapon high. "Everyone, fire at will!"

A barrage of gunfire erupted as the survivors unleashed their determination upon the approaching shadows. The camp lit up with flashes of light, illuminating the charging figures and the raw expressions of fear intertwined with fierce resolve.

Deacon positioned himself at the forefront, sending shots at the nearest Hound as it lunged toward the defenses. "Don't let them in! We can't let them breach the camp!"

WOODS - NEAR DEACON'S CAMP - NIGHT

Just then, from the edge of the woods, a group of raiders emerged, seizing the opportunity amid the chaos.

"Charge!" one of their leaders yelled, eyes wild with rage and desperation as they rushed toward the weakened defenses.

"Oh no, not now!" Deacon exclaimed, realizing the monsters were not their only threat.

"Stay together!" Colonel Stone yelled, pivoting to face the incoming raiders as the survivors found themselves caught between two monstrous threats—the Nightmare Hounds and the unexpected raider attack.

"Fall back! We need to regroup!" Deacon shouted, his heart pounding in his chest.

ABANDONED WAREHOUSE - NIGHT - CONTINUOUS

Inside, Emily and the others quickly exchanged worried glances as they heard the sounds of chaos erupting outside.

"What are we going to do?" Rachel asked, adrenaline rippling through her as she gripped her weapon tightly.

"We need to prepare to defend the warehouse," Emily replied. "If they break in, there won't be any escape."

Just then, a loud crash resonated again, sending shivers down her spine.

DEACON'S CAMP - NIGHT - CONTINUOUS

Outside, the chaos unfolded. Deacon regrouped with his team, determination mingling with the adrenaline racing through them.

"Hold your ground!" he bellowed, rallying the group. "They think they've won, but we will not back down!"

Lila positioned herself next to Deacon, eyes fierce with determination. "Let's push! We can drive them back, both the Hounds and the raiders!"

The group advanced collectively, pushing forward against the Hounds while simultaneously facing the surge of raiders.

"The right flank's getting overwhelmed!" Frank shouted; his voice laced with urgency as he took aim.

"Reinforce the right!" Colonel Stone commanded, guiding the survivors with practiced authority, creating a united front against the incoming wave.

Every shot fired sent a message—they were not going to succumb to panic; they were reclaiming their right to exist.

NEARBY WOODS - NIGHT - CONTINUOUS

In the turmoil, the raiders began to realize they were caught in a snare of their own making.

"Fall back! The Hounds are coming for us too!" one raider shouted, a note of panic creeping into his voice as they faced the brunt of the Nightmare Hounds.

The Hounds, emboldened by the fray, lunged at both groups, their predatory instincts driving them into a frenzy. They sensed the tensions, the inability to find safety, and they thrived on the chaos.

ABANDONED WAREHOUSE - NIGHT - MOMENTS LATER

Inside, Emily felt the chaos closing in around her. She hurriedly surveyed the entrance, adrenaline mixing with desperation. "We have to reinforce the door! Everyone grab what you can!"

As the group scrambled to push furniture into position, the sounds of battle roared outside—the growls of the Hounds as they clashed with the cries of the raiders filled the air.

"Just hold on!" Frank yelled, trying to anchor the group.

But the sounds of the struggle echoed louder, and panic began to lace through their ranks as the fear of doom crept closer.

DEACON'S CAMP - NIGHT - CONTINUOUS

Amid the chaos, Deacon caught sight of an injured survivor trying to escape from the flickering light of battle but faltering, desperate eyes searching for safety. He felt a surge of instinct kick in.

"Get him!" Deacon shouted to Lila and Jacob. "We can't leave anyone behind!"

Together, Lila and Jacob dashed into the fray, narrowly dodging the chaos as they made their way to the survivor, determined to bring him back.

"Stay close!" Lila shouted, her heart racing as they navigated through the madness.

DEACON'S CAMP - NIGHT - MOMENTS LATER

Deacon continued to lead their defense, the collective force of the remaining survivors bolstering his determination.

"Regroup! We push these creatures back!" he yelled. The camp erupted with renewed fervor as they closed ranks, working as a cohesive unit against the encroaching shadows and battling both the raiders and the Nightmare Hounds with fierce determination.

Just as the chaos began to settle slightly, the raiders showed signs of disarray. Some turned to flee as the Hounds pressed against their flank, capturing their worst fears and threatening to turn the tide of the battle against them.

"Push forward! Don't let them regroup!" Colonel Stone

shouted, moving to cut off any raiders attempting to escape back into the woods.

DEACON'S CAMP - NIGHT - CONTINUOUS

Deacon watched as the group pressed forward, the Hounds and raiders locked in their own battle as the survivors formed a united front. "We have to reclaim what is ours!" he shouted, adrenaline propelling his movements.

Lila and Jacob, hand in hand with the injured survivor, forged their way back through the tumult. "Come on! We can make it!" Lila urged, shooting at an approaching raider just in time to hold him back, the shot finding its mark.

The formed alliance fought fiercely; each member ignited with the will to protect who they could. Amidst the flashing gunfire and the cacophony of the fight, the Hounds darted back, agitated by the overwhelming resistance.

Jake, standing shoulder to shoulder with Deacon, took careful aim. "We need to focus on those Hounds; they're getting too close!" he yelled, adjusting his aim as another Hound lunged.

"Together! On the count of three!" Deacon shouted, rallying both new and old survivors. "One! Two! Three!"

In a synchronized volley, they unleashed their firepower, striking down the advancing Hounds, each pull of the trigger fueling their resolve. The shadows of fear began to dissipate as the monsters howled in pain, retreating into the darkness.

ABANDONED WAREHOUSE - NIGHT - A MOMENT LATER

Inside the warehouse, the activity slowed as they awaited news of the battle outside. Emily, heart pounding, gathered remaining supplies to reinforce their barricades, shouting orders to the injured survivors who had found refuge within.

"We need to hold this door! Stay vigilant!" she shouted to the ragged group. As she was rushing around, a chilling thought crossed her mind—what would happen if they couldn't hold on?

Suddenly, the room shuddered as a loud crash echoed just outside the door—a signal of the violence that raged uncontrollably just outside.

"Keep it together!" Emily yelled, urging everyone to maintain focus amidst the fear.

DEACON'S CAMP - NIGHT - MOMENTS LATER

Outside, the battle raged on, and incoherent shouts filled the air. Deacon took a moment to glance at Colonel Stone, both men sensing the shifting tide of the fight.

The Nightmare Hounds, wounded but relentless, roared anew, aggression laced with primal energy. Deacon's heart sank as he saw Lila struggling to pull the injured survivor toward the safety of the camp.

"Cover her!" he shouted, instinctively pushing forward to provide protection, but the shadows at the tree line began to shift again. More raiders emerged from the darkness, emboldened by the chaos and ready to take advantage.

"Fall back! We need cover!" Colonel Stone bellowed, recognizing the strategy unfolding before them—a two-pronged attack threatening to unravel all they had fought for.

"Get inside!" Deacon yelled, adrenaline surging as he repositioned himself at the center of the fray. "Hurry!"

ABANDONED WAREHOUSE - NIGHT - CONTINUOUS

Inside, Emily worked with urgency, commanding the injured survivors to help brace the door in preparation for the fight they knew was coming. Anxiety swirled in her chest as she felt the pressure of the moment grow.

"Get that barricade reinforced!" she shouted, shoving crates against the door. "We'll hold the line!"

Just then, a loud bang echoed, making everyone jump. The heavy door shuddered against the impact. "They're coming!" a survivor yelled, wide-eyed and filled with fear.

DEACON'S CAMP - NIGHT - CONTINUOUS

Out on the battlefield, Deacon caught sight of the escalating chaos around him. "We need to fortify the perimeter!" he called out, his heart racing wildly as the raiders advanced, weaving through the shadows as the Hounds howled.

"Get the injured back to the warehouse!" Colonel Stone shouted, leading the charge forward. "We can't risk anyone getting cornered!"

In quick succession, each survivor responded to the command, moving as fluidly as a single organism as they tried to push back against the mounting threats. Lila, holding the injured survivor close, helped others pull back into the safety of the warehouse.

"Come on! Almost there!" she called out, urging everyone to move quickly.

As the group surged back, Deacon felt the ground beneath them settling into darkness, but their will remained unyielding.

DEACON'S CAMP - NIGHT - MOMENTS LATER

As the camp erupted in chaos, the raiders pushed forward fiercely, challenging anything that stood in their way. Deacon and the survivors fought with resolve; each shot fired intensifying the urgency of their plight.

The fear of despair and loss began to swell within Deacon, but rather than allow it to envelop him, he drew strength from his team.

"Don't give in!" he shouted, pushing forward against the onslaught. "Fight back with everything you've got! We can't let them win!"

With collective spirit ignited, the group surged forward, unleashing another volley of gunfire that descended upon the raiders.

ABANDONED WAREHOUSE - NIGHT - CONTINUOUS

Inside the warehouse, Emily ensured that everyone worked together to barricade the entrance, determination burning in her chest. The tension hung palpably as the survivors banded together, forming a united front against whatever clawed at their resolve.

"Breathe!" she urged them, working tirelessly to maintain their spirits. "We're not done yet!"

Suddenly, a loud blast erupted from outside, sending a tremor through the air, making it clear that the raiders were not yet finished with their fight.

DEACON'S CAMP - NIGHT - MOMENTS LATER

Outside, the chaos continued to swell. The raiders had begun smashing against their defenses even as the survivors regrouped, their determination fortifying with each breath.

The Hounds, emboldened by the disarray, pushed closer, drawn to the adrenaline and fear. Each howl echoed like a haunting reminder of the horrors they had battled to survive.

"Hold steady!" Deacon shouted, stepping into the fray with Colonel Stone beside him.

The remnants of darkness pressed against them, shadows swirling threateningly. Deacon's heart raced as he aimed at the threatening figures, knowing that the battle for survival loomed on the horizon.

With one last fierce push, they took their stand, refusing to yield to the fears that clawed at the edges of their souls—a new dawn hung on the horizon, but it would demand the strength of their human spirit and collective courage.

CHAPTER 31: THE BATTLE WITHIN

DEACON'S CAMP - NIGHT

The chaos of battle raged as the raiders and Nightmare Hounds collided with the survivors. Shadows danced beneath the flickering campfire light, fear intermingling with determination. Deacon stood resolutely at the forefront, his heart pounding as he prepared to face the encroaching darkness.

"Don't let them break the line!" he shouted, rallying the survivors as they clung to their weapons. Every heartbeat resonated with the knowledge that together, they could face the storm.

"Regroup!" Colonel Stone echoed, positioning himself alongside Deacon as they turned to face the snarling Hounds, their eyes glowing like molten fire in the night. "We need to push back; these beasts thrive on fear!"

As Deacon fired into the fray, his mind raced with the urgency of survival. He felt the heat of adrenaline coursing through him, awakening every instinct to defend those around him. The Hounds lunged, snapping their jaws, but the survivors stood firm.

With rapid precision, Lila and Jacob covered their retreating comrades, a fierce resolve igniting their every action.

"Keep firing!" Jacob shouted, reloading swiftly as he took aim at an advancing Hound, shooting it down before it could reach them.

ABANDONED WAREHOUSE - NIGHT - MOMENTS LATER

Inside the warehouse, Emily worked quickly, ensuring the barricades held strong while hearing the shouts and gunfire outside.

"It's just a matter of time," she whispered to herself, determined to maintain focus. "We can't let them break through."

Turning to the survivors alongside her, she reminded them, "Stay strong! We'll make it through this night together!"

Suddenly, another loud crash reverberated, sending waves of discomfort through the building as the door rattled. "What was that?" one of the survivors asked, eyes wide with panic.

"Just hold fast!" Emily replied firmly, trying to remain calm amid the rising frenzy, maintaining focus on bolstering morale. "We'll wait for them to signal back!"

DEACON'S CAMP - NIGHT – CONTINUOUS
Outside, the battle morphed; the tide crashed furiously against their defenses. As Deacon aimed again at a charging Hound, he felt the emotional weight of their plight collide with the bitter edge of survival.

Suddenly, he caught sight of one of the raiders approaching him, weapons drawn. "This is our time!" the raider shouted, attempting to break through, eyes wild with desperation.

Deacon squared his shoulders, stepping into the fray, fueled by instinct. "You think you can take what's ours?" he roared, standing firm. "You're mistaken!"

"Enough of this—it's survival or surrender!" the raider

retaliated, swinging his weapon as the clash erupted between them.

Deacon ducked swiftly, returning fire as Colonel Stone moved to reinforce him. "Focus, Deacon!" Stone called. "We can't let them weaken our defense!"

As they fought back against the raider, Lila shouted from nearby, "The Hounds are circling! They're using the uncertainty against us!"

WOODS NEAR THE CAMP - NIGHT

From the trees, more shadows crept closer. The sound of rustling leaves hinted at more dangers lurking just beyond the camp's borders.

Deacon looked toward the woods, feeling the weight of eyes upon them from the shadows. "We have to secure the perimeters!" he commanded, realizing that their unity was being tested at every turn.

"Everyone, stay tight!" he bellowed, pushing them back against the encroaching dangers. "We don't fall apart now!"

The raiders pressed in with renewed fury, and the Hounds continued to encircle them, preying on their panic. Every moment felt precarious; fear was palpable.

ABANDONED WAREHOUSE - NIGHT - MOMENTS LATER

Inside, Emily and the remaining survivors worked together, reinforcing the barricades. The sounds of chaos beyond the walls echoed ominously, tightening the knot of dread within her.

"Hold steady!" Emily shouted to the group. "Stay focused on the task—we can't let the fear in!"

Then, a faint sound drifted through the cracks; it was the low growl of a Nightmare Hound, barely discernible but laden with sinister intent.

"Get ready!" one of the survivors warned, glancing nervously toward the entrance.

"We need to shout if anything breaches!" Emily commanded, her resolve hardening as she prepared for a fight on two fronts —against the raiders and whatever darkness the nightmares brought.

DEACON'S CAMP - NIGHT - CONTINUOUS

As chaos evolved outside, Deacon saw one of the more fearful survivors falters, his aim wavering. "Stay strong!" Deacon shouted, urging the group to close ranks and push back against both the Hounds and the raiders. "Remember why we fight!"

Resilience surged as the group found their footing, rallying against the oppressive darkness surrounding them. Frank and Colonel Stone stood firm, providing coverage as the team reorganized.

But just when it seemed they were regaining momentum, the Hounds lunged in a coordinated attack, springing forth from various angles, their grotesque forms merging into the shadows, and suddenly splitting their defenses.

"Watch out!" Frank yelled, swinging blindly as a Hound lunged toward him, narrowly missing before he regained his balance.

Deacon took aim, sending fire into the horde with a rapid cadence, heart racing as the nightmares came alive amid the chaos. "Together!" he shouted again, rallying his crew. "We've faced this darkness before!

ABANDONED WAREHOUSE - NIGHT - CONTINUOUS

Inside, back among the survivors tending to the barricades, Emily felt the tension surge again as the growls intensified. "We have to hold this edge!" she shouted, emboldening those around her.

Suddenly, the noise of the raiders' assault echoed in the dim walls of the warehouse, crashing into any semblance of calm they had tried to cling to.

"We need to be ready; if they breach…" one of the younger survivors whispered, his eyes wide with fear.

"Then we will push back!" Emily declared, her voice rising like a clarion call. "Every ounce of courage, every breath—together, we fight!"

DEACON'S CAMP - NIGHT - MOMENTS LATER

Outside, the battle reached new heights, gunfire mixing with the hounds' howls, a chaotic symphony resounding through the cold night. The combined forces of raiders and Nightmare Hounds surged against the survivors, each moment intensifying their struggle for survival.

Just then, Deacon caught sight of the raider leader pushing forward through the tumult, his eyes blazing with fury and desperation. The moment felt charged with danger as the raider pivoted, realizing they might just take advantage of the chaos surrounding them.

"We can't let them break through!" Deacon shouted, raising his weapon, but the situation had heightened to indecision—as shadows sliced through the air, and the growls of the Hounds echoed through the cacophony around them.

"Steady!" Colonel Stone urged as he took aim, determined to maintain focus amid the confusion. "Don't let their numbers intimidate you."

The raider leader repositioned himself, trying to rally his comrades and break through the survivors' defenses. "Push forward! They're weak — we can take it!" he bellowed, fury fueling his newfound resolve.

With a spontaneous shift, the Hounds lunged, dashing against the barricades, clawing and snapping at anything within reach. Chaos erupted again as the combined forces of raiders and nightmarish creatures collided against the line of survivors.

"Watch your backs!" Lila screamed as the creature's jaws narrowly missed her, scratching the air just beside her. Jacob fired at the Hound, narrowly bringing it down.

"Keep fighting!" Deacon shouted, aiming at the approaching raider leader, whose eyes blazed with unhinged ambition. "We can't let them in! Do not falter!"

ABANDONED WAREHOUSE - NIGHT

Inside the warehouse, the tension reached a boiling point. As the sounds of battle penetrated the thin walls, Emily and the remaining survivors busily worked to reinforce the shelter against the encroaching darkness. They structured barricades and prepared for the worst.

"Get the heavier supplies! We have to hold this!" Emily urged, rallying the team as the noise around them heightened.

"The barricade won't hold forever!" a younger survivor exclaimed, panic rising in his voice as he tightened his grip on a weapon.

"We have to stay calm!" Emily reassured them, her heart pounding, focused on the incoming danger. "This is just another trial we can face together!"

DEACON'S CAMP - NIGHT - CONTINUOUS

Outside, Deacon's heart thundered, and his resolve hardened as the sight of the raider leader emerged again amidst the chaos. "You'll regret this!" the raider yelled, swinging blindly at the nearest survivor before setting his sights on Deacon.

"Let's see if you have what it takes!" Deacon shouted as he closed in on the raider, aiming directly at him. With a steadying breath, he pulled the trigger.

The shot rang out—hitting the raider squarely in the shoulder. The man stumbled back, a cry of pain escaping his lips.

"Reinforce the center!" Colonel Stone commanded, his voice cutting through the noise as he positioned himself next to Deacon, readying his weapon for whatever came next.

Just as they began to push back, a sudden movement caught Deacon's eye—a figure slipping through the tree line, cloaked in shadows. "We have more coming!" he yelled, recognizing the looming threat just beyond the edge of the firelight.

The shadows multiplied, and Deacon felt his heart drop. Just then, the howl of another Hound joined the fray, merging with the chaos that had once felt like a tangible storm.

"Prepare yourself!" Colonel Stone shouted, scanning the area. "Everyone, stay alert!"

WAREHOUSE - NIGHT - CONTINUOUS

Inside, Emily continued to rally those around her, her determination emboldening the others. "We need to hold fast! If they break through, we retreat together into the depths!"

"There's nowhere left to retreat to!" one of the survivors replied, panic lacing his words. "What do we do?"

"Trust in each other! We can do this!" Emily insisted, steeling herself against the uncertainty around them. "Remember why we're fighting!"

DEACON'S CAMP - NIGHT - MOMENTS LATER

Outside, chaos reigned as the tension between raiders and Nightmare Hounds collided in a chaotic maelstrom. Deacon pushed back against the emerging threats, standing resolute with Colonel Stone.

"Don't lose focus!" Deacon commanded, his voice rising above the noise. "Together, we can cut through this chaos!"

With renewed fire in their hearts, the survivors fought back against the darkness, but uncertainty still lurked in the shadows. Just as they worked to bring down the raiders, a sudden shout rang out.

"They're breaking in!" one of the raiders yelled.

"Push back!" Colonel Stone barked, directing his fire toward the flanking Hounds as the survivors rallied against the surging tide of danger.

ABANDONED WAREHOUSE - NIGHT - CONTINUOUS

Inside the warehouse, Emily led the survivors into a tactical formation, readying themselves to reinforce the entrance as the sounds of battle escalated outside.

"Everyone, hold together!" she shouted, feeling a surge of adrenaline. As the barricade quaked under the pressure, they braced themselves against the impending breach.

Suddenly, the door shook violently as a deafening growl tore through the night air.

"Hold on!" Emily yelled, heart racing as the noise echoed, the tension peaking.

DEACON'S CAMP - NIGHT - MOMENTS LATER

Outside, Deacon's voice rose above the chaos. "We cannot falter! We are stronger than this!"

As they fought side by side, the boundary of primal fear began to dull. With every shot fired, and every cry of defiance, the darkness began to recede, even if only slightly.

A glimmer of hope started to pulse through them, a soft light breaking through the oppressive shadows besetting them.

As they pushed back with a united force, Deacon felt the heavy chains of doubt begin to loosen. They could do this; they had faced hell before and would rise again, together.

"Give them our strength!" Deacon yelled as the camp rallied behind him, a fierce spirit igniting in them all as the Hounds retreated, and the last of the raiders fell back from the barrage of their united front.

As they pushed onward, everything felt possible—a brighter future illuminating just beyond the chaos and the pain.

And as the night wore on, they would continue to fight for what they held dear, emerging anew from the shadows—their hearts intertwined in hopes of a new dawn.

CHAPTER 32: THE CALM BEFORE THE STORM

DEACON'S CAMP - NIGHT - LATER

As the smoke cleared and the howl of the Nightmare Hounds faded into the distance, the survivors of the camp found themselves standing amidst the remnants of chaos—a landscape transformed by battle.

Deacon surveyed the scene, still reeling from the adrenaline of the night's events. Bodies of the defeated Hounds and raiders lay scattered, stark reminders of the confrontation they had just overcome.

"Check that perimeter!" Colonel Stone ordered, his voice cutting through the post-battle silence. "Make sure there are no stragglers left behind."

The survivors split into small groups to assess the damage and regroup. The air, once heavy with panic and fear, now carried a breath of tentative relief.

"We held the line," Frank said, moving to Deacon's side. "But it's not over yet. We need to fortify before they return, emboldened."

"Agreed," Deacon replied, wiping sweat from his brow, feeling the weight of leadership settling heavily on his shoulders.

"We need to gather everyone and formulate our plans for tomorrow."

As the other survivors finished securing the area, Lila approached, her eyes filled with both pride and concern. "How did we do?" she asked, her voice steady despite the chaos around them.

"We survived," Deacon said, his chest swelling with admiration for the tenacity of his team. "But this was just a taste of what we face. We need to remain vigilant."

ABANDONED WAREHOUSE - NIGHT - MOMENTS LATER

Inside the warehouse, the energy shifted as survivors began discussing the immediate needs of the camp. Emily moved among them, her heart filled with both relief and unease.

"We need to tend to the injured," she instructed, directing some of the survivors to gather medical supplies while others checked on those who were hurt in the fray.

Rachel joined her, a determined glint in her eye. "I'm ready to help however I can. We need to make sure everyone is taken care of."

As they worked diligently, laughter echoed through the space, infused with the spirit of camaraderie. For a brief moment, the weight of death and loss was pushed aside as they remembered the strength they drew from one another.

DEACON'S CAMP - NIGHT - CONTINUOUS

Outside, Deacon and Colonel Stone gathered everyone around the fire to assess their situation. The flickering flames illuminated their faces, revealing a mixture of exhaustion and resolve.

"Everyone, listen up!" Deacon called, commanding attention as the survivors gathered closer around. "We faced true danger tonight, and we came out standing. But we can't let our guard down just because we've won this fight."

"Tonight was a victory," Colonel Stone added, leaning forward in seriousness. "But we're still vulnerable. We have to anticipate that the raiders may regroup and return to test our defenses again."

Kira stepped forward; her brow furrowed with concern. "What if they come back while we're unprepared? We can't afford to lose anyone else."

"That's why we need to split our resources effectively, reinforce the perimeter, and maintain watch schedules," Deacon replied firmly. "We've survived because we've fought together, but we must remain proactive."

WOODS NEAR DEACON'S CAMP - NIGHT - MOMENTS LATER

As the planning discussions continued, Lila stepped aside, feeling the enormity of the night weigh heavily on her heart. She moved toward the edge of the camp where shadows lingered, longing for a moment of solitude to gather her thoughts.

Suddenly, she caught a movement from the trees—a flicker of light danced in the distance. Curiosity suddenly turned to unease.

"What was that?" she whispered, peering into the darkness.

Just as she pulled her weapon closer, the sound of footsteps cracked through the underbrush again. Her heart raced, adrenaline coursing through her veins as she prepared for another potential assault.

"Lila!" a voice called out, and she relaxed slightly at the sound of Jacob's voice, following her.

"Did you see that light?" she prompted, her voice barely above a whisper.

"No, but I heard something. It sounded like whispers," Jacob replied, tension lacing his tone. They exchanged worried glances, sensing the impending danger that felt ever-looming.

ABANDONED WAREHOUSE - NIGHT

Inside the warehouse, Emily knelt beside the injured survivor they had brought back from the previous skirmish, working methodically to clean and dress their wounds.

"We'll get through this," she whispered soothingly, meeting the survivor's weary eyes, trying to imbue them with strength. But doubt lurked just beneath the surface.

Suddenly, the loud crack of wood splintering broke through the silence, sending a ripple of fear through Emily. She glanced up sharply, feeling the tension ripple through the air.

"What was that?" Rachel asked, looking around nervously.

"We need to stay on guard," Emily replied, her heart racing as she exchanged anxious glances with Rachel and the others. "We've fought too hard to let anything destroy our home now."

DEACON'S CAMP - NIGHT - MOMENTS LATER

Outside, as Deacon finished addressing the group, he felt the weight of uncertainty creep into his heart again. The tension hung thick, reminding him that survival could tilt at any moment.

Suddenly, the howl of a distant Nightmare Hound echoed from the woods, mixing eerily with the sound of whispering voices that seemed to drift through the trees.

"Did you hear that?" Frank asked, stiffening his posture as he turned to Deacon.

"Everyone, stay alert!" Deacon commanded, a sense of deep

unease clawing at his stomach as eyes darted around the camp.

As they rallied, it became evident that the night was not yet done with them; shadows writhed at the edges of the light, haunted by the presence of fear that threatened to consume them all.

The terrifying thought settled within Deacon: they must be ready for whatever awaited them, for the true battle was far from over, and the enemy—both internal and external—was closing in.

CHAPTER 33: CONFRONTING THE DARKNESS

DEACON'S CAMP - NIGHT

The atmosphere among the camp was electric with anticipation, the air heavy with uncertainty and the whispers of shadows curling at the edges of the firelight. The howl of the Nightmare Hounds muted slightly, replaced by the distant sounds of rustling leaves and ominous shifts in the tree line.

Deacon, standing at the forefront of the gathered survivors, tightened his grip on his weapon, his senses heightened as he stared into the darkness. "We've faced fear before, and we'll do it again," he declared, drawing the eyes of his companions.

"Stay vigilant!" Colonel Stone added, scanning the perimeter with focused intensity. "If they think we're weak now, they'll try to exploit it."

Frank kept his weapon steady, adrenaline pulsing through him. "What do we do if they come back—if they breach our perimeter?"

"We stand united," Deacon stated firmly. "Our strength lies in our numbers, and together we can push back against whatever approaches us."

Suddenly, a series of howls erupted closer, each sound a

chilling reminder of the creatures stalking them. The hairs on the back of everyone's necks stood on end.

"Here they come!" Lila shouted, bracing herself as she took position among the other survivors.

WOODS NEAR DEACON'S CAMP - NIGHT - CONTINUOUS

From the shadows of the woods, groups of Nightmare Hounds began to emerge, their eyes gleaming like twin suns against the backdrop of darkness. They slinked through the trees, moving with eerie grace, their howls a symphony of terror matched only by the waves of dread that crested through the camp.

"Fire at will!" Deacon shouted, raising his weapon as the first Hound lunged into the clearing.

A storm of gunfire erupted as shots rang out, hitting the Hounds as the survivors united against their fears. Deacon's heart raced; each shot fired was a declaration of their determination to survive against the dark.

"Don't give in to fear!" he bellowed, trying to rally everyone as they concentrated their firepower on the approaching figures. "Aim for the heads!"

ABANDONED WAREHOUSE - NIGHT

Inside the warehouse, Emily felt the echoes of chaos engulfing them. "We need to stay focused!" she urged, as the air felt thick with unsettling tension. "If we can reinforce the barricade, we'll buy ourselves time."

Rachel was at her side, aiding in assembling makeshift barriers made of crates and debris. "How much longer do you think we can hold this?" Rachel asked, her breath quickening.

"Until we have no choice but to fight back," Emily replied calmly, though trepidation laced her words. "We need to protect what's inside. Every life matters."

DEACON'S CAMP - NIGHT - CONTINUOUS

Outside, the Nightmare Hounds pressed fiercely against the defenders. The shadows writhed, and the chaos erupted into a savage clash as the Hounds fought against them, fueled by primal instinct.

"Hold your ground!" Deacon urged again, moving to flank the Hounds as they circled like predators. Just then, a particularly large Hound lunged toward him, teeth bared and snarling.

Deacon's reflexes kicked in; he sidestepped the attack and fired, striking the beast square in the side, causing it to yelp in pain. The Hound staggered but quickly regained its focus, turning its gaze on him as a new threat emerged from the shadows.

"Push back!" Frank shouted, rallying the group as they pressed against the waves of fear that enveloped them. "We can't let them break through!"

Within moments, the Hounds began to waver, their snarls mingling with the cries of the raiders still engaged in combat.

WOODS EDGE - CONTINUOUS

But then, a chilling howl echoed once more, deeper and more ominous, causing everyone to pause. It felt almost like a call to arms among the nightmare creatures.

"They're regrouping!" Colonel Stone called out as the Hounds began to retreat into a darker part of the wood, a heavy sense of foreboding creeping alongside.

Deacon felt a tight knot in his stomach. "What are they doing?" he asked, almost to himself, as an overwhelming dread pressed in on the edges of his mind.

"Whatever it is, we need to be ready," Lila said, tightening her grip on her weapon. "We've held them off, but they might come back with something more."

Just then, Ethan, who had quietly been scanning the surrounding landscape, called out. "We should be prepared for a bigger wave. They won't stop retaliating until they've taken what they want from us."

ABANDONED WAREHOUSE - NIGHT - MOMENTS LATER

Back inside the warehouse, Emily and Rachel had finally reinforced the entrance, but the clamor outside served as a reminder of their vulnerability.

"They're going to try and take this away from us," Emily said, her voice low and filled with determination. "They won't let this go easily."

As the sounds of chaos began to recede, a sudden burst of energy flooded through the group—a realization that they needed to stay together.

"We have to stick together," Rachel said, hope lacing her words, despite the tension that threaded through everyone. "We have faced fear and uncertainty before, and we've overcome it."

DEACON'S CAMP - NIGHT - CONTINUOUS

Outside, Deacon turned to his team, adrenaline still pumping through his veins. "We hold the line and prepare for whatever comes next. If they attack, we respond with everything we have. We are stronger as one."

The group nodded, a unified front against the chilling reality of their existence. The night lay heavy around them, shadows creeping in as the haunting echoes of uncertainty whispered in the wind.

But in the heart of the chaos, a flicker of defiance ignited—the unyielding spirits of those who refused to be easily defeated as they prepared to embrace whatever darkness threatened to engulf them.

ABANDONED WAREHOUSE - NIGHT - MOMENTS LATER

Just then, the war cries of the Hounds erupted once more. The ground shook slightly as everyone felt the dread clutching at their hearts—a prelude to chaos.

"We've got incoming!" Frank shouted, anxiety lacing his voice as he prepared to respond.

"Get ready, everyone!" Deacon shouted, rallying together with Colonel Stone, their resolve unwavering despite the impending chaos.

As they stood together, adrenaline coursing through them, the group knew they had to face the oncoming shadows as a united front—a collective spirit born of fear yet tempered by hope.

In the face of impending danger, the will to confront their fears surged like a beacon against the night. They knew they were fighting not just for survival, but for the chance to reclaim and reconstruct what had been shattered—a chance at resilience and unity forged stronger through the fire of their shared battles.

CHAPTER 34: THE RECKONING

DEACON'S CAMP - NIGHT

The remnants of the camp stood defiant under a canopy of stars; the air thick with anticipation as the howls of the Nightmare Hounds escalated into a chilling chorus. Shadows danced just beyond the flickering light of the campfire, creating a labyrinthine escape of fears and uncertainties that no one could entirely understand.

"Hold your ground!" Deacon shouted to his team, gripping his weapon tightly as the sounds of the encroaching threat intensified. Adrenaline surged through him as he prepared for whatever challenge lay ahead.

"Count of three!" Colonel Stone urged, positioning himself strategically alongside Deacon. "We shoot on my mark!"

Deacon's heart pounded in syncopation with the anxious murmurs of the other survivors as they gathered around, weapons raised, ready to confront the wave of darkness barreling toward them.

"Take the Hounds first, then focus on the raiders," Colon Stone clarified, steadying his gaze. "We need to keep them separated as best as we can."

As the group steadied themselves, a sudden rush of heavily padded paws came crashing through the darkness, drawing nearer—shadows morphing into the fearsome figures of the Nightmare Hounds.

"Now!" Stone bellowed, and an eruption of gunfire rang out, illuminating the silhouette of the Hounds as they lunged forward.

DEACON'S CAMP - MOMENTS LATER

The camp was enveloped in chaos as the Nightmare Hounds charged, teeth bared and eyes glowing like spots of molten coal in the darkness. Deacon kept his focus sharp, firing as he moved between the survivors.

"Push them back! We can't let them in!" he yelled, his voice rising above the howl of winds and the growls of the beasts.

The spirits of the survivors ignited, each shot delivered with determination as they stood shoulder to shoulder, an unyielding wall against the encroaching fear. Despite the chaos, they had forged a bond stronger than darkness—a unity to fight against their worst fears.

"Watch your left!" Lila shouted, darting around as another Hound lunged, narrowly avoiding its snapping jaws. Her adrenaline surged as she retaliated with her weapon.

Jacob covered her back, firing at the Hound, while Nadine stood resolute, aiming at another threat, pushing forward with every ounce of strength.

ABANDONED WAREHOUSE - NIGHT - CONTINUOUS

Inside the warehouse, Emily and the few survivors who had remained behind heard the chaos erupt outside.

"Listen to the sounds. They need us," Rachel murmured, her heart heavy with concern for everyone outside. "We can't just hide away."

"We need to reinforce the entrance just in case they breach!"

Emily insisted, moving with purpose to help. "Our survival depends on each of us facing our fears."

DEACON'S CAMP - NIGHT - MOMENTS LATER

Outside, the cacophony escalated, the Hounds crashing against the defenses relentlessly, trying to claw their way into the heart of the camp. Deacon felt the pressure weighing heavily around him as he yelled orders amidst the chaos.

"Everyone, flank the right! Push them back!" he commanded, adrenaline coursing through him as the glow of gunfire mingled with the shadows.

But just then, a wave of raiders broke through from the darkness—caught off guard by the Hounds but determined to fight. "They're coming for you!" one raider shouted, seizing the moment to advance.

"Form up! Protect the center!" Colonel Stone yelled, glancing at Deacon with urgency as they prepared to face the dual threats.

Deacon's heart sank as he saw the formation fracture under pressure. "Hold steady!" he shouted, rallying his companions toward the center. They needed to unite to fend off both the Nightmare Hounds and the advancing raiders.

With each clash, the battle unfolded—a frenzied dance between visceral nightmares and desperate survival. The air thickened with chaos, courage fighting against the uncertainty that plagued them.

DEACON'S CAMP - NIGHT - MOMENTS LATER

Suddenly, amidst the howling winds and chaotic splashes of gunfire, one particular Hound broke through the frontline, darting directly toward Deacon, a flurry of fangs and claws.

"Get back!" Deacon shouted, moving to dodge its grasp, but the creature was faster, adrenaline kicking in as he fired.

The shot connected, but the Hound merely staggered. It howled in response, the sound reverberating through the night—a deep, guttural echo that struck right at the center of his fears.

"Deacon, watch out!" Lila called out, rushing to his side.

But momentum surged forward; the Hound lunged again, determination etched on its feral face while a strange, unpleasant pressure filled the atmosphere, feeding on the anxiety rippling through the survivors.

As Deacon pushed back against the Hound with all his strength, the darkness almost felt tangible—a living nightmare wrapped in fear.

ABANDONED WAREHOUSE - NIGHT - CONTINUOUS

Inside the warehouse, the sounds of chaos reverberated loudly. Emily and the others worked tirelessly to ensure their spots held firm against any potential threat, fear settling in their stomachs.

"Just hold on! They can't last forever," Emily assured the group as adrenaline heightened awareness.

Suddenly, someone burst in through the door—one of the wounded survivors from the earlier skirmish. "They're breaking in! We have to hurry!" he urged, gasping for breath.

"The barricade!" Rachel shouted, moving quickly with the others to reinforce their defenses as shadows loomed outside.

DEACON'S CAMP - NIGHT - CONTINUOUS

Outside again, together, Deacon and Lila fought side by side against the remaining Hounds and the influx of raiders surging into the camp. Each shot fired rang out like thunder, illuminating the chaos.

"Break their ranks!" Lila shouted, ducking and weaving as she flanked a raider trying to disrupt their line.

"Keep moving forward! This isn't the end!" Deacon shouted, each moment deepening his resolve.

Colonel Stone directed the others with his shouts, commanding their movements while maintaining composure. "Push back against the creatures! We're stronger as a unit!"

As the battle raged on, fatigue began to creep in, but determination surged within them as they fought against both nightmares and raiders.

"Get down!" Deacon shouted as a Hound lunged dangerously close, narrowly missing him as Lila fired in retaliation, her shot true.

Just then, with a burst of adrenaline, they felt a wave of ferocity—it enveloped them, igniting the energy needed to shift the tide.

DEACON'S CAMP - NIGHT - MOMENTS LATER

With fierce resolve, Deacon led the charge, weapon raised as he pressed forward, cutting through the remnants of their fears and struggles. "We fight for each other! We will not bow to darkness!" he shouted, feeling the energy build among the survivors.

The team rallied, taking courage from his words as they surged forward, a united front against the chaos surrounding them. Each shot fired marked not just a defense of their camp, but a declaration of their indomitable spirit.

The Hounds began to waver, their advances faltering as fear turned into aggression. The combined force of the survivors pressed harder against them, the movement synchronized with instinctive resolve.

"Don't let them break our line!" Colonel Stone shouted, locking eyes with Deacon as they fought back-to-back. "Time to turn the tide!"

Just then, another howl split the air—a sound more chilling than the others. It was deeper and reverberated through the earth itself. Deacon momentarily froze, dread pooling in his gut. "What was that?" he murmured, feeling a dark premonition grip him.

"Something worse is coming!" Frank warned, alerting the group. "Stay on guard!"

WOODS NEAR THE CAMP - NIGHT - CONTINUOUS

As if responding to the call, a heavier presence loomed from the depths of the woods—a larger, more menacing Nightmare Hound materialized through the shadows. Its size was staggering, glowing eyes surveying the camp with predatory intent.

"Look out!" Lila shouted, pointing toward the massive creature as it emerged, a manifestation of their darkest fears and unresolved anxieties.

"What do we do?" Jacob asked, voice thick with dread, fear cascading through him as he recognized the new threat.

Deacon felt his heart race as he faced the creature, understanding the terror it represented—not just to him but to the entire camp. "We stand our ground!" he shouted, lifting his weapon to face the monstrous Hound head-on, adrenaline surging as the creature locked its gaze onto him, its presence almost paralyzing.

"Together, we can overcome this!" Colonel Stone encouraged, rallying the group as fear and resolve collided, igniting a fire in their hearts.

ABANDONED WAREHOUSE - NIGHT

Inside the warehouse, Emily and the other survivors listened to the chaos unfold outside, the sound of gunfire and the haunting howls of the creatures' sending chills down their spines.

"We have to help them!" Rachel insisted, her eyes darting to the front door.

"No! We can't put ourselves at risk!" Emily replied, composed but shaken, trying to keep the group steady. "We must hold this position!"

Just then, another loud CRASH resonated against the door, shaking the wooden frame. The roar of the monstrous Hound echoed from outside, signaling that they were not safe yet.

DEACON'S CAMP - NIGHT - MOMENTS LATER

Outside, Deacon faced the massive Nightmare Hound, feeling the weight of the camp on his shoulders. "Focus fire!" he commanded, orchestrating their defensive maneuvers as every survivor rallied around him.

The attack against the larger creature became both instinctual and fluid. Deacon took aim, firing directly at the beast's skull, but the Hound seemed impervious, unfazed by the shots, charging forward relentlessly.

"Everyone, push back!" he shouted, driving determination among his comrades. "We don't take a step back! They live on fear; we have to fight our way through these shadows!"

Lila and Jacob provided critical support, firing at the creature's flanks as they danced away from its splayed claws, refusing to yield ground.

The Hound lunged, its massive body moving swiftly and with predatory grace, sending shockwaves through the survivors' defenses. It snapped ferociously, narrowly missing Lila and Jacob but catching Frank as he tried to gather himself.

"Frank!" Colonel Stone yelled, firing rapidly at the Hound, forcing it to retreat momentarily. "Get up!"

ABANDONED WAREHOUSE - NIGHT - CONTINUOUS

Farther back, Emily heard the cries of concern and desperation. Holding her breath, she caught sight of the barricade trembling under pressure. "We can't let fear take us!" she called, her voice rising above the chaos. "We have to push through!"

The survivors inside braced themselves, tension coursing through them. They could hear the muffled sounds of the battle—howls, gunshots, screams—serving as a reminder that they could not hide forever.

"Stay sharp and be ready!" Emily urged, feeling the weight of their fate pressing against her.

DEACON'S CAMP - NIGHT - MOMENTS LATER

Deacon felt the pressure of panic starting to rise as the beast seemed to absorb their firepower.

"Move!" he shouted, redirecting himself behind cover as the Hound lunged again, this time with more conviction. "We need to find a way to drive it back!"

"Look at its eyes!" Lila shouted as her instincts kicked in. "They're filled with rage but also confusion. Let's exploit that!"

With newfound bravery, the survivors took a step back, trying to ensure they weren't attacking blindly. "Together!" Deacon roared, aiming at the creature once more.

In a synchronized effort, the group pushed forward and unleashed another barrage of shots, a volley aimed to create pressure and move the beast away from their ranks.

"Push! Push!" Frank shouted, rallying the others as they regained their footing.

ABANDONED WAREHOUSE - NIGHT - CONTINUOUS

"You can do this!" Emily cried inside the warehouse, the tension rising within her. Each thud of gunfire echoed through the structure, each howl driving fear into them, but they would not yield.

"Breathe, everyone!" Rachel instructed, holding the shoulders of one of the scared survivors. "We've overcome fear before—together!"

DEACON'S CAMP - NIGHT - MOMENTS LATER

Outside, the sheer volume of sound escalated as the Hound howled in frustration, the realization that it was losing ground. Deacon saw a flicker of hope as the creature staggered from the constant assault—determined to force it into retreat.

With a final surge of adrenaline coursing through him, Deacon aimed and fired one precise shot that struck the large Hound in the side. The creature howled again, reeling in pain as it began to shrink away from the camp's defenses.

"Now! Press the advantage!" Colonel Stone called, surging forward with the group as the Hound turned, its body melting into the darkness of the trees.

Amidst the chaos, Deacon felt a powerful sense of relief wash over him—they had held the line against the darkness.

ABANDONED WAREHOUSE - NIGHT - MOMENTS LATER

Inside the warehouse, those gathered began to catch their breath, the sounds of battle dwindling as they steadied themselves.

"Are we safe?" one survivor asked, looking toward Emily with wide eyes.

Emily nodded, though her heart was still racing. "For now. We've held our ground—together."

DEACON'S CAMP - NIGHT - MOMENTS LATER

As the tension receded, Deacon turned to his team, the weight of relief merging with a sense of responsibility. "We must remain vigilant. The danger may have passed for now, but they'll return. We need to fortify our defenses and prepare for any possible retaliation."

Lila wiped the perspiration from her brow, her gaze steadfast. "We should also reunite with those inside," she suggested. "They've been holding their ground just as we have."

"Agreed," Deacon replied, the warmth of camaraderie strengthening their resolve. "Let's check on everyone and make sure we're ready for whatever comes next."

ABANDONED WAREHOUSE - NIGHT - MOMENTS LATER

As Deacon and the others entered the warehouse, the atmosphere shifted. Inside, the survivors were visibly shaken, but relief washed over them as they realized the battle had subsided.

"Is everyone accounted for?" Deacon asked, scanning the faces within the room.

"We've managed, but a couple are wounded," Emily reported, moving closer to Deacon, concern mirrored in her eyes. "They took some hits, but nothing we can't handle."

"Let's assess everyone and look into what we need for healing," Deacon said firmly. He felt the collective weight of leadership pressing heavily on him, a reminder that their survival was tied intricately to each other.

As they tended to the injured, bandaging wounds and sharing

stories to distract from their pain, Lila caught Emily's eye from across the room and offered a reassuring nod. With unspoken trust growing, they were all determined to battle their fears together.

DEACON'S CAMP - LATER THAT NIGHT

Outside, the campfire flickered as the night deepened, shadows dancing among the survivors. The group gathered around, sharing a communal meal, the warmth of the fire juxtaposed against the cold remnants of nighttime terror.

"Tonight, we faced darkness," Deacon called out, raising his voice to bring attention. "But we stood together and pushed back. We're stronger than any creature that haunts our dreams."

The group murmured in agreement, feeling the fire of determination rekindle within them. Yet, in the corner of his eye, Deacon noticed Frank lingering toward the back, a storm brewing behind his eyes.

"Frank!" Deacon said, motioning him forward. "Come join us. This is a moment for celebration."

Frank approached slowly, face a mask of conflicted emotions. "How can we celebrate with what still haunts us?" he asked, anger threading through his voice.

Deacon paused, sensing the rising tension. "What do you mean? We fought hard for our survival."

"But we're still vulnerable. You kissed Emily earlier!" Frank said, frustration spilling over. "You can't let personal feelings distract you from your responsibilities as leader!"

Deacon felt the accusation hang heavily between them. "This isn't just my fight; it's ours. My affections don't change the fact that we're together in this," he replied firmly but with a hint of fatigue in his tone. "We all have emotions. This moment requires unity, not divisiveness."

"Unity, right," Frank scoffed, his expression hardening. "What happens if your emotional ties compromise that unity? What if it puts the group at risk?"

Colonel Stone stepped in, sensing the rising conflict. "We can't afford to let this turn into infighting. Deacon has shown leadership through the chaos. We need to support him."

Frank scoffed, unsure of where the discontent inside him was coming from. "I'm just saying we can't ignore the truth of our fears—even those in our camp."

"It's not about ignoring our fears, Frank. It's about facing them," Lila spoke up, passion igniting her words. "We all have scars from battles fought and lost. We must rally together, not apart."

ABANDONED WAREHOUSE - NIGHT - MOMENTS LATER

Inside, the survivors shifted uneasily, feeling the tension reverberate.

"We're still a family here," Emily said softly, stepping forward to connect with the group. "We can choose to strengthen those bonds instead of letting fear divide us."

Just then, a loud thud echoed from outside the warehouse, freezing everyone in place. The tension escalated once more as they exchanged worried glances.

"Prepare yourself!" Colonel Stone barked, looking toward the source of the sound, adrenaline kicking in again.

Deacon moved to the entrance, instincts flaring. "Stay alert," he ordered quietly.

As they cautiously made their way outside, the icy grip of foreboding wrapped around them.

DEACON'S CAMP - NIGHT - CONTINUOUS

What they saw sent a chill down Deacon's spine. A large shadow loomed near the edge of the camp, indistinct yet undeniably threatening—another Hound but much larger, revealing its monstrous form against the flickering light.

"Not again," Lila whispered, fear creeping into her voice.

This Hound, larger than any they had faced before, stepped forward, its presence overshadowing the camp. The air crackled around them, charged with a malevolent energy—a physical embodiment of their fears, bold and monstrous.

They had fought bravely, but now they faced a new darkness that felt insurmountable.

"Hold your ground!" Deacon commanded, lifting his weapon high. "We can do this!"

As the creature stepped closer, baring its teeth, the night shifted—their resolve was tested once again, binding them together against the encroaching darkness.

CHAPTER 35: THE ULTIMATE CONFRONTATION

DEACON'S CAMP - NIGHT

The air hung thick with tension as the massive Nightmare Hound loomed at the edge of the camp, its glowing eyes locking onto Deacon and the rest of the survivors. The creature's growl resonated through the darkness, a deep and ominous sound that sent chills down their spines.

"Don't show fear!" Deacon commanded, stepping forward to face the beast head-on. He could feel the hearts of his companions racing behind him, their breaths hitching in anticipation.

"We need to work together!" Colonel Stone shouted; his stance resolute. "Aim for the head, and don't back down!"

As the Hound took a menacing step forward, Lila instinctively moved closer to Deacon, gripping her weapon tightly. "We can't let it intimidate us," she whispered, trying to rally the group around her. "This is just another challenge we can overcome."

"Let's remember, this creature feeds on fear," Deacon said, feeling the resolve swell within him despite the terror washing over the group. "If we unite our spirits and confront it as one, we can push it back into the darkness."

DEACON'S CAMP - NIGHT - MOMENTS LATER

With a loud howl that echoed through the night, the Hound charged, lunging toward Deacon, jaws snapping ferociously.

"Now!" Colonel Stone shouted, and a barrage of fire erupted as survivors aimed their weapons at the approaching beast.

Deacon steadied his aim, heart pounding as he focused on the Hound. "We do this together!" he yelled, squeezing the trigger, the deafening roar of gunfire ringing in his ears.

The Hound was hit, staggering back, but it quickly recovered, fueled by the flickering shadows that danced among the firelight. It howled with rage and lunged again, a horrifying visage that seemed to embody every fear they had tried to confront.

"Fall back! Regroup!" Deacon shouted, but the creature was relentless, pushing through the barrage of bullets like an unstoppable force.

WOODS NEAR DEACON'S CAMP - NIGHT

The shadows behind the Hound began to shift again, revealing the lurking forms of additional Nightmare Hounds, drawn to the commotion. Their guttural growls resonated, signaling the emergence of a larger threat.

"They're not alone!" Lila yelled, panic creeping into her voice as more figures emerged like specters from the depths of the woods. "We need to get everyone inside the warehouse!"

As the group fought against the first Hound, another howl echoed—a signal that more danger was approaching quickly.

ABANDONED WAREHOUSE - NIGHT - MOMENTS LATER

Inside the warehouse, Emily had been anxiously listening to the chaos unfold outside. Suddenly, the door rattled, and she turned to see the injured.

"We need to fortify here!" she demanded, urgency lacing her tone. "If they breach the warehouse, we're done for!"

"Let's get everything we can against the door!" another survivor suggested, rushing to help as they gathered crates, furniture, and anything sturdy enough to create an additional barricade.

Suddenly, a terrified look washed over one of the survivors. "What if they come in while we're not prepared? We can't let them overrun us!"

"Stay focused! We've faced darkness before. We can do this!" Emily insisted, working expertly to reassure everyone around her as determination sparked.

DEACON'S CAMP - NIGHT - MOMENTS LATER

Outside, the battle raged on and Deacon felt an overwhelming pressure building within him—fear threatening to seep back in as more Hounds emerged from the shadows, surrounding their camp.

"Steady, everyone!" Deacon shouted. "We've bin fighting hard and we won't let this darkness take us. Keep firing!"

With that rallying cry, the survivors locked into the perimeter focus, holding their ground and pushing back against the assault. Each gunshot rang out like a challenge to the darkness.

But as the Hounds lunged and snapped at their heels, it became clear they could not hold them off indefinitely.

"Pull back to the warehouse! We need to regroup!" Colonel Stone shouted, realizing they were losing ground.

ABANDONED WAREHOUSE - NIGHT - MOMENTS LATER

As Deacon and the other survivors retreated into the

warehouse, the atmosphere grew thick with anxiety. Emily led them inside as they quickly barricaded the door behind them.

"We're holding this place!" she declared, determination ignited in her eyes. "No matter what comes for us!"

"Don't let fear overtake us," Deacon said, feeling the weight of their survival pressing against his heart. "We've faced the darkness. We need to harness our will!"

Just then, a loud crash filled the air as a Hound launched itself against the door. The survivors jumped back, adrenaline surging as fear threatened to claw at their insides.

"Get ready, everyone!" Colonel Stone ordered, positioning himself near the barricade as everyone took up defensive positions. "They'll come for us. Let's show them we can protect what's ours."

DEACON'S CAMP - NIGHT - MOMENTS LATER

Outside, the Hounds continued to pound against the barricade, howls mixing with the panicked breaths of the survivors still outside, caught in a struggle against their own fears.

"Keep focused! We can drive them back!" Deacon shouted outside, determination surging as they unleashed a flurry of shots, attempting to drive the monsters away.

But with every pull of a trigger, it felt as if the battle was pulling them further down—a whirlpool of dread drawing them in.

ABANDONED WAREHOUSE - NIGHT - CONTINUOUS

Inside, just as the survivors braced for an overwhelming onslaught, Emily strategized with the others, calling out orders amidst the tension. "We've got to hold on! They're not going to win!"

As the pounding against the door escalated, a chilling realization hit everyone—the volatile merge of their fears was coming to fruition, a tangible manifestation of darkness lurking just beyond the barricade.

"Stay together!" Emily insisted, her voice steady in the face of uncertainty. "Speak your fears! If we stand united, we can resist them!"

With each heartbeat, the tension surged as shadows flickered across the walls of the warehouse—an impending doom that hovered in the air, intertwining with their deepest anxieties.

The Hounds trembled against their surroundings, insatiable hunger reflected in their glowing eyes, and just beyond their defenses, it felt like the very essence of despair crept closer.

DEACON'S CAMP - NIGHT - MOMENTS LATER

Back outside, the tensions reached a fever pitch. Deacon stood at the front; his eyes locked on the swirling shadows. "Hold steady!" he chanted, rallying his group. "Push back the darkness!"

Suddenly, the door to the warehouse rattled violently as if something immense was trying to break in. Desperation clawed at Deacon's gut as he turned to the group, fear spreading like wildfire through the survivors.

"Get ready! If they break through, we fight!" he shouted, adrenaline surging through him like a live wire.

The pounding continued, the air thick with anticipation and anxiety. Each thud echoed like a drum, keeping everyone on edge, their breaths held tight as they prepared for the inevitable clash.

ABANDONED WAREHOUSE - NIGHT - MOMENTS LATER

Inside the warehouse, Emily could feel the atmosphere grow

heavier with each passing moment. "We're going to need everyone to be ready," she said firmly, her heart racing. "Each of you has faced darkness before; this isn't our first challenge."

"Why don't we have a plan for if they get past the door?" Rachel asked, fear lacing her voice. "We can't just let them overwhelm us!"

"Listen!" Emily called, raising her voice above the murmurs of anxiety. "We reinforce with everything we have. If they manage to breach, we regroup toward the back and push them into a corner."

"What if they overwhelm us before we can regroup?" another survivor asked, voice shaking.

"We'll find a way," Emily replied, her confidence grounding those around her. "This isn't just survival—this is living. We must overcome our fears together!"

DEACON'S CAMP - NIGHT - CONTINUOUS

Back outside, the Hounds' howls mingled with the sounds of chaos as Deacon prepared for the next wave of assault. Relying on the bond forged through their struggles, he rallied the defenders one more time.

"On my count! One! Two! Three!" he bellowed, and as the Hounds shifted toward the barricade, he felt a surge of adrenaline ripple through the camp.

Deacon readied himself alongside Colonel Stone as they coordinated their shots, the crack of gunfire illuminating the night with every pulse of energy.

"Hit them with everything we've got!" Stone shouted; his tactical experience evident as he navigated the fray.

The Hounds lunged again, the darkness that emanated from them feeding into the hearts of those who dared resist. A fierce growl echoed through the camp as one particularly large Hound broke through the line of defense, slashing at the nearest survivor.

"No!" Deacon yelled as he rushed forward, but he was too late.

ABANDONED WAREHOUSE - NIGHT - CONTINUOUS

Inside, urgency electrified the air as Emily and Rachel prepared for any possible threat. The warehouse shook as the Hounds clawed their way toward the entrance.

"Hold the line!" Emily shouted, scrambling to ensure their barricades remained intact. As she did, the sound of chaos from outside intensified, sending shivers down her spine.

"You're not getting through!" one survivor yelled outside, clashing against the darkness with unwavering determination.

But just as Emily prepared herself to face whatever horror lay beyond, the door shuddered violently and then—a loud crash sent splintered wood flying, and the Hounds surged inward.

DEACON'S CAMP - NIGHT - CONTINUOUS

Outside, chaos erupted as the survivors faced the tide of darkness. The Nightmare Hound that had broken through was joined by others, and the camp felt like it was on the verge of collapse.

"Fight!" Deacon shouted, desperation lacing his voice as he pushed forward. "We're not losing anyone else tonight!"

The assessment of their situation turned to instinct as they fought fiercely against the incoming wave. The shadows had come alive, but so too had the spirits of those who refused to be cowed.

ABANDONED WAREHOUSE - NIGHT - MOMENTS LATER

Inside, the battle against despair surged like a tidal wave. Emily had gathered everyone near the back, ensuring they stood together, their defenses forming a resilient front.

"Whatever happens, we stick together!" Emily called, holding tight with resolve. "Each of you is stronger than the darkness outside, and I believe in you all!"

The whispers of ghosts past began to rise, but together, they fought their way through the haunting memories. One by one, they recounted their fears and turned them into a collective promise—together they would emerge victorious.

DEACON'S CAMP - NIGHT - MOMENTS LATER

Back outside, Deacon felt the intensity of battle wash over him like a storm. His instincts pushed him forward; he needed to protect his group, protect everyone who was now a part of his fight.

"Form up! We're not letting them win!" Colonel Stone called out, guiding his team in energy and precision against the Hounds.

Just then, one particularly fearsome Hound turned its gaze toward Deacon, and in that moment, a connection sparked—a phantasmal vision creeping into his heart. The creature began to snarl, reflecting deep-rooted fears back at him.

"You'll never win, Deacon!" it seemed to howl, its voice echoing with haunting familiarity. "You've lost everything you hold dear!"

But instead of shrinking back, Deacon took a deep breath, holding firmly onto his conviction. "You're just a shadow!" he roared. "I have my team, my people, and I'll fight for them! You don't control me!"

With a surge of momentum and unwavering resolve, Deacon

fired again, striking the Hound with newfound strength as the combined forces of survivors rallied behind him.

DEACON'S CAMP - NIGHT - MOMENTS LATER

The noise of battle drifted into a frenzy as the Hounds recoiled against the united front of survivors, the shadows that had promised to drown them in fear beginning to wane.

"Keep pressing! We can drive them back!" Frank shouted, despair giving way to determination as the camp began to find their footing.

The Hounds retreated slowly, driven by the resilience that pulsed through the survivors' unity. They could feel that something was changing; the chaotic energy of battle was shifting back toward hope.

ABANDONED WAREHOUSE - NIGHT - MOMENTS LATER

Inside the warehouse, Emily inhaled deeply, driven by the rising courage she felt coursing through her companions. "We've survived worse," she said softly, her heart lightening.

Just outside, the howls of retreating Nightmare Hounds echoed through the night, a haunting reminder of their struggle—a battle won, but not yet over.

As they emerged victorious, Deacon stood tall amidst the chaos, knowing the promise of tomorrow would bring new challenges—but together, they had forged a new dawn in their hearts.

CHAPTER 36: THE ECHOES OF TOMORROW

DEACON'S CAMP - NIGHT - AFTERMATH OF THE BATTLE

As the chaos gradually faded and the last echoes of the raiders' howls dissolved into the hush of night, Deacon took a moment to gather himself. The adrenaline that had propelled him through the fight began to ebb away, leaving behind a potent blend of exhaustion and relief.

"Is everyone alright?" he called out to the group, scanning the survivors who stood in a tight huddle, breathing heavily and recovering from the fray.

"Mostly okay," Frank replied, wiping sweat from his brow. "A few scrapes and bruises, but nothing serious."

Lila stood beside him; her face illuminated by the fading light of the fire. "We fought them off. Together," she said, her voice steady yet filled with emotion. "That means something."

"We've proven we can stand against them," Deacon affirmed, looking around as the reality of their triumph began to settle in. "But we need to reinforce our defenses immediately. This attack won't be the last."

ABANDONED WAREHOUSE - NIGHT - MOMENTS LATER

As survivors filtered into the warehouse after the battle,

Emily assessed the scene. The atmosphere was heavy with the aftermath of confrontation, but the spirit among them was filled with a spark of resilience.

"Let's check everyone's wounds and make sure no one needs immediate care," she instructed, her voice firm and calming amid the bustling previous tension.

Rachel crouched down beside a wounded survivor, carefully wrapping up a limp arm. "We're all in this together; we can't afford to lose anyone now," she said, her determination unwavering.

Emily nodded appreciatively, grateful for Rachel's unwavering spirit. "Even the smallest injuries can escalate if we don't take care of them now."

DEACON'S CAMP - NIGHT - CONTINUOUS

Outside, Deacon gathered the team once more, his heart heavy with the burden of leadership. "We need to assess the perimeter and ensure we've reinforced every possible entry point," he directed.

Colonel Stone stood beside him, surveying the camp with keen eyes. "We'll set shifts for watch. Given the attack we just faced, we need to stay vigilant. Everyone in the camp deserves a chance to recover," he stated, his voice carrying the authority of experience.

As they organized into shifts, the moon hung high above, casting an ethereal glow upon the camp. The survivors stayed close, sharing stories of bravery while nursing lingering fears of the Hounds and the raiders.

WOODS NEAR DEACON'S CAMP - NIGHT - MOMENTS LATER

As the survivors prepared for the watch shifts, Lila and Jacob moved to check the perimeter. The events of the night had illuminated their bond, propelling them forward together through fear and darkness.

"Do you think that's the end of it?" Jacob asked, his tone cautious. "What if they come back with reinforcements?"

Lila looked toward the woods, uncertainty nagging at her heart. "It's hard to say. But we have to be prepared. Even though we drove them back, we can't afford to let down our guard."

"Yeah... and the Hounds," Jacob added quietly, his voice revealing the shadow cast by their fears. "They'll find a way to haunt us again. They always do."

"Then we face them together," Lila asserted, her voice filled with resolve. "We'll overcome our fears—because that's what we do."

ABANDONED WAREHOUSE - NIGHT - MOMENTS LATER

Back inside the warehouse, Emily worked diligently among the survivors, helping to patch up wounds and offer comfort.

"Thank you," one survivor murmured, eyes filled with gratitude. "You've really been a lifeline for us in this hell."

"I'm just doing what I can," Emily replied, giving a gentle smile. "We've all faced our shadows tonight, but together we can strengthen each other."

As she moved around, tending carefully to anyone needing assistance, a determined fire seemed to ignite within her. As darkness threatened to consume them, she knew they held the power to forge light through solidarity.

DEACON'S CAMP - NIGHT - MOMENTS LATER

Just as the group began to settle back into their routines, the deafening howl of a Nightmare Hound surged out from the shadows, sending a tremor of fear rippling through the camp.

"On your guard!" Deacon shouted, instincts kicking back in.

"Everyone, take your positions!"

But as they prepared, another sound broke through—the creaking of branches and the crunch of leaves. The energy thickened, and from the woods emerged a silhouette.

"Who's there?" Frank shouted, aiming his weapon toward the figure emerging from the darkness.

"Don't shoot!" a voice called, filled with exhaustion. "Please, don't shoot! We mean no harm!"

Deacon felt a wave of uncertainty wash over the camp. As the figure stepped into the dim light, revealing a young woman with dirt-streaked skin and wild hair, the tone shifted.

"Are you from the other camp?" Lila asked cautiously, sensing the fear and fatigue radiating from the newcomer.

"Yes! I'm... I'm Sarah. I barely made it out before they were overrun by raiders and the Hounds," she gasped, her breath ragged with panic. "I had to find safety; I thought I was going to die out there."

Deacon eyed her with a mix of concern and caution. "What does that mean for us? You need to understand we can't let anyone in who could put our lives at risk."

"I swear, I'll do whatever it takes to prove I can help you," Sarah insisted, desperation edging her voice. "I'm lost and terrified; I've seen too much."

Deacon exchanged skeptical glances with his team, uncertainty roiling through him. But the promise of upheaval lingered in the air, and they couldn't dismiss the hopes of survival she represented.

"Let's hear her out," Colonel Stone finally said, assessing the situation with a glance. "If she's survived, she might have useful information."

Deacon nodded cautiously. "Alright, Sarah. You're welcome to join us, but understand this: we operate on trust and we remain vigilant. One misstep could cost us everything."

As Sarah stepped cautiously into the camp, tension wrapped itself tightly around Deacon's heart. They had faced overwhelming darkness tonight, and now they had to navigate new dangers—including those within their community.

As the moon hung suspended in the sky, a sense of both fear and hope intertwined in a delicate dance, reminding everyone of the danger that lurked both outside their perimeter and within themselves.

CHAPTER 37: SHATTERED ILLUSIONS

DEACON'S CAMP - NIGHT - MOMENTS LATER

The atmosphere in the camp shifted as Sarah stepped into the flickering light of the campfire, her appearance stark against the shadows. The murmurs among the survivors grew louder, uncertainty mingling with curiosity.

"Welcome to our camp," Deacon said cautiously, studying her features closely. "But we expect honesty. What happened to your camp?"

Sarah nodded; her eyes wide with fear as she glanced into the faces around her. "We were attacked; it all unfolded so quickly. Raiders came with those... those Hounds. We split up when things got chaotic. I just ran," she said, her voice trembling at the memory. "I didn't want to die like that."

Deacon exchanged glances with Colonel Stone and Lila, each considering the implications of what she had just shared. The survivors held their breaths, caught between empathy and caution.

"Do you know how many were left?" Lila asked, needling deeper as concern knotted in her stomach. "Are there others out there—more survivors we could help?"

"I... I don't know," Sarah admitted, tears glistening in her eyes. "I saw some trying to escape, but I couldn't look back. I didn't feel safe."

"Let's not jump to conclusions; we need a strategy," Deacon said firmly, pushing aside his own worries about the absolute reality of their safety. "We can't risk another attack when we're still recovering. We'll have to keep our guards up."

ABANDONED WAREHOUSE - NIGHT - MOMENTS LATER

Inside the warehouse, survivors worked tirelessly to tend to the injuries from the night's battle. Emily felt the uncertainty of the situation creeping back in as she moved between the injured, bandaging wounds and offering comfort.

"Did you hear the howl of the Hounds earlier?" Rachel murmured as they bandaged a survivor's arm. "What if they come back, or what if the raiders regroup?"

"Stay focused," Emily said with a quick smile. "We have to remain calm. There's strength in unity."

The sound of whispers began to swirl through the room, the heavy weight of dread lurking in the corners as the night wore on. Emily exchanged glances with Rachel, worry creeping back into her stomach.

"Do you think we can trust Sarah?" Rachel asked quietly, her voice barely above a whisper. "What if she draws trouble down on us?"

"We have to play it smart," Emily replied, her resolve hardening. "But we also need more hands. If she's truly alone and scared, we can't turn our backs on her."

Just then, the warehouse door creaked slightly, and a loud hitting noise sounded, startling both women. "What was that?" Rachel gasped, looking toward the entrance.

DEACON'S CAMP - NIGHT - CONTINUOUS

Outside, Deacon gathered the survivors close, feeling the tension thicken in the night air. "Tonight was a reminder of how quickly danger can emerge from the shadows," he began, his voice steady yet solemn.

"But we also fought back as a united front!" he continued passionately. "We protected our home, and together we won! We need to remain vigilant, reinforce our strengths, and keep communicating. Our survival hinges on our ability to trust and rely on one another."

As the group murmured in agreement, a cold breeze sent shivers through the camp. The fire flickered, casting unsettling shadows that reminded everyone of the fear lingering just beyond the tree line.

"Stay sharp," Colonel Stone interjected, scanning the darkness. "Nightfall brings its own dangers."

A distant howl rose again, slicing through the air. This time, it was lower, almost mournful—a sound that sent the hairs on the back of Deacon's neck standing on edge.

"Almost like they're challenging us," Lila said, her expression tight with concern.

"We won't back down," Deacon replied, a steely determination settling in his chest. "What we face is a collective fight, and we will rise above it all."

Within the camp, however, the shadows felt particularly thick, wrapping around them like a heavy cloak. Each survivor felt the pressure of tension mounting, a reminder that they were teetering on the edge of uncertainty as night deepened.

ABANDONED WAREHOUSE - NIGHT - CONTINUOUS

Back inside, Emily and Rachel continued tending to the injured as the sounds of the camp intensified outside. They exchanged worried glances as the echoes of battle played through their minds.

"What if those creatures find a way in?" Rachel asked quietly, anxiety lacing her words.

"We'll find a way to fight back," Emily said, her voice steady but soft. "We've dealt with darkness before, and we can do it again. We have to believe in ourselves and in each other."

DEACON'S CAMP - NIGHT - MOMENTS LATER

As the group prepared for the possibility of further attacks, Deacon felt the weight of responsibility pressing heavily upon him. He pulled Colonel Stone aside, determination etched across his features.

"We need to strengthen all defenses now," Deacon urged. "I don't care about bruised egos; we must present a united front to any that may come against us."

"I support your focus," Stone replied, crossing his arms. "But we need to establish clear lines of authority—if you're overwhelmed with emotion or distraction, it could cost us."

Deacon felt a flicker of frustration but quickly quelled it, recognizing that the pressure of the moment weighed on everyone's hearts. "I'll do what I must to protect this camp," he said fiercely. "We can't falter in our resolve. Not now."

Just then, the ground beneath them trembled slightly. "What was that?" Lila asked, glancing nervously around.

"Something's coming," Colonel Stone said, gripping his weapon tighter, eyes sharp in the flickering light. The atmosphere thickened, permeated with dread as they awaited the next wave of darkness.

WOODS NEAR DEACON'S CAMP - NIGHT - MOMENTS LATER

From the tree line, the creature's growls intensified, a chorus of malevolence that filled the air with chilling certainty. Something was amiss, and Deacon could feel it.

"Prepare yourselves!" he yelled to the camp as shadows danced at the edges.

Suddenly, the Nightmare Hounds broke through once again, their forms dark and menacing. This time, they were not alone.

A pack of raiders followed closely behind, emboldened by the chaos outside. It was a strike from two ferocious fronts—an overwhelming wave that tested their resolve.

"We're not done yet!" Deacon shouted, stepping to the forefront, sustaining his message of unity and resistance. "We've faced our fears before, and we'll face them together again!"

CHAPTER 38: THE RECKONING BEGINS

DEACON'S CAMP - NIGHT

The atmosphere electrified with tension as the camp prepared itself for the imminent onslaught. The howls of Nightmare Hounds fused with the shouts of raiders, creating a cacophony of impending doom. Deacon drew in a deep breath, grounding himself as he focused on the encroaching shadows.

"Everyone, take your positions!" he shouted, rallying the survivors as they gathered into a defensive line. The flickering firelight cast long shadows across their faces, revealing lines of fear mingled with determination.

"We hold this ground!" Colonel Stone echoed, stepping beside Deacon. "Aim true, stay sharp, and remember your training!"

Lila positioned herself near the perimeter, gripping her weapon tightly as adrenaline surged through her veins. "We're ready!" she called out, looking back at her comrades. "We've faced worse!"

Just then, the Hounds broke through the tree line, moving with an unnerving speed and joined by a wave of raiders who spilled into the camp like a tide of chaos. The instant the figures came into view, Deacon felt his heart race; they were not alone, and fear gripped him anew.

"Now!" Deacon yelled as gunfire erupted, the air filled with flashes of light and the sounds of resistance against the approaching darkness.

WOODS NEAR DEACON'S CAMP - NIGHT - CONTINUOUS

The Hounds bounded forward, snapping at anything in their path. One of them lunged dangerously toward Frank just as he pulled the trigger, the shot hitting it squarely in the side but failing to slow its frenzied charge.

"Behind you!" Lila shouted, moving to intercept the threat, her weapon raised high. "Stay focused!"

As chaos erupted outside, the survivors responded with a force of collective energy—each pull of the trigger a statement of their resolve against the creatures and raiders alike.

"They're overwhelming us!" Jacob shouted, struggling to maintain his aim as the Hounds pressed in around them.

"We need to push them back!" Deacon commanded, moving with fierce determination. His heart surged with the need to protect everyone he had come to care for. The battle felt visceral, primal—a dance between survival and despair.

ABANDONED WAREHOUSE - NIGHT - MOMENTS LATER

Inside the warehouse, Emily and the remaining survivors prepared for a potential breach. They huddled near the barricades, feeling the vibrations from the chaos outside coursing through the walls.

"What if they come here?" Rachel whispered, anxiety lacing her tone. "We can't let them find us unprepared."

"Stay calm," Emily replied, her tone steady. "If they get in, we fight back, just like they are at the camp. We won't be easy prey."

As the growls and roars of the Hounds fused with the sounds of gunfire, everyone inside felt a tight knot of fear twisting in their hearts. The intensity of the situation was palpable, pressing down on them like an oppressive weight.

DEACON'S CAMP - NIGHT - MOMENTS LATER

Back outside, the clash grew fiercer. Deacon worked his way through the chaos, exchanging fire alongside Colonel Stone as they faced the Hounds pressing from the woods.

"We can't let them break through!" Colonel Stone shouted, aiming at an approaching raider who sought to take advantage of the chaos.

But just as they pressed forward, a shudder ran through the ground—the sound of more footsteps crashing through the underbrush, escalating the urgent sense of dread.

"More are coming!" Lila screamed, panic lacing her voice as shadows extended and multiplied.

"We stand united!" Deacon shouted, even as his heart raced. "Push them back! Hold your ground!"

ABANDONED WAREHOUSE - NIGHT - CONTINUOUS

Emily felt the tension rise in the warehouse as the crashing continued outside, and fear began to creep into the hearts of those nearby.

"Hold tight!" she urged. "If we can withstand this, we can thrive. Every person here matters!"

Just then, the sound of a loud BANG echoed through the warehouse as a section of the barricade shook violently. "They're trying to break in!" someone shouted, panic rising among the survivors.

"We've got to reinforce this door!" Emily shouted, moving swiftly to gather more supplies. "We are not going to let them in!"

DEACON'S CAMP - NIGHT - CONTINUOUS

Outside, the energy shifted as the Hounds, now landing blows on the camp's defenses, drew strength from the fear swirling among the surviving group.

"This is it; we will not give in!" Deacon roared, moving to bolster the group's morale. "We've fought for our lives! Remember what we've lost to darkness! We will not let that happen again!"

But the raiders began to realize what lay ahead—a chance to capitalize on the chaos. They pushed forward, emboldened by the uncertainty.

"Deacon, look out!" Frank shouted, noticing a raider attempting to flank from the left.

"On it!" Deacon murmured, turning just in time to face the threat. He fired, hitting the raider squarely, but others continued to press closer, taking advantage of the commotion.

ABANDONED WAREHOUSE - NIGHT - CONTINUOUS

Back inside, Emily's heart raced as she heard another loud crash resonate from outside. Sweat trickled down her forehead as she motioned for Rachel to help.

"Get everything we can to hold this line!" she commanded. "I won't let them take what we've built!"

"On it!" Rachel replied, taut determination lighting her eyes.

Suddenly, just as they settled back into the rhythm of reinforcing their defenses, a sudden tremor shook the warehouse, making them all jump.

DEACON'S CAMP - NIGHT - CONTINUOUS

Outside, Deacon felt the ground shift as well. The Hounds lunged forward again, clawing against the barricades while the raiders pressed in on all sides, a tumultuous wave threatening their fragile defenses.

"Focus!" Colonel Stone barked, trying to regain control of the chaos. "Front line—fire! Back line—watch for breaches!"

Despite their efforts, the combination of Hounds and raiders was beginning to fracture their defenses. Deacon noticed a growing number of Hounds retreating only to flank back into the encroaching darkness—a strategy meant to prey on their fear.

ABANDONED WAREHOUSE - NIGHT - MOMENTS LATER

Emily felt her heart race in sync with the chaos outside. "If they breach," she reminded the others, "we enter together, and we fight."

"Are you ready for this?" one of the survivors asked, his hands shaking.

"Yes! We've fought too hard, too long to let fear snatch away our chance!" Emily spoke with a fierce resolve. "Every one of us matters. We do this together!"

DEACON'S CAMP - NIGHT - CONTINUOUS

Outside, Deacon pushed back against the relentless tide of chaos, his focus unwavering despite the rising tension. "Hold the line! We can do this!" he shouted, rallying his team as they fired retaliatory shots into the advancing Hounds, holding firm against the pressures of the battle.

The Hounds, emboldened by the sheer chaos that enveloped them, began to advance in a synchronized rush, pressing as closely as they could to the survivors' defenses. Their guttural growls echoed in the night—the sound clawing at every survivor's nerves.

"Focus fire on the Hounds!" Colonel Stone yelled, taking careful aim once more, intent on striking down the first beast that breached their defenses. "We can't let them close in!"

As they fired, Deacon felt the ground beneath them tremble again—not just from the force of the Hounds, but also from the thunderous approach of more impending dangers from the woods.

WOODS NEAR DEACON'S CAMP - NIGHT - CONTINUOUS

The shadows writhed, and the alarming sounds only intensified. "More are coming!" one of the raiders shouted from the outskirts of visibility. "We need to consolidate or we'll lose this entire camp!"

Deacon glanced around at his allies, each person struggling against the palpable waves of anxiety that threatened to tip them over into despair. "Stay together!" he shouted. "Fear does not claim this ground!"

But as the raiders regrouped and the Hounds pressed closer, their determination began to falter. With a mighty roar, one of the larger Hounds lunged toward Frank, snapping its powerful jaws just inches from his face.

"Frank!" Lila screamed as she pulled him back, adrenaline pushing her to act, but the Hound was undeterred, turning its attention to her instead.

"Shoot it!" Deacon bellowed, heart racing as he saw Lila struggling to keep her footing in the shifting chaos.

Lila fired her weapon, hitting the beast squarely in the chest, but it barely staggered, driven by some primal instinct as the monsters' ferocity seemed to only intensify.

ABANDONED WAREHOUSE - NIGHT - MOMENTS LATER

Inside the warehouse, panic surged anew as the sound of chaos pressed against the walls like an impending tide. Emily's heart raced, and each howl reverberated like a warning sign, pushing her own fears to the surface.

"It's time!" she shouted, gathering the remaining survivors. "We may need to fight our way out if they breach!"

"Are we ready for that?" Rachel asked, worry shadowing her previously steady demeanor.

"Yes! We face fear head-on, together, as we always have!" Emily proclaimed passionately, determination solidifying within her heart. "That's how we ensure we survive!"

DEACON'S CAMP - NIGHT - CONTINUOUS

Outside, Deacon encouraged everyone forward, feeling the resolve building within them as they fought tooth and claw against the advancing Hounds and raiders alike. Their unity illuminated the darkness cast by the chaos, each survivor standing strong beside one another.

"Move back to the barricade!" Colonel Stone yelled, coordinating the defense. "Hold the line at all costs!"

Lila continued to fire, pressing against the Hounds with an intensity fueled by desperation and determination. "They're not taking us without a fight!" she shouted, as the shadows closed in around them.

Suddenly, the noise from outside intensified—a loud crash echoed through the night as the Hounds broke through the makeshift barriers. For a moment, time seemed to slow, and the realization struck.

"They're inside!" Frank yelled, wide-eyed with fear.

INT. ABANDONED WAREHOUSE - NIGHT - CONTINUOUS

Inside, Emily prepared to take charge alongside Rachel as they gathered with the others near the entrance. "We'll hold this line!" she declared.

Just then, more noise erupted from outside—the raiders and Hounds converging upon them, and the sounds of chaos filled the air like dark clouds brewing.

DEACON'S CAMP - NIGHT - MOMENTS LATER

Back outside, Deacon steadied his breath, locking his gaze on the encroaching shadows. The Hounds surged forward, clawing at his soul, but he was steadfast.

As the raiders pressed onward, a pale shadow moved behind them—another raider even more menacing. "You fought well, but this is where your strength ends," the figure growled ominously.

"Not if we have anything to say about it!" Deacon roared back, a surge of protective energy coursing through him. "We will not cower in the face of fear!"

With that declaration, the battle surged back into full swing; their struggles blending into one—the primal fight against the nightmares, both physical and existential.

ABANDONED WAREHOUSE - NIGHT - CONTINUOUS

With the onslaught escalating, Emily and Rachel braced themselves against the barricade. "This is it!" Rachel shouted as they heard the sound of the Hound's claws scraping against wood, each strike a note of impending dread.

"We stand together!" Emily shouted, clenching her weapon tightly as urgency surged through her veins.

DEACON'S CAMP - NIGHT - MOMENTS LATER

Outside, Deacon narrowed his eyes and took aim at the advancing raiders, adrenaline surging once more as they fought fiercely against the tide.

"Hold!" he ordered, each pull of the trigger propelled by the will to protect their sanctuary. "We push through together!"

The collective roar of voices melded with the growls of the Hounds and the cries of the raiders, creating an overwhelming rhythm of determination that surged against the desperate darkness.

He felt a pang of hope as the group worked seamlessly together, each individual weaving their fears into a fabric of strength and resilience—orchestrating a dance against the chaos.

ABANDONED WAREHOUSE - NIGHT - MOMENTS LATER

Back inside, the tension mounted as the stripped barricades began to tremble under the weight of the Nightmares' assault.

"Now or never!" Emily shouted, driving her fear into action. "Everyone stick together!"

The air was electric with anticipation as they adapted and pushed against the boundaries of fear, driven by the hope that they held within their hearts.

DEACON'S CAMP - NIGHT - CONTINUOUS

Outside, Deacon felt a shift in the energy as the Hounds began to retreat slightly, their snarls contrasting with the renewed vigor among the defenders.

"Press the attack!" Colonel Stone shouted, rallying the troops. "We take back what is ours!"

With emerged confidence, they charged forward, reclaiming the ground that had once felt lost as they faced down the encroaching darkness with fierce defiance.

The flames of determination roared, illuminating the camp once more as the survivors forged forward in a unified front against the fear that had plagued them, ready to face whatever awaited them in the depths of night.

CHAPTER 39: INTO THE DEPTHS

DEACON'S CAMP - NIGHT - CONTINUOUS

The charge from the survivors pushed back against the raiders and Nightmare Hounds, determination mingling with adrenaline as the battle unfolded around them. Deacon fought alongside his allies; every shot fired igniting the collective strength within the camp.

"Keep pushing!" Deacon shouted, his voice fierce above the clamor of gunfire and howls. "We're reclaiming our home!"

Colonel Stone echoed his sentiment, moving strategically to cut off the retreating raiders. "Don't let them regroup! They're desperate now—let's take advantage!"

Lila and Jacob worked in tandem, providing cover fire while helping to draw the Hounds away from vulnerable group members. "Look out for those flanking!" Lila called out, her aim unwavering as she sheared down a Hound that lunged at her side.

The camp echoed with a symphony of defiance—their voices rising against the darkness that sought to reclaim them, a resonating reminder of hope amid the brewing storm.

ABANDONED WAREHOUSE - NIGHT - MOMENTS LATER

Inside the warehouse, Emily and the survivors braced for whatever came next; the sounds of battle just beyond the walls were both exhilarating and terrifying.

"We have to be prepared for when they inevitably breach!" Rachel exclaimed; her voice shaky.

"I know! Stay calm, focus on securing our area!" Emily urged, rallying the group around her. "We can't lose sight of each other."

Another crash resonated from outside, followed by a chilling howl. Fear rippled through the survivors, and they all exchanged anxious glances, feeling the uncertainty of the battle seeping into their bones.

Suddenly, a shout echoed through the chaos outside. "It's time to reinforce our position!" one of the other survivors bellowed. But sure enough, the barricades began to tremble.

DEACON'S CAMP - NIGHT - MOMENTS LATER

Back outside, Deacon caught a fleeting glimpse of the relentless Hounds retreating momentarily, but noticed that the raiders were beginning to regroup.

"Push them back!" Deacon shouted, rallying the group again. "We won't let fear take this camp!"

In response, the surrounding defenders surged forward, united in their purpose. But deep inside, he recognized the danger had not dissipated; it loomed like a storm ready to break.

Suddenly, the larger Hound re-emerged from the darkness with a terrifying snarl, causing the ground to shake beneath its feet—a harbinger of the nightmares that threatened to swallow them whole.

"It's not going to give up!" Colonel Stone shouted, stepping forward to join Deacon. "This creature is here for blood!"

"Then we give it no ground!" Deacon cried, adrenaline setting his battle instincts ablaze as he aimed again, focusing on the massive beast that threatened to overwhelm them once more.

ABANDONED WAREHOUSE - NIGHT - CONTINUOUS

Back in the warehouse, the wild sounds and distant howls served as a constant reminder of their vulnerability. Emily rallied those inside, urging everyone to stay ready.

"They're coming!" she warned. "We need to be prepared for the fight of our lives!"

Just as she finished speaking, a loud crash echoed through the walls, rattling every survivor inside the warehouse, moments before their own darkness pressed dangerously close.

"Push everything against the door!" Rachel shouted; eyes wide with fear. They scrambled to secure the entrance, feeling the pressure mount.

DEACON'S CAMP - NIGHT - CONTINUOUS

Outside, Deacon watched as the large Hound lunged toward a fellow survivor, jaws snapping dangerously close. Without hesitation, he shot, the bullet hitting its mark and causing the creature to stagger back, but it hardly seemed fazed.

"We need to draw its attention away from the camp!" Deacon shouted, feeling the tension begin to break through their wall of combat.

Suddenly, a group of raiders rushed in, taking advantage of the distraction and trying to flank the camp. "Guard the left!" Colonel Stone yelled, focused on managing the chaos around them.

"Watch your backs!" Frank shouted, feeling the fear about to overwhelm him again, racing to steady his aim.

The survivors tightened their formation, all fighting back against the encroaching wave, rallying on Deacon's leadership despite the overwhelming odds.

ABANDONED WAREHOUSE - NIGHT - MOMENTS LATER

Inside, the warehouse felt like a pressure cooker, the sounds of battle beyond intensifying with each passing second. Emily glanced at Rachel and the others, her heart pounding.

"Are we ready?" she asked, determination lighting her eyes.

"Yes! Let's do this together!" Rachel affirmed, nervously glancing back at the door as the crashing continued.

DEACON'S CAMP - NIGHT - MOMENTS LATER

"Move back into the camp!" Deacon yelled, coordinating his team as they took aim. "We'll push them into a corner—together!"

Deep in his heart, Deacon knew that they had to confront their inner demons, but the tangible fear of the Hounds and raiders threatened to drown them all.

As they regrouped, resolve pulsed through them, igniting a fire to push back against the darkness.

Just as they prepared for another round of combat, a sharp howl rang out, echoing through the night with primal force—something deeper and darker than they had faced before, a reminder that there were scars yet unseen that haunted the night.

"Get ready!" Colonel Stone shouted, urgency flooding his voice. "We need to resist whatever force is coming for us now!"

With determination etched on every face, Deacon took a deep breath, locking eyes with each member of the camp. "We hold this ground together—no matter what they throw at us!"

A fierce fire ignited within their hearts as they charged toward the onslaught, ready to face both the Nightmares and the fears they had long struggled to conquer.

CHAPTER 40: INTO THE ABYSS

DEACON'S CAMP - NIGHT

A sudden charge of energy surged through the camp as Deacon grasped his weapon tightly, ready to face the oncoming wave of raiders and Hounds. The air crackled with the intensity of battle—fear and resolve mingling as darkness pressed in upon them.

"Stand your ground!" Deacon shouted to rally the survivors, whose adrenaline surged with anticipation. The flickering fire illuminated their determined faces, a fierce reminder that they wouldn't back down without a fight.

The large Nightmare Hound, now fully enraged, lunged forward, its pack of smaller Hounds close behind. As they closed in on the camp, the air filled with frantic growls and distant yelps, the oppressive chaos reminding them of every fear they had fought to overcome.

"Fire!" Colonel Stone commanded, resolutely lining up with Deacon, aiming at the advancing Hounds. Gunfire erupted in a deafening chorus, lighting up the night sky as they targeted the oncoming threats.

"We can't let them through!" Frank yelled, steadier now, each shot reflecting his determination. The rest of the survivors joined in, their collective strength pushing back the tide of fear that threatened to crush their morale.

ABANDONED WAREHOUSE - NIGHT - MOMENTS LATER

Inside the warehouse, Emily steeled herself alongside Rachel, feeling the tremors from the ongoing battle. The noise of chaos outside served as a reminder of their vulnerability.

"They're still fighting out there," Emily said quietly, glancing at the reinforced door. "We need to be prepared for anything."

"We can't let the fear overwhelm us," Rachel replied, determination illuminating her eyes. "We have to support them however we can."

"Agreed. Let's gather any supplies we can find here to help reinforce our defenses," Emily urged, urgency rushing through her veins.

DEACON'S CAMP - NIGHT - CONTINUOUS

Outside, the battle raged on, each survivor standing resolute as they pushed back against the surging tide. Deacon felt a swell of pride in his heart as he fired another round at the nearest Hound.

"Don't give in!" he shouted. "We've come too far to let fear take hold!"

With each shot, the Hounds began to falter, their shadows darting back into the darkness of the trees, the survivors gaining momentum. But just as hope began to seep back into their hearts, a loud crash resonated, vibrating through the camp.

Overhead, the moon hung low, illuminating a figure emerging from the shadows—a colossal raider stepping forward, his eyes wild with madness. "You think you can defend against us? This ends tonight!" he shouted, raising his weapon high.

"Focus fire!" Colonel Stone yelled, redirecting his aim at the new threat. "We can't let him take advantage!"

ABANDONED WAREHOUSE - NIGHT - MOMENTS LATER

Inside again, Emily and the remaining survivors were still gathering supplies, their nerves taut with anticipation. Suddenly, the door shuddered again, the howl of a Nightmare Hound emerging from the far side, mingling with the chaotic noises of the battle outside.

"They're coming for us!" one survivor shouted, panic spreading through the room.

"No! We hold this line!" Emily insisted, stepping forward with resolve. "We brace ourselves and fight back!"

DEACON'S CAMP - NIGHT - CONTINUOUS

Outside, Deacon quickly turned his attention to the raider. "We stand firm against you!" he shouted, aiming the weapon toward the assailant. "You won't claim us tonight!"

As the raider charged forward with harsh intent, Deacon adjusted his aim—heart pounding fiercely. "We fight for our home, for our lives!"

The sound of gunfire erupted again, colliding with the howls of the Hounds echoing through the night air. As Deacon fired at the advancing raider, the creature staggered but kept pushing through the chaos.

"Line up!" Colonel Stone encouraged, moving deftly to take his shot, the coordinated effort among the survivors becoming a bond capable of withstanding the darkness.

Lila fired again toward the raider, catching him flush but noticing that he remained determined, fueled by adrenaline and madness. "This guy just won't go down!" she exclaimed, frustration lacing her tone.

"Don't give up!" Deacon shouted, feeling the urgency swell among them as the raider grew ever closer.

ABANDONED WAREHOUSE - NIGHT - CONTINUOUS

Inside, the soldiers braced themselves, the atmosphere almost suffocating as Emily turned back to the barricaded door. "We have to be ready for when they push through," she urged again.

"Let's secure this place and make sure that we're prepared," Rachel affirmed, moving quickly to join her side.

DEACON'S CAMP - NIGHT - MOMENTS LATER

Outside, the fight intensified—the Hounds began to regain their ground, and the raider pushed closer still.

Deacon swiveled toward the two threats, feeling the weight of the moment press heavily against him. "We fight together! Don't lose sight of what this means!"

With that proclamation, the group erupted into action. The commotion experienced first in the warehouse echoed outward; even enemies felt the connection, the tension firing back and forth.

Just as Deacon prepared for another shot, the raider lunged at him, weapon raised, but as he turned, the weight of the creature's chaos crashed inward. "You'll regret standing against us!" the raider shouted.

"Not if we fight as one!" Deacon cried, the sudden fire of determination surging through him as he aimed the weapon squarely at the raider.

ABANDONED WAREHOUSE - NIGHT - CONTINUOUS

Back inside the warehouse, Emily and the remaining survivors focused on sealing off their positions, helping to secure barricades and check supplies. As they prepared for potential chaos to unfold inside, each heartbeat resonated with urgency.

"Everyone stay alert!" Emily insisted, feeling a swell of

uncertainty mingle with strength. "This is our home, and we will defend it!"

"Ready ourselves!" Rachel affirmed, her breath steady and resolute.

DEACON'S CAMP - NIGHT - MOMENTS LATER

Outside, the moment had arrived—the raider stood poised, intent on breaching their defenses while the Nightmare Hounds recounted their skirmishes. Deacon pressed forward, taking aim. "We push back and defend what is ours!"

With a roar of defiance echoing through the night, they fought back, unified against the tide of madness that threatened to engulf them. Each shot fired ignited a flicker of hope—every move a testament to their resolve.

And as the battles raged on in the depths of night, Deacon knew that whatever darkness awaited them, they would confront it together—and face whatever horrors lingered in unseen corners with their fierce love for their home and each other.

CHAPTER 41: SHADOWS OF DOUBT

DEACON'S CAMP - NIGHT

The chaos outside continued as Deacon and his survivors faced the relentless onslaught of both raiders and Nightmare Hounds. The air was electric with fear and resilience, crackling as bullets and growls pierced the darkness, intertwining the two opposing forces in a brutal struggle.

"Push forward!" Deacon shouted, the echoes of bravery mixing with the rising tide of tension. "We can't let them breach our defenses!"

As shadows loomed and the night felt thicker, he could sense the fear creeping back into the hearts of his comrades. They had fought valiantly, but the howls of the Hounds seemed to amplify the anguish within them, feeding on the very essence of anxiety coursing through the camp.

"Regroup at the fire!" Colonel Stone called, urgent in his commands as he provided cover for Frank and Lila, who were busy watching for any signs of retreating Hounds.

With a fierce determination, the defenders rallied closer to the central area around the campfire, where the flickering light served as a beacon against the dark. Each shot echoed the promises of survival—each flame flickering against the shadows illuminating their united front.

ABANDONED WAREHOUSE - NIGHT - MOMENTS LATER

Inside the warehouse, Emily felt the familiar pressure of worry creeping in as she listened to the cacophony of violence outside. "We can't allow ourselves to be overwhelmed; we need to hold this place!" she instructed, her heart racing.

"Every turn now feels haunted," one of the survivors muttered, his voice low but trembling with uncertainty.

"We're standing strong against fears," Emily replied, firm in her belief. "If they breach, we're ready to face them together. We'll fight for our home!"

Suddenly, another loud CRASH echoed through the wall, sending adrenaline coursing through her veins. The sounds of chaos pushed at the door, intensifying the pressure against their defenses.

DEACON'S CAMP - NIGHT - CONTINUOUS

Outside, Deacon caught sight of the large Hound breaking through, its hulking body crashing against the barriers as strands of chaos painted shadows against the flickering firelight.

"Get ready to fire!" Deacon shouted, heart racing. "Aim high!"

As the Hound lunged again, snapping its jaws, soldiers steadied their aim, ready to retaliate. The air was thick with the tension of their collective fear as they steadied themselves against the assault.

"Push back!" Colonel Stone roared, adrenaline sharpening everyone's focus. "We fight for what is ours!"

As they released a volley of shots, the Hound staggered back, but its resolve remained. It roared again, its eyes filled with hunger, and the Hounds surrounding it continued their relentless charge.

"Oh no, more are coming!" Lila cried out, glancing toward the tree line where even more monstrous figures began to emerge, their eyes eager and intent.

"Fall back!" Deacon ordered, instinctively moving closer to his team as the pressing tide threatened to overwhelm them.

ABANDONED WAREHOUSE - NIGHT - MOMENTS LATER

Back inside, Emily and Rachel worked frantically, pushing crates and furniture against the door to reinforce the entrance. The sounds of battle outside intensified, and she felt the walls around them tremble.

"They're trying to break in!" Rachel exclaimed, feeling panic rise within her.

"Stay focused!" Emily ordered, her heart steady against the storm of fear threatening to wash over her. "We hold this line—we won't yield!"

Just then, the door rattled violently again, sending a surge of adrenaline through the group. Each echo resonated with the reality that they could be trapped if they weren't vigilant.

DEACON'S CAMP - NIGHT - MOMENTS LATER

Outside, Deacon felt the tide of the battle shift again. He noticed Lila and Jacob darting toward him, determination lining their features as they prepared to flank the advancing foes.

"This is it!" Lila exclaimed as they pushed forward. "If we don't redirect their focus, they'll overwhelm us!"

"Then let's use that to our advantage!" Deacon replied, adrenaline also coursing through his body as he surveyed the battlefield. "We have to draw them into the center!"

Pulling their focus together, they moved through the camp

strategically, trying to leverage any position they could in order to regain control. The bond they had forged felt palpable as they worked together, united against the rising tide of terror.

ABANDONED WAREHOUSE - NIGHT - MOMENTS LATER

Inside, the barricades rattled under the continued assault as the echoes of chaos settled heavily in the air. Emily turned toward the door, feeling resolve surge inside her. "We won't let them take this from us!"

Suddenly, one of the injured survivors looked up, fear etched deeply across his features. "What if they get in? What will we do?" he asked, his voice cracking under pressure.

"We make a stand!" Emily replied, locking her gaze with each of them. "We fight back—together!"

Back outside, Deacon took a deep breath, his heart steadying as unity surged within him. "Together, we can push these shadows back into the nostalgia of nightmares," he declared, pulling everyone close, grounding themselves against the chaos that threatened.

DEACON'S CAMP - NIGHT - MOMENTS LATER

As the Hounds lunged once again, Deacon prepared for the charge. With one final rush of adrenaline, he fired into the cluster, hitting one of them squarely as they pressed forward.

"They can't take us!" Frank shouted, standing shoulder to shoulder with Lila and Jacob. The shots rang through the night air, a fierce chorus resonating against the oppressive shadows.

Then, as the air crackled with energy, another Hound broke through, roaring. It lunged toward Deacon but fell short under the combined force of their gunfire.

"That's it! Hold them off!" Deacon urged, feeling the heartbeat of battle intensifying yet again. "Don't give in to despair!"

The Hounds and raiders began to retreat slowly, realizing they faced an unyielding force. They sensed the fierceness of the survivors' resolve, amplifying the cries of frustration seeping through the night.

Finally, with one last howl, the remaining Hounds began to scatter back into the woods, and the raiders made their retreat, the symphony of chaos slowly receding into silence.

ABANDONED WAREHOUSE - NIGHT - MOMENTS LATER

Feeling the stillness envelope the camp, Emily allowed a moment of caution to rise and walked carefully to the entrance. The battle had quieted, but doubt still lay beneath their skin.

"Has it really passed?" Rachel murmured near her, shaky but hopeful.

"I don't know," Emily admitted, peering into the night, determined to remain vigilant.

DEACON'S CAMP - NIGHT - MOMENTS LATER

Outside, Deacon took a deep breath, surveying the aftermath around the flickering campfire. They had survived; his heart swelled with pride as he looked at the faces of his companions, who now shared in the fragile victory of the night.

"We did it!" Frank exclaimed, his voice filled with a mixture of disbelief and exhilaration. The tension that had gripped the camp began to dissipate, replaced by a sense of camaraderie forged in fire.

Deacon stepped forward, trying to capture the moment. "Let's not forget what we faced and the victory we've claimed together. Each one of you fought bravely and proved that fear has no place among us."

Lila nodded, walking to his side. "We've all shown our mettle. But we can't become complacent; this battle is just the beginning. We need to reinforce everything we have here."

The group murmured in agreement, the shadows of the night still lingering but slowly being illuminated by the flickering campfire.

"Let's get to work," Colonel Stone suggested, already moving toward the supplies. "We'll need to assess the perimeter, gather anything we can, and ensure that we're fortified against whatever may return."

ABANDONED WAREHOUSE - NIGHT - MOMENTS LATER

The survivors moved to the entrance of the warehouse, preparing to check outside for any remnants of raiders or Hounds that might still pose a threat. With each cautious step forward, Emily felt an invigorating energy pulse within her.

"Stay together," she instructed, her voice steady and reassuring as they ensured that no one was left behind. "Let's see what we can gather and work out a plan for the night. We can't let fear govern us again."

DEACON'S CAMP - NIGHT - CONTINUOUS

As the team moved to assess the perimeter of the camp, the air filled with purpose. Deacon led them, vigilant against any further signs of danger and determined to ensure their safety.

"Lila, Jacob, check the southern edge," Deacon instructed, pointing toward the tree line. "Frank, you and Stone cover the east side. I'll take the west."

They nodded, moving quickly to cover ground while the adrenaline from the fight still buzzed in their bodies.

WOODS NEAR DEACON'S CAMP - NIGHT

As Lila and Jacob made their way toward the southern edge of the camp, the weight of the night pressed against them. "Do you think they'll come back?" Jacob asked, concern marking his features.

"I don't know," Lila replied, her voice steady but thoughtful. "We just need to prepare for whatever might happen. They may regroup and try again; we'll be ready."

As they approached the tree line, a sudden rustling caught their attention. Lila tensed, instinctively raising her weapon and peering into the darkness.

"Did you hear that?" Jacob whispered, eyes darting to the shadows around them.

Lila nodded, tense but focused. "Stay on your guard. We need to see what it is."

DEACON'S CAMP - NIGHT - CONTINUOUS

Meanwhile, Deacon, along with Stone and Frank, surveyed the other perimeter, glancing around for any signs of movement. The buzz of adrenaline began to fade away, replaced with fatigue as they assessed the havoc left behind.

"This place is a mess—," Frank muttered, kicking some rubble from the raiders' assault with a frown. "Can't believe we're still standing."

"That's because we worked together, Frank. Don't underestimate the bond we've formed," Deacon replied, locking eyes with his friend. "It's what's keeping us strong through all of this."

Suddenly, the shrill howl of a nearby Hound shattered the stillness, hammering familiarity deep into their fears. "It's still out there!" Colonel Stone growled, tightening the grip on his weapon.

"Let's finish securing this area," Deacon said, pushing urgency through his veins. "We can't let fear take hold."

WOODS NEAR DEACON'S CAMP - NIGHT - MOMENTS LATER

As Lila and Jacob crept slowly through the underbrush, shadows danced restlessly around them. The quiet rustles grew louder, folding over each other, and Lila could feel the palpable tension rising in her chest.

"Whatever it is, it's not far away," Jacob whispered, sweat beading on his forehead as they moved in close.

Just then, the bushes parted, and a figure emerged—a gaunt survivor, dirt streaked across their face, eyes wide with terror.

"Help me!" the figure gasped, fear lacing his voice as he stumbled forward. "I barely escaped! They're still coming!"

Lila and Jacob exchanged shocked glances, instinctively moving to intercept the survivor, concern etching deeper into their features. "Who are you? Are you alone?" Lila asked cautiously.

"Just... just me. My group was taken by the Hounds! They're here! They're coming!" the survivor pleaded, breathing heavily as panic surged. "You have to believe me!"

DEACON'S CAMP - NIGHT - CONTINUOUS

Back at the camp, Deacon and Colonel Stone shared a worried glance. The energy of the camp shifted again as the echoes of the distant howl returned and uncertainty clawed at their hearts.

"Do you think they're really coming back?" Frank asked, trying to steady his aim as tension flooded the air.

"They wouldn't retreat for long; they'll be looking for another chance," Colonel Stone replied grimly. "We have to prepare ourselves for whatever approach they take."

Suddenly, Lila and Jacob burst into the camp, breathless. "Deacon! We found another survivor! He says more are coming!"

"What? More?" Deacon replied, his throat tightening. "We need to figure out what we're facing."

ABANDONED WAREHOUSE - NIGHT - CONTINUOUS

Inside the warehouse, Emily felt the atmosphere shift again as concern loomed heavy over them. She turned to Rachel. "We have to adapt; we can't let this moment define us," she urged, feeling every heartbeat echoing with uncertainty.

"Whatever comes next, we can face it together," Rachel replied, her voice solid as the tension in her words cracked.

DEACON'S CAMP - NIGHT - MOMENTS LATER

Deacon gathered the group together, feeling the intensity of the moment peak. "We've survived chaos—time and again. Each moment has brought us closer together," he said, locking eyes with every survivor present.

"We need to unify our defenses. No one stands alone—if they come, then we confront it as one!"

As they prepared for the next challenge, Deacon felt a flame of determination reignite in everybody. They were bonded through battle, through fear, and through the strength of fighting for their future together.

With resolve coursing through their veins, they held firm against whatever darkness awaited them, ready to reclaim their hope once and for all.

CHAPTER 42: INTO THE UNKNOWN

DEACON'S CAMP - NIGHT – MOMENTS LATER

The air hung heavy with anticipation as the survivors rounded up for a brief council amid the flickering firelight. Shadows danced around them, but their spirits remained anchored in unity and determination. Deacon stood at the forefront, trying to capture the resolve burning brightly in their hearts.

"We need to reinforce our defenses now," he said, urgency threading through his voice. "If any remnants of Hounds or raiders return, we have to be prepared."

"Let's set up more barricades around the entrance," Lila suggested, glancing toward the tree line, the fear of another attack still fresh in her mind. "We need solid positions for everyone to retreat to if needed."

Frank stepped forward, determination etching his expression. "We need a schedule for watch offs. We can't let anyone sleep too deeply. If they come, we need to be ready."

Colonel Stone nodded in agreement. "And we should consider scouting out the woods as well. If more survivors are out there, we may be able to bring them back and strengthen our camp."

Just then, the survivor they had brought back from the woods, still shaky and trembling, stepped closer. "Please," he urged, desperation lining his features. "I know the woods well—I can help you—just let me prove myself."

Deacon shared a glance with Colonel Stone, weighing the possibility of bringing another person into the fold. The very air around them felt charged with the weight of the night's events, and the consequences of any decision now loomed larger than ever.

ABANDONED WAREHOUSE - NIGHT - MOMENTS LATER

Inside the warehouse, the emotional toll of recent battles weighed heavily on those preparing to gather their strength. Emily gathered supplies, her heart racing with urgency.

"Everyone, stay focused," she called out, trying to maintain a sense of calm as people filed in from the depths of the camp. "We can't let fear engulf us."

"Do we have enough supplies?" one survivor asked, worry evident in her tone as she grabbed bandages and rations.

"Yes, but we have to make every item count," Emily replied, rallying her courage. "Tonight, we face the darkness—again—and we cannot afford to break."

The atmosphere pulsated with intensity as they reinforced their positions, determination pooling within as each individual rallied to contribute.

DEACON'S CAMP - NIGHT - MOMENTS LATER

As the camp began to settle back into a cautious routine, Deacon addressed the gathered survivors around the campfire once more. "Let's form two groups for scouting," he suggested, surveying the faces before him. "One goes to the east side, the other to the south. We'll need to assess any signs of danger or potential refuge."

"I'll go on the east side," Lila volunteered, her resolve strengthening. "If there are any signs of raiders or Hounds, I want to be the first to know."

"I'm with you," Jacob said, stepping forward, his expression fierce. "I want to make sure we stay vigilant against any potential threat."

Deacon nodded, feeling a swell of strategy emerge within him. "Fine. We have to keep our watches overlapping. No one goes into the woods alone—stay in pairs at all times."

"Aye, and I'll head up the southern perimeter," Colonel Stone confirmed. "I'll make sure we keep an eye on the main threat while you scout."

As they divided into teams, Deacon felt the strength of their resolve pooling within him; this was who they were—a family forged in darkness, ready to face whatever awaited them.

WOODS NEAR DEACON'S CAMP - NIGHT - LATER

As Lila and Jacob ventured into the quiet of the woods, the air felt impenetrable amidst the otherworldly silence that surrounded them. The moonlight illuminated their path, but shadows lurked at the edges, reminding them that danger could emerge at any moment.

"Let's stay alert," Jacob said, scanning the trees as they made their way deeper into the wilderness. "Even the slightest sound could be trouble."

"Right," Lila replied, feeling a thrill run through her at the thought of what might lie ahead. With every cautious step forward, they had to remind themselves to stay focused and grounded, casting aside the echoes of fear that had stalked them through each battle.

Suddenly, a rustle broke through the silence—a sound too close for comfort. Lila's heart raced as she turned her weapon toward the source, and her instincts flared.

"Did you hear that?" she whispered, body tense and ready.

"Yeah, I did," Jacob replied, his gaze narrowing in concentration. "It's coming from over there."

DEACON'S CAMP - NIGHT - CONTINUOUS

Back at the camp, the remaining survivors remained on high alert, exchanging wary glances as they anticipated the sound of chaos returning upon them. The air was thick with tension as Frank joined Colonel Stone near the edge of the camp.

"We need to ensure the perimeter is completely secure," Frank said, his voice steady but filled with urgency. "The Hounds could come back at any moment."

Colonel Stone nodded, surveying their surroundings. "We have to remain vigilant and cover all avenues. If they manage to get in, it could spell disaster for everyone."

Suddenly, a howl echoed from deep in the woods—this one more haunting than the rest, resonating with the kind of darkness that struck fear into the hearts of the bravest among them.

"Get ready!" Colonel Stone commanded. "That might be a sign that they're regrouping!"

WOODS NEAR DEACON'S CAMP - NIGHT - MOMENTS LATER

Back in the woods, Lila and Jacob pressed closer to investigate the sounds they'd heard. The air around them felt charged, vibrating with foreboding energy.

"What if it's another Hound?" Lila whispered, feeling the weight of anxiety creeping into her body.

"Then we'll deal with it together," Jacob said, determination shining brightly in his eyes. "We've stood up to worse."

Suddenly, a figure darted through the underbrush, almost too fast to be identified.

"Lila!" Jacob exclaimed, tensing as the shadow moved closer. Heart racing, Lila aimed her weapon, a mixture of adrenaline and fear flooding her senses.

"Who's there?" she shouted, not lowering her weapon. "Identify yourself!"

The figure paused, and in the faint light of the moon, they recognized the silhouette—another survivor, weary and traumatized. "I'm not here to hurt you!" the newcomer called out, stepping closer, hands raised. "I'm just trying to find everyone!"

As Lila and Jacob exchanged wary glances, they felt the tension shift. "What is your name?" Lila demanded, keeping her weapon raised as she processed the sudden appearance.

"I'm Mark. I was with a group a few miles from here, but we were attacked by the Hounds and ran," he explained, desperation etched across his features. "I'm trying to find safety!"

DEACON'S **CAMP - NIGHT - CONTINUOUS

Back at the camp, the unease continued to spread as the remaining survivors locked onto the sounds echoing from the woods.

"We can't afford to trust easily," Frank cautioned, scanning the periphery nervously. "Not after everything we've faced."

"We won't know unless we give him a chance," Colonel Stone replied, a stoic determination etched into his expression. "We have to be open to possible allies if we want to survive."

As the howl of the Hounds resonated in the distance, the group felt the weight of their collective fears—each anxiety manifesting as the shadows pressed closer. Deacon stepped forward, heart resolute, determined to protect those beside him.

"We need to stay united. If Mark is here, then we'll bring him back and assess his situation. Trust needs to be built among us," Deacon said firmly, ushering them back to prioritize the group's survival.

WOODS NEAR DEACON'S CAMP - NIGHT - CONTINUOUS

Lila lowered her weapon slightly as she observed Mark, reading the desperation etched into his features. "Are you sure you're alone?" she asked, her voice a blend of curiosity and wariness.

"Yes! I didn't see anyone else. I just ran when the Hounds attacked," Mark replied, his eyes darting toward the shadows. "Please, I don't want to be alone out here. I can help you."

"Help us how?" Jacob pressed, skepticism lingering in his voice. "What can you offer that we haven't figured out ourselves?"

"I know the woods. I've traveled these areas for longer," Mark explained, earnestness spilling from his voice. "I can help scout—the safest paths, where to find food or potential threats."

"Could he be leading us into a trap?" Lila whispered to Jacob, concern creeping into her thoughts as shadows continued to dance around the edges of perception.

"We need to weigh our options, Lila," Jacob replied quietly. "But we also can't let fear dictate our actions."

Taking a deep breath, Lila stepped back to Mark. "Alright, but you stay in sight of us—no wandering off, got it?"

"Okay, I promise," Mark assured, relief flooding his features as he nodded in understanding.

DEACON'S CAMP - NIGHT - MOMENTS LATER

They made their way back toward the camp together, and as they neared the perimeter, the atmosphere changed subtly—the sense of dread that had filled the air lingered still, whispering of the threats lurking just beyond the light.

"Deacon, we found another survivor," Lila announced as they reached the firelight, her eyes scanning the unfamiliar face during the tense introduction.

"Another survivor?" Deacon asked, locking eyes with Mark. "And what is your name?"

"Mark," he replied, standing tall despite the weariness clinging to him. "I survived a Hound attack and want to help."

Deacon could feel the apprehension swirling around him, but he also sensed a flicker of hope. "We value survival here," he said firmly. "Join us, but know that trust must be earned."

ABANDONED WAREHOUSE - NIGHT - CONTINUOUS

Inside the warehouse, Emily, Rachel, and a few other survivors continued to fortify defenses, the sound of the ongoing battle resonating outside.

"Are we ready?" Rachel asked, gripping a weapon ready. "If they break in, we will need to be stronger than ever."

"We are," Emily replied confidently. "We've banded together before, and we will do it again."

Suddenly, a loud crash erupted from the entrance, rattling the place. Everyone froze, their hearts pounding in unity, uncertainty weaving through their ranks, but they steeled their hearts against panic, prepared to respond.

DEACON'S CAMP - NIGHT - MOMENTS LATER

Back outside, Deacon felt the energy shift again as the raider leader observed their preparations from a distance, weighing his options. "They're regrouping!" Deacon shouted, not wanting to underestimate what lay ahead.

"We push them back!" Colonel Stone shouted as he directed the group closer to the firelight for cover.

Suddenly, the raider turned to run, but just as he did, the Hounds surged forward, their snarls and howls mixing in a chaotic symphony that tested the very core of what they fought for.

"Here they come!" Frank shouted, readying himself. The air felt charged with an impending storm, tension wrapping tightly around each survivor, hearts pounding as they prepared to face whatever darkness wound its way toward them.

"Ready!" Deacon shouted, his voice calling for strength as the line held steady, defending against both encroaching raiders and the nightmares circling them.

As the battlefield settled, the darkness crescendoed around them, and the clash of desperate survival surged in both haunting growls and revolutionary shouts. Together, they braced for the storm—every heart beating in unison against the dangers that lay ahead.

CHAPTER 43: SHADOWS OF BETRAYAL

DEACON'S CAMP - NIGHT

The battle had shifted into an uneasy silence as the survivors regrouped, exhausted yet resolute after holding back the initial wave of Hounds and raiders. But amidst the flickering campfire light, concern began to coil tightly in Deacon's gut.

"Where's Frank?" Deacon asked, glancing around at the survivors, but the faces that met him were filled with confusion and worry.

"He was right here a moment ago!" Lila exclaimed, her brow furrowing as she looked around the perimeter. "He must have gone to check on something."

"Great, just what we need," Jacob muttered, his eyes scanning the treeline. "Another problem to deal with."

"Let's not panic yet!" Emily interjected, stepping up beside Deacon, her voice steady. "We can't have anyone wandering off..."

But as the night settled deeper, shadows fell across the camp like dark promises, and a creeping dread began to worm its way into Deacon's heart. "Everyone! We need to form up and check the perimeter," he commanded, his voice firm. "Make sure he's not in danger."

ABANDONED WAREHOUSE - NIGHT - MOMENTS LATER

Inside the warehouse, the atmosphere felt heavy, and whispers began swirling. The remaining survivors viewed each other with tense expressions, uncertainty gnawing at their edges.

"Could something have happened to him?" Rachel asked, her voice barely above a whisper.

"It's a dangerous world," Emily replied, urgency spilling into her tone. "We need to find him; he could be hurt or worse."

With that thought, Emily turned to Deacon, determination gleaming in her eyes. "Where do we start?"

DEACON'S CAMP - NIGHT - MOMENTS LATER

Deacon broke into action, adrenaline sharpening his instincts. "We'll split into groups. Search the surrounding areas in pairs. Lila, Jacob, you check the east side. I'll team with Emily to scan the woods."

"Take your time," Lila urged. "Be careful; the Hounds might still be lurking."

As the groups dispersed into the shadows, Deacon felt the weight of responsibility settle heavily on his shoulders. Frank's absence gnawed at him, and he couldn't shake the feeling that something wasn't right.

"Let's move!" Deacon urged Emily; his voice low as they made their way toward the tree line. "We need to be quick and quiet. I'll call out if I see anything."

The cool night air hung thick around them as their footsteps crunched against the leaves. A sense of unease settled in, reminding him of the dangers that lurked in the shadows.

"Do you think Colonel Stone knows anything?" Emily

whispered cautiously as they advanced, the tension palpable between them.

"He might. He often seems one step ahead; it's unsettling," Deacon replied, his voice tinged with suspicion. "I can't shake the idea that he's hiding something."

WOODS NEAR DEACON'S CAMP - NIGHT - MOMENTS LATER

As Deacon and Emily moved deeper into the woods, the darkness felt heavy, each rustle adding to the weight of uncertainty. "Frank!" Deacon called out softly, hoping that somewhere in the night, his voice would reach his missing friend. But silence swallowed the sound, leaving only the rustle of night creatures moving in the underbrush.

"Could he have wandered too far?" Emily asked, a frown plastered on her face. "If he sensed danger, it's possible he instinctively retreated, but…"

"He would've told someone where he was going," Deacon said, frustration bubbling beneath the surface. "This doesn't feel right. He wouldn't just disappear."

Just then, another faint howl echoed through the trees, a reminder that the night was far from safe. They shared a worried glance, adrenaline surging as they pressed forward.

NEAR THE RIVERBANK - NIGHT - MOMENTS LATER

As Deacon and Emily reached a small clearing near the riverbank, they discovered signs of a struggle—broken branches and disturbed earth hinted at something amiss.

"Deacon, look!" Emily pointed toward the ground, a frown deepening as she knelt closer. "This doesn't look good."

"Footprints," Deacon murmured, examining the ground where Frank's unmistakable tracks sunk into the earth. But oddly, they faltered, vanishing as if he had been pulled into the shadows.

"Does this mean he was taken?" Emily asked, a tremor of fear underlying her words.

"We have to assume he's in danger," Deacon replied, standing up sharply. The weight of urgency pressed against him, re-igniting the fire of determination. "We need to get back and regroup."

DEACON'S CAMP - NIGHT - MOMENTS LATER

As they returned to the camp, Deacon felt the heaviness of unspoken worries settle in around him. The survivors gathered around the campfire, shoulders tense, eyes wide.

"Did you find him?" Lila asked urgently as Deacon approached.

"No, but we found signs he was here," Deacon said, trying to keep his tone steady. "We need to talk about where Frank could be and what that means for us."

The murmurs of concern spread through the group as Deacon locked eyes with Emily. "And we need to figure out if Colonel Stone knows anything," he said, suspicion swirling deeper within him.

"I'll confront him," Lila said, stepping forward. "If he's hiding something, I'll get to the bottom of it."

"No," Deacon replied quickly. "We need him now as a leader, so let's tread carefully."

"Fine," Lila conceded reluctantly. "But we can't let anyone hide information from us. We have to protect ourselves."

As the essence of doubt settled in, Deacon could feel the shadows pressing around them—a darkness creeping in as their struggle against the night deepened.

Suddenly, the sharp cry of a Hound echoed in the distance,

sending tingles of fear reverberating through the camp. "Everyone to your posts!" Deacon shouted, urgency igniting within him once again.

As they prepared for another confrontation, doubt mingled with hope, reminding them that the fight was far from over. With each moment that passed, Frank's absence became a haunting reminder of the dangers lurking just beyond the shadows—a relentless foe that could emerge at any moment.

CHAPTER 44: FRACTURED TRUST

DEACON'S CAMP - NIGHT

The atmosphere around the camp felt heavy with uncertainty as the sound of the distant howl echoed through the trees. Survivors stood around the flickering fire, their faces shadowed with doubt and fear. Deacon, still reeling from the unsettling discovery of Frank's tracks, felt the weight of each gaze upon him.

Colonel Stone's voice rang out, slicing through the tension. "We've faced chaos tonight, and now another battle lies within our camp!" He stepped forward, his expression severe. "Frank's disappearance is a matter of great concern, and I believe we must ask who bears responsibility for his fate."

"What are you implying?" Deacon shot back, feeling a chill creep up his spine. "You think I'm responsible for Frank's disappearance?"

"Yes," Colonel Stone replied, his tone firm and unyielding. "You were the last person with him. While we fought to protect this camp, how do we know you didn't lead him into danger?"

The murmurs grew louder among the survivors, suspicion weaving into their words like a dark thread through the fabric of their unity. Lila looked at Deacon, her expression torn between disbelief and worry.

"Deacon wouldn't do that!" she defended, stepping forward to protect him. "He led us through the chaos, kept us safe! This isn't fair!"

"While I appreciate your loyalty, Lila," Stone said, his voice calm but lacking warmth, "the evidence speaks for itself. We need to scrutinize our leadership in times of crisis."

Deacon's heart raced as he stepped forward, ire bubbling within him. "I'm not responsible for Frank's fate! This is madness—"

Stone raised a hand to silence him. "I think you are a danger to this camp," he declared, a steely resolve piercing through his words. "We must take precautions for everyone's safety. Until we uncover the truth, I'm placing you in custody."

"Custody?" Deacon echoed incredulously. "You can't just—"

"Enough!" Stone interrupted, stepping swiftly toward Deacon with intent. "You're coming with me."

In a swift motion, the Colonel signaled to several of the survivors, who moved to subdue Deacon, their hands firm as they escorted him away from the heart of the camp.

WAREHOUSE - NIGHT - MOMENTS LATER

Inside the warehouse, the atmosphere grew even more charged with tension as Deacon was brought to a small holding area. He could sense the disbelief among the onlookers, but uncertainty flowed freely as Stone locked the door behind him.

"Once we gather more information, we will hold a trial to decide your fate," Colonel Stone said coldly, turning away from Deacon. "In the meantime, consider how your actions have led to this."

"Stone, you're making a mistake," Deacon said urgently,

pressing against the bars of the small cell. "I'm innocent! Frank is missing, and I would never put him in danger. You know me!"

"Do I?" Stone replied with an edge. "In uncertain times, we must question even those we consider allies. It's possible you've deceived us in means beyond what we can see."

As incarceration settled around him, Deacon felt the walls close in. "You cannot let paranoia cloud your judgment! This isn't right!" he called after Stone, but the Colonel turned, eyes narrowed and resolute.

"Stay here until the truth is determined," he replied coldly, marching away into the depths of the camp.

DEACON'S CAMP - NIGHT - MOMENTS LATER

Outside the holding area, murmurs buzzed through the survivors gathered around the fire. Emily watched as Colonel Stone walked away, her mind racing with thoughts of uncertainty and betrayal.

"Is he really responsible for Frank disappearing?" Rachel asked hesitatingly, looking around at the gathered group with apprehension.

Emily felt a pang of distrust shoot through the atmosphere. "I don't believe so," she replied, conviction glazing her eyes. "Deacon has always fought for our safety. We can't let fear guide our thoughts."

As she stood among the group, she noticed Nadine lingering by Colonel Stone, her posture somewhat submissive but eyes glinting with intrigue. It struck Emily that perhaps this could be a chance to glean information.

"I'll be right back," Emily said to Rachel, stepping aside to discreetly approach Nadine while focusing on the tension unfolding around the camp.

"Nadine!" Emily called softly but urgently, trying to catch her attention, her mind racing with suspicion. "Can we talk?"

Nadine turned; her expression wary. "What is it?"

"Is there something you know about this?" Emily asked, glancing at Colonel Stone before returning her gaze to Nadine. "There's tension in the air, and I feel like something isn't right with Frank's disappearance."

"I don't know anything for sure," Nadine replied hesitantly, glancing back toward Stone. "But you have to understand that Stone seems determined to keep the camp secure by any means necessary. He genuinely believes Deacon's actions have endangered us."

"But he's not the threat!" Emily argued, frustration creeping into her voice. "We need to remain united, not divided by doubts and accusations!"

"I'm trying to help," Nadine said, a flicker of resolve in her eyes. "But you must understand, Stone has his reasons. There's a lot at stake here. We cannot disregard the weight of his concerns."

"Maybe you should talk to him," Emily suggested, desperate to glean anything useful. "See if he's willing to listen and trust Deacon."

Nadine looked concerned for a moment, the shift in energy palpable. "I will," she promised, her tone softening. "But we all need to prepare ourselves for the worst."

WAREHOUSE - NIGHT - MOMENTS LATER

Back in the holding area, Deacon paced, frustration simmering beneath the surface as he attempted to process the situation. The shadows within felt thick, and he could feel the weight of doubt settling in.

He could hear the muffled sounds of conversations outside,

uncertainty threading through the camp like a gathering storm.

"Damn it, Frank…" he muttered, the weight of worry gnawing at him. "Where are you?"

Just then, a familiar voice called out from beyond the bars. It was Lila, leaning toward him with concern. "Deacon, are you okay?"

"I'm fine, but this isn't fine!" Deacon replied, pacing back and forth. "I need to clear my name. They can't believe I would endanger Frank."

"Emily's fighting for you. She believes you didn't do anything wrong," Lila reassured him, determination shining through her words. "We all do. Don't lose hope."

"Hope has a way of becoming a double-edged sword," Deacon said, his heart heavy with the weight of surrounding uncertainties. "And right now, I'm the scapegoat."

"You have to hold strong. We'll find a way to get you out of here," Lila insisted, her voice cutting through the darkness that wrapped around his spirit. "We've come too far to let doubt destroy us now."

"Thank you, Lila," Deacon said, feeling the shared resolve fill him with strength. "Just keep pushing for the truth. I trust you to help Emily, and I need you to keep an eye on Stone."

"Don't worry. We'll figure this out," Lila replied, determination lighting her eyes. As she stepped back, Deacon watched her go, the shadows of uncertainty creeping back in.

DEACON'S CAMP - NIGHT - MOMENTS LATER

Outside, the atmosphere among the survivors hummed with tension. Gathered around the fire, whispers floated through the air, each person echoing doubts about Deacon, questioning what they truly believed.

Emily moved through the group, maintaining a facade of calm even as confusion swirled around her. "We need to trust each other," she stated firmly. "We can't let paranoia tear us apart."

"Do you really think Deacon had anything to do with Frank's disappearance?" Rachel asked, concern painted across her face.

"No! I know him," Emily insisted, her voice rising with conviction. "He would never betray us. We have to stand together against this chaos."

But just as she finished, another group of raiders emerged from the shadows—pale and gaunt, their eyes sunken from the struggles they faced in the night. "We'll give you what's coming for you!" one of them shouted, their voice carrying the weight of betrayal.

"Get ready! We need to prepare to defend ourselves!" Emily yelled, the tension ricocheting through the camp as everyone galvanized against the new threat, buzzing with urgency.

ABANDONED WAREHOUSE - NIGHT - CONTINUOUS

Inside, Deacon felt the temperature drop as the sounds of battle echoed from outside—howls morphing into desperate cries and gunfire. He paced the small confines of the holding area, his mind racing.

"Come on…" he muttered to himself, frustration flaring as he thought about Frank, wondering where his friend had gone. But beneath it all, a sinister thought crawled to the surface: Was there more to Colonel Stone's actions than what he let on?

"Why would he want to lock me up?" Deacon whispered, glancing around the shadows, feeling trapped not just physically, but emotionally.

DEACON'S CAMP - NIGHT - MOMENTS LATER

Outside, the camp erupted into chaos once more as the new raiders descended, clashing against the defenders. Emily and the surviving members screamed commands to each other amid the disarray.

"Hold the line!" Emily shouted, heart racing in adrenaline-fueled solidarity. "We can't let them overrun us again!"

The sound of gunfire filled the air as another Hound broke through, its eyes filled with hunger. As they faced this new tide of chaos, Emily felt her resolve deepen, knowing they couldn't afford to lose the ground they'd fought so hard to reclaim.

ABANDONED WAREHOUSE - NIGHT - CONTINUOUS

Meanwhile, Deacon remained restless within the confines of the holding area, frustration boiling over as he pondered the odds. "I need to know the truth," he whispered to himself, pacing back and forth.

Suddenly, he heard a noise—a familiar sound that creaked against the silence of his confinement. He turned to see a figure cloaked in shadow from the far side.

"Who's there?" he called, grasping the bars. The figure stepped closer, revealing itself to be Emily.

"Deacon!" Emily exclaimed, urgency flashing in her eyes as she approached the bars, urgency underscoring her presence. "I came to make sure you're okay. They're trying to tear us apart out there!"

"Is it the raiders?" he asked, heart racing. "What's happening?"

"No, it's more complicated than that." Emily's voice tinged with anxiety. "We're facing internal threats, too. Stone... he's convinced everyone that you're responsible for Frank's disappearance!"

"Of course he is," Deacon replied bitterly, feeling the anger churn in his stomach. "That man... He's twisting everything to control this camp."

"He's rallying support against you. We need to prove your innocence; we can't let him make this about fear," Emily said passionately, determination lacing her voice.

"I need you to listen to me," Deacon urged, locking eyes with her. "If Stone is manipulating this situation, we have to find proof. Frank's disappearance could hold the key to all of it."

"What do you mean?" Emily queried, realization dawning.

"If Stone knows something about Frank's whereabouts, we'll need to confront him," Deacon said, his mind racing. "We might be facing something worse than just the outside threats."

"Then we have to act fast," Emily replied, determination igniting in her gaze. "We'll figure out how to expose him and prove you're innocent."

DEACON'S CAMP - NIGHT - MOMENTS LATER

As the camp continued to erupt into chaos, Deacon gripped the bars of the holding area, determination surging in him. "Emily, make sure the others are okay. We need to keep them safe while we figure this out."

"All right," she agreed, glancing toward the growing commotion. "Let me see what's happening. Stay strong!"

As she moved back into the fray, Deacon steeled himself for whatever was to come. The night still loomed heavily around them, shadows wrapping through the trees like a dark shroud, but he refused to surrender to despair.

DEACON'S CAMP - NIGHT - MOMENTS LATER

Emily rejoined the group around the fire, urgency pulsing

through her. "We need to keep pushing back. We can't let fear divide us!"

"Did you speak to Deacon?" Lila asked, tension woven tightly into her voice.

"He knows about the threat we're facing," Emily replied, her heart racing. "But we can't let Colonel Stone continue to manipulate this situation."

"We need to unite against this!" Frank shouted, trying to keep the spirit of defiance alive. "If we don't trust each other now, we'll never survive!"

"Stick to the plan!" Emily shouted, the knot of determination tightening within. "We stand together against both the external threats and the shadows creeping inside our circle!"

As the night deepened, pulses of fear and unity flowed through the group, reminding each survivor that they were in this fight together.

HOLDING AREA - NIGHT - MOMENTS LATER

Meanwhile, back at the holding area, Deacon could only listen as the chaos continued outside, the din of battle rising and falling. He had to trust that Emily and the others would hold the line.

As he paced, memories of Frank flashed through his mind—their moments of shared laughter, the bonds they had forged against the darkness. He refused to let anything take that from him.

"I'll find out the truth," he vowed quietly to himself. "I won't let fear take this camp."

With that determination firmly in place, Deacon braced himself for the challenges ahead, plotting how to confront the lurking shadows with his friends rallying together for their safety.

DEACON'S CAMP - NIGHT - MOMENTS LATER

Back outside, the chaos continued to unfold as the survivors fought back against both the Hounds and raiders. The flickering campfire illuminated the fierce expressions on their faces as they locked their focus on the oncoming threats.

"Cover the right flank!" Lila shouted, taking her place beside Jacob who was aiming at a group of raiders that had strayed too close.

"We need to maintain formation!" Colonel Stone commanded, sweat glistening on his brow as he moved through the chaos, directing his team with the precision of a seasoned leader.

But as the sounds of growls and shouts filled the air, the threat of betrayal crackled at the edges of their unity—deeper tensions rising among the group.

"Watch your backs!" Frank shouted, spotting a raider darting toward a vulnerable position. His shout energized the survivors as they turned their focus, instinctively banding together again against the pressure that threatened to pull them apart.

With gunfire reverberating through the night, the surviving defenders pushed back against their enemies, their collective strength illuminating their path amid the shadows threatening to engulf them.

WAREHOUSE - NIGHT - CONTINUOUS

Inside the warehouse, Emily paced, her heart heavy as she tried to reassure the remaining survivors. The noise from outside echoed ominously, a constant reminder of their vulnerability.

"We've come through so much," she said, trying to bolster

their spirits. "We have to keep holding on! Just remember we are not alone!"

"Do you really think we can hold off the onslaught?" Rachel asked, her voice trembling as she clutched her weapon tightly.

"Yes! If we remain united and believe in each other, not just ourselves, we can win this," Emily replied firmly. "We must keep testing our limits and fighting back!"

Just then, several loud thuds against the warehouse door sent shockwaves through the air. "They're trying to get in!" one survivor yelped, eyes wide with fear.

"Brace!" Emily yelled, adrenaline surging as they hurriedly moved closer to the entrance, preparing for the oncoming storm.

DEACON'S CAMP - NIGHT - MOMENTS LATER

Outside, the situation continued to escalate. Deacon felt the raw energy of the fight meld together—Hounds snarled, and raiders shouted amidst the chaos that wove dangerously close.

Suddenly, the dark raider leader emerged again, his expression twisted with determination. "You think you can stand against us? You're nothing but shadows in the dark!" he mocked, stepping forward to confront Deacon.

"Not tonight!" Deacon shot back, raising his weapon once more. "We stand as a united front—you won't take this camp!"

The tension in the air thickened as the raider and his followers charged forward, emboldened by their earlier chaos, and Deacon could feel the storm of fear gathering at their edges once again.

"Hold your ground!" Colonel Stone shouted, aiming at the advancing raiders. "Don't let him break our ranks!"

With a renewed focus, the survivors tightened their

formation, standing tall against the insane tide overwhelming them. As the growls of the Nightmare Hounds merged with the raiders' battle cries, it felt as though they were caught in a whirlpool of chaos.

WAREHOUSE - NIGHT - MOMENTS LATER

Meanwhile, inside the warehouse, the atmosphere throbbed with unease as Emily and the survivors stood ready, hearts racing with anticipation.

"Do you think they'll win?" Rachel asked, dread creeping into her voice. "What if they break through?"

"We will fight!" Emily asserted, grounding herself. "They're counting on our fear to break our spirit, but we won't let them."

Suddenly, the door shuddered violently—a loud crash rippled as if something enormous were forcing its way through. The hallowed space filled with a frenzied energy.

"Get ready!" Emily yelled, adrenaline surging as she prepared to confront whatever came next.

DEACON'S CAMP - NIGHT - MOMENTS LATER

Outside, Deacon felt the tide shift as the raider leader charged, scramble growing as he rallied for an attack. A roll of gunfire erupted against the advancing captors as Deacon pushed forward.

"Together! We fight as one!" Deacon shouted, sensing the unity among them flare once more, the bond solidifying through the fire of battle.

The fight unfolded before him in a blur of desperation and courage, shadows clashing against the flickering light, but still, he could see the fear gripping his team.

But realization struck within him—Deacon knew that beyond

this battle, betrayal lay in wait. "Keep an eye on Stone!" he shouted, the thought seeping in beneath the chaos.

Fear fueled Deacon's instincts as the raider chaos continued to rage; they would not back down.

ABANDONED WAREHOUSE - NIGHT - CONTINUOUS

Back in the warehouse, Emily felt the energy ripple through as the door rattled violently, sending tingles of panic through the remaining survivors.

"Remember, we stand together!" she called out as another loud crash echoed from outside. Their eyes went wide, courage blooming even as doubt threatened to creep in.

As more sounds reverberated through the walls, a sense of urgency propelled their movements. "Get ready to fight!" Emily ordered, adrenaline surging as they braced for impact.

DEACON'S CAMP - NIGHT - MOMENTS LATER

Deacon felt the shadows closing in as the Hounds once again charged the perimeter, a collective force threatening. "Everyone, back to the fire!" he yelled, sensing their courage unsteadily wavering.

As they stumbled back, he noticed Frank's absence gnawing deeper now, the uncertainty surrounding that feeling becoming palpable.

"Stay together," Deacon shouted, holding them close. "We can't lose anyone else; we must push back. This night isn't over yet!"

With that declaration, adrenaline surged within the group as they prepared to respond to the unrelenting darkness. Together, they steeled themselves for whatever lay ahead, embracing the uncertainty while digging in their resolve to confront their fears and the dangers looming just beyond the light.

And as the echoes of chaos surged like a storm, they all knew they would have to choose hope over despair—in this battle, in this fight for their lives and their home.

CHAPTER 45: THE TRIAL OF FAITH

DEACON'S CAMP - DAYBREAK

As dawn broke over Deacon's camp, the first light of day illuminated the remnants of night's chaos. Shadows began to recede, but a palpable tension remained, wrapping tightly around the survivors as they prepared for the challenges that lay ahead.

The survivors gathered near the fire pit, where Colonel Stone had set up a makeshift area for the trial. Deacon stood, confined within a small area made from crates, his heart heavy with the weight of uncertainty and betrayal. He watched as his friends assembled, knowing they were preparing to decide his fate.

"The trial of Deacon will begin shortly!" Stone announced, his voice commanding the attention of the group. Everyone fell silent, the atmosphere thick with unease as they turned their focus to the proceedings. "We must determine whether he is responsible for the recent events, including the disappearance of Frank."

Deacon felt a wave of concern ripple through the crowd, uncertainty etched on the faces he once called allies. He steeled himself, knowing he had to fight not just for himself, but for the unity of their camp.

"Look, I'm innocent!" Deacon called out, trying to capture

everyone's attention. "Frank disappeared when we were attacked. I had no part in that!"

DEACON'S CAMP - MOMENTS LATER

Colonel Stone raised a hand to quiet him. "We will hear your defense in time, Deacon. First, we shall hear from the accuser."

Lila stepped forward, her expression a mix of determination and anxiety. "I don't believe Deacon would ever put us in danger. He's fought for our survival more times than I can count. This feels wrong."

"Is it not true, Lila, that he was the last one with Frank before he went missing?" Stone countered, his tone cold, trying to sow seeds of doubt.

"Yes, but so were many of us during the battle! We were all fighting for our lives!" Lila insisted, her voice rising in defiance. "This is insane! We can't blame one person when we've all been through this nightmare!"

Frank's absence loomed heavy in the air, and murmurings of doubt began to swirl among the survivors. The tension rose, each voice echoing doubts that Fedora had begun to settle over the camp.

DEACON'S CAMP - MOMENTS LATER

One of the older survivors, a grizzled man named Martin, stepped forward. "I trusted Deacon. He led us through darkness," he said, voice gruff yet steady. "But if we're questioning loyalty, we ought to look at everything."

Deacon felt a flicker of hope. "Thank you, Martin," he said, desperation dripping from his words. "None of us can afford to let fear guide our actions. We fought together last night to protect our home."

"Let's hear Deacon's side then!" Rachel chimed in, stepping up beside Martin. "We can't forsake him without hearing what he has to say."

"Very well," Stone replied, conceding somewhat as he turned to Deacon. "Make your case, then."

As Deacon began to speak, his heart raced with urgency. "I want to assure everyone here that I am not responsible for Frank's disappearance. I stood beside him during our fight, and I would never put my friends in jeopardy. We learned to survive in the face of darkness together."

There was a moment's pause as the group contemplated his words. "Frank was like family to me. I understand the fears spiraling in this camp after last night, but we need to focus on what truly matters: survival."

"Then why did you not go searching for him when he went missing?" Stone asked, interjecting sharply. "You had a chance to lead, yet here you are, locked away."

"Because I was engaged in fighting for our lives," Deacon retorted, frustration prickling at the end of his temper. "We were surrounded! If I had left, it could have ended poorly for everyone present."

"You didn't think it would be prudent to check afterward?" Stone pressed, his eyes narrowing.

"I didn't think we would face these monsters without a plan!" Deacon shouted, fueling his resolve. "I thought about the all too familiar price of sacrifice! Those Hounds are attracted by fear, and we can't let paranoia tear us apart!"

Emily stood nearby, catching Deacon's eye, her own heart aching with the weight of uncertainty. "We're all scared," she said softly, stepping forward. "But I believe in Deacon. We're a family here, and family means not only standing together but trusting each other."

DEACON'S CAMP - DAY - MOMENTS LATER

"Do you trust Colonel Stone?" Deacon challenged, eyes burning with urgency. "Is he representing our collective best interest or merely trying to seize power during chaos?"

The crowd murmured, the tide of opinion shifting as doubt threaded through like fragile filaments of doubt.

"I may be a leader. But I will not let fear dictate my direction!" Stone asserted, trying to maintain control of the growing unease. "We need to decide if Deacon is a threat to our future."

"Or if he's the key to our survival," Lila interrupted, stepping closer to Deacon with unwavering resolve. "To condemn him without proper evidence could destroy what we have all fought for!"

Just then, from the tree line, a loud crack sounded—a branch snapping abruptly. The surrounding chatter ceased as the group turned toward the noise, eyes wide and hearts racing.

"What was that?" someone whispered in fear, eyes darting to the gathering shadows.

ABANDONED WAREHOUSE - NIGHT - CONTINUOUS

Inside the warehouse, Emily sensed the weight of uncertainty growing dire. "Everyone, stay close!" she urged, determination rising as shadows flickered at the edges of perception. "We're not facing this alone!"

She felt empowered; they had to hold their ground against the tide of darkness.

DEACON'S CAMP - NIGHT - CONTINUOUS

As the tension mounted outside, Suspicions started to bubble again within. "We need perimeter check—everyone standing strong!" Colonel Stone commanded, eyes narrowing. "No distractions now!"

Deacon felt a surge of urgency as another shadow slunk across the treeline's edges, growing nearer and more menacing. "This can't be a coincidence," he muttered to himself, alarm bells ringing in his heart.

"Deacon, stay with us!" Lila urged, fear flashing through her eyes.

"I'm fine! We face what lurks beyond our line!" Deacon insisted but inside felt the shadows creeping closer with each beat of the heart.

"Now!" Stone barked, refocusing the crowd. "Report back what you find—immediately!"

As the noise settled outside and suspicion crept back into the hearts of the survivors, both fear and uncertainty threatened to tear them apart, echoing louder than the howls of the night.

In the heart of chaos, truths began to intertwine with lies, and as the shadows drew near, their resolve surged—the survivors stood ready, determined to face whatever darkness lay ahead, even as doubts threatened to fracture their foundations.

DEACON'S CAMP - NIGHT - MOMENTS LATER

"Everyone move to the fire!" Deacon shouted, commanding attention as the team instinctively closed ranks around him, forming a protective barrier against the darkness that encroached from the trees. "Stay together! We can't afford to lose anyone else!"

As they rallied near the firelight, Lila gripped Deacon's arm, her gaze intense. "You have to figure out what's happening with Colonel Stone! We can't allow this division to fester if we're going to survive!"

"I will," Deacon promised, determination reflecting in his eyes.

"But right now, we can't let him sway our unity with fear. We must protect each other."

Suddenly, a loud rustle broke through the air, causing everyone to draw their weapons, eyes wide as they prepared for the worst. Just a few feet away, shadows flitted through the underbrush, and then, before their very eyes, a figure stumbled into the firelight.

"Frank!" Lila gasped, relief flooding through her as the missing survivor emerged, disheveled and visibly shaken.

"You're alive!" Deacon exclaimed, rushing to his side, relief mingling with concern as he surveyed his friend for injuries.

"I... I'm sorry I disappeared," Frank gasped, breathless and shaken. "I got separated during the chaos. I was lost in the woods."

"Where are you hurt?" Lila asked, stepping closer, worry radiating from her.

"I'm not... I'm just tired," Frank replied, his eyes darting nervously around the camp. "But they know we're here. The Hounds—they're gathering!"

The revelation sent shockwaves through the group once more, a reminder of their tenuous grip on safety.

DEACON'S CAMP - NIGHT - CONTINUOUS

"Gather everyone! We need to verify what Frank saw!" Colonel Stone shouted, trying to bring order amid the chaos forming again. "Don't let fear drag us into despair!"

Deacon felt a pang of frustration at the Colonel's commanding tone. "We need to hear Frank's account," he said, stepping toward the center of attention. "We all fought through the darkness; let's hear what he has to say about what he witnessed."

Frank nodded, brushing off the dirt and grime from his clothes. "I was caught in the woods as Hounds closed in, but I saw the raiders—they seemed to gather nearby."

Deacon's heart sank. "Gather where?"

"Towards the old logging road... I could barely make out their shadows, but they seemed to just linger, waiting for a moment to strike," Frank reported, his voice trembling. "I feared they would find their way back to the camp."

"Then we fortify our defenses! We'll prepare for both the raiders and Hounds," Colonel Stone stated authoritatively, though Deacon felt a flicker of suspicion still lingering in the back of his mind.

"Frank is back, and that means we can set a broader watch. We must be prepared—together," Deacon responded firmly. "Let's not allow fear to force us apart."

Lila stepped closer to Deacon; concern etched across her features. "Have you considered that Colonel Stone may know more than he's letting on?"

"I—" Deacon started but was cut off by a sudden commotion from the tree line.

WOODS NEAR DEACON'S CAMP - NIGHT - MOMENTS LATER

From beyond the edges of their camp, the unmistakable sound of deep growls rose again, reverberating through the trees.

"Get ready!" Deacon shouted, urgency filling the air as everyone braced themselves for the impending storm.

The sound intensified, as a massive silhouette emerged from the shadows—a larger Hound, more menacing and fiercer than any they'd faced before, trotted out into the clearing. The air thickened with anticipation—this was not just a menace; it was a manifestation of their worst fears.

"Here they come!" Lila cried; her weapon raised high as she steadied herself.

Fires blazed around the camp as Deacon's gaze darted between the approaching creature and the tumult of raiders lurking in the shadows. He felt the weight of responsibility crush down on him as he readied himself to protect his team.

DEACON'S CAMP - NIGHT - MOMENTS LATER

"Hold the lines!" Deacon yelled, the moment coming alive with urgency as the Hound approached, snarling and snapping its jaws menacingly.

"Ready! Aim!" Stone shouted, marshaling everyone together in a unified front.

The survivors worked together, taking aim at the impending threat, waiting for the right moment to strike. The air was taut with anticipation, the growls of the Hound echoing through the camp like a fierce wind.

"This is it!" Deacon shouted as the Hound lunged forward, the air filling with the tense energy of the gathering storm.

ABANDONED WAREHOUSE - NIGHT - CONTINUOUS

Meanwhile, within the confines of the warehouse, Emily and the remaining survivors continued to ready themselves for any potential threat.

"Stay close!" Rachel urged, shifting anxiously as she tried to maintain focus.

Regardless of the chaos outside, they clenched their weapons, waiting for the sounds of an imminent assault while drawing strength from one another.

Then, just as the volume outside crescendoed, a fierce crash echoed again through the walls of the warehouse, enough to send everyone jumping back instinctively.

"Brace yourselves!" Emily shouted, gripping her weapon tightly.

The door rattled under impact, and the pounding intensified, a reminder that the night was far from over.

DEACON'S CAMP - NIGHT - MOMENTS LATER

Back outside the camp, chaos intensified; the Hound collided with the defenses, pushing as the first line began to fracture beneath the assault. Deacon focused on the creature as it lunged toward the survivors at the front.

"On my mark!" Stone shouted, firmly positioned beside Deacon, both leaders ready to direct the fight ahead.

"Now!" Deacon yelled, and as one, they unleashed their barrage of gunfire, determined to push back against the monstrous Hound.

The creature staggered, momentarily thrown off balance—but it quickly rallied, eyes blazing with fury.

"Reform! Stay back!" Colonel Stone commanded, feeling the pressure of battle mount as shadows loomed heavier—reinforcements were approaching.

The air quaked as anticipation buzzed like electricity in the darkness, and in that moment, Deacon and the other survivors realized that the stakes of the night were higher than they'd ever imagined.

With the shadows closing in, and their fears threatening to overwhelm them, they had to band together—fight to retain what they had built and protect one another from whatever awaited them in the dark.

CHAPTER 46: BETRAYAL AMONG SHADOWS

ABANDONED WAREHOUSE - NIGHT

The atmosphere inside the warehouse felt charged with uncertainty as Emily paced, her mind racing with a mix of worry for Frank and confusion about the growing tensions among their group. Shadows flickered along the walls, the aftermath of the chaos lingering like a bad memory.

Emily's gaze settled on Nadine, who stood slightly apart from the rest of the survivors, her expression inscrutable. Sensing an opportunity to delve deeper, Emily approached her.

"Nadine," she said, keeping her voice steady despite the turmoil swirling within her. "Can we talk?"

Nadine looked up, her brows knitting together slightly. "Is everything alright, Emily?"

"I need to understand... these shadows among us, the tensions," Emily said, searching Nadine's face for any hints of what lay beneath her calm exterior. "You seemed close to Colonel Stone. Is there something going on that we're not aware of?"

Nadine hesitated, the weight of Emily's words hanging between them. "You know how things get in chaotic times.

Everyone's on edge," she said at last, defending her stance but not quite meeting Emily's gaze.

"It's more than that, isn't it?" Emily pressed, a mix of apprehension and curiosity creeping into her tone. "You've been standing too close to him. What do you know?"

Nadine's expression shifted slightly, a flicker of something indecipherable crossing her features. "I might know more than you think," she replied, her voice low and cryptic.

Emily's heart raced as she read between the lines. "What do you mean, Nadine? Is it about Frank?"

"Maybe," Nadine said slowly, sizing Emily up. "But there are things best left unspoken, you know? Knowledge can... complicate things."

"Complicate how?" Emily asked, unease crawling across her skin. "We're in the middle of a crisis! If we're hiding things from each other, it could cost us dearly!"

Nadine stepped closer, lowering her voice. "Listen, Emily. If you want to find out the truth about your brother, we need to approach this delicately. There are forces at play you're clearly unaware of."

"What forces?" Emily replied, growing wary as she started to grasp the underlying tension.

Nadine leaned in conspiratorially, her expression shifting. "You and I can uncover what happened to Frank. If you come with me now, I promise, we'll find the answers."

Emily narrowed her eyes, suspicion gnawing at the edges of her thoughts. "What do you really want from this? Are you suggesting we sneak out in the middle of the night?"

"They won't let you search. If we stay hidden in the shadows, we can find out the truth without stirring panic," Nadine insisted, her voice silky with persuasion. "It's the best chance you'll have."

"Fine," Emily said slowly, hesitating, "but I need to know I can trust you. What's your true motivation here?"

Nadine's demeanor shifted again, an unreadable mask settling over her features. "Let's focus on finding out about Frank first, and then we can address trust."

The tension swelled as Emily contemplated the proposition, knowing it could lead her deeper into murky waters. But the thought of learning about Frank propelled her forward. "Alright, let's do it. But if something feels off… I'll know."

Nadine smiled, a hint of darkness flickering in her eyes. "Trust me, Emily. This will be worth it."

ABANDONED WAREHOUSE - NIGHT - MOMENTS LATER

As they slipped out of the warehouse, the cool night air washed over them. Emily felt a mix of excitement and dread swirling within her. She cast a last glance at the camp's security; their makeshift barricades stood firm, but uncertainty held the dark night.

"Where do we even start?" Emily asked, glancing over at Nadine, who seemed to know the direction they needed to take.

"Follow me. I have a place in mind," Nadine instructed, leading the way into the forest with a measured pace.

As they moved deeper into the woods, Emily felt an unsettling knot in her stomach, the shadows looming larger as the trees closed in around them. "You mentioned forces at play. What did you mean?"

Nadine turned; her expression oddly calm though her eyes flickered with something darker. "Let's just say some truths are better left hidden. Not everyone here wants what's best for the camp."

"What do you mean?" Emily pressed, confusion rising. "Are you saying Stone is hiding something?"

Nadine hesitated, a flicker of contemplation crossing her face. "There are threads that connect us all... and some of those threads lead to places you'd rather not tread."

"Is this about Frank?" Emily insisted, alarm bells ringing in her mind. "What are you not telling me?"

Nadine smiled in a way that sent a chill down Emily's spine. "Everything will become clear soon enough. But right now, we must find the answers without drawing too much attention."

Emily felt a profound unease settle in her chest as they moved deeper into the forest, feeling as if they were crossing an invisible line. But the thought of uncovering the truth about Frank propelled her, driving her forward despite her rising dread.

WOODS NEAR DEACON'S CAMP - NIGHT - MOMENTS LATER

As they neared a clearing, the eerie stillness of the woods enveloped them. Nadine paused, her expression shifting to one of stern resolve.

"This is where we can talk," she said quietly, glancing around to ensure they weren't being watched.

Emily looked around, feeling the tension weave itself through the trees. "What's about to happen?" she asked cautiously.

Nadine turned back, her eyes narrowing into focus. "Truth can be a heavy burden, Emily. It can change perceptions and alliances."

"What do you mean?" Emily pressed, anxiety tightening within her. "What's coming?"

With a sudden shift, Nadine stepped closer, her demeanor darkening. "If you want the truth about Frank—and the matters we need to discuss—you may find it comes at a cost."

Emily's heart raced, suddenly grasping that something was terribly amiss. "What cost?"

Before she could react, Nadine's expression darkened further, and her voice lowered to a whisper. "You need to understand that some answers come with silence. And I'm afraid it's time to seal your lips."

"What are you talking about?" Emily gasped, her breath coming quick as she sensed the shift from ally to threat rapidly unfolding in front of her.

But before she could back away, Nadine lunged forward, her hand reaching for Emily's throat, eyes cold with a calculated resolve.

"Sorry, but in this world, trust is a luxury!" Nadine hissed.

In an instant, adrenaline spiked through Emily, a visceral instinct to survive igniting within her. She pushed back, pivoting on her heel to break free just as Nadine grabbed for her.

"Stay away from me!" Emily shouted, scrambling back toward the tree line, her heart racing as she realized the true nature of the danger she faced.

Nadine's expression hardened, a chilling smile creeping across her face. "You had to know too much. I can't let you expose what's really happening, not to anyone in the camp."

WOODS NEAR DEACON'S CAMP - NIGHT - CONTINUOUS

Emily's instincts kicked in as she bolted deeper into the trees, the sounds of the camp fading behind her. The adrenaline coursed through her body, propelling her forward as she tried to navigate through the brambles.

"Emily!" Nadine shouted, her voice sharp as she began to pursue, the menace clear in her tone. "You don't want to make this harder for yourself!"

Panic flared within Emily, but she couldn't lose hope. "I won't let you take me down! I'll expose you!" she yelled back, determination steeling her nerves.

Suddenly, Nadine lunged forward, easily darting through the underbrush. "You don't know what you're playing with!" she hissed, her eyes glinting in the dim moonlight.

DEACON'S CAMP - NIGHT - MOMENTS LATER

Back at the camp, Deacon felt the sudden shift in the atmosphere as he sensed that something was off. "Where's Emily?" he asked, his heart racing.

"She went after Nadine; they headed into the woods," Rachel replied, anxiety threading through her voice. "Something's wrong!"

"Gather everyone! We have to get them back!" Deacon shouted, urgency igniting once more. "Stay alert; they could be in danger!"

He quickly moved toward the forest, eyes scanning for any signs of his friend. Doubt began to creep in—whether they were facing simply a physical threat or something deeper lurking in the shadows.

WOODS NEAR DEACON'S CAMP - NIGHT - CONTINUOUS

Emily sprinted through the underbrush, each branch and twig clawing at her arms as she tried to escape Nadine's grasp. The darkness loomed around her, threatening to swallow her whole, but she refused to back down.

In a moment of fury, she turned, adrenaline surging. "You can't silence me!" she shouted, defiantly bracing herself against the tree.

Nadine collided into her, sending them both crashing to the ground in a tangle of limbs. "You think you have a choice?" she hissed, attempting to pin Emily down, but Emily fought back with all her strength, pushing against Nadine's weight.

"Get off me!" Emily screamed, finally managing to shift to the side and kick out, catching Nadine in the stomach.

The impact momentarily stunned Nadine, allowing Emily to scramble back to her feet. "You're not going to win!" she exclaimed, adrenaline fueling her.

"I'll do what I must to protect myself!" Nadine spat, her eyes narrowing with rage as she resumed the chase.

DEACON'S CAMP - NIGHT - MOMENTS LATER

Meanwhile, Deacon and a group of survivors emerged from the tree line, determination etched across their faces. "We need to spread out and search for them!" he commanded. The palpable sense of urgency surged as they fanned out into the woods.

"Head toward the sound!" Rachel urged, pointing toward distant shouting once she caught a hint of noise.

They followed the echo of the struggle deep into the forest as they sprinted, every heartbeat in sync with their collective determination.

WOODS NEAR DEACON'S CAMP - NIGHT - CONTINUOUS

Emily pressed onward, heart racing as she tried to put distance between herself and Nadine. She could hear the branches snapping behind her, the sound of breathing growing closer.

"Don't fight me, Emily!" Nadine shouted; frustration tinged with malice. "You need to understand that this is bigger than you!"

Ignoring her words, Emily continued to push forward, determination fueling her escape. "You can't keep me quiet! I won't let you! You're a liar!"

Suddenly, Emily stumbled, falling into a shallow ravine where damp earth and slippery rocks sent her feet slipping.

Nadine saw the opportunity and lunged. "This is your last chance!" she yelled, reaching for Emily, fingers just inches from grasping her.

DEACON'S CAMP - NIGHT - MOMENTS LATER

Back at the camp, Deacon heard the distant shouting intensify, growing closer. The anxious murmurs of the group surrounded him as they made their way through the woods.

"They have to be near!" Deacon urged as they pressed onward, urgency carrying them through the shadows.

Just as they rounded a bend in the trees, Deacon caught a flash of movement—he turned to see two figures struggling in the darkness just ahead. "Emily!" he called, pushing past the trees.

"I'm here!" Emily shouted back; her voice strained but fierce.

WOODS NEAR DEACON'S CAMP - NIGHT - CONTINUOUS

Deacon rushed toward the sound, heart pounding as he burst into the clearing where he found Emily grappling with Nadine, who was trying to overpower her.

"Get off her!" Deacon shouted, adrenaline surging as he charged forward, urgency guiding his actions.

As he surged forward, his presence ignited Emily with a surge of hope and strength. "Deacon! Help!" she cried out, pushing back against Nadine with renewed vigor.

With one swift motion, Deacon lunged, grabbing Nadine by the shoulder and pulling her away from Emily easily. "What are you doing?" he yelled, anger boiling beneath the surface.

"You don't understand! I was trying to protect us!" Nadine said defensively, regaining her composure as tight fear washed over her features.

"Protect us? Or yourself?" Deacon shot back; his voice steady yet filled with betrayal. "You can't just hurt people because of whatever paranoia you've conjured up!"

Emily, breathless and shaken, got to her feet, stepping closer to Deacon. "I won't let you hurt us, Nadine. We're here to find the truth, not to kill each other!"

Nadine took a shaky breath, eyes darting between Deacon and Emily. "You don't get it!" she cried, vulnerability trembling in her voice. "If Deacon reveals what he knows, everything will fall apart! I had no choice!"

The gravity of her words settled heavily in the air as Deacon and Emily exchanged glances filled with horror.

"What do you mean?" Deacon pressed, his heart racing as he realized the depth of Nadine's hidden motives. "What do you know about Frank's disappearance? What are you hiding?"

"I... I've seen things," Nadine said, stumbling over her words, uncertainty creeping back into her expression. "Things I shouldn't have witnessed... secrets that could cost lives!"

Emily stepped closer, determination filling her voice. "You either tell us everything, or we're confronting this together— no more secrets, no more lies."

"I thought if I didn't say anything... it'd keep everyone safe," Nadine murmured, her voice trembling as the weight of her choices began to unravel around her. "But now it's all slipping away..."

Deacon's heart sank. "Nadine, you're only bringing more

danger on us with your silence. We need to unite. If you have information that could help us find Frank—or reveal the truth behind Stone's manipulation—we can face it together."

Nadine looked back at the shadows of the trees, uncertainty flickering in her eyes. "There are forces in play here that are beyond us. Frank... he was digging too deep, and I think he uncovered something—something Stone was trying to keep hidden."

"Then tell us!" Emily urged, taking a step closer, her heart racing. "We can turn this around!"

"I can't—not yet! If I do, it could endanger everyone," Nadine said, her voice quaking. "But I was approached by someone—someone who offered me information in exchange for loyalty. Stone's agenda isn't what it appears."

"Who approached you?" Deacon pressed, the knot of understanding tightening in his chest. "What's going on?"

Nadine shuffled her stance, breathing heavily as she glanced between Deacon and Emily. "I can't say yet, but it has to do with Frank. Everything is connected."

"Then we'll find Frank ourselves," Emily declared, determination surging within her. "We will uncover what's gone on in this camp—together."

Suddenly, the distant howls of the Hounds pierced through the stillness again, sharper and more ominous than before. Deacon tightened his grip on his weapon once more, readying himself for whatever threat lay lurking among the shadows.

"We don't have time," Deacon urged, glancing back toward the camp. "Those Hounds will be drawn by the ruckus. We need to move!"

DEACON'S CAMP - NIGHT - MOMENTS LATER

As they made their way back toward the camp, Nadine aligned herself closer to Deacon and Emily, uncertainty etched in her features. The air felt heavy with tension, and the shadows hung thick as they navigated through the trees, their hearts racing.

"Just stick together," Deacon instructed, determination coursing through him as they returned to the heart of the camp. "We have to confront whatever lurks beyond our defenses."

Coming back into the light, the camp buzzed with anxiety as survivors prepared themselves against the imminent threat. Lila dashed toward Deacon and the others, worry overwhelming her expression.

"You're back! We need to be on guard—the raiders were sighted again!" she exclaimed, eyes darting nervously toward the trees.

"Then we need to fortify, now!" Deacon declared; the urgency palpable as the atmosphere thickened with tension. "We can't afford to let fear break our unity!"

As the group rallied around the fire, Deacon caught a glimpse of Colonel Stone watching the chaos unfold, the remnants of earlier conversations flickering in his mind. There was something about him—something hidden beneath the surface that felt like a fracture in their already tenuous trust.

"Remember, we're in this together!" Deacon shouted, trying to solidify their resolve. "We've faced darkness before and survived by relying on each other!"

But just as hope began to kindle again, the first signs of movement from the woods came to life—the growls of Hounds rising ominously, the distance tightening like a noose around their collective spirits.

"Everyone ready!" Colonel Stone called out, urgency lacing his commands. "We hold this line!"

The survivors took their places, forming a circle of defense, each person standing resolutely alongside another. Deacon felt the weight of responsibility surge within him, a fire igniting his determination to uncover the truth.

DEACON'S CAMP - NIGHT - MOMENTS LATER

As the Hounds howled from within the darkness, the shadows morphed into monstrous forms darting toward the survivors. The sound of frantic paws echoed against the silhouettes of the trees, the Hounds' presence a tangible nightmare.

"Here they come!" Frank shouted, gripping his weapon tightly, heart pounding with adrenaline.

"Take aim!" Deacon called, the adrenaline coursing through him as he prepared to face the oncoming tide of darkness that threatened to sweep them away.

With a surge of gunfire echoing through the night, they unleashed their collective strength, pressing tightly against the shadows threatening to consume them.

But in the back of his mind, Deacon couldn't shake the suspicion that the greater threat lay not just in the monstrous forms attacking from the woods but also in the shadows lurking within the camp itself—waiting for the opportune moment to strike.

"Beware the Hounds, but also watch your backs," he called out fiercely, his voice ringing with urgency. "Tonight, we confront more than one enemy!"

As the whispers of the past and tangled truths floated just beyond their reach, the battle roared to life around them, and the fight for survival stretched far beyond the immediate danger, paving the way into an unknown abyss.

CHAPTER 47: THE PRICE OF BETRAYAL

DEACON'S CAMP - DAYBREAK

As dawn broke over the camp, the survivors gathered around the makeshift tribunal formed around the flickering embers of the fire. Deacon stood at the center, the weight of his fate pressing down heavily upon him. Anxiety rippled through the crowd—fingers fidgeting with weapons, eyes darting with uncertainty.

Colonel Stone stood across from Deacon, his expression stern, as he presided over the trial with an air of authority that felt more like a shroud of malice. "The council has convened, and we must determine how to address the accusations against Deacon for the disappearance of Frank," Stone declared, his tone strong. "Is this man guilty of endangering our camp?"

A murmur of agreement rippled through the onlookers, each sharing glances that revealed the divide forming within their ranks. Frank's absence loomed heavily, underscoring the tension in the air.

"He has led us through battles," Lila protested, stepping forward from the crowd. "Deacon has always fought for us! He would never betray Frank!"

"We can't ignore the fact that Frank is gone, and the last person seen with him was Deacon," Stone countered, his tone cold and calculated. "How can we trust anyone who puts themselves in positions that endanger the rest of us, especially when we face real threats from every corner?"

As murmur groups began to share opinions among themselves, Deacon could feel the shadows creeping back into their hearts. "Fear cannot guide our decisions!" he called out, desperation blooming in his chest. "We need unity, not division!"

But the air around him thickened with mistrust, leaving the crowd hanging on the precipice of decision.

DEACON'S CAMP - LATER - MOMENTS AFTER THE ACCUSATIONS

Eventually, the verdict came through the crowd like a death knell. "Guilty," several voices chimed, and the crushing weight of betrayal bore down on Deacon as the murmurs rippled through the gathered survivors.

"No! This isn't right!" Lila yelled, stepping forward defiantly. "Deacon doesn't deserve this judgment! We've fought through hell together!"

But as anger and despair brewed amongst them, a sense of finality settled. "We can't risk our camp's safety; he put us all in danger," Stone declared, treachery woven within his words.

"Deacon," Lila began, but the camp shifted with the presence of cruel inevitability. The shadows of distrust began to thicken —the looming threat of darkness surrounding their very existence.

"Whatever happens, I know the truth," Deacon replied firmly, though the urgency sounded weak against the mounting tide. "You'll see I didn't do it."

And just then, a chill crept over the camp, echoing through the air like a warning sign—a reminder of the darkness that loomed beyond.

ABANDONED WAREHOUSE - NIGHT - MOMENTS LATER

Meanwhile, inside the warehouse, Nadine and Emily found themselves standing amid the remnants of the earlier chaos, both feeling the palpable weight of tension in the air.

"Nadine, where have you been?" Emily asked, concern lacing her tone. "We need to figure out why this trial is happening so rush.

"I was trying to assess the commotion when I... heard things," Nadine admitted, hesitating as her eyes darted nervously around the room. "Stone isn't who he appears to be."

"What do you mean?" Emily pressed, sensing the urgency unraveling in Nadine's expression. "He's trying to pin everything on Deacon!"

"He has a motive, Emily!" Nadine hissed, urgency seeping into her voice, moving closer. "He's playing a dangerous game with everyone's lives. If we don't act now, it could destroy our camp."

DEACON'S CAMP - NIGHT - MOMENTS LATER

Meanwhile, as tensions rose, the sounds of trouble intensified outside. Shadows darted between the trees, and a feeling of dread settled deeper within.

Colonel Stone stepped forward, firm in his stance. "We will hold Deacon accountable for his actions—he will be confined until a suitable plan is devised," he said with a tone that suggested absolute authority.

But before any new measures could be enacted, the cacophony of noise erupted—a chorus of anguished cries resonated through the forest like a death knell.

"What was that?" someone shouted, fear piercing the air as the shadows thickened, almost alive with malevolence.

Suddenly, a new breed of demons emerged from the depths of the dark—**Wrathful Spirits**—vengeful ghosts with bitterly contorted faces, their forms shifting as they rippled through the shadows.

"Look!" Lila cried, pointing as the spirits swirled into view, their voices a haunting melody of anger and sorrow. "What are they?!"

"They seek retribution!" Stone shouted, stepping back instinctively as fear began to ripple through the crowd.

The spirits surged toward the camp, eyes filled with rage and vengeance, twisted mouths howling demands for retribution against the living.

"Do not let them in!" Deacon shouted, realizing the encroaching danger. "We have to fight back!"

DEACON'S CAMP - NIGHT - CONTINUOUS

The survivors armed themselves, the palpable tension mingling with fear and anxiety as the Wrathful Spirits pushed closer, reaching out with ethereal hands, an anguished chorus that echoed their own regrets.

"Stay together!" Deacon bellowed, trying to keep his composure as the spirits neared. "We must face this to survive!"

But the specters began trying to invade the minds of those present, whispering their fears and regrets, clouding the air with doubt. Shadows of the past leached into hope, threatening to tear them apart.

"Fight them!" Colonel Stone shouted; his voice almost cracking as panic threatened to take hold. "Do not let them win; uphold the bonds of life!"

With that rallying cry, the survivors gathered their strength amid the chaos, pushing back as a collective heartbeat surged against the encroaching spirits.

Deacon felt the darkness stirring, and through the haze of uncertainty, he resolved to fight back—not just for himself but for everyone who had stood by him.

"Take aim at your regrets and doubt!" he shouted, a fiery defiance igniting within him. "Remember—fear is only a shadow! Push back with everything you have!"

As they stood their ground, the battle erupted again, but this time against the very specters of despair threatening to consume their souls. With the Wrathful Spirits storming forward, the camp now faced a battle on multiple fronts—a reckoning of both the living and the dead.

ABANDONED WAREHOUSE - NIGHT - MOMENTS LATER

Back inside the warehouse, with the sounds of chaos unmistakable, Emily looked at Nadine with realization. "We have to help them! We can't let the camp fall to despair!"

"But how?" Nadine replied, urgency flashing in her eyes. "We're outnumbered, and we're still vulnerable. There's nothing we can do to fight those spirits!"

Emily scoured the room for any tools, any weapon they could wield against the encroaching threat. "We've faced darkness before," she said, her resolve hardening. "We need to draw strength from each other! If we can gather the remaining survivors, we can fortify our stance!"

Finally, determination surged within Emily again as she moved toward the door. "Come on! We've got to give them something to fight for!"

DEACON'S CAMP - NIGHT - MOMENTS LATER

Outside, the chaos reached a fever pitch. The spirits swirled through the camp, shrieking for vengeance, their forms shimmering in and out of existence—wrathful, helpless spirits echoing painful cries.

"Stand strong!" Deacon shouted as he stepped forward, instinct driving him to confront the nightmarish visions. "Remember the strength we've built together!"

Gathering around the fire, the survivors joined in retaliation against the spirits, their voices rising in a fervor of determination. Deacon could feel the bond strengthening as his companions drew closer, their collective resolve igniting a fire within.

"Let the light guide you!" Colonel Stone shouted, desperately rallying his troops against the invading force. "We are not defined by our past; we fight for our lives!"

The survivors focused their energy, working to push the spirits back as they channeled their fears into unyielding resolve, each rallying cry becoming an anthem of empowerment.

But as the battle persisted, the spirits pressed closer, wrapping around the edges of their defenses and whispering haunting memories that threatened to fracture their collective strength.

ABANDONED WAREHOUSE - NIGHT - CONTINUOUS

Inside the warehouse, Emily moved swiftly, gathering supplies and weapons, ready to bolster the others outside. "We won't let the camp fall!" she declared, determination pulsing through her veins as she prepared to embrace whatever darkness awaited her.

"If you get close enough, we can drive the spirits away!" Rachel urged, anxiety hanging in the air like a thick fog.

Emily paused, feeling a surge of hope rise. "We'll give them something to focus their rage on—something to give them clarity!"

DEACON'S CAMP - NIGHT - MOMENTS LATER

Outside, the fight raged on, and the Hounds lunged forward, driven by the wrathful spirits' cries. "Keep pushing!" Deacon called, trying to keep the spirits at bay while the survivors shot at the Hounds nearby.

Just then, another writhing spirit broke through the perimeter, and Deacon felt a chill race down his spine. "It knows our weaknesses!" he shouted. "It's feeding on our doubts! Don't let it in!"

Lila stood steadfast beside him, readying her weapon. "We're all we have—all of us!" she yelled. "We fight now!"

But with every howl, the shadows shifted, and the lingering memories of doubt weighed heavily, forcing the group to confront the pasts they hoped to leave behind. The spirits spiraled closer, weaving their despair among the survivors like a suffocating mist.

Suddenly, Deacon spotted Nadine emerging from the woods, urgency etched across her features. "Emily! We need to get back!"

"Where is she?" Deacon demanded, scanning the forest's edge.

"Inside the warehouse, trying to gather supplies!" Nadine shouted, anxiety growing as she glanced over her shoulder. "But we have to hurry!"

Just then, a piercing howl echoed from in front of them, the spirits stretching closer. The ground shook as the Hounds lunged forward again, the shadows closing in, demanding vengeance amidst the chaos.

DEACON'S CAMP - NIGHT - MOMENTS LATER

Deacon, Lila, and Frank rallied together as they prepared to defend against the oncoming onslaught. "We can't let the spirits overwhelm us—focus on what keeps us strong!" Deacon shouted, locking eyes with each of his companions.

Audible breaths echoed in the air as the group faced down the encroaching darkness. "We're not just fighting for ourselves, but for each other!" Lila called out, fire in her voice as they charged forward.

Determination surged as they stood resolute against the shadows, the weight of the spirits bearing down but unable to break their unity. Each gunshot and rallying cry became a flicker of light against the oppressive forces surrounding them.

ABANDONED WAREHOUSE - NIGHT - MOMENTS LATER

Inside the warehouse, Emily moved with urgency, adrenaline surging as she prepared to aid her camp. "Rachel! We need to be ready! Grab anything heavy we can use as weapons!"

"On it!" Rachel replied, her hands shaking slightly as she rummaged through the remaining supplies.

The distant sounds of battle reverberated through the sheltering walls, urging Emily to push past the fear collecting around her—a relentless reminder of their struggle.

DEACON'S CAMP - NIGHT - MOMENTS LATER

Outside again, Deacon felt hope igniting within him as he grasped the resolve of his companions. "We fight together!" he shouted. "We will not back down!"

But the Hounds continued to press close, spurred on by the whispers of vengeful spirits. The shadows seemed to pulse with a life of their own—a living reminder of everything they battled through.

Suddenly, another shadow detached from the spirit horde, drawing closer—a twisted visage unmistakably familiar.

"Frank…" Deacon whispered, heart plummeting as he recognized the spectral presence of his friend, a haunted expression reflecting the pain of his absence.

"Deacon…" the shimmery voice echoed, heavy with sorrow. "You let me down… your decisions drove me away!"

"No!" Deacon cried, anguish overtaking him as he faced the vision of his friend. "I would never betray you!"

But the spirit of Frank only lingered closer, shadows coiling around him like chains. "Your choices have fatal consequences!" The words echoed through the night, reverberating in the hearts of everyone present.

WAREHOUSE - NIGHT - CONTINUOUS

Inside the warehouse, Emily's heart twisted at the sounds that reached her ears, realizing the torment that had unfurled outside. "We need to get out there!" she urged. "We can't let them face it alone!"

"I know, but we must be careful!" Rachel responded, determination swelling within her. "We can't afford to let more spirits or Hounds take hold!"

DEACON'S CAMP - NIGHT - CONTINUOUS

Outside, the confrontation intensified; anguish creased through Deacon's expression as he faced the spirit of Frank, the pain etched deeply in his heart. "You have to fight this, Frank! You're not lost—you're still with us!"

"Is it too late to change?" the spirit echoed, despair washing over, tangled within shadows that stretched far and wide. "You decided to leave me…"

"No! I fought for you!" Deacon shouted; sorrow laced with determination. "I've always fought for us! We can still unite against the darkness!"

The spirit flickered, caught in a vortex of emotions, its form wavering between the ethereal and the corporeal. "You must confront the truth. Stop letting fear guide you."

Deacon could feel the shadows closing in around him, whispers escalating into a cacophony of anguish. The weight of doubt pushed hard against his resolve, but he refused to let it consume him. "I won't lose faith! We will reclaim what was taken!"

In that moment of defiance, the air around Deacon vibrated with energy. With compassionate conviction, he reached forward, trying to make contact, envisioning a connection through the pain. "We fight together, Frank! We can defeat this darkness!"

DEACON'S CAMP - NIGHT - CONTINUOUS

As the spirit of Frank flickered before him, the shadows began to swirl, mixing with the encroaching Hounds and the growing band of raiders. The camp felt charged with chaotic energy.

"Hold the line!" Colonel Stone shouted, trying to regain control of the fighting spirit as desperation swelled around them. "This is our home; we won't let anyone take it from us!"

As the Hounds lunged against the barricades, survivors pressed forward, determination rooted deep within them as they faced the rising tide of chaos. Together, their energies converged into a powerful front, igniting fierce flames of hope against the shadows threatening to drown them.

From within, Emily emerged from the warehouse, determination shining through her eyes as she called out, "Everyone! Stay united! We can win this fight!"

The survivors instinctively turned toward her, hearts warming against the cold grip of fear.

"Yes!" Deacon roared, using the moment to rally. "We can push back against all of this! We're strong together!"

The group felt resolute, pushing forth, uniting against not just the Hounds lurking in the darkness but also against the haunting specters of their fears.

WOODS NEAR DEACON'S CAMP - NIGHT - CONTINUOUS

As the chaos unfolded, Emily joined the others, a fierce energy pulsing through her. "We can't let the darkness drown us!" she shouted, locking eyes with Deacon. "We need to confront these spirits together!"

"We fight for our unity! We've fought for each other!" Deacon exclaimed, feeling the power of their bond solidifying their defenses. "We're the light in this darkness!"

The group surged forward, pushing back against their enemies as the night seemed to shimmer with resilient energy. Each pull of the trigger fueled their determination, each cry a testament to their unity against the relentless shadows.

But as the sheer battle intensified, Deacon noticed something shifting in Colonel Stone's demeanor—a flicker of uncertainty slipping in amid the chaos.

"Stone!" Deacon called out, trying to catch his attention. "What are you really hiding? What do you know about Frank's disappearance?"

"I'm focused on saving the camp!" Stone shot back, voice sharp, eyes flaring with uncertainty.

But Deacon sensed the cracks forming in Stone's façade, a shadow of doubt creeping in. "If you are hiding something, it could cost us! We need transparency to survive!"

Colonel Stone hesitated, and for the first time, doubt flickered across his features. Yet the remnants of authority hung heavy on him as the battle waged on.

DEACON'S CAMP - NIGHT - MOMENTS LATER

As tensions escalated, the Hounds began to retreat, some pulled back by the advancing waves of survivors. But just as victory threatened to shimmer at the edge of the darkness, a chilling howl stretched through the air.

"What is that?" Lila shouted, dread mingling with confusion.

From the shadows, another wave emerged, a new, twisted breed of demons rising from the depths—Wrathful Spirits, their forms shifting and changing, swirling with vengeful anger. The air thickened with sorrow and rage as they stepped closer, their manifestations echoing the haunting cries of those lost.

"Back to the camp!" Deacon shouted, fear knotting in his throat as the spirits moved like smoke, seeking vengeance against the living. "We need to regroup!"

The overwhelming sounds of grief and anger mixed with the air around them, increasing the sense of dread settling in.

"Form up! We need to face this!" Colonel Stone urged, his voice losing the edge of control as panic began to thread through the group.

With the arrival of the Wrathful Spirits, doubt surged anew, threatening to swallow the camp whole in its wake. Spirits grieved for loved ones lost, seeking retribution against the living for perceived transgressions, their ethereal forms flickering through the shadows.

WAREHOUSE - NIGHT - MOMENTS LATER

Inside, Emily turned to Rachel, urgency igniting her thoughts. "We must find a way to confront these spirits!" she declared. "They won't just disappear!"

Rachel's face paled, but determination sparked in her eyes. "We need to gather anything that can help—ideas, protection, something to ground us!"

DEACON'S CAMP - NIGHT - CONTINUOUS

Outside, the spirits surged, moving toward the gathered survivors, their forms swirling around them, whispering ancient grievances that haunted the night.

"Fight back!" Deacon commanded, sensing the stakes rising as the waves of shadows pressed closer. "Remember your strength!"

But as the darkness loomed nearer, vicious growls mingled with the haunting cries of the spirits, creating a dissonance that threatened to tear them apart.

"We push back, together!" Deacon shouted, desperation igniting within him. "We cannot lose hope!"

With that declaration, they surged forward, ready to confront not just the physical threats—but the darker specters that embodied every fear they faced, refusing to let the echoes of betrayal or loss extinguish the bond forged through their struggle for survival.

CHAPTER 48: FRACTURED REALITIES

DEACON'S CAMP - NIGHT - MOMENTS LATER

The battle intensified as the Wrathful Spirits surged forward, their anguished wails intertwining with the growls of the Nightmare Hounds. Deacon felt the air thrum with the weight of their desires for retribution, and fear slithered through his heart.

"Remember why we fight!" he shouted, trying to center the group's panic. "We protect each other! We've come through shadows before; we can do it again!"

Survivors tightened their ranks, firing into the encroaching spirits and Hounds, but the twisted forms of the spirits shimmered, distorting their attacks. The growing cries of vengeance mixed with the snarls of beasts, creating a suffocating cacophony that threatened to drown out their resolve.

"Stay together!" Colonel Stone yelled, trying to regain control of the chaotic energy. "Don't let your fear break our lines!"

But as the spirits drew closer, a creeping despair began to unfurl within the ranks of the survivors. Shadows darted between them, whispering memories and grievances that burdened their minds.

"Deacon!" Frank shouted; eyes wild with panic as he swung his weapon at a writhing spirit. "They're feeding on our fear!"

"We have to confront them! Lean into each other's strengths!" Deacon cried out, his mind racing frantically for a solution as he fought the proximity of despair closing in.

Suddenly, Deacon caught a flicker of confusion from Colonel Stone as he faced the growing tide of spirits. "What do we do?" Stone asked, his authoritative demeanor wavering for the first time.

"We stand strong!" Deacon insisted, rallying the remaining strength within himself. "These spirits are lost, caught between worlds. If we can connect with their memories, maybe we can help them find peace!"

ABANDONED WAREHOUSE - NIGHT - CONTINUOUS

Inside the warehouse, Emily felt the tumult of chaos outside, her heart racing as the distant cries echoed through the walls. "We can't just stand here!" she urged Rachel and the others. "If there's a chance to help, we can't ignore it!"

"We don't have a plan!" Rachel exclaimed, fear thickening the air. "What if those spirits turn on us, too?"

"We'll approach it carefully—together!" Emily said, determination scrambling through anxiety as she prepared to face whatever awaited them. "If we can offer comfort, maybe they'll respond differently."

DEACON'S CAMP - NIGHT - CONTINUOUS

Back outside, Deacon watched as the spirits surged forward, the air thick with malevolence. "Get ready!" he shouted, adrenaline flooding his bloodstream.

"Hold strong, together!" Lila echoed, gripping her weapon ready as they took aim at the advancing forms.

But fear surged in waves, and as the spirits came closer, Emily could feel their dark intentions pressing against her heart. "We're not here to harm you!" she shouted out, stepping forward despite the danger, desperate to connect.

"Come on!" Deacon shouted, realizing Emily was stepping away from their protective line. "Get back!"

But Emily's resolve fueled her courage, her voice strong even as the spirits drew nearer. "We can help you! We hear your pain!"

The spirits halted, flickering in place but remaining an intangible force. Each survivor felt the weight of their own memories coursing through the air, folding into whispers that pressed down on them like a weight.

"Deacon!" Lila shouted, gripping him tight. "We have to protect her!"

But Deacon could only watch in horror as spectral forms began dancing around Emily, whispering echoes of the memories they clung to. The connection she sought surged through the air, wielding anguish and heartbreak like blades.

"Emily, get back!" he barked, but his voice was drowned by the growing wails of vengeful spirits, a dark tide rising against their makeshift defenses.

WOODS NEAR DEACON'S CAMP - NIGHT - MOMENTS LATER

Suddenly, a new presence rippled through the crowd—an immense figure stepped toward the chaos, emanating a powerful aura that compassed both fear and despair.

"Leave her alone!" Nadine shouted, rushing from the shadows, determination digging deeper into her features as she rushed to intervene, standing between Emily and the swirling spirits.

"Nadine, what are you doing?" Deacon called out, concern lacing through his voice, but her expression was fierce—like a knight standing guard to protect against overwhelming odds.

"Let me help!" Nadine insisted, stepping closer to Emily, who remained rooted in place, fear and pain mingling in her eyes.

"Get out of here!" Deacon shouted, ready to move, but the moment spun into chaos as the spirits lashed out, desperate for vengeance.

Suddenly, the spirits surged with renewed rage as Nadine stepped forward. "You need to stop!" she cried, grounding her voice.

In that instant, the atmosphere shifted as the spirits took a poised stance, the collective energy swirling with unresolved grief.

"Nadine!" Deacon shouted, his heart racing as he felt the shadows stretching and wrapping deeper. "What do you know about this?"

"Nothing that doesn't put our entire camp in danger!" she cried back, her resolve shaking but her fear settling behind a determination not to yield.

ABANDONED WAREHOUSE - NIGHT - MOMENTS LATER

Back inside, Rachel glanced at the door, heart racing as the impending confrontation unfolded beyond the walls. "What if they break through?" she whispered, anxiety rising.

"We have to hold together! We will not be consumed!" Emily shouted, feeling the determination surge within her as shadows began to weave through the corners of the room.

DEACON'S CAMP - NIGHT - CONTINUOUS

Around the camp, the atmosphere felt alive with chaos. Deacon, Nadine, and Emily stood firm against the growing tide of spirits threatening to break through, the weight of vulnerability threading heavier as uncertainty coursed through them.

"Hold strong!" Deacon urged, trying to keep the group focused amidst the rising doubts.

"I can't contain this forever!" Nadine shouted, feeling the pressure forcing her to the brink, uncertainty flickering in her resolve.

The tension pulsed in waves as the spirits lingered, demanding their claims, and just then, a loud HOWL pierced through the gloom—their cries echoing louder in waves of urgency.

"They're pushing in!" Lila shouted, instinctively tightening her grip around her weapon. "We need to do something now, and fast!"

The spirits began closing in on the camp like a storm cloud ready to unleash its fury—a new intensity rising in the air, threatening to sweep everything away.

"Together!" Emily yelled, defiance pulsing through her heart as she locked eyes with Nadine. "We confront this darkness as one! We can't let fear dictate our actions!"

With that powerful declaration echoing in the night, they stood resolute against the encroaching shadows—with the weight of the past urging them forward and the flickering flames of determination illuminating their path.

DEACON'S CAMP - NIGHT - CONTINUOUS

As the Hounds and Wrathful Spirits converged, Deacon and the survivors rallied next to the campfire, adrenaline surging as they prepared to confront the chaos. The air filled with the scent of smoke and the sense of urgency weighed heavily on their shoulders.

"Keep your focus!" Deacon yelled, raising his weapon. "We know how to fight! Stand together and push back!"

The group formed a protective circle around the fire, weapons aimed at the approaching spirits. Each survivor steeled themselves against the turmoil, grounding their resolve in the bonds formed through countless battles fought together.

"Do not let the shadows consume us!" Colonel Stone shouted, leading the charge. "This is our home, and we must defend it!"

Lila turned to Deacon; concern etched on her features. "What if the spirits have a way of getting inside our minds? They'll prey on our fears!"

"Then we fight them with the truth!" Deacon replied fiercely. "We're not alone; we have each other. Remember what we've fought for!"

Suddenly, the first wave of spirits surged close, their forms phasing in and out as they reached out with cold hands. Desperate whispers filled the air, echoing the regrets of the living.

"You abandoned us..." they cried in unison, their voices chilling and pained. "You let the pain consume you!"

"What do you want?" Emily shouted, stepping forward with raw conviction. "You need to find peace! You're lost, but you don't have to lash out at the living!"

Deacon could feel the energy shift. The spirits hovered closer, their presence thickening around the survivors, yet he could see a flicker of repression in their forms. They were caught in the depths of anguish, and somehow, there existed a link—a way to reach them.

"Listen to us!" Lila called out, voice strong but gentle. "We understand your pain. We've lost loved ones too. But anger won't solve it!"

Deacon locked eyes with Emily and Lila, both sharing a

determination that flowed between them. "We are the living!" he urged. "You don't have to stay trapped in this cycle of revenge! Let us help you find closure!"

As their words reached the spirit horde, the chaos surged. Some of the spirits began to pause, their movements slowing as if torn between their vengeful nature and the hope offered before them.

WOODS NEAR DEACON'S CAMP - NIGHT - MOMENTS LATER

Amidst the shadows, a spirit caught the faint glow of the campfire, flickering as it hovered—its features became indistinct, reflecting a life lost. "We just want to be free..." it whispered, pain etched in its voice.

"That's what we all desire!" Deacon replied, stepping forward with courage. "We can unite in our shared grief. We will help you find peace!"

The spirits paused, the swirling mass of anguish flickering with uncertainty. The whispers of their rage shifted, becoming almost mournful, and Deacon felt the air change—a fragile bond forming between the living and the dead.

"Together, we can heal," Emily said, heart pounding with urgency as she moved alongside Deacon, reaching for their hands as a gesture of unity. "You're not alone in this!"

DEACON'S CAMP - NIGHT - CONTINUOUS

With each word spoken, the tension shifted as the group stood firm against the encroaching shadows. The spirits flickered before them, the rage beginning to ebb slightly.

"Let go of your anger!" Frank shouted, stepping forward despite the shadows, determination fired in his voice. "We'll honor those you lost! We'll fight to protect those still here!"

The back-and-forth continued as survivors rallied together,

emotions intertwining with the grievances surfacing from the past. The spectral forms began to waver, their anger muted against the light of dawning understanding.

As they projected unity and empathy, a pulse of warmth began to emanate from the campfire. The spirits ventured closer, caught between two worlds—living and dead, seeking solace in the presence of understanding.

WAREHOUSE - NIGHT - MOMENTS LATER

Meanwhile, inside the warehouse, Emily felt the tug of anticipation rushing through as the sounds of the struggle echoed outside. "We can't stay here forever!" she urged Rachel, determination soaring within her. "Let's move!"

As the two stepped closer to the door, the distant sounds of battle reached them, mixing with the echoes of longing and sadness permeating the air.

DEACON'S CAMP - NIGHT - CONTINUOUS

Outside, the moment of connection began to ripple through the camp as the spirits hovered, caught between the realm of vengeance and the warmth of acceptance.

"Will you help us?" a spirit whispered, its form shimmering as it lingered in the flickering light.

Deacon stepped into the breach, heart pounding as he reached out. "Let us help you find peace. You deserve to rest, just as we do. Together, we can break these chains!"

As the last echoes of their plea mingled through the night, the spirits trembled, caught in the weave of understanding. "Freedom..." they whispered, their forms flickering as if torn between worlds.

WAREHOUSE - NIGHT - CONTINUOUS

Inside the warehouse, Emily and Rachel could feel the vibrant energy of the battle shift, stirring with the heavy weight of expectation as they ventured toward the opening.

"We need to hurry!" Emily insisted, steeling bravery.

DEACON'S CAMP - NIGHT - CONTINUOUS

Back outside, Deacon locked eyes with the spirits, a layer of connection unwrapping further beneath the surface, the shadows around slowly dissipating. "We'll fight for you," he promised, anchoring his resolve to the frail spirits.

But suddenly, the air sharpened—another figure emerged from the tree line, the menacing form woven in darkness as a new breed of terror approached the camp.

"No… no, not again!" Lila shouted, her voice shaking as she pointed toward the approaching figures emerging from the darkness.

A new wave of figures stepped forward—darker shadows woven into the multitudes—Wrathful Spirits oozed with malice in stark contrast to the earlier spirits.

"We will have revenge!" they shrieked, voices spiraling through the air like the roar of a tempest as they advanced, their forms twisting and swirling toward the living.

"Everyone, we need to defend ourselves!" Colonel Stone shouted, grabbing his weapon and moving to the frontlines.

Deacon felt the air shift, a sharp realization striking him again. "This isn't over!" he affirmed, rallying against the shadows. "We should stand united! We will fight for our home!"

The survivors maneuvered together, their sense of purpose igniting into flames as the shadows closed in.

As the battle raged on, and darkness threatened to swallow

them whole, new connections began to unfold—both among the living and the spectral forces that surged forward, weaving sharply in and out of visibility.

And as Deacon prepared to confront this new wave of darkness, he knew they had to find a way to bridge the gap between the worlds of the living and the dead, facing their fears head-on.

DEACON'S CAMP - NIGHT - CONTINUOUS

The shadows of the Wrathful Spirits closed in, their hungry cries slicing sharply through the night air. Their forms twisted and writhed, driven by vengeance, their faces contorting into masks of anguish and rage.

"Steady!" Colonel Stone shouted, taking control amidst the chaos. "Aim for the Hounds first. Keep the lines tight!"

Deacon tightened his grip around his weapon, heart racing. "We can't let the spirits overwhelm us!" he yelled, trying to rally the group. "They're feeding on our fear; we must push forward!"

The defenders steeled themselves, standing shoulder to shoulder, but Deacon could see doubt flicker in their eyes, the shadows of fear creeping back.

"Fight for each other!" Lila urged, determination flashing across her face. "We're stronger together!"

As the campfire's light flickered, illuminating the fearsome specters, the group became a beacon against the impending tide of despair. Deacon spotted the dark forms pouncing toward the fire, a relentless wave testing their resolve.

"One! Two! Three!" Stone shouted, and a chorus of gunfire erupted as they unleashed their volleys against the oncoming

Hounds while simultaneously facing the wrathful spirits.

ABANDONED WAREHOUSE - NIGHT - MOMENTS LATER

The camp surged with energy as Deacon led the charge, pushing back against both the Hounds and spirits, encouraging the others to stand firm. "Together, we reclaim our light!"

"Do not let their cries drown you!" Colonel Stone ordered, his voice firm as he tried to maintain discipline in the ranks. "Focus on what you are fighting for!"

Deacon felt the spark of unity igniting within the group, a powerful force weaving through them. "Push forward! Don't let fear take the helm!"

Suddenly, as the battle raged on, a new howl broke through the cacophony, chilling the blood in every survivor's veins. The dark figure of a Hound peeled away from the shadows—a ghastly sight that loomed larger than the rest, its eyes glowing like fire.

"There's more than one!" Lila shouted, pointing toward the added threat.

Without hesitation, Deacon focused on the new beast, aiming for its head. "Aim true!" he yelled, watching as their firepower rattled against the oncoming force.

But as they fought bravely, Deacon's heart sank. The spectral forms of the vengeful souls drew closer, swarming against the heat of the flames, seeking the living for their own closure.

WAREHOUSE - NIGHT - MOMENTS LATER

Meanwhile, Emily and Rachel gathered additional weapons inside the warehouse, knowing they wouldn't be able to remain hidden for long.

"They're going to find us!" Rachel said, gripping a nearby

crowbar tightly. "What will we do if they break down the door?"

"We'll fight! We won't let them take us down without a struggle," Emily replied, heart pounding as she prepared to stand her ground.

"Let's move!" Emily shouted urgently, leading the charge toward the exit of the warehouse. The sounds of battle echoed outside, igniting a fire within her.

DEACON'S CAMP - NIGHT - MOMENTS LATER

Emerging from the warehouse, Emily could see the chaos unfolding with clarity. Deacon's team was pushing back against the horrors surrounding them—but the conflict intensified as the Hounds and spirits surged toward him.

"Come on!" Emily shouted, her resolve surging as she raced toward the fray. "We're in this together!"

With Rachel right beside her, they pushed forward, ready to join the fight.

"Cover the left side!" Deacon shouted as he ducked under a clawing Hound, squeezing the trigger again with fervor. "We can't let them overwhelm us!"

Colonel Stone moved alongside Deacon, their focus aligning as they confronted the dark forces together—not as enemies but as a strategic battleground against the encroaching shadows.

Corners of the camp flickered with firelight as the shadows blurred with chaos, each move a reminder of the stakes heightened in their struggle.

DEACON'S CAMP - NIGHT - MOMENTS LATER

As the battle reached its boiling point, Deacon could see glimpses of hope amidst the struggle. The greater unity crafted through their struggles began to shine, igniting strength among them.

"Fight back!" he shouted, rallying everyone even deeper. "Remember those we fight for! Let's reclaim our space!"

Determined and united, the survivors surged forward, meeting the Hounds and spirits with renewed vigor. As fury surged against the spirits' vengeful cries, the tides began to shift—their anger muted against the light of their combined resolve.

But just as victory seemed within reach, the air trembled with a new energy, and yet more spirits began to emerge, drawn to the growing strength among the survivors.

"We will not falter!" Lila called out loudly, locking eyes with others around her. "Together, we'll drive them back!"

DEACON'S CAMP - DAYBREAK - MOMENTS LATER

As the first light of dawn began to break through the horizon, the camp felt alive with determination. The survivors pressed on, the shadows of spirits rising to challenge them.

Deacon's heart surged with hope as he aimed, striking fiercely into the heart of the chaos. "Come on, together! We can pull through this!"

Each spirit that grew closer only heightened their resolve; reborn from the ashes, they stood ready against the ominous tide pressing upon them.

But as dawn approached, revealing the struggles played out under the veil of night, Deacon couldn't shake the unease gathering in his gut. The spirits weren't merely seeking vengeance—they were entwined in their lingering pain, and the past threatened to tear their unity apart.

And somewhere deep within the shadows, there lingered a glimmer of truth—a danger lurking far beyond what they could see—a truth that awaited its chance to emerge and linger within their ranks, poised to disrupt their fragile unity when they needed it most.

CHAPTER 49: THE UNRAVELING TRUTH

DEACON'S CAMP - DAWN

The first rays of sunlight broke over Deacon's camp, illuminating the battlefield with a soft golden hue. The shadows of the night began to recede, but the remnants of chaos lingered in the air, palpable and heavy. Survivors stood firm, weapons still drawn, but the frantic energy surrounding them slowly started to cool.

Deacon looked around, surveying the faces of those who remained, each etched with fatigue and resolve. "We held the line," he said, allowing his voice to echo the pride of their collective effort. "But the threat isn't over. The spirits—and the raiders—could return."

Lila stepped forward, breathing heavily. "What do we do now? Are we just supposed to wait for them to strike again?"

"No," Colonel Stone interjected, his tone measured. "We need to fortify the perimeter and gather more supplies. We've survived this round, but we must be prepared for any further threats."

"Frank is still out there," Emily said quietly, her heart heavy with uncertainty. "We have to keep searching for him."

"Let's check the woods for any signs," Deacon said, glancing at the trees that loomed ominously nearby. "If we can find anything... a clue or something from Frank's account, we might be able to piece together what's really happening."

WOODS NEAR DEACON'S CAMP - DAWN - MOMENTS LATER

A small group, including Lila, Jacob, and Frank, followed Deacon as they cautiously stepped into the woods once more. The remnants of night hung in the air, but he felt a renewed energy from the light of dawn pushing them forward.

"Stick together," Deacon urged, gazing at the shadows still lingering among the trees. "We've got to stay vigilant."

As they pressed forward, each crackling branch beneath their feet heightened their awareness and reminded them of the dangers that lurked around them.

DEEPER IN THE WOODS - DAY - MOMENTS LATER

With each step, however, a feeling of dread crept into the group. The woods felt different this morning, the air heavy with an unshakable tension.

A low growl reverberated through the trees, causing every one of them to freeze. Deacon raised his hand, signaling them to stop. "What was that?" he whispered, straining to listen.

"It sounded close..." Lila said, eyes widening as shadows shifted just beyond their line of sight.

Suddenly, from the depths of the trees, another cackling howl broke through the morning mist. This one felt deeper, more menacing—a warning that sent chills racing down their spines.

"They're here!" Jacob shouted, instinctively raising his weapon. "We need to move!"

DEACON'S CAMP - DAY - MOMENTS LATER

Back at the camp, Colonel Stone began directing survivors to reinforce the barricades. Tension hung in the air as everyone sensed something was terribly off—and he felt it, too.

"Nadine! Everyone to their posts!" Stone barked, his eyes scanning the treeline.

Nadine stood quietly nearby, her expression anxious, clearly wrestling with something unspoken. She seemed distracted, eyes flickering toward the woods while the camp buzzed with hurried preparations.

"Are you alright, Nadine?" Stone asked, noticing her unrest.

"Yeah. I'm... I'm fine," she replied, but Stone sensed that her mind was elsewhere.

"Listen, there's something going on that I can't pin down," he replied, trying to maintain control. "I need everyone focused, including you."

As the sound of another growl echoed through the woods, a feeling of urgency surged through Stone. This wasn't just a typical raid—they needed to confront whatever darkness could be approaching.

DEEP IN THE WOODS - DAY - MOMENTS LATER

Deacon, Lila, and Frank continued deeper into the woods, moving cautiously as a subtle tension thickened around them. They knew they were not just facing physical threats anymore; shadows of doubt hung on the air, reminding them of the fragile trust that had begun wilting in the wake of accusations.

"Why do you think Colonel Stone is acting so strangely?" Lila suddenly asked, concern etched across her brow. "It's like he knows something we don't."

"I don't know, but I feel like we're scratching the surface of something bigger," Deacon said, kneeling to examine the ground where Frank's tracks had faltered. "There's more happening beneath the surface, and we need to figure it out before it's too late."

As Frank stepped beside Deacon, he paused, his expression suddenly turning grave. "You think Stone could be hiding something about Frank?"

"I can't be sure yet—but I won't disregard anything," Deacon replied, feeling the weight of suspicion fuel a fire of determination within him.

DEACON'S CAMP - DAY - MOMENTS LATER

Back at the camp, the atmosphere began to shift again, the uneasy tension palpable as residents prepared for the unknown once more.

Colonel Stone scanned the tree line, feeling the grip of disquiet tighten in the air around him. "We've got to keep our lines steady! There's no way we can let fear dictate our survival!"

But beyond the layers of bravado, he felt a nagging worry blossom in his gut—a realization that his own secrets might come back to haunt him.

Just then, a rustling sound broke through the trees at the edge of camp, drawing his attention sharply. "What's that?" he barked, instinctively raising his weapon toward the disturbance.

WOODS NEAR DEACON'S CAMP - DAY - CONTINUOUS

Back in the woods, Deacon and his group continued their search, tension wrapping tightly around them as they pressed forward. The feeling of unease was almost suffocating, heavy with the scent of impending danger.

Suddenly, a flash of movement caught Lila's attention, causing her to raise her weapon instinctively. "There! At the tree line! I saw something!"

Deacon turned quickly, heart pounding as they moved toward the source of the movement, ready for anything that lurked among the shadows. But as they reached the edge of the clearing, they were met not with animals or raiders, but with an overwhelming sight that halted them in their tracks.

A mass of **Wrathful Spirits** began to coalesce, their forms twisting and howling in a dance of vengeance, both ethereal and horrifying as they surged forward, a tempest of unresolved wrath.

DEACON'S CAMP - DAY - CONTINUOUS

Back at the camp, the atmosphere thickened as the survival against darkness continued to press in. Stone held his ground, his senses heightened as he watched the haze of spirits dissipate into the earth.

One figure emerged from the shadows, a lingering sense of dread radiating from its presence.

"Stone," the figure whispered, voice low and tinged with unease. The apparition hung at the border of the camp, eyes piercing with memories unsung.

DEACON'S CAMP - DAY - CONTINUOUS

Colonel Stone felt the chill of the specter wash over him, instinctively gripping his weapon tighter. "Who goes there?" he demanded, trying to maintain authority despite the unease creeping beneath his skin.

The figure stepped forward, revealing itself as a gaunt white figure, a translucent shade that shimmered with sorrow—a **Wrathful Spirit**, its face twisted in a grimace of pain and longing.

"I am one lost among shadows—one who remains tethered by the ties of anger," it said, voice echoing with sadness. "You bear the weight of decisions made in darkness. Will you face your truth?"

"Ties of anger?" Stone repeated, confusion knitting his brow as he observed the spirit's haunted expression.

"Many have suffered because of betrayal," the spirit intoned, sadness lacing its words. "You will feel the echoes of those who have passed—those seeking solace."

As the spirit drew close, the essence of wailing spirits surged, their psychic energy fraying at the edges of reality. The atmosphere bristled with emotion, memories of the lost ascending to confront the living.

DEEPER IN THE WOODS - DAY - CONTINUOUS

Back in the woods, Deacon, Lila, and Frank stood frozen, observing the spectral turmoil rising from the camp. "This is bad," Frank muttered, anxiety threading through his voice. "The spirits... they're moving differently."

"They're feeding off the chaos, turning it into vengeance," Deacon replied, determination quickly replacing fear. "We need to foster light against their darkness!"

"This isn't anything we've faced before," Lila cautioned, eyes wide as the masses of spirits surged closer toward the camp, their mournful cries echoing through the trees. "They're not just angry, they're vengeful!"

Deacon felt dread wash over him. "If they connect with Stone, they might amplify his fears, his anger. We can't allow that to happen."

Suddenly, a loud howl echoed through the woods again, a dark foreboding reminder that the connections between the living and the lost were deteriorating even further.

"We need to get back! We have to warn them!" Lila urged,

pulling Deacon and Frank forward as they rushed toward the camp.

DEACON'S CAMP - DAY - CONTINUOUS

Upon returning to the camp, the tension hung thick in the air. The whispers of the spirits echoed louder now, filling the survivors' hearts with despair.

"Don't give in!" Stone shouted, his voice trembling slightly but trying to maintain control. "We face them, united! We will not let our past haunt us!"

Deacon pushed through the crowd; eyes wide with urgency. "Stone! We need to confront their pain, not let it consume us!" he called out, desperate to make his voice heard amidst the chaos.

Stone turned sharply, a flicker of doubt crossing his face. "You think you can reason with them?" he spat back; the line of distrust still etched between them. "You've lost your right to lead here!"

But just then, the mass of Wrathful Spirits surged forward into the clearing, their spectral forms coiling into the light. They chanted, their voices piercing through the ambient noise—a haunting melody of loss and lament.

"We thirst for justice!" the spirits cried in unison, their incorporeal forms twisting and shifting in living anger. "Release us from this torment!"

DEACON'S CAMP - MOMENTS LATER

Deacon felt the atmosphere thrum with tension as the spirits drew closer, their wailing filling the air. "We need to find a way to reach them!" he shouted, trying to keep the survivors focused amid the rising chaos.

"They're not just spirits," Frank exclaimed, fear surging

through him. "They're reflections of the pain we've caused—the anger of those who suffered! They want retribution! We need to honor those lost!"

As the spirits began to close in, the air thickened with despair and rage. Deacon braced himself, knowing that they needed to confront the emotions tied to the spirits to break their hold.

"If you see Frank, let us help you!" Deacon shouted, grounding himself against the encroaching darkness. "We can't lose sight of who we are!"

Suddenly, the leading spirit flickered, and its sorrowful visage shifted before them—a faint echo of Frank's face emerged from the darkness. "You will pay for your choices!" it cried, voices intertwining in a chorus of anguish.

"No!" Deacon cried, stepping forward as if to reach into the spirit's breast. "It doesn't have to be like this! We can fight for resolution! You don't need to bring vengeance against those still living!"

But the spirit continued to pull back, shadows coiling tighter as it hovered, anger boiling to the surface. "You abandoned the ones left behind!" it screeched, the words striking like daggers into Deacon's heart.

WAREHOUSE - NIGHT - CONTINUOUS

Inside the warehouse, Nadine stepped back as the shadows pressed in around her, feeling the weight of despair sweep through her. She knew that confronting Deacon's fate could bear heavy consequences, the shadows thickening around her heart with every passing moment.

"Help them, Nadine," she muttered to herself, the burden of betrayal feeling heavier. "You owe it to everyone."

With a determined breath, Nadine moved toward the exit of the warehouse, overcoming the shadows of doubt that clung to her. She would confront the encroaching chaos; she would find a way to turn the tide.

DEACON'S CAMP - NIGHT - CONTINUOUS

Back outside, while chaos erupted around him, every fiber of Deacon's being screamed for resolution. "This isn't the end," he vowed silently, watching as the spirits struggled against their own unresolved pain. "There must be a way to find clarity. A way to honor those we've lost instead of letting shadows divide us."

But as the turmoil deepened and the cries of vengeance rose into a crescendo, Deacon felt the shadows closing in on every side, enveloping him in a darkness that threatened to extinguish the light of hope flickering just beyond.

And somewhere amid the grasp of impending darkness, secrets lingered yet to be revealed—truths twisted in the shadows that could change the course of everything they fought to build and protect.

With a determination forged in the fire of battle, Deacon prepared to once again confront the darkness, prepared to uncover the truths hiding within the chaos. The battle stretched beyond the physical—and for each soul, the reckoning loomed ever closer, begging for resolution amid the shadows of despair.

CHAPTER 50: THE CONVERGENCE

DEACON'S CAMP - NIGHT

The air trembled with the tension of impending confrontation as Deacon stood at the forefront of chaos, surrounded by the Wrathful Spirits, their anguished wails echoing through the camp. The sun dipped below the horizon, allowing shadows to stretch longer, deepening the dread that hung over them like a heavy fog.

"Don't let them overwhelm us!" Deacon shouted, fervently pressed between fear and determination. "We must find a way to understand their pain, to help them find closure!"

The spirits flickered in the dim light of the camp, swirling with anger and sorrow, their voices weaving into a haunting melody. "You abandoned us! You must pay for your choices!" they echoed, each word a sharp reminder of the loss they represented.

"Listen to me!" Deacon yelled, stepping closer, heart pounding in synch with the rising tension. "We grieve, too! We know the pain of having loved ones… of loss! You are not alone!"

As the spirits drew nearer, their energy pulsed with a chaotic amalgamation of sorrow, entwining itself with unrelenting rage. The Hounds, emboldened by the ghostly cries, became restless, their snarls mingling ominously with the ethereal whispers.

"Hold steady!" Colonel Stone barked as he shifted to the frontlines, steadying his weapon against the approaching darkness. "We won't allow this chaos to consume us!"

But despite his commanding presence, Deacon sensed the unease stirring among the survivors; every passing moment weighed heavily on their resolve. The chants and howls from the spirits grew louder, filling the air with palpable despair.

In an attempt to offer an olive branch, Deacon stepped further into the threshold between the realms. "You have power! We want to help you find peace. We can honor your memories—yours and those lost!"

For a brief moment, the spirits hesitated, their forms flickering as they appeared to contemplate his words. Yet the darkness, led by the greater Wrathful Spirit that had taken form again with Frank's ghost, clutched tighter, threatening to drown them in fury.

DEACON'S CAMP - NIGHT - MOMENTS LATER

Suddenly, another howl rose from the core of the forest, louder and more menacing than any before. The sound cut through the air like a knife—filled with raw hunger.

"Nadine! I need you!" Deacon shouted, spotting the dark figure still lingering at the edges of the camp—a witness to the unfolding chaos.

But just as he turned toward her, a wild figure emerged from the darkness behind her—a grotesque form of what once was human, its body twisted and wretched, radiating an overwhelming aura of hatred.

"No! It can't be!" Colonel Stone gasped, eyes going wide as recognition washed over him.

"Let's act!" Deacon shouted, urgency rippling through him as he prepared to defend against the new monstrosity, realizing with horror that this creature fed on the darkness of their past—perhaps it was a manifestation of all their hidden fears.

The twisted spirit lunged forward, ready to engage the camp, a howling wail of anguish escaping from its lips.

As the spirit leapt toward the gathered survivors, Deacon instinctively aimed his weapon, heart racing. "Everyone, focus on the spirits! They're using our fears against us!"

WOODS NEAR DEACON'S CAMP - NIGHT - A MOMENT LATER

Emily and Rachel had just emerged from the warehouse, weapons drawn, ready to face whatever lingered outside. They moved quickly toward the source of the commotion, their hearts pounding.

"Are you ready?" Emily called to Rachel as they maneuvered toward the chaos.

Rachel nodded, steel in her voice. "Ready as I'll ever be!"

Suddenly, the shadows thickened around them as the air filled with small whispers. "What's going on?" Rachel asked, worry lacing her tone.

"We need to keep moving forward!" Emily insisted, determination shaping her words. They hurried onward toward the growing sound of chaos, sensing they were on the cusp of something tremendous.

DEACON'S CAMP - NIGHT - CONTINUOUS

Back at the camp, the battle erupted fiercely. The army of spirits surged ahead, and the spectral beast clashed against the defenses. Deacon shouted commands, desperately trying to maintain control amidst the chaos.

"Protect each other!" he called, feelings of responsibility propelling him to action.

The campfire flickered violently, shadows and light intertwining in a dance of chaos, and just as Deacon felt hope waning, he sensed another presence nearby—a ghostly form partially shrouded in the spirits, a visage of Frank emerging from the chaos.

"Deacon!" Frank cried out, his voice filled with urgency. "You have to be careful! They're drawing strength from your fear—and Stone! He... he knows something!"

"No! Frank!" Deacon yelled, desperate to reach him. "Come back! You can't let them pull you in!"

But the shadow of anguish that wrapped around Frank tightened, pulling him back as torment surged through the air.

Suddenly, Nadine stepped closer into the fray, her eyes blazing with an intensity that was equal parts fear and malice. "Stop! All of you!" she demanded, trying to push against the tide of chaos surging forward.

"You don't understand!" Emily yelled, panic threading her voice. "We can't back down!"

In that moment, just as the looming shadows began to crush against the survivors, the chaos shifted unexpectedly. A piercing light began to seep from Deacon's heart, radiating throughout the camp in waves of warmth that began to push back the least of the spirits.

"Fight for those we've lost! Stand for each other!" Deacon shouted, rallying every ounce of strength within him.

But as the overwhelming energy surged, the scene became fraught with danger—a realization creeping in that as much as they fought their external battles, shadows of betrayal still lingered amid friends.

DEACON'S CAMP - NIGHT - MOMENTS LATER

In the throes of the turmoil, the murmurings of anger echoed through the spirits as they pressed closer, the truths woven between them demanding to be revealed.

Stone stepped back, uncertainty flickering across his expression. Deacon locked eyes with him, suspicion igniting anew as everything culminated. "What do you know about this?!"

But instead of responding, Stone's resolve seemed to waver. "I...I'm trying to protect the camp—from all of you! You don't see what's at stake!"

WAREHOUSE - NIGHT - CONTINUOUS

Meanwhile, Nadine's face twisted into a cruel smile as she sidled closer to the gathering crowds, drawing attention away from the surging chaos. Her eyes gleamed with a predatory sharpness.

"Let them tear each other apart," she hissed, a low murmur escaping her lips. She edged closer to Emily, desire palpable in her gaze. "After all, in chaos lies opportunity..."

DEACON'S CAMP - NIGHT - MOMENTS LATER

As the battle raged, the air electrified with the tension of survival and betrayal twined together. Deacon felt the shifting tides of conflict strangling their unity. Shadows coiled around the camp, pulling tightly, threatening to rend their bonds apart.

The specter of Frank hovered nearby, flickering between worlds, his eyes filled with anguish. "Deacon!" he shouted, his voice carried away by the chaos. "You must learn the truth! Colonel Stone's intentions are not what they seem... he has hidden motives!"

"What do you mean?" Deacon called back through the chaos,

desperation tightening its grip around him. "Tell me! What's Stone hiding?"

But as he tried to reach the wavering form of Frank, the weight of the surrounding spirits surged forward, howling their pain and regret, drowning his words in a cacophony of despair.

"Don't let them consume you!" Deacon yelled, rallying everyone around him.

But just then, a loud crack shone through the air, as a burst of intense light shot up from the campfire—a beacon of hope and anger erupting as the light challenged the gathering shadows.

"They are twisted by grief! They need compassion!" Lila shouted, urging them forward with renewed resolve. "We need to confront the darkness together!"

Suddenly, Colonel Stone's face twisted with uncertainty as he raised his weapon against the oncoming tide of spirits. "This is madness! You are all digging your graves!"

"Madness is not fighting for our lives!" Deacon responded, heart racing as he observed Stone becoming increasingly agitated. "You've become what you once stood against!"

Just as the tension reached its peak, Nadine moved closer to the fire, her intentions obscured. "It's all so clear now," she whispered, her voice as soft as silk against the roaring chaos. "You've betrayed the camp, Deacon, and you'll pay the price."

WOODS NEAR DEACON'S CAMP - NIGHT - CONTINUOUS

The shadows intensified as a new wave of vengeful spirits emerged, howling and swirling in anger. The air thickened with electric energy, a palpable reminder that the fight was far from over.

"Stay close!" Deacon commanded, rallying the survivors once more against the raging spirits. "Don't let doubt take hold!

Focus on what's right in front of you!"

But as the spirits surged, Emily felt a pang of realization tightening in her chest. "Nadine, you're hiding something! What do you know?"

Nadine smiled, a chilling glint in her eyes. "What I know will save you—but only if you're willing to pay the price."

"Enough of this!" Lila shouted, trying to keep the spirit from consuming them once more. "We don't have time for games!"

Suddenly, the ground trembled again, and from the shadows, a terrifying entity emerged—an even darker spirit, larger and more grotesque than the others, lurching toward the camp like a gathering storm.

"Revenge!" it bellowed, its voice a twisted echo of the past. "You shall pay for your transgressions!"

The specter lunged forward, and with it came a wave of despair that crashed against the survivors, threatening to crush their spirits underfoot.

DEACON'S CAMP - NIGHT - MOMENTS LATER

"Fight back!" Deacon hollered, gripping his weapon as he took aim at the approaching threat. "Remember who we are!"

The survivors surged forward, united with the flickering energy of the campfire behind them, desperate to hold off the tide of darkness that sought to devour them whole.

But as the spirit pressed against their defenses, the weight of the world seemed to turn heavy once more. The air buzzed with impending darkness as the scene spiraled into disarray.

"Do not let despair take hold!" Lila shouted, each word a beacon of hope amid the chaos. But as she stepped closer, the twisting shadows reached toward her, threatening to consume her spirit.

"Lila!" Deacon cried, feeling panic flare as he reached out to grab her, fighting against the tide.

WAREHOUSE - NIGHT - MOMENTS LATER

Unbeknownst to him, inside the warehouse, Nadine seized upon the emotion swirling between them, her expression hardening with a predatory edge.

"Emily, join me," she said softly, her voice wrapping around Emily like a serpent. "Together, we can capture this power. You've felt it, haven't you? You know you long for something more."

"No! I won't betray them!" Emily shouted, realizing the magnitude of Nadine's treachery rapidly unfurling.

Nadine stepped closer, her presence chilling. "But they've already faltered. You have the chance to rise above it, to choose your path."

The sounds of chaos from the camp dulled in Emily's ears as she fought against the spellbinding lure of Nadine's offer. But in that moment of vulnerability, she noticed something flicker in Nadine's eyes—an emptiness that mirrored the very darkness they faced.

DEACON'S CAMP - DAYBREAK - CONTINUOUS

Back outside, Deacon struggled against the tide of despair, the writhing shadows and vengeful spirits threatening to envelop them completely. "Fight through it!" he cried, urging Lila and Frank to continue battling against the oncoming darkness.

But as the darkness surged forward, layers of betrayal and anguish began to peel back the unity they had built, as doubt threatened to drown them all.

Through the cacophony, Deacon suddenly caught a glimpse of Colonel Stone—his face twisted with conflict, doubt battling within him like a tempest.

"Stone!" Deacon shouted, "What are you really hiding?!"

But before Stone could respond, the larger spirit lunged, a ferocious roar echoing through the night that drowned out Deacon's voice, sending shockwaves of horror through the survivors.

In that pivotal moment, as the fight surged with fervent energy, the weight of the past, the looming darkness, and the fracturing bonds threatened to tear them apart in one single moment—and the encroaching shadows stood ready to seize their chance.

As Deacon gripped his weapon tight, heart pounding, he realized that everything they had built could shatter in an instant if they didn't find a way to confront the demons of both the living and the deceased.

WOODS NEAR DEACON'S CAMP - NIGHT - MOMENTS LATER

Suddenly, from beyond the shadows of the trees, new forms emerged—more Hounds, more Wrathful Spirits, enveloped in darkness!

"More of them!" Jacob cried, panic rising in his voice as he instinctively aimed at the approaching figures.

But as the darkness loomed, Deacon's heart sank—I don't know if we can hold them back any longer. With shadows rushing to overtake them and betrayal lurking within their ranks, the camp could very well unravel into chaos.

"Stand together!" Deacon shouted, fear and anger mingling together. "We refuse to give up this fight! This darkness will not consume us!"

Just as the cacophony reached a breaking point, a sudden explosion echoed from the trees beyond the camp, forcing all heads to turn. Flames erupted against the dark sky, illuminating the horrors around them.

"Get down!" Lila shouted, instinctively pulling Frank to the ground as debris flew through the air.

Deacon's heart raced as the camp vibrated against the force of the blast, shadows undulating with the flames illuminating the spirits as they recoiled momentarily. "We can't let the past drag us down!" he yelled, rallying the survivors again.

"Look!" someone cried, pointing toward the edge of the forest as a new figure emerged, shrouded in smoke. "Who is that?"

Deacon squinted through the chaos, trying to make sense of what he was seeing. The figure stepped forward into the flickering firelight, revealing an unexpected ally. It was **Emily**, forcing her way through the wreckage alongside Rachel.

"I'm back!" Emily called, voice steady amid the chaos. "I found some weapons! We can fight!"

"Thank goodness!" Frank shouted, relief washing over him as he pushed back to his feet.

But as the flames roared, the overwhelming presence of vengeful spirits surged forward again, fueled by the chaos of the moment.

"Not again!" Deacon yelled, knowing they were on the precipice of catastrophe. "They're drawing even closer! We have to break this cycle!"

Colonel Stone shot a glance at Deacon, realization dawning in the heat of the moment. "We need to unite on all fronts—take the fight to the spirit realm!"

With that fervent rallying cry, a wave of energy filled the camp as survivors prepared to surge against the oncoming tide.

The air vibrated with tension as they embraced their fateful moment, everything they had fought for hanging in a delicate balance.

DEACON'S CAMP - NIGHT - MOMENTS LATER

Deacon stood shoulder to shoulder with Emily, Lila, and Frank as they readied themselves against the overwhelming rush of spirits and Hounds. "We must engage the spirits with the memories they cling to!" he shouted, trying to focus their thoughts. "Remember those we've lost!"

"Let's do it!" Emily cried back, energy surging through her veins as she called every survivor to rally deeper.

As they readied their weapons, a panicked glance darted between Nadine and Colonel Stone, who lingered slightly apart. Emily's heart quickened, suspicion blooming anew as she saw the way Nadine watched the Colonel, her expression oddly hungry.

But that thought flickered away as the spirits surged forward, monstrous shadows closing in around them.

"Charge!" Deacon shouted, leading the charge against the wave of darkness, eyes focused on breaking the spectral connections that threatened to tear them apart.

As the group surged forward, the combined might of the survivors met the spirits with renewed fury, interwoven with their shared memories.

"Remember why we fight!" Lila cried out, pushing against the tide. "Let's honor those lost, not let bitterness consume us!"

The air shimmered with energy as they confronted the growing spirits, the ethereal shadows flickering, caught between anger and the light forged by memory and loyalty.

But amid the clash and the turmoil, a jarring silence fell across the camp—a collective gasp echoed through the group as the ground beneath their feet began to tremble unexpectedly.

"Oh no!" Deacon shouted, glancing down just as the earth shuddered violently. "What's happening?"

As the ground shook, the darkened forms of the Hounds lunged forward, fueled by the chaos of the spirits growing stronger. They were no longer simply facing shadows of the past but a full-fledged assault from every angle.

DEEPER IN THE WOODS - NIGHT - MOMENTS LATER

And just as the chaos reached a fever pitch, Deacon noticed a flicker of movement in the trees just beyond the camp—a familiar gleam catching his eye.

"Someone's out there!" Deacon shouted, trying to pinpoint the source amidst the uproar.

But before anyone could respond, a bone-chilling howl erupted above them—a cacophony of despair intermingling with the cries of the angry spirits, echoing louder and louder until it drowned out every rational thought.

The earth ruptured below them, shadows swirling around like a tempest, threatening to consume everything as the night climaxed into a terrifying confrontation between the living and the dead.

"Deacon!" Emily cried, panic flaring in her voice, arms outstretched as shadows loomed ever closer.

As the spirits converged, the tenuous thread of trust hung in the balance. Deacon's mind raced with the reality that all they fought for could vanish in the abyss if the darkness consumed them.

"Everyone, hold fast!" Deacon yelled, fear dancing across his features. "We gather together! Remember what binds us—the fight is not just against the darkness beyond, but the betrayal lurking among us!"

The spirits surged, and the darkness began to swirl around them, encroaching in a tightening grasp, as trust became a fragile promise hovering on the precipice of despair.

DEACON'S CAMP - NIGHT - MOMENTS LATER

In that moment, the earth buckled violently, and from the depths of the shadows, a wave of them surged forth—spirits and demons coalescing into a tempest of chaos and retribution that threatened to shatter everything they had fought to hold together.

"Stand strong!" Deacon shouted, fighting the rising tide of despair as the camp threatened to unravel beneath them.

But as the spirits howled for vengeance, the shadows cast their final grip, pulling at the threads of unity, and one simple, devastating thought echoed in the mind of the survivors— Could this truly be the end?

Just as the tide threatened to consume them, a piercing shriek echoed from deeper within the forest, shattering the air with the echoes of lost souls rising in fury.

In that exact moment—amidst the chaos of battle and the weight of betrayal—the survivors faced the realization that something far darker loomed just beyond their sight, ready to unleash an unimaginable torrent upon them. The battle was only just beginning, and the true test of their bonds and resilience awaited within the heart of the shadows.

Epilogue: The Weight of Tomorrow

The sun hung low on the horizon, casting a warm glow over the remnants of Deacon's camp, now filled with a cautious optimism. After the fierce confrontation with the Wrathful Spirits and the spectral echoes of the night, the survivors had worked tirelessly to rebuild what had been lost. The air was thick with the scent of fresh earth and the distant sound of laughter echoing among the trees—a welcome reminder of life overcoming despair.

Deacon stood at the edge of the camp, watching as his friends began to restore a semblance of normalcy. It was a stark contrast to the darkness that had threatened to consume them only days before. Lila, Frank, and Rachel were clearing the debris, toiling together with newfound resolve, and even Colonel Stone seemed to soften, his gaze shifting from suspicion to one of cautious acceptance.

Yet, as the embers of the past faded into the background, a gnawing unease settled in Deacon's chest. He had fought so hard to keep their community alive, but the scars of betrayal and the whispers of those they had lost still lingered in the hearts of the living.

"Deacon!" Emily called from behind him, her voice breaking through his thoughts. She approached, her expression a mix of determination and vulnerability. "We need to talk about what's next. About everything we uncovered."

Deacon turned to face her, noting the fire in her eyes. "I know. We need to figure out how to deal with the aftermath, not just with the demons we faced but with our own internal struggles as well."

As they walked deeper into the camp, Deacon felt the weight of the community resting on his shoulders—each soul intertwined, each person bearing their burdens. They had survived, but at what cost?

"We also need to talk about those mysteries we uncovered," Emily said, her voice steady. "Nadine's revelations—I can't shake the feeling that she knew more than she let on."

"Yes," Deacon replied, recalling the moment they had confronted the darkness together, the myriad connections between the spirits' rage and their own hidden regrets. "Her words felt tinged with reluctance. She must have realized something that we—"

Before he could finish, a chilling wind swept through the camp, causing the branches of nearby trees to creak ominously. The laughter and camaraderie fell silent as a haunting aroma of decay filled the air, turning the whispers of the past into a hushed murmur.

"What was that?" Frank asked, his expression shifting into one of concern.

"It's... nothing," Deacon said uncertainly, but doubt crept in. "Just the remnants of the past. We need to remain vigilant."

As the group gathered around the fire, Colonel Stone handed out supplies, a strange tension lingering. "We have a chance to make this work," he said, looking out at the camp with renewed focus. "We need to build stronger ties, to become better than we were."

But beneath the surface, shadows flickered in the corners of Deacon's mind—memories of vengeful spirits and the sense of betrayal layered within their ranks. Would they truly be able to stand united after the darkness they had faced?

Just as hope began to rise, a sudden low growl echoed from the distance, chilling the air around them. It was followed by a piercing howl that resonated through the night, a vivid reminder that danger still lurked beyond the tree line, waiting for the perfect moment to strike.

"Everyone stay alert! Get ready!" Deacon shouted, adrenaline surging within him as the camp drew tight, weapons raised against the unseen threat.

In that moment, the fragile peace that had settled over them shattered, and Deacon felt the familiar tension of apprehension coil around his heart. The shadows of the past would not remain buried easily.

As the darkness spread through the trees, a flicker of malevolence emerged from the depths—a massive shadow creeping closer, heralding something even more sinister than before. The specters of the lost weren't ready to let go, and the battle was far from over.

In the heart of chaos, Deacon knew they would have to confront their fears once more, their unity tested against the encroaching darkness.

With stakes higher than ever, and the echoes of the past whispering through the leaves, one truth pressed heavily upon them: the real fight for survival was just beginning.

To be continued...

Preview of the Next Book in the Series: Echoes of Reckoning

In the wake of the climactic battles faced in Hell Left Behind, the survivors of Deacon Sawyer's camp regroup, grappling with the remnants of their harrowing experiences. But when dawn breaks, the world remains fraught with uncertainties, shadows lurking in the corners of their newfound refuge.

As they seek to rebuild and heal from the wounds of loss and betrayal, whispers of a greater darkness begin to surface —an ancient evil that stirs beneath the earth, hungry for vengeance. Amidst their efforts to restore their camp, Deacon and his companions discover cryptic messages left behind by the Wrathful Spirits, hinting at a deeper connection to the land they inhabit and the horrors that once thrived there.

As tensions resurface between the camp's leadership, old wounds fester, and new allegiances are formed, Deacon must navigate the complexities of trust in a world riddled with exposed secrets and hidden agendas. The loyalty of his closest friends is tested as suspicions arise, threatening to tear their fragile community apart yet again.

When a mysterious figure appears with knowledge about the origin of the demons and spirits haunting the world, it becomes clear that the battle is far from over. This enigmatic stranger offers a revelation—an ancient prophecy that suggests a reckoning is upon them, one that will determine not only their fate but the fate of the world itself.

As they set out on a perilous quest to uncover the truth, Deacon and his allies must confront the very embodiments of their fears—hellish creatures that embody the darkness of their past decisions. The stakes are higher than ever, and they quickly realize that the echoes of their choices will reverberate throughout their journey, challenging their will to survive and the bonds of loyalty they share.

In Echoes of Reckoning, the fight for survival is reignited as Deacon grapples with his inner demons while leading his friends through a perilous landscape of betrayal, revenge, and existential dread. With the shadows deepening and the forces of darkness tightening their grip, the survivors must rally together once more, pushing through the emotional turmoil that threatens to tear them asunder.

As the line between ally and enemy blurs, can Deacon and his friends hold onto their humanity, or will they succumb to the darkness they've fought so hard to escape? The echoes of the past are rising to shape their future, and only by confronting their truths can they hope to forge a new dawn.

Prepare for a gripping journey into the heart of a world where the shadows grow longer, and every choice shapes the delicate balance between light and dark. The reckoning is here, and the echoes will be heard.

Echoes of Reckoning invites you to delve deeper into the intertwined destinies of its characters, grappling with the complexities of trust, loss, and the unfaltering power of hope in the face of darkness. Are you ready to face the haunting echoes of what lingers just beyond the shadows?

Copyright © 2024 by Eric Wright

All rights reserved. No part of this book may be reproduced or transmitted in any form or by any means, electronic or mechanical, including photocopying, recording, or any information storage and retrieval system, without prior written permission from the author.

For permissions, contact:
Email: fish4himentertainment@gmail.com
Website: www.fish4himentertainment.com

Made in the USA
Columbia, SC
19 January 2025

7cfe1201-b222-47d7-8d43-6237fb7b6d81R01